D1629830

THE HOLLOW GODS

The Sun's Devices

Rebecca Levene is an experienced author of fiction and non-fiction and has written scripts for TV and video games. She began her career writing media tie-ins for properties ranging from *Doctor Who* to the *Final Destination* movies before moving into television to work on *Emmerdale Farm*. She is currently writing for Amazon Prime's adaptation of *The Power* and is narrative producer for the hit app *Zombies, Run!*. You can follow her on Twitter @BexLevene.

REBECCA LEVENE

The Sun's Devices

THE HOLLOW GODS
BOOK 3

HODDER &
STOUGHTON

First published in Great Britain in 2020 by Hodder & Stoughton
An Hachette UK company

1

Copyright © Rebecca Levene 2020

A CIP catalogue record for this title is available from the British Library

Hardback ISBN 978 1 444 75379 0
Trade Paperback ISBN 978 1 444 75380 6
eBook ISBN 978 1 444 75381 3

Typeset in Plantin by Palimpsest Book Production Limited,
Falkirk, Stirlingshire

Printed and bound in Great Britain by Clays Ltd, Elcograf S.p.A.

Hodder & Stoughton policy is to use papers that are natural,
renewable and recyclable products and made from wood grown
in sustainable forests. The logging and manufacturing processes
are expected to conform to the environmental regulations
of the country of origin.

Hodder & Stoughton Ltd
Carmelite House
50 Victoria Embankment
London EC4Y 0DZ

www.hodder.co.uk

For Rupert Laight
I miss you, Ru

Prologue

Yetunde rose with the dawn on the day he didn't die. His window stood open and the rising sun shone so bright he closed his eyes, blinking away his tears. His mistress had two faces, and only one could be looked on without pain.

His bed was soft, but his back still ached when he left it. The physicians said that something was broken inside him, and they frowned and looked away when he asked how long. He washed himself in the gold-rimmed basin and slipped into his silk robes. He hadn't been born to such luxury. Before She came his family had been miners, but his talent for the runes had bought him all this silver and gold, all the silks. All these things he would lose when he was gone, and his beloved Emilohi along with them.

Mizhara's chambers were near to his, as they had been in all the years since She came to them, the little golden-eyed girl whose birth had changed the world. He and his fellow priests had been all she had back then, parents and friends and siblings all in one, but now there were others. Her Servants waited outside her chambers, skin and hair glowing bright. The one called Bachur stood to attention before her door. He thought she meant to block his way, but she smiled and stood aside.

'She is waiting for you,' Bachur said.

Mizhara sat on the stool by her window, gazing out on the city into which she so seldom ventured. She ruled from a distance and through her priests. Unlike his, the room in which she spent so much of her time was plain. She might have had all the gold and jewels she wanted, but she preferred polished wood and sharp-angled metal, each object around her purely practical.

'How goes my land?' she asked him.

'All is well.' His words caught in his throat and he doubled over, coughing.

'All is not well with you.' Her face was very like a person's, only her eyes to mark her out. But as she studied him, he thought that she was more strange by far than her golden-skinned, sharp-eared Servants.

'I've lived seventy years,' he said. 'Long enough to see you grow into a woman. But all things must end.'

'Must they?' She frowned down at her city, its hectic streets reduced to order by distance. 'What does my coming mean, if not an end to endings?'

'Well, perhaps you are right. Only time can reveal it.'

Such an answer had silenced her before, but now she glided towards him, tread light on the marble floor. 'I have been studying the runes.'

'There's no need to trouble yourself. Your existence is sufficient.'

'Sufficient for whom?'

For us, he thought. *For your priests, who use the runes in your name.* But that was a truth it was best not to speak.

'I have been studying the runes, and I believe I understand them.' She smiled. He knew that there was no better smile in the world. The worship he felt for her in that moment was so profound it could consume him entirely, until he was nothing but love for her. He held on to the feeling, making sure to remember it. Without it, the runes would not answer him.

'I can have instructors sent—' he began.

She held up one finger to silence him. 'The runes are mine. I understand them better than any instructor. You mages hold them in your minds. That is well, but there is a better way. I believe they can be put out in the world, made permanent and strong.'

'Engraved? No, my dearest, we considered this but never found a way. When the rune faded from the mind its power faded from the object on which it had been carved.'

'Because you chose the wrong runes. The permanence must be written into them.'

They'd tried that too, but he saw that there was no way he would persuade her. Better to let her try and fail, and then maybe she would leave the runes to those who understood them.

'You do not believe me.' Her expression was jarringly adult. It reminded him that she was no longer the child he'd helped to raise. If she'd been an ordinary woman, she might have had a child of her own by now. 'Perhaps I'm wrong, Yetunde. We will see.' She knelt by the chest at the foot of her bed and pulled a golden sphere of metal from it.

There were runes scribed all across the sphere's surface: markings he didn't recognise and whose meaning he couldn't puzzle out. The glyphs of being and becoming were twisted together in complex, unfathomable ways. 'You asked for gold to make jewellery,' he said.

'I asked for gold to make something beautiful,' she corrected, 'and this is it. Here – take it.'

For a moment it felt just what it appeared: cool and smooth, warming as he held it. But slowly the warmth grew, hot and hotter until he couldn't bear to hold it. He cried out but found he couldn't let go. It had fused to him, no longer metal but flesh growing into flesh. As the pain grew, something came from it, burrowing through his skin and wriggling up his veins, flowing into every part of him. He tried to scream but all that emerged was a hoarse croak.

She took his hands in a gentle grip. 'I'm sorry. I didn't know that it would hurt.'

Hurt was too small a word for this agony. He fell to his knees, barely feeling the impact amidst the greater cacophony of pain. Then he felt it all rushing back again, soothing what it had burned until all sensation was gone, sucked back into the golden sphere. His fingers loosened at last and he dropped it to the floor, shuddering.

'What did you do to me?' he whispered. 'Why did you do it?'

'I wanted to fix you.' She pulled him to his feet with inhuman strength. Her golden eyes studied him; they seemed to look through him. 'I've mended what was broken inside you.'

The hope blossomed in him, its own sort of pain. 'My illness?'
'Gone.'

He turned his attention inward, focusing his mind on his joints,
the internal processes that others couldn't feel but mages had
learned to heed. The growth was gone; the tumour that no rune
he'd summoned could touch had melted away and left only
healthy flesh behind.

'That shouldn't be possible!' he said.

'For you, perhaps. But my power is the greater whole of which
yours is only a fragment. The sphere's merely a beginning. I'll
make another one, a much more powerful one, and set it at the
centre of the city. No one will have to suffer or die before their
time. I will bring life and happiness to my people.'

Her people. It was the first time he'd ever heard her call them
that.

'Come,' she said. 'There's more I've been working on.' She
strode towards the door and he strode after, his body moving
with an ease and fluidity he thought had been lost to it for ever.

★

Emilohi sat in the prow of the barge as it floated towards the
eastern gateway of the Garden. She alighted before they reached
it and waved to the bargemaster. He signalled his men to pole
backwards, away from the sacred ground. None but Yron's priests
were permitted to enter here.

She'd pretended reluctance when she parted from Yetunde two
days past. In truth, the parting did pain her. He was so frail now,
his remaining days so few. But in his absence she could remember
the man she'd married. When she looked at his ravaged body, all
she could see was the day very soon when he'd be gone.

It was hard to think of such things in Yron's Garden. As familiar
as it was to her, as many times as she'd been here, she returned
each time a stranger. The path she walked between drooping
willows had once led to a rose garden, but now it ended at a
small lake scattered with clumps of lily and crowded with violet-
bloomed reeds. Music drifted over it and she knew that she'd
find Yron beyond.

It took another hour. The route wasn't straight; no route through this garden was. She passed statues of beasts that had never been, a sundial that told the time in a distant land and a maze whose prickly walls swayed forward to entrap her as she passed. By the time she emerged into the broad field on the far side of the lake, she was sweating and displeased.

Yron stood at the centre of a crowd of his Servants, their ash-grey skin very different from his healthy black, but their eyes the same moon-silver. They all turned to her as she approached, unblinking. She might have found it threatening, but she remembered when each of them had been born. She'd dripped blood into their greedy toddler mouths and wiped their noses. She'd comforted them when they cried for the parents who'd given them up when they saw what their children were.

'You came!' Yron sounded surprised, as if she'd ever have ignored his summons.

'You said it was urgent.'

'Did I?' He grinned, his expression hovering between wicked and innocent as it so frequently did. 'Well, I found myself desiring your company – craving it – and what could be more urgent than that? Come, I've something to show you.'

When she was with Yetunde, standing beside his failing body, her sixty-five years seemed like nothing at all. Beside Yron's youthful exuberance she felt old.

His hand beneath hers was like any man's: warm and soft. He cupped her elbow and supported her as they walked to the far side of the field and into the orchard beyond. The boughs of each tree were bent beneath the weight of fruit, far more than was natural.

'You've been experimenting again,' she said.

He pressed a finger into one of the fruits and the overripe flesh parted, dripping juice down his arm. 'Yes. I heard that the mountain people were starving. After my sister's armies—'

'Your armies too,' she said firmly.

'We live in the Eternal Empire of Mizhara, don't we? *Her* armies conquered the mountain people, and the war left them no time to plant. I heard there was starvation.'

She wondered who he'd heard it from. Yron's Garden was a refuge of sorts, an island isolated from the troubles of the world, or so it had been intended. 'Shipments of grain are being sent,' she reassured him.

'But growing their own would be better. I've been working on plants that can feast on barren soil. See?'

She followed his pointing finger and saw that the fruitful orchard had its feet in dry, sandy soil. 'Impressive. But their land is cold. What thrives here won't grow there.'

'Oh.' He looked stricken. 'I hadn't thought of that. Cold? As cold as last winter here, when the rain fell so much?'

'Far colder.'

In moments like these he still seemed the child he'd quite recently been. But then he smiled again, wide and challenging, and was far from young. 'I'll work on it more. Perhaps I'll work on changing the weather first. If I can make it as cold here as it is there, I'll be able to judge things better.'

'You wouldn't like the cold. And besides, working the weather is hard and dangerous. Why don't you leave such concerns to your priests and enjoy your revels without guilt?' She gestured back to the field, where more of the Servants were congregating. The grass was littered with trays of food and many flagons of drink, and pipes to smoke the purple sorghum of which they were so fond.

'And will you enjoy our revels with us?' He laced his fingers through hers as he led her back.

'Of course, my boy.'

'Ha! Am I a boy to you still? Let's see what I can do today to change that.' The fingers of his free hand rose to trace the lines of her face, the crow's feet at her eyes and the deeper grooves that framed her mouth.

'Really!' she said, laughing, but his expression only grew more serious.

'Yes, really.' He bent his head to kiss her.

She thought of telling him she had a husband, but he knew that and he knew her age too. 'We brought you women and men,' she said, but he shrugged.

'I've yet to try a priest. And the women and men you sent are only pretty on the outside. Your mind shines.'

After that, he didn't seem to want to speak and she didn't have the breath for it. He was a skilful lover, gentle and harsh at the right times. When he pulled at her nipple just the way Yetunde liked to do, she wondered if he'd learned the trick from her husband.

Afterwards they lay side by side in the grass and stared up at the flat blue sky. The moon had risen to sit pale and overawed beside the too-bright sun.

'Everything I ask for, I'm given,' he said.

'We can deny you nothing,' she agreed.

'Then bring me people from the mountains. Bring me some of the prisoners – if I speak to them, perhaps I can fathom how to help them.'

★

She and Yetunde met three days later, in their villa by the banks of the Kanad. She already knew what Mizhara had done for him, and she didn't gasp when she saw his upright back and easy stride and his body unravaged by disease. She only threw her arms around him and squeezed until the tears pushing from behind her eyes retreated.

'Yron was well?' her husband asked.

'He was . . . enthusiastic. He's become interested in the fate of the mountain people.'

'Mizhara concerns herself with our own.'

She sighed and sat beside him on a bench that looked out over the burbling river. 'He's been studying the runes.'

'They both have.' Yetunde laughed, an unamused sound. 'No, not studying them. *Mastering* them. You were right – you were right all along and I should have listened.' He laughed again, even more harshly. 'I suppose now at least I have time to try to correct my mistake.'

'We're agreed then?'

He nodded, his gaze on the water. 'We are, but not many of the others will be. This must be done in secret.'

It was a beautiful day, the sky pure and cloudless and the sound of birds all around. 'They'll understand soon enough – one day they'll realise that Yron and Mizhara need to be stopped. And when they come to us for an answer, we'll have the God Killer ready.'

PART I

The Mortal Lands

I

The borderlands were ugly, uninhabited and unloved. Renar could see that they displeased her male sib. Lanalan's face wore the frown of a man who'd discovered a fly in his palm wine as he stared at the flat brown landscape from the prow of their canal racer. The canal ran low here, a mere fifty strides above the earth – low and lonely. No other waterways remained this far north. The ruins of a few were visible here and there, piles of crumbling brick half overgrown with the prickly plants that alone seemed to thrive in this nowhere place.

Behind them the canal was a perfect straight line, blue-black against the brown, running to the horizon. A mere five other boats clove the water, sailors straining at their oars. They lumbered low, weighed down by the many knick-knacks and gewgaws her male sib had insisted on bringing with him on this long journey. He would have brought his pets, too, if she hadn't persuaded him they were sure to perish when exposed to the foreign airs of their destination.

Lanalan disliked the land they travelled through, but it thrilled Renar. She'd ridden the canals often and even sailed on the broad sea on more than one occasion. She'd toured the insectariums of Makat and the windmills of Vien as had many others before her. But this would be a voyage none but she had made in a thousand years.

Their destination lay ahead, a mile or two beyond the termination of the canal. The wall had been built nearly two hundred years ago in the aftermath of the Supad Krik, but it looked untouched by time, its resin bricks glowing orange as the setting sun lit them. It alone was tended in all this wilderness, kept strong and whole as their best defence against the god-sick peoples beyond it.

The end of the canal approached and the rowers slowed their strokes, allowing the boats to drift on the north-flowing current of the water. Ahead the brick walls bulged to form a large pool where the current swirled round to flow south on the left-hand side of the canal. Some hidden mechanism must have lain beneath the water to move it in so convenient a way, but no one had ever dived down to examine it. It was no doubt magic that powered it, a relic of a long-gone era, but what wasn't seen needn't be known.

There was a sudden flurry of movement as the sailors rushed to tie their boat to the small dock, leaping across the gap to secure the knots. Their faces were tense as they laughed and talked too loudly, as if to drown out some unwelcome noise, though around them was nothing but silence.

'Why, we've reached our destination,' Lanalan said, as if this had somehow come as a surprise to him.

A staircase led down from a hatch in the dock, a narrow spiral. Beside it a platform hoisted by ropes and pulleys sat ready to carry cargo. It made its first journey as Renar descended the stairs, which creaked with the rusty sound of long disuse. They looked fragile, the wooden treads riddled with small black wormholes and the bannisters made spongy by centuries of rain and rot.

'La, are these quite safe?' Lanalan asked.

'We'll soon see, won't we?' she told him, which kept him quiet until they'd reached the ground.

Sailors swarmed down after them and began the task of unloading, piling Lanalan's many boxes and crates in untidy heaps that had her male sib frowning again. 'A little care with those, I beg of you,' he said. 'Each is worth a year of your wages.'

'Well, that should certainly motivate them,' Renar said drily.

The very last boat contained their wagon. It was a marvel of construction, specially commissioned by Renar for the journey. She'd known it wouldn't occur to Lanalan to consider such a thing. She'd had it made in pieces small enough to fit inside the canal racers, yet quick to reassemble. A few of the sailors were doing so now.

They moved slowly at the task. She saw one glance between her and the landscape and smirk. Renar scowled. She understood the problem quite as well as the smirking sailor. There was no road here at the end of civilisation, only a rocky track. The wagon was sturdy and well sprung but it was made for travelling on lacquered ways. Its wheels would be quite incapable of carrying them here.

'Stop!' she said. 'You know as well as I that it will serve no purpose. You'll have to carry the packs, I'm afraid. We'll pay you extra, don't doubt it.' It would be Lanalan's coin, naturally.

'You want us to go there?' The captain of their little fleet stared at the amber glitter of the wall ahead.

Her male sib smiled that sunny smile of his. 'Why yes, of course. And beyond, I suppose, until a decent road can be found. I believe they have roads in the god-sick lands, do they not?'

'Yes,' Renar said. 'They have roads. They're not entirely savage.'

The captain watched his crew place the last of their packages on the pile. It teetered in the shadow of the canal, absurdly large for just two travellers. 'To the end of the water and no further. That was the job. We've done it.'

Lanalan's smile remained as carefree as ever. He didn't believe himself a man who could be refused. 'I'll pay more, we've already said. Why, I'll pay you and your crews the full fee for the voyage all over again, and it's just a short walk. You'll have the cubes in your purses within the hour.'

The captain looked at his crew, his eyes measuring them. Renar knew what he saw: sullen, fearful expressions. She wasn't surprised when he shook his head. 'No. There's no amount of cubes. We've done our work and now we're leaving. And you'd do the same if you had any wisdom in you.'

'This is an outrage!' Lanalan's smile faded at last. 'How do you expect us to transport our baggage without you?'

The captain wiped his brow, flicking the sweat to the ground.

He'd taken a turn at the oars alongside his crew and Renar respected him for it. She'd respect him more if he managed to refuse her male sib. Sometimes it seemed that all but she were powerless to resist his charm. It was his helplessness, she thought, that weakened people so. Like a small child, he seemed in such need of care that others were always willing to provide it.

But not the captain. 'I suppose you'll have to carry it across one piece at a time. It could take a few days, but if it's so important to you . . .' He shrugged, then turned to his crew. 'What are you loitering for? There's a long way back to civilisation and no game to be had for leagues. Move, you vagabonds – I don't pay you to idle.'

The oarsmen must have been exhausted after so long a journey, but they were as lively as grasshoppers as they rushed back up the stairway and to their boats. One moment she and Lanalan were surrounded by sailors, and the next they were surrounded only by their orphaned possessions. Nothing but the splash of oars above told that they were not entirely alone in this empty land.

'They can't do that!' Lanalan said, his tone more hurt than angry. 'How can they leave us so?'

Renar was already on her knees beside her two crates. A pack lay inside one, filled with her most essential possessions. She hadn't known this would happen, but she'd known something might, and she didn't enjoy being unprepared.

'Just take clothes and a little food,' she told Lanalan. 'I have our gold – they value it hugely where we go. With gold we'll be able to purchase all else we need, and we don't have far to go.'

'Not far!' His woeful expression would have moved her if she hadn't known him so well. 'Why, the walk to the border is long enough and who knows how much further we must go beyond before we find another living creature. And I'm thirsty already!'

'Then bring water. And hurry. I'd like to cross before the sun leaves us.'

He brought water and a lot else beside. He laboured under a heavy pack with two more in his hands as Renar strode ahead.

She'd brought only food, clothes and the books she'd carefully selected before leaving Täm. Even so, her back and legs were aching before they'd covered half the distance to the wall. Lanalan was an even sorrier sight, his white skirt darkened by dust and his chest lightened where the dust had smeared into pale mud in his sweat.

They were being watched. Only here in the borderlands were there people to be found, guards dotted along the length of the wall, and a whole troop of them at the gate they approached. She saw their homes, small cubes little bigger than the shacks of the poor of the park. This was a hard service, chosen by lot and undertaken for only a quarter of a year. No wonder their expressions were so grim.

Their leader was a Mortal, black-robed and veiled. 'Where are your oxen?' she asked. 'Where are your goods?'

'We bring none. It's not the purpose of this journey,' Renar told her.

'There is no other purpose that should bring a traveller here. Turn back.'

'We have papers of transit,' Lanalan declared.

He fumbled in his packs, cursing, until Renar drew out the papers from her own.

'Signed by Remembrancer Bruyar.' She handed them to the Mortal's servant. 'I trust you'll find them in order.'

The Mortal's expression couldn't be seen. There was a long silence as she scanned the papers held out for her by her servant, longer than it could possibly take to read them. The guards shuffled and fidgeted but made no move to reach for the long-bladed falces slung at their sides. Renar didn't suppose she and Lanalan looked particularly threatening, dusty and weary as they were. Besides, the guards weren't there to prevent people leaving. Their job was to keep out what lay beyond the wall.

'That's Bruyar's seal,' the Mortal said, though Renar doubted she'd ever seen the Remembrancer's mark to compare. One didn't get posted to so distant and dry an outpost for being high in the favour of one's superiors.

'This voyage has been properly authorised,' Renar agreed.

'So what is your business beyond the wall?'

'Why,' Lanalan said, 'we go to—'

'We go about our own business,' Renar interrupted. 'Now if it won't trouble you too much, perhaps you could let us pass? The day draws to its end and we'd prefer not to travel in darkness.'

The Mortal would have liked to argue. Renar didn't need to see beneath her veil to know it. But she had no cause and grudgingly stepped aside. Four soldiers lifted the bar that held shut the gates, staggering beneath its weight as they carried it aside. Six more grasped rings set into the gates and heaved them open.

When they were still open only a crack, the fear hit her. It must have been there all along, waiting for the moment to pounce. Her throat was thick with it and her scalp aprickle. The gates swung easily on their hinges so that what lay beyond was revealed to her in an eerie silence.

Everyone knew of the Great Rift. It was marked on all the maps. But to see it – to finally see its size. She wondered why the wall was needed at all, when they had this to guard them from the god-sick.

The edges of the canyon were ragged, as if the two sides had been torn apart in some monumental fit of rage. It must have stretched a mile wide and more than a mile deep. The bottom was lost in darkness at this late hour of the day, but she could hear, echoing from the cliffs that bracketed it, the sounds of a wild river flowing. And on the far side was another wall, as pitiful as their own when seen atop the grandeur of the Rift.

A person might have climbed down the sides with ropes and strength and courage, but it would have taken almost inhuman strength to climb back up again. No wonder the invasion of the Supad Krik had failed so miserably and the god-sick had never tried that madness again.

There was only one wise way to cross the Great Rift and it lay ahead of them, the same cheerful amber as the wall. The bridge stretched in a straight line from their side of the Rift to the other. There was no visible means of support beneath it. Against the vastness of the canyon it seemed terrifyingly thin, but as she and Lanalan walked closer she saw that it was wide enough to bear three carts travelling abreast.

No railing guarded the bridge's sides. She swallowed and took her first footstep onto the lacquered surface as close as she could judge to its middle.

'La, we have arrived,' Lanalan said.

Her sib's voice was shaking. She felt a flush of unaccustomed sentiment and reached to take his hand. He clung to her as they walked on.

The wind blew strongly in the bridge's centre and she fancied she felt it tremble. She trembled too, at the wind and the great drop beneath them and the unknown that lay ahead. There was a scent on the wind she didn't recognise, some flower or herb that didn't grow in Ofiklanod. They were truly beyond the borders of civilisation.

'We could turn back,' Lanalan suggested, though he kept on walking forward. 'No one would think the less of us.'

They would, but that wasn't what kept Renar striding on. There was a *purpose* to this visit, and Renar would see it done. And besides, beneath the overwhelming fear she could still feel her excitement. She might have lived her whole life, each day forgettably like the last, but *this* she would remember.

If, of course, she lived to remember it.

The end of the bridge approached at last, and another gate. The wall stretched into the distance to either side and she saw eyes peering at her from atop its rough bricks and mortar. It was altogether a more primitive thing than their own, and a little of her confidence returned. She held tight to it and raised her fist to knock on the wood of the gate.

These gates creaked as they swung inward. Renar had an instant's warning to brace herself and then the crowd descended on them, shouting in a gabble of foreign voices and reaching out grasping hands for the packs on her and her sib's backs.

'We have no goods!' she shouted. The press of people didn't

abate and she realised she'd spoken in her own tongue. She said it again more loudly in each of their barbaric languages, but they still paid her no mind until one of their own roared and gestured them back, leaving her room to breathe at last.

The man who'd rescued them was short, a head at least shorter than her and two shorter than her sib. His skin was light and his black hair entirely straight, but he might have walked the streets of Täm almost unremarked. Not so those around him. Their skin was as pale as milk and some among them had hair the colour of ripe corn. She'd known to expect it but it was still a shock to see it.

'Forgive us,' the short man said, in the language of the eastlanders. 'It's just that so few of you have come here lately, and we've wagonloads of goods to trade and no market.'

She could see their wagons now, circled in a ring behind them. Beside them ran a road, if you could call it that: unlacquered, muddy and deeply rutted.

Beyond stretched the beginning of the god-sick lands, a muddled patchwork of fields hemmed by low stone walls and more of these churned-up tracks between them. No wonder they were so desperate for the goods of Ofiklanod.

'We did not come to trade,' she said.

'Didn't you?' The short man frowned. 'Why else would you come?'

'To see your prince,' she told him. 'The one they call Krishanjit, who is Yron reborn. The people of Ofiklanod, which once was the Eternal Empire of Mizhara, have need of him.'

2

Krish had pictured this moment as a boy. Poor and ignorant and landborn as he'd thought himself, he'd imagined one day walking down from the mountains into the heart of Ashanesland where the King ruled. He'd pictured it again when he'd learned the truth about his birth. In those visions he'd been returning a conqueror and the King, who was also his father, had been on his knees, begging for a mercy Krish wouldn't give.

In all his imaginings, he'd never pictured this. He and his father rode side by side on black stallions, brothers with the same fleck of white on each of their cheeks. They'd been chosen to match. Nothing was supposed to get in the way of this show of unity as they returned from a campaign that was meant to be the end of one of them. But Krish knew he and his father weren't such a matched pair. His slender, hollow-cheeked form was like a parody of the King's, a sickly mirror to his robust health. And his silver eyes would mark him as different whoever he stood beside.

Their army marched behind them, much smaller now. As they'd passed through the mountains and into the fertile lowlands, their troops had left in dribs and drabs; Krish knew they'd gone to work the fields left fallow in their absence. He'd have been much more at ease sharing that labour than where he was now. Only the core of the army remained, troops trained and loyal to his father and the carrion riders flocking above them, grey as ash against the bright sky.

The surviving shiplords had returned to their forts and Krish had sent the Yronim back to the land that was once again their own. It had been his father's suggestion and it had seemed sensible at the time. The savage tribe of the mountains was feared by the lowland Ashane. If Krish had come to his people backed by the Yronim, they would never have accepted him as their own. It was the same reason he'd told the beast Rii to fly only at night and left the monkey Adolfo in Mirror Town. He wanted his people to see him as a man.

Now it didn't seem so wise. He had barely a dozen of his own people around him: freed slaves of Mirror Town. They were a ragged and mismatched bunch, still wearing the scraps of armour they'd scavenged from their former masters' stocks. They weren't a group designed to intimidate, though Krish had seen them fight. He remembered them laughing as they killed for him. It had horrified him at the time, but now it gave him a little comfort.

Their destination lay ahead. Ashfall. It was a name he'd heard all his life, the greatest shipfort in the land, seat of the Oak Wheel and home of their King. It would be his home now: this lake, and the steep, conical mountain that formed an island in its centre. The waters of the lake were very dark and from this distance they seemed quite still. The whole scene was frozen, as lifeless as a painting. Overhead, the carrion flock flew past with a great rushing of wings towards the fort.

The mammoths who pulled Ashfall were as small as mice in the distance, their coats the same grey. The base of the fort was red, while its many turrets shone a patchwork of a hundred different colours that resolved into images of flowers and ships and elegantly dressed people as they drew near. Nearer still and he could hear the creaking of the mammoths' harnesses as they laboured to pull the shipfort on its circuit of the huge lake.

Krish remembered with sudden sharpness the village in which he'd spent the first seventeen years of his life: a ring of tents with the jagged rocks and mountains all around. It was strange to long to return to a place in which he'd been so unhappy, but it had been a simple sort of misery. He'd spent the last two years discovering that there were worse things than being hungry and bruised.

His father's gaze was fixed on him as he studied the fort. King

Nayan's face was riven by lines that had only grown deeper on the long journey back from Mirror Town, and his hair was a steely grey, but there was nothing weak about him.

'Ready to return home?' his father asked. A twist to his lips said he understood the irony of the question.

The bridge that led from the lakeshore to the fort was long and lined with people. These were the ones who'd been left behind, the women and the children and the old and the sick. Their eyes on Krish weren't friendly. They'd seen husbands, fathers and sons march to a war against him from which they hadn't returned. And now he sat at his father's side, their dead for ever unavenged.

But these were the people who'd served his father for years, even after he'd proclaimed a sentence of death on his own unborn son. Krish didn't think he owed them anything.

'Hold your head high. You are their prince and they must know it,' his father said quietly.

'But will they like it?' Krish asked.

'They must.'

★

Rii seemed to labour through the air, her wings creaking as they swept up and her chest heaving with effort as they swept down. Eric patted her flank encouragingly, though she probably couldn't feel it through the thick fur. It was far cleaner than it had been when he'd first met her, regularly washed and brushed and fussed over by the grooms Prince Krishanjit had assigned him. The men had been terrified at first, and then fascinated and finally honoured that they'd been chosen to tend to the Prince's Monster. They gave her everything she asked.

Rii was pampered now, that was the problem: pampered and fat. He'd noticed her sides swelling in the last few weeks and was it any surprise, the amount of food she put inside her? Who could have guessed, in the cold north where only reindeer and bears thrived, that she had a weakness for sweet pastries?

She wasn't the only one growing soft. Since the Battle of Mirror Town, Eric had also discovered a taste for the finer things. He had silk shirts that showed off the blond of his hair to perfection and rings to wear on the fingers that hadn't been mutilated by the ice of the far north. The silver torc around his neck chafed, but he wouldn't have parted with it for the world. Prince Krishanjit himself had given it to him, to mark the part he and Rii had played in winning the battle for him. He suspected it came from the neck of one of the lords of Ashanesland killed before the unlikely peace had been made.

Now they'd returned to the heartland of Ashanesland. He'd returned to the place from which his very long journey had begun, not that he could see it. Prince Krishanjit had asked him to come at night. Rii didn't tend to make a happy first impression on people.

The moon was bright enough and the stars clear. There was light below too, firelight in scattered villages and then, ahead, the far brighter blaze of Ashfall itself. Rii had learned better than to land anywhere near the poor mammoths tugging the shipfort around. The beasts of burden who'd accompanied the army had never warmed to her, and he'd sometimes caught her staring at their meaty flanks with a hungry eye.

She alighted a few hundred paces behind the fortress, which quickly became a few hundred more as the mammoths trudged onward. Eric slid from Rii's back and slapped her neck affectionately. 'Sorry, Rii, but you're gonna have to stay here till morning.'

'If the Lord Yron desireth it.'

'He does. But I don't reckon he'll complain too much if you find yourself a cow to keep you going till we can sort you out a proper meal. Just try not to be seen.'

Arwel whimpered as Eric freed him from his makeshift cradle among Rii's saddlebags, but his mouth split into a wide grin when he saw his father. He gurgled in pleasure and Eric felt the same thing shift inside him that always did, pouring a warmth into all his veins. What did it matter that his son's teeth were sharp or his eyes grey? He was the most perfect baby that had ever been born.

Though not as much a baby as he had been. He was a solid weight now, legs and arms chubby and strong enough to move him in a crawl. He wriggled in Eric's arms until Eric turned him on his back and tickled his stomach. Arwel's arms reached out, grasping for Eric's nose, and Eric gave him a finger to suck on. Sharp little teeth dug into it and he felt blood flow out. His fingers were prickled by teeth scars but there was hardly any pain.

When he drew nearer to the bridge across the water and the men guarding it, he pulled the swaddling clothes up to cover his boy's face.

The guard at the gate saluted as he approached. 'Lord Eric?'

Eric preened a little at that. *Lord* Eric, and he a boy not yet twenty. 'Yeah, that's me.'

'Welcome, my lord. The prince asked me to show you to your rooms.'

His *rooms*? Well then. He followed the man down a long spiral corridor winding inward and marvelled at how much posher this place was than the one other shipfort he'd ever seen: clapped-out old Smallwood. They passed a hall bigger than the Great Temple of the Worshippers in Smiler's Fair, though there were only five idols in this one, the unfriendly-looking prow gods of the Ashane. Another room was filled floor-to-high-ceiling with books, and there were tapestries studded with jewels on all the walls of the corridor.

No wonder it was in such good nick. There were servants everywhere, polishing the wood and the precious metal and watering flowers that grew in pots. Even so, the red of the walls made it gloomier than Eric cared for. The colour seemed designed to dull the glow of the lanterns hung at every corner. Smiler's Fair had been far brighter, but that was like comparing the lipstick of a lady and a whore.

They walked past a ladder with a servant on it, dusting the corners of the ceiling. As the lad climbed down, Eric admired the lean solidity of his legs and the way his blouse hung open, showing the muscles of his stomach.

The servant seemed to feel Eric's gaze. He met his eyes with a smile, then winked and took his ladder away. Eric remembered with a flash of pain how Lahiru had spoken of flings with servants in far-off forts. Now Eric could do the same thing if he chose, but he knew he wouldn't. His son stirred against his chest and made those little whimpers that meant he was ready to eat.

'Here, my lord,' the soldier said, holding open a wooden door for Eric. The room was luxurious beyond anything he'd ever seen before. The bed was draped with velvet, the furniture all richly carved and the floor scattered with furs, but he didn't have much time to enjoy it. When Arwel was hungry, he didn't have any patience.

'Listen, if it ain't too much trouble, do you think you could bring me a bite to eat?' Eric asked the guard. 'Meat if you've got it. And . . . and blood as well from the carcass.'

'Blood?'

'That's right. Don't you know it's a delicacy in the Moon Forest? All the thegns love it.'

The man's stern face was caught in a struggle not to look disgusted by one of his betters. He won the battle, nodded and left Eric in peace.

Arwel's whimpers were growing into howls and Eric gave him his own thumb to suck on to ease him. There was a pleasure in feeding his boy that he'd never known was possible.

But then again, a whole lot had happened to him that he'd never for a moment have guessed. He'd left Ashanesland a slave and returned a conqueror. He remembered Babi's doll-like face twisted in dislike as she'd sold him to the Servants. She'd acted so high and mighty, but she'd have to bow to him now he was an admiral and a favourite of Prince Krishanjit. How was that as a job for a sellcock of Smiler's Fair?

But if he went to her, he'd have to tell her Lahiru was dead. It didn't seem nice to crow when bringing news like that. They should be mourning together, not fighting. Except Eric didn't think Babi would shed too many tears for Lahiru, and all Eric's were done. There hadn't been as many as he expected. When he tried to bring his lover's face to mind, all he got was a sort of handsome brown blur. Wasn't that funny? He remembered the woman who wronged him better than the man he'd once thought he loved.

The door swung open but he didn't look up, too lost in his memories as Arwel suckled. And then a heavy body bowled into him, knocking him to one side and Arwel to another.

Arwel screamed and Eric didn't see the blade the guard had drawn until after he'd thrown his body in front of it. He screamed too as the blade pierced him, but the guard must have stopped the thrust the moment he realised it would strike Eric, and it didn't go too deep. Eric gasped, clasping his hands against the wound in his side.

'Out of the way,' the guard yelled, his voice high-pitched and scared. 'There's a worm man!' The guard grabbed his shoulder, trying to pull him away, and Eric finally understood.

'It's my son!' he shouted.

Arwel wailed. His face was pale with crying as Eric scooped him into his arms. He held Arwel to his chest, rocking him and whispering 'there, there'. His back itched with the fear of a sword blade, but his spine would stop the metal from cutting through to his boy.

No blow came, and after a moment there was the sound of metal clattering onto wood as the weapon must have been dropped. Eric turned, Arwel cradled against him, to see the guard frozen with fear and horror.

'Your . . . your son, my lord? But he's . . . he's . . .'

Eric wasn't a fool. He understood the horror. He knew how his boy looked, the ash-grey skin, the hairless head and the nails curved into claws. He knew and it still enraged him that anyone could look at his beautiful boy and see a monster. 'Get out!' he shouted, and the guard only hesitated a moment before stooping to retrieve his sword and scrambling to obey.

He'd dropped the tray of food he'd brought. Eric's meal lay scattered across the floor, a slab of meat half in and half out of the hearth, one half burned and the other red, and peas rolling everywhere. But by some small stroke of luck, the jug of blood had fallen on its bottom.

Eric's hand was shaking as he poured it into his palm for Arwel to lap at with his thin tongue. Daydreams about living it high as a thegn of Ashanesland were all fine and dandy for a boy fresh out of the fair. But he was a man with other responsibilities. And enough to love right here in his arms.

★

A knock on his door woke Krish at daybreak. He expected to see one of the many servants who'd poked and prodded and stared at him last night as they bathed him, but it was his father. Dinesh stirred at the foot of his bed, cracking open a wary brown eye to watch. He'd slept with his sword naked beside him. Krish shook his head sharply when he saw Dinesh's fingers creeping towards the hilt.

There was an uncomfortable silence before Nayan said, 'You look tired. Did you not sleep well?'

Krish shrugged. He felt near naked in the silk gown his servants had left for him. 'I'm not used to sleeping in a bed.'

'Well,' Nayan said. 'Well. That will soon change, I'm sure.'

Two guards stood at attention behind his father, stern-faced men in full metal armour. Dinesh moved to stand at Krish's shoulder, naked and weaponless with the dazed smile he wore near-constantly. His father's guards eyed him and then cut their eyes at each other, clearly containing smiles. It occurred to Krish they thought Dinesh was his lover.

'Do you need me?' Krish asked. 'Is there business to attend to?'

'Not business, no. There's something I'd like to show you.'

'Oh. Then I should dress.'

His father and his men turned their backs while Krish pulled on the thick woollen trousers, pearl-embroidered tunic and blue-and-green cloak that were the first items that came to hand when he opened his wardrobe. His father eyed him critically but said nothing. Krish suspected he'd chosen wrong somehow. He was sure it was only the first of many mistakes he'd be making.

The guards watched him with judging eyes until his father waved his arms at them and snapped, 'Go! Go! Return to your duties.' He raised a thin brow at Krish until he nodded at Dinesh to leave them too. Dinesh looked unhappy, but he didn't have it in him to disobey Krish.

His father's eyes were tight and his hands fidgeted at his belt. It startled Krish to realise that it was the first time they'd been alone together. In all their long journey here, Krish had taken care never to be in his father's presence without a guard. And his father had always done the same – until now.

'Where are you taking me?' Krish asked.

'I want to talk to you about your mother.' His father didn't elaborate. Only the sound of their footsteps accompanied them, loud then soft as they moved between wooden floor and fur coverings.

Nayan led them through the fort to another doorway, simpler than the one through which they'd entered. There was misty daylight beyond, blocked by a steep-sided mountain. They must be on the fort's inner side, facing the island at the lake's centre rather than its outer shore. The bridge here was just as long, wavelets slapping against its wooden boards as the mammoths towed it onward. When they'd crossed, they stood in the shadow of the mountain.

'How did she die?' Krish kept his eyes on the winding, grassy path that led them upward.

He felt the flutter of fingers against his shoulder, but his father must have thought better of resting his hand there. 'Your mother was very dear to me. I mourned her when she died.'

Krish didn't turn to face him. He couldn't bear to. It wasn't his womb mother he thought of. It was his ma, who'd saved his life and sent him off, not caring that it would cost her own. Now he was prince he could send to the mountains and learn her fate, but he wasn't sure that he would. It was easier not to know.

'This was your mother's favourite place,' his father told him. 'She walked here often. Her rooms were filled with the flowers she picked.'

There were a few early spring flowers already, white and purple droplets in the grass. But if this was a garden, it was one that had long ago fallen to neglect. What might have once been hedges trimmed into fanciful shapes had grown bulbous and unformed, and there were brambles everywhere, crawling up the trees and choking the bushes. Only the path remained clear. Krish wondered if his father walked here often.

'I never imagined she might do what she did,' Nayan said. 'I know the rumours that have run free in the kingdom ever since, but the truth is she chose her death herself. She gave her life for yours.'

'I'm sorry,' Krish said, though he wasn't quite sure what he was apologising for. The sacrifice would never have been needed if his father hadn't planned to kill him the moment he was born.

Now Nayan did touch his shoulder, turning him so they were face to face. 'You didn't ask to be who you are. None of us had any choice. Your mother acted for love of you and I . . . I acted for love of my kingdom. The prophecies said your coming would bring strife and death, and can you say that it hasn't?'

'That wasn't my choice either.'

'No. And we must live with how we chose. But there are always new choices to make. Because of what happened I have no heir. I took another wife after your mother. Did you know that? It isn't spoken of. She died in the fourth month of her pregnancy and my people whispered that I was cursed. I could have found another woman to wed. I'm a king. But I saw the fear in the eyes of all the shipborn ladies. How could I have married a woman who was afraid to share my bed?

'If you wish to rule after me, you may. My people – our people – need a leader. But they don't love you now. You'll need to win them over. I can teach you how to do that. I can teach you how to rule.'

'I'm your son.' Krish looked into his father's face, so tired and worn. 'If you can't love me, how will the people?'

His father gave a wintry smile. 'You slaughtered half my lords and thousands of my soldiers.'

'You attacked me.'

'And I don't imagine you love me either.'

'Why did you bring me here then? To Ashfall, I mean? Was it just to save your life?'

Nayan sighed and walked onward. The path switched back along the mountain's flank and for a few paces the lake lay in front of them. Its waters were restless, stirred into white peaks by a growing wind. Birds dipped and dove above it.

'I wasn't ready to die,' his father said. 'But I was resigned to it. I'd lost, as the prophecy told me I would. Then you offered me a different way. I don't love you, it's true. But I respect you. I don't believe I would have done as you did, had our positions been reversed. I want to teach you how to rule, so my kingdom will thrive when I'm gone. But I believe there may be things you can teach me too.'

His smile was less wintry this time, though not yet warm. Krish thought of his da, who'd never spoken to him so plainly or without contempt. This might not be love, but maybe it could become it. Maybe he could love this man. Yet gods had no need of this sort of love, or so everyone seemed to think.

'Was this what you wanted to show me?' he asked. 'This place my mother loved.'

'Not quite. Just a little further now.'

The mossy path twisted round again, back under the shade of the winter-bare trees. Then, quite unexpectedly, the trees ended and they'd reached the peak. It wasn't flat as Krish had expected, but scooped out into a shallow hollow. Nothing grew here, the ground dusty and grey.

Nothing grew but something had been planted. The spikes were taller than a man, as thick as an arm and cruelly pointed on their tops. The bodies that hung impaled on them had long since rotted down to the bone. Krish looked far below, towards the lake and the shipfort. These bodies must be visible to anyone standing on its battlements or walking its bridges. He could have seen them himself, if he'd known to look.

'Who are they?' he asked.

'Your mother chose what she did, but she didn't do it alone. Her maid helped her. It was her maid who cut her open and took you away, and the maid's son who smuggled you out.'

'And that's why you executed them?' Krish had seen horrors at the Battle of Mirror Town, but the sight of those skeletons made his bile rise. Their pain had been given them in cold blood, not in hot.

His father rested his hand on Krish's shoulder, a far heavier weight than before. 'For that and for what they did afterwards. Your mother gave them a purse of gold to care for you, but they decided the gold would be easier to spend without the burden of a fugitive prince. When we caught them, they told me that they'd thrown you in the river to die. It didn't even require torture to extract the confession. They thought I'd be pleased that they'd killed you as I'd commanded.'

'And weren't you?' Krish studied his father's face and tried to see the man he'd been back when all these choices had been made. It was impossible. All that he'd done had changed him too profoundly.

'One day you'll understand,' his father said, and Krish didn't know if it was a reassurance or a warning.

3

The dusty streets of Mirror Town had grown familiar to Dae Hyo in the months he'd been here, but he couldn't say he'd grown any more fond of them. The debris of the battle had been cleared and the corpses had long ago been given desert graves, but half the buildings remained wrecked. The dead were in no fit state to mend them and the survivors seemed to have lost the will. He missed the plains of his home fiercely and the simple warrior life he'd lived there. The tribes knew that reputation was more sturdy than stone, and the grass would grow to cover them all in the end.

As he crossed the central square, he saw the only things that had been growing here since Krish had taken his army back to Ashanesland. There had only been a dozen pillars in the sun-baked square before Krish had come. There must be a hundred now and others being built – and every one had an occupant. Dae Hyo hadn't believed it at first, when he'd been told the mages would climb the poles and stay there for months or even years. But while he'd been here he'd come to recognise their faces, the same faces on each pillar, though they grew more gaunt and dirtier with time.

They weren't happy faces. Why would they be? Who could find joy standing in the moisture-sucking sunlight from dawn till dusk? Then again, the people walking the streets didn't seem too overjoyed with their lives either. It was a thin crowd, slow-moving and listless. Many stopped to watch the lunatics on their pillars with yearning eyes.

Dae Hyo had thought that when Krish left they might all cheer up, but something more was broken here than the buildings.

He saw two blind women being led stumbling by small children, and others with faces so horribly disfigured he had to look away. Mirror Town's people had paid a steep price for the magic that had saved them.

But not all who lived here were sad. His destination lay ahead, the city's largest park. It had once been carefully tended, flowers arranged in pleasing swirls of colour. The ragged outline of those designs was still visible, but the plants had been left to grow free and weeds had invaded the beds. Now both plants and weeds were being crushed heedlessly underfoot by Mirror Town's new army.

The slaves of Mirror Town had always outnumbered their masters. If the mages had asked Dae Hyo's opinion of it, he'd have told them it wasn't wise. Now the slaves had been freed, the city was under their rule, and their former masters climbed up to rot on pillars rather than face the new way of things.

A thousand or more of the former slaves were in this park today, their white robes hidden beneath armour of metal or leather or some substance that looked like amber, with swords and knives and axes and the occasional trident strapped to their sides. They'd arranged themselves into a neat square, and they chanted as they marched in step from one side to the other and then back again. They might have kept at it all day if the thin Ashanewoman at the front hadn't seen Dae Hyo and shouted at them to stop.

She smiled when he turned to her. 'Commander! We've done as you asked!'

He *had* asked them to do this. It was something Yemisi had insisted on reading to him from one of the books in the Great Library, a military history of nations long gone. He couldn't see the point of it himself – all this walking backwards and forwards wouldn't do you much good in a battle – but the book said it taught soldiers to think and fight as one unit.

Besides, he hadn't any better idea what to do with the army he now commanded. Krish had told him to fashion the slaves into a true fighting force, and he didn't mean to let his brother down.

'Yes,' he said, 'it's very impressive. But what about the bow work and sword work?'

Her expression fell. 'I'm sorry, commander. We thought you wanted us to practise our walking.'

The slave army had stopped in their march, facing sideways. A thousand pairs of eyes slid leftward to see his reaction in a thousand faces as woeful as hers.

'No, no, you did well,' he told her.

She smiled, and a thousand faces behind her smiled too. Dae Hyo suspected they'd have stood there all morning grinning like idiots if he let them. The rune Krish had ordered tattooed on their cheeks had freed them from the grip of bliss, the drug that had kept them enslaved, but only to make them prisoners of Krish's will. And when Krish wasn't here, it was Dae Hyo they followed so blindly.

He sighed. 'Why don't you practise this one day, bow work the next and sword work the day after?'

'One day walking, one day with bows and one day with swords.' The woman nodded. 'Yes, commander.'

He turned on his heel, only to find himself facing another group of former slaves, all grinning that same idiotic grin at him. These had no armour, but they'd fashioned red sashes to tie around the waists of their robes, marking them as part of the force he'd set to watching over Mirror Town itself – and its unhappy residents in particular.

One of those residents was with them, hanging limp between two slaves. Dae Hyo couldn't see her face, but he could see the blood dripping from it.

'What happened here?' he asked.

'A traitor!' the slaves said in a cheerful chorus and one of them added, 'She betrayed Lord Krish.'

He cupped his hand beneath the woman's chin to raise her face. It was very badly beaten. Her eyes were swollen shut and

her lips split against her teeth, which were smeared a gory red.
'What did she do?'

'We heard her,' a flabby youth said. 'In the wine vendor's on
Victory Street. She was . . . she was speaking against Lord
Krishanjit.'

Dae Hyo leaned closer to study the woman. When his shadow
passed over her, she flinched away.

'What did she say?' he asked the flabby youth.

'I wouldn't like to repeat it.'

'Belbog's balls, boy! If you don't repeat it, how will I know
what to do about it?'

The youth swallowed. 'She said that Krish was a peasant. That
he was as ignorant as a slave.'

Dae Hyo couldn't really claim any of that was untrue. The
woman shifted and groaned in the grasp of the slaves. Her tongue
licked bloody lips and she croaked, 'I'm sorry.'

She probably was, which wasn't the same as saying she hadn't
meant it. No doubt given the chance she'd do what she could to
hurt Krish. But Krish was a thousand miles away and she wasn't
in much of a state to hurt anyone. Dae Hyo was no strategist,
but he knew that beating its citizens wouldn't make the people
of Mirror Town love Krish more.

'Let her go,' he said. 'I tell you what, I think she's learned her
lesson.'

The boy's face was an interesting study: mulish determination
warring with his desire to obey the commander his Lord had set
above him.

'Keep an eye on her if you like,' Dae Hyo told him. 'Only
don't hit her again unless you really have to. The elder mothers
always told us it's bad for the spirit to torture your captives.'

He felt suddenly too weary to deal with them any longer.
The sounds of the pointless walking up and down started up
again as he walked away. He supposed if that kept them busy,
it was better than dragging people from their homes.

When Krish asked him to stay here it had seemed to make
sense. Krish was heading across the mountains to an uncertain

future as Prince of Ashanesland and leaving behind a city he and his newfound father had wrecked. It wasn't a pretty situation and asking a brother to make sure it didn't turn ugly was exactly what Dae Hyo might have done. And there was Olufemi, scouring the Great Library in search of the secrets of the runes. She needed Dae Hyo to guard her against her own family, who hadn't taken too kindly to the carnage she'd brought with her.

But the longer time stretched, the less useful Dae Hyo felt. The slaves didn't need him. They were happy to walk backwards and forwards all day and beat bloody those who didn't love Krish as much as they did. They sat on Mirror Town like a man on a wild pony he had tamed – unloved but in control.

It itched at Dae Hyo. He didn't like to be useless. He'd occupied too much of his life with it already. Thanks to the rune that stopped his body from turning drink into fun, he could see that clearly. He could see everything clearly. His thoughts went on and on with nothing to shut them up, and the least that Krish could do after forcing him to feel this way was to give him something to occupy his mind. Maybe Dae Hyo would tell him so, the next time he wrote to him.

His house loomed ahead of him. It was quite absurdly large: ten storeys high, the storeys stacked improbably on top of each other, some square, some round, some rectangular and each painted a different colour. They weren't nice colours to look at – too bright and sharp. They were the colours venomous animals wore to warn you not to touch them.

Yemisi was waiting for him in the fourth-floor lounging room. She'd said yesterday that she'd visit, but her magically returned youth had made her flighty and he hadn't been sure she'd come. He'd filled the place with cushions and rugs and wall hangings looted from the homes of those who no longer had any need of them. He'd told Yemisi they reminded him of the tents of his childhood, and she'd mocked him for his barbarian tastes.

She was reclining on one of the cushions, a half-empty jug

of rice wine in front of her as she sipped from a crystal glass. She looked guilty when she saw him. She knew he didn't like watching others drink when the pleasure was denied him. But she emptied her glass all the same. She drank a lot. Olufemi said she never used to, but many things had changed since the Battle of Mirror Town.

'The general returns triumphant,' she said snidely. Her mouth was less pretty when it twisted that way.

He didn't know why he put up with her, except that the mages shunned him, Olufemi held him in contempt and the former slaves had as much conversation as vegetables. Any company was better than none, even hers.

He sat beside her on the cushions. 'Not much to triumph over. The ground was beaten into submission by the slaves' boots and one sorry mage by their fists, but none of it had anything to do with me. I tell you what, a man could feel quite useless around here.'

'Well, I have news.'

'What's happened?'

'I don't know. But a bird fetched you a letter from Prince Krishanjit. Olufemi brought it over.'

She handed him a roll of parchment small enough to be strapped to a bird's leg and grubby from its long journey.

He unrolled it with enthusiasm. His brother had learned to write since Dae Hyo had first met him, but he hadn't learned it well. The parchment looked as if a spider had fallen into ink and then crawled across it.

'What does it say?' Yemisi asked.

'My friend Dae Hyo,' he read, and smiled. 'We are in Ashanesland. There's been fever in the army and desertions since we left the plains. We're half our size now. I hope my army in Mirror Town is doing better. We should reach Ashfall by the time you read this. I'll write again when we do.'

'That was pointless,' Yemisi said. 'He told you no more than you could have guessed.'

'Not true. He might not have reached Ashanesland. Another army might have attacked him. Disease might have killed him. Now we know he's safe.'

'Or that he was safe three weeks ago.'

He scowled at her, though she was right. The birds were fast but Ashanesland was a very long way away, across the plains and over the mountains. Still, Dae Hyo found it a comfort to hear from Krish. His absence had been growing larger the longer it went on.

'Are your duties done for the day?' she asked.

The sun streamed through the room's east-facing window, only an hour or two above the horizon, but he nodded.

She smiled and stretched, as lazy and contented as a well-fed cat. 'Well then, we'll have to find some other way to pass the time.'

She said the words in the tribes' tongue. He'd taught her the language on a whim at first, not expecting her to learn it, but enjoying the sound of the familiar words in his own mouth. She'd sucked them in as easy and as eager as a babe drank milk. It was her youth, he supposed, that made her so apt to learn. She'd come to this life near a hundred years past, but magic had given her back the body of a woman barely into adulthood with all the life and liveliness that went with it.

She was beautiful. It was irritating. More irritating because she knew it, but he couldn't deny the perfection of her figure and face. Her skin shone from the oils she rubbed into it and into the stormcloud of her hair. Her lips were plump and moist and she pouted them now, enjoying that she'd caught him in a moment of appreciation for her.

'What is it you want to do?' he asked gruffly.

She sighed and stood. 'A walk perhaps to clear my head.'

★

Later, she slipped her hand into the crook of his elbow as they walked through the orchard that had once been a desert, where Olufemi had performed the first true magic of the new age. The trees had grown and ripened fruit in the space of moments, and for a few weeks after the Battle of Mirror Town every survivor had gorged on them.

The brief spring in which they'd flourished had passed. The magic faded and the summer sun had withered them. What fruit hadn't been picked had rotted on the bough into husks too dry even to draw flies.

'This isn't a cheerful place,' he said.

She shrugged, less carefree than she'd seemed earlier. 'I like it. A thing both old and new.'

Like me hung between them, unsaid.

'Have you tried reading your journals?' he asked. 'You said that might bring the memories back.'

'It didn't. They were just words on a page. I read about the party my family threw me when I reached my sixtieth year and it might as well have been a tale of Abayomi the Lecher. Worse even. When I read those tales as a youth I used to picture them in my mind. I'd see her face and the room she sat in and the way she'd smile when she spotted a pretty boy. It's a great work, truly, you should read it. But when I read the recounting of my own past there was . . . nothing. I could make no pictures of it in my mind.'

He remained silent as they walked further, through the bones of the trees. He'd learned that she'd mock him if he spoke without thinking. 'Well,' he said at last. 'Then you don't know if the memories were good or bad.'

'It was a party. Of course it was a good memory.'

'Svarog's cock, I've been at festivals so awful they left people dead. And maybe you were sad that day, or maybe you had your moon blood and your stomach pained you.'

'I didn't. The journal said it was a good day.'

'So?' He snapped a twig from one of the trees and rubbed it absently between his fingers. 'We lie to ourselves about the past. I did, and then I drank until the lies seemed real. I used to tell myself that life among the Dae was a paradise. I remembered my childhood as endless spring and endless sun. But when

Krish . . . when he did what he did to me, I saw it all clearly, exactly the way it had been.

'When I was seven there was illness among the rabbits and half of them died. We went hungry that year and the baby who would have been my youngest brother was born dead. The elder mothers said it was for the best and my mother wept and raged. I didn't understand at the time, but I see it now.

'I was thirteen when I rode on my first raid. I was too young, but I'd always been big. And I was strong and a decent fighter and the tribe needed all they could find. We'd always been weak. I'd forgotten that too. At the start of the fight an arrow grazed my arm, and I felt so proud of the scar I'd have. But then my pony threw me and there I was in the middle of all those legs and axes. I was so scared I pissed myself and the others laughed at me all the way home. The next fight I killed three men and hid behind a prick-leaf bush when I threw up.

'And I remember . . . I've spent so many years trying to forget how the camp looked after the Chun came. If you put enough wine inside you, even the memory of the way your sister's body looked with half its guts hanging out and a knife shoved in her . . . even the memory of that will fade. But not any more. Now I have them all back. I could tell you the colour of the beetles that were crawling across her face. If I could give all my memories away, I would.'

They'd reached the centre of the orchard. This was the place where it had happened: where the long-dead magic had been reborn. The strange rune-sculpture that had sparked it all was surrounded by a ring of ripples, frozen into the earth, as if some mighty stone had been dropped there. That's how it was all over Mirror Town. The benefits of magic had faded, like the dried-out branches of these trees, and only its unwanted after-effects were left.

Yemisi knelt to brush away the windblown sand that half-obscured the rune. He wondered if he'd angered her. He'd always had a talent for saying the wrong thing. He'd thought it might be the drink that made his tongue wag too loosely, but it seemed it was just him.

Yemisi didn't look angry, though. Without the mask of lines that age put on it, her face was easy to read. She was melancholy. No doubt the wine she'd drunk was partly to blame. 'I asked Olufemi what kind of person I was,' she said. 'Before the Battle of Mirror Town.'

'A grumpy one,' Dae Hyo told her. 'You thought I was a fool.'

That won a small smile from her. 'I still do. But Olufemi couldn't tell me much. She spoke about how great a mage I was, and how short-tempered a teacher. She spoke about what I did, but not who I was. She didn't know me, except as the woman who taught her magic. I wonder if anyone knew me.'

'Your family?'

'No. They scorned me when I chose to study the runes.'

'There you go then. Better to have a fresh start. And you're living with your cousins now, aren't you?'

'With strangers. My memories end long before they were born. Everyone I remember is dead.' She laughed jaggedly. 'We're a sorry pair, aren't we? A sober drunk and a mage without her magic.'

She meant to lighten the mood and it would be easy to let her. But this was the first time they'd spoken so honestly. It was better, he'd come to realise, to face your problems than to run from them. Problems always had stouter legs than you imagined.

She stepped away from the rune, leaving it still half-covered in sand. He used his sleeve to clear it all, until the full shape was revealed. Krish told him that Olufemi had a slave dig it into the earth for her, and he'd done a neat enough job, but not a perfect one. There were places where curves wobbled and straight lines bent. Still, Dae Hyo felt that he could see the true shape of it, hidden within this imperfect copy. He didn't understand it but he felt its power.

He looked up into Yemisi's eyes, so dark and wide. 'You learned it once. You could learn it again.'

She didn't look surprised. The thought must have occurred to her. 'It took me a lifetime to study the runes before. It would take me as long again to re-master them. And besides, your Lord Krishanjit has forbidden it.'

He had. Dae Hyo had seen the horror in his friend's face when he'd surveyed the damage done by the Battle of Mirror Town, and much of it self-inflicted. Krish had said no more magic should ever be performed in his name. But Krish was over the mountains in Ashanesland and besides, he'd spoken in haste and without thought for when even such a dangerous weapon might be needed.

'Just try it,' he said to her. 'Where's the harm?'

'Where's the harm? When Olufemi did this magic her family's mansion collapsed. People died!'

'Well, maybe do it less then. Not so strongly.'

'That isn't how it works,' she snapped.

'My apologies for trying to help. I'll leave you to your misery.'

He made to stand, but she took his arm and pulled him back. 'Don't. I've . . . I've thought it myself. If I can do a little of what I did before, if I knew that I could get it back with trying . . . Then if I become something else, I'll know it's my choice. Does that seem like sense?'

He nodded. It made more sense than he was comfortable with.

'I've been trying to learn again how to clear my head – to make it peaceful and empty,' she said. 'It's hard. My head is so noisy. But I've been getting better, and maybe . . .'

She took the twig he'd plucked from between his fingers and scratched a shape with it into the hard-baked earth.

'A rune?' he asked. It was barely more than a line and a circle.

'A simple one. It's meant to make just one flower grow. I found it in a book. A mage of old used it to woo his sweetheart, but the more flowers he grew for her, the less she cared for him. It was the price of his magic.'

He scowled at the rune. 'I don't want you hating me even more. You're hardly bearable as it is.'

'It's just one flower. I won't do it again – and besides, each person has their own price to pay. It's never the same. Now be quiet. I can't empty my mind if my ear is full of your talk.'

He watched her face as she settled into the cross-legged crouch he'd seen Olufemi take. It didn't look very comfortable, but he supposed she knew what she was doing. Her face didn't look too peaceful, though. Her eyes were screwed shut with the force of her concentration.

He was glad she was trying, truly. Despite her awfulness he didn't enjoy seeing her sad. But sitting here in the dry desert heat was no entertainment. The dead trees all around weren't much of a view. For want of anything better to study, his eyes were drawn back to the rune.

It was strange to think that so simple a thing held so much power. Although from the little Olufemi had bothered to tell him, it was Krish who held the power and the rune merely drew on it. But then again, Krish didn't look much like a person of power either.

The form of the rune was pleasing. There was something just right in the balance of its lines. Its meaning tickled at him, present but intangible. He found it easy to fill his mind with the thing. The feeling was strangely soothing and he closed his eyes so that the rune would be the only thing there. When he focused on the exact shape of it, he didn't need to think about anything else. He felt as if it emptied his mind, tipping all other thought out and leaving only itself behind.

For a moment there was nothing. Dae Hyo didn't exist; there was only the rune. The freedom of it felt wonderful, and in experiencing that wonder Dae Hyo returned. With him came a rush of something he couldn't identify but that washed through him with the force of a flood.

He opened his eyes, shocked. The rune was still in front of him, imperfect as the version in his mind hadn't been. And in its centre was a flower: a golden rose bobbing on a thin, thorned stem.

'You did it!' he said, grinning at Yemisi.

She reached out to cup the flower between two fingers – and then with a brutal twist she pulled it out and threw it away.

'No,' she said. 'I didn't do that. You did.'

4

It was only because Alfreda leaned forward to row that the arrow struck the boat's side and not her back. She froze in shock as another flew, better aimed, to graze her side. And then the pain jolted her into motion and she turned and dived into the water, oozing a cloudy trail of blood behind her.

She made herself stay under, near the muddy bottom of the marsh. It was thick with long-leaved plants that twined around her and tried to trap her as she moved. The breath was already growing short in her lungs and she forced two more strokes from her arms, a push with her legs. She could only hope she'd come far enough.

She hadn't, not quite. When she surfaced, she could see her attacker crouched on one of the low, reed-fringed hillocks that dotted the marsh. His head swung round at the sound of her, his bow followed and she dived again. She wasn't quick enough to stop another arrow lodging in her shoulder, soon torn painfully from it by the tangling weeds.

He knew where she was now and he knew her path. More arrows followed, slowed by the water but still lethal. Her large, ungainly body made for an easy target. She weaved from side to side and every one of them missed, but now her breath was growing short again and she wasn't there yet. There was more water ahead of her, so cloudy with dirt she could see barely one hand in front of her eyes. Was she even swimming the right way?

She pushed onward until her chest felt on fire and she knew that soon she'd breathe in water just to relieve the terrible burn. She hadn't reached land but she dove upward anyway. Her head broke the surface and she gasped desperately for breath and clawed at the slimy leaves draped across her eyes.

She'd emerged behind him. He must have heard her. He was beginning to turn, but she was near him now, only paces away. The water was waist-deep, the mud solid enough to stand. It was wet and clinging but she forced herself forward. She scrabbled up the hillock in a sodden rush and flung herself on her attacker.

His bow was caught between them, the already nocked arrow scratching the skin along her collarbone as they grappled. He was a big man, nearly as tall as her and almost as heavily muscled. But blacksmithing had left her stronger. Her weight bore him to the ground. The arrow pushed deeper into her and she felt the blood flow as he struggled beneath her.

There was no finesse to the fight. They were both slippery with mud and they rolled and struggled, first one of them on top and then the other. The fight would only be won by chance this way, and Alfreda didn't trust it.

She used her waning strength to throw him from her. He landed on his back, winded. He pushed himself up on his elbows as she staggered towards him. His hand reached for his knife and she brought her booted foot down hard on his chest and then again. She heard the sound of his ribs snapping, and when she stamped again he screamed and then went silent as she crushed the heart beneath them.

He looked absurd in death. His arms were splayed above his head as if he'd tried to surrender too late and his mouth gaped in surprise, caked in blood. His shirt had torn in the fight and she saw that his chest had three long white scars and one redder and more recent, crossing the others. She didn't doubt he'd been a soldier in King Nayan's army.

There was a splash behind her and she turned, still panting, to see Marvan rowing their boat towards her. His arms stretched wide across its breadth to handle both oars.

'You look a sight,' he said as he beached the boat on the small hillock. He grinned at her beneath the absurd hook of his nose. 'Is that Alfreda of the Moon Forest folk, or the Beast of the Swamp?'

He often joked. Only killing seemed to leave him serious: serious and sated. 'You might have helped,' she told him. 'It isn't just me they're hunting.'

'I, unlike you, am wise enough not to dive into these waters. Is the man truly dead?'

She knelt to rummage through a pack that had rolled to the far edge of the hillock during their struggle. 'Aye. And there's bedding here for one and no sign of a larger camp. Looks like he was alone.'

'Then come back to the boat and let me examine you. You're bleeding. And you've ventured into waters that are best not swum in.'

The wounds had already stopped hurting. She felt quite numb, but she did as he said. It was best they left the hillock anyway. The swamp was also home to hunters of the non-human kind, and the fresh corpse would draw them.

The boat sank deeper into the mud of the shore when she stepped inside it, and some squelched through into the bottom of the vessel where their meagre belongings lay, already filthy. She rose, meaning to push the boat off before getting back in again, but Marvan grabbed her hand.

She found the touch of his skin against hers shocking, as she'd found all human contact since Cwen. It froze her, and she let him pull her back down onto the wooden seat.

'Take off your trousers. Your tunic too.' His hands began to work at the ties around her waist until she slapped them away.

'You'll see why if you do it,' he said patiently, and for once he didn't seem to be joking.

They had no modesty in front of each other. They'd been too long in each other's company too far from civilisation. Edred had been abandoned leagues and days ago, lamed by the impossible pace they'd driven him to. Alfreda had wept as she'd released him from his harness and then yelled at him as he tried to follow her. He and Algar had been almost exactly of an age, but the horse had outlived her brother.

Edred couldn't have come into the marshes anyway. And he'd

be safer far away from her. Horses were valuable. No doubt some churl family had been glad to take him in. Her anvil she'd sunk into the muck of the marsh. She couldn't bear the thought of another person working it.

The buttons of her shirt were slippery with slime and the cloth half-rotted from the persistent wetness. It ripped as she fumbled with it and she shrugged and tore the whole thing off. She'd go back and take the dead man's. It was of better quality anyway.

'Worse than I thought – there must be a score of them, and that's only your top half,' Marvan said, tutting.

She saw that her chest was covered in black lumps. She brushed at them without thinking and cried out at the pain it brought. Two of them wriggled and she realised that they were alive: horrible, bloated black worms with their heads buried inside her flesh. She understood the numbness now. It must be some poison they'd injected into her to allow themselves to feast in peace.

She pinched one between thumb and forefinger, meaning to pull it off, but Marvan grabbed her hand before she could. 'Don't do that. You'll leave the head behind and before you know it you'll be sick with the marsh fever, and then where will we both be? They'll need to be burned off. And from your legs too.'

There were a score more on her legs and, when she removed her smalls, three hanging from the flesh between them. Marvan blushed at the sight of them, as shy as a maid, and dropped his gaze to the tinderbox. He soon had an ember glowing and she took it from him without a word, pressing it one by one against the creatures on her legs. The tiny hairs on her skin singed as she worked, but the ember did its job. Creatures of water, the little worms clearly didn't care for fire.

They shrivelled as they died and dropped into the boat's bottom, where Marvan crushed them beneath his heel. Each left a tiny wound behind, star-shaped like their mouths. And each was a little pinprick of pain that burned brighter the longer their venom was gone from her blood.

She offered her back to Marvan so he could burn them there,

and then took the ember from him before he could baulk, to press it against the creatures feasting on the blood that fed her cunt.

'Our pursuers aren't stopping,' she said, when the job was done. She rose, still naked, and went to pilfer the dead man's shirt, then returned to push the boat out. She was far more wary than she had been of the filthy water.

Marvan passed over her trousers and an oar, pausing until the hillock was out of sight before replying. 'There's a bounty on us. A good one according to that boy we took back near North Star, and I don't think he was lying. Men who scream that loud are usually truthful.' His lips quirked into a brief smile of pure pleasure at the memory. He liked to kill. She'd seen that in him from the start.

'We shouldn't have killed so many on the journey here,' she said. 'They were bound to notice. And we shouldn't have killed those injured men they left on the plains. That was what did it, I think. When they sent back for them and found them slaughtered. That was what really upset them.' She didn't bother to suggest they shouldn't have killed at all. Marvan seemed to need bloodshed as much as he needed food, and these were all men who'd fought with Cwen's people and then turned their backs on them when peace was offered. They deserved to die as Cwen had. It was the least revenge she could take for the betrayal of her only friend.

'I don't know how they even guessed it was us,' he said. 'Those men were easy prey. The whole army was. The tribes raided them often enough and I didn't see a bounty set on them. How did they know to lay all the killings at our door?'

'It was the wounding, the knife wounds. They could see you killed for sport. And I told you we should have taken gold from them to make it seem like robbery.'

'I'm not a common thief!' He looked scandalised at the idea.

'Aye, but that's how they knew it was us. And now there's a hundred gold wheels or more for our heads and a pack of desperate men out to win it.'

The sun was low on the horizon, no longer quite a perfect circle. It sank out of sight as they rowed on. Midges rose from the marsh as they always did at dusk, biting what skin they could and flying into eyes and mouth. Alfreda waved her hand to shoo them off but there was little point.

Around them, the noises of day gave way to the louder chorus of night. The marsh slumbered when the sun was in the sky, but now its many inhabitants were waking. Ripples rocked the boat as some hidden animal dived into the water. The moon was a silver sliver above them and it left them in a world of shadows.

There were nocturnal birds here too. Their shrieks had alarmed her at first, but now she barely noticed them. They seemed to be in some unspoken competition with the croaking of the bullfrogs.

She must have drifted into a restless sleep, dream-haunted. She woke with only scraps of it remaining: her brother's face and the cries of a baby that in the dream she'd known was his. Marvan was already ashore, preparing what camp he could from their scant supplies. There was a fire burning and a small bird on a spit above it. The smell of it turned her stomach. Her eyes were clouded and when she put a hand to her forehead she felt its heat.

'You've a fever,' Marvan said.

She pulled up her tunic to see that several of the bite marks beneath were redly inflamed. One oozed a noxious green-yellow substance. 'Infection,' she said, or tried to say, but the words turned to mush in her mouth and her head dropped back weakly against the wood of the boat.

'Yes,' he said. 'That's what I thought.' The words stretched like softened metal and then the glow of them faded in her mind and left her nothing.

★

Marvan's strength began to fail him on the third day. He hadn't quite appreciated Alfreda's muscles until he no longer had the use of them and was forced to row alone. She lay in the bottom of the boat, twitching and flushed. She'd fouled herself on the first day and her clothes were crusted with shit. He'd tried to clean her, but she was too big to move and after a while the smell had faded. Now she took nothing in but the water he dribbled into her mouth and nothing but the occasional dribble of piss came out.

He thought the fever might be breaking. He *hoped* it was. It was certainly rising, and if it rose much higher she must surely die. It was a wonder she'd lived this long, but she was a tough one. It took toughness to survive in these marshes. He'd forgotten that.

He'd left here half a lifetime ago and never thought to return. Yet here he was. Everything felt stiflingly familiar, from the drab brown flies that stung like wasps to the startling pink wading birds. He remembered that they took their colour from the fish they ate, and turned an even brighter purple in the summer when the shoals of pricklefish were washed into the marshes by each spring tide.

And now the land he passed through was more familiar still. The twisted tree on the hillock to his left, long dead and half decayed, had been the first he ever climbed. Behind it was a shallow pool in which he'd often swum, though he'd known enough to rub himself in rotleaf oil before attempting it.

The stream narrowed up ahead. He pushed hard at the oars for two more strokes and then pulled them inward to keep them free of the bulrushes that leaned in on either side, shaking their dried-out heads at him. He had memories of this place too, where the water ran deeper than you'd guess and a corpse weighed down with stones might never be found.

Alfreda groaned, reaching out with her arm for something he couldn't see, only to groan again and drop her hand limply back down to her side. He thought, not for the first time, of heaving her body over the side of the boat and rowing quickly back the way he'd come, far away from this place and all its memories. He could tie stones around her ankles and she'd lie beside his brother's bones, a meal for the water snakes and the flesh newts.

The idea offended him, though. His brother had deserved every painful moment of his death, and Marvan had enjoyed giving it to him more than he'd enjoyed any other death since. Alfreda, however . . . There was something in the huge, pale-skinned Aerlithwoman that fascinated him. There was a fire, scorching hot but banked in ashes. He longed to set it free.

He would go on. There was one more pool to pass, this one crowded with red-tailed geese who reared and honked in rage as his boat pushed through them. And then the waterway widened at last, the reeds retreating on either side until, imperceptibly, what had been a river became a lake.

The shipfort was at its far side today, carried there by winds that filled the sails above its roof. Marvan well remembered the creak of them. That sound had been the constant accompaniment to his childhood, in concert with the scraping of the salt-encrusted ropes and the shouts of the sailors whose job it was to move them. His father had often spoken of filling the margins of the lake with inland soil and buying mammoths to pull their shipfort round as other shipforts were, but it had been no more than talk. His family had lacked the coin and his father lacked the will.

Marvan's wasn't the only boat on the lake. The people of this land were fisherfolk and the richest haul was to be found here. A group of skiffs clustered together, racing with the wind on the far side of the water, and knew they must have found a shoal. He'd seen fights break out between crews when the catch was rich.

The shortest route lay across the deepest water at the lake's centre, but he didn't take it. Only the strongest boats would venture there, where the water serpents grew three times the length of a man, with jaws that could swallow him whole. As he skirted the lake's rim, careful to keep his oars from tangling in the browning lilies, he saw the serpents' heads peek up from time to time to spot their prey and then sink lower, almost invisible but for the nostrils that they always kept in the air. An unwary mallard, too eager for a fish, dived too close to one. The serpent threw its body from the water with terrifying speed, flinging its coils around the bird to drag it under.

He was exhausted by the time he reached the shipfort. His skin was sticky with the insects he'd crushed against it as they bit him, and his hands were cracked and bleeding. It wasn't how he would have chosen to return here.

When he was within forty strokes of the front gate, the guards who stood to either side turned to watch him, uninterested at first and then with more attention as his boat drew nearer.

'Clear off!' one of them shouted. 'You know you're not to fish so close to the fort.'

It was an accent he hadn't heard in more than a decade and it went through him as sharply as a blade.

'I'm here to see the lady of the fort,' he said.

One of the guards laughed, but the other studied Marvan with more care. His own accent had never ceased to be that of a shipborn lord.

'She isn't taking visitors,' the first said. 'Specially not the likes of you.'

Marvan'd reached the small jetty that led to the shipfort's gate. It was a risk, but he climbed from the boat, arms held far from his own tridents. 'She'll see me, that I promise you. Tell her Marvan's here.'

They might have run him off despite his words. They looked as if they meant to. But at that moment the fort's gates opened behind them and she walked out.

Age had been kind to her. Her hair had turned from black to silver and her body had thickened around its middle, but her face had barely been touched by the years. It had never been beautiful, with its long thin nose and narrow eyes, but it had a dignity that time had only increased. Her presence shook him in a way he hadn't anticipated. He felt like a child again, weak and afraid, and it took a great effort to straighten his spine and speak as a man.

'Hello, Mother,' he said.

*

Alfreda woke from dreams of fire to a soothing darkness. She blinked, disorientated, and tried to rise, only to find that she was pinned down. The sensation of confinement frightened her. It was too like the fever dreams that had consumed her and she struggled against it until a hand reached out to push her down.

She couldn't resist it. She was far too weak. She sank back down into what she realised was a bed. The sheets were damp and there was a musty smell all around her, the stink of long illness.

The hands released her once she stopped struggling. There was the sound of struck flint and a lamp flickered into brightness. Her eyes didn't want to focus. She had to blink them twice before the fog cleared and she saw that it was Marvan bending over her. The room around him was dark but she could make out enough to know they weren't in any simple wagon or hut.

'Where are we?' she asked. Her voice was no more than a husk of itself.

'We're in Fell's End.'

The rocking motion she felt must be real, and not a vestige of her illness. 'A shipfort?'

'Indeed.'

'And they took us in.'

'Well, they had reason to. Welcome, Alfreda Sonyasdochter, to the home of my youth.'

'Your family lived here?'

A smile twisted beneath his beak of a nose. 'They're mostly dead. But my mother is its ruler – for now.'

Her thinking felt as clogged with mud as the waters of this land. 'You're . . . you're the son of the shiplord.'

'The son of the shipfort's former lord, yes. But here's the thing you might find interesting. Here's the stroke of luck we've been waiting for.' His body, she realised, was tense with excitement, his fingers fidgeting in that way he had when he was yearning for blood. 'You see, the ill-fated Battle of Mirror Town took the last but one of my family, my youngest brother. And with him gone, there's none of my father's line to rule here. They'll certainly not have me after all these years. A distant cousin from Fellview is set to inherit the place and of course there must be an investiture.'

He paused, as if this should mean something to her. 'So . . . we have to leave before then?'

'I hardly think so, unless you've changed your mind.'

'About what?'

'About Krishanjit, of course. No new shiplord can be named without the say-so of the Oak Wheel, and King Nayan is sending his own son to give it. In a week's time this place will have the honour of a visit from Prince Krishanjit himself. And you will finally have your chance to kill him.'

5

Eric had taken to sleeping with Rii, enveloped by the scent of mouldy cinnamon. It was the only place he felt safe. They'd built her a hall of sorts, ill-made with green wood and draughty. Even so, it rose nearly as high as the shipfort itself. Servants and soldiers gave it the side eye, unhappy to have their King's home overshadowed.

It didn't much please Rii either, but there was straw on the floor and a crib that he'd brought out from the fort. Rii's body kept it warm and, best of all, her simple presence kept it empty of all but them. No one dared come here with Rii inside, and he could leave Arwel to sleep in his crib without fear that anyone else would come at his baby with a knife.

It wasn't quite the high life he'd been imagining on the journey here, but when had his life ever travelled in the direction he'd supposed it would? That's why you had to look forward and not back. A boy needed to watch his step.

It was still early. There were enough cracks in the wood of the hall to let through shafts of daylight, but they were greyish and feeble, signs of a sun not yet above the horizon. He'd made himself a little nest of furs and he didn't much feel like leaving it, with the chill of winter still frosting the planks and icing up the water in his bucket. Arwel grizzled but he wasn't yet wailing. He could wait a little longer.

'Wilt thou not attend to thy son?' Rii said, piping loud enough to chase the last sleep from his mind.

Eric sighed. 'He won't starve.'

'He hungers.'

Her tone brooked no argument, and he rolled from his bedding, shivering.

Rii had hunched herself above the cradle, peering down at Arwel with her dark, half-blind eyes. Arwel's chubby fingers reached up for her and she dipped her head lower until he could pull at the fur of her face. Her fangs were inches from his nose and her mouth was large enough to swallow him whole, but there was no fear in him. He'd even stopped crying.

'He likes you,' Eric said.

She sniffed, sounding so much like a person that Eric laughed.

'Thy son hungers,' she said again, nagging like a person too.

She watched intently as Eric fed him. The flagon of blood they brought him every day had congealed in the night, but Arwel had three teeth now and he chewed at the rubbery lumps happily, pausing only to burp.

Rii craned her head to inspect the baby from each side. *'He hath grown, hath he not?'*

'No, he ain't – not since the last time you asked.'

'But there is no doubt he flourisheth.'

'Yeah, he's beautiful.'

She hummed contently, a sound almost like a purr, when he took Arwel and sat down in the crook of her wing to rock him to sleep. That was the position King Nayan's guard found them in when he entered. He came in without so much as a by-your-leave and it was only the creak of the huge gates swinging open that woke Eric from his pleasant doze.

The man had a determined scowl on his face, but his fists were clenched so tight the pale of his knuckles showed. He looked cold, too, as if he'd spent a good long while outside the door, gathering his courage to come in.

Eric smiled. His son was in his arms and he wanted the guard's eyes on him instead.

'What is thy business?' Rii piped.

The apple of the guard's throat bobbed up and down a full three times as he swallowed. 'The King has a message for you.'

He held out a scroll to Eric, sealed with wax. His eyes widened as Eric came to take it from him, fixing on Arwel.

'My son,' Eric said quickly. 'He ain't gonna do you no harm.'

The guard swallowed again but his weapons stayed sheathed as he handed Eric the scroll.

Eric unrolled it, then handed it back.

'It's for you,' the guard said.

'Then you're gonna have to read it to me.' Eric raised his chin so the guard didn't think he was ashamed of it.

★

Five days later, and half the country away from Ashfall, Eric wondered how instructions so simple had turned out to be so hard to obey. *There's an ambassador from the Eternal Empire,* the orders had said, only in fancier language. *He wants to speak to Prince Krishanjit. Find him and bring him to Ashfall.*

It was the finding him that was the problem. Rii had brought him all the way down south, through warming weather and with only a little complaining, right to the Great Rift that marked the edge of Ashanesland. And Eric still hadn't clapped eyes on the man.

Even from the air, the depth and width of the Rift were shocking. It looked like a person the size of a mountain had dug his fingers deep into the earth and ripped it apart. If you fell from the top you'd have a good long time to regret it before you hit the bottom.

But now they were here, where were they supposed to look? What exactly did an ambassador from the Eternal Empire look like that any other cully didn't from hundreds of paces up in the air? Dark-haired, he supposed, like the mages of Mirror Town. But then so were the Ashane.

It seemed such a hopeless task he wondered if that was precisely why he'd been sent. Krishanjit was off touring the shipforts. Eric hadn't been sent with him because no one thought it was sensible for people to be introduced to their prince in the company of a great smelly monster. But Rii wasn't much welcome at Ashfall either. Every time she flew to feed, the churls screamed and ran for their caravans. Rii seemed to quite enjoy it, miserable sod that she was.

'Shall we land then?' he shouted to her. The sun still had a way to go before setting, but he was aching from his arse to his shoulders after days of flying, and he wouldn't say no to supper. They'd just flown over a flock of sheep that would do nicely for a roast.

'*We are almost at our destination,*' Rii said. '*We may not yet stop.*'

That was the first she'd mentioned that she knew where they were going. The note from the King hadn't told them, but soon he saw why she sounded so certain. There was a bridge across the chasm, impossibly long and thin and with nothing at all holding it up in the middle. Eric didn't think there was any amount of gold that could have made him cross it, but it must have been the way their visitors came.

'You've been here before,' he shouted to Rii.

'*Ahead lies the land of my birth, morsel, in the age that is long past.*'

There were wagons drawn up round the Ashane side of the bridge, brightly coloured in the manner of the Wanderers. The horses shied and whinnied as Rii flew over, but their owners seemed less shocked, only watching Eric with cautious eyes as he dismounted.

The Wanderers always had been the first with any news, and the quickest to spread it. They'd probably heard talk of the Battle of Mirror Town already and of Rii's part in it. It was strange to think that something they'd done could be spoken of on the other side of the world.

The Wanderers weren't the sort to have leaders, but one of the wagons looked larger than the others. The woman holding the horse's halter stood with the sort of pride that came with wealth. And wealth always walked hand in hand with power. Eric hadn't learned much in his life, but he'd learned that.

Halfway towards her, he got a nasty shock when he finally noticed the painting on the side of her wagon. It was the Hunter. Of course it was. The Wanderers always decorated their wagons that way, only he'd forgotten it. He owed her Arwel's life, but he couldn't say he felt too fond of her.

'You're here for the strangers?' the Wanderer asked.

'That's right. How did you know?'

'You come from the Ashane King.'

He was going to ask how she knew that too, until he remembered the new saddle and armour they'd made for Rii, that she'd grumbled about wearing. The sign of the Oak Wheel was embossed on it. Eric was a King's man now, a person with an official place in the world, and a high one at that.

'That's right,' he said. 'Do you know where they've got to?'

'I know where they've gone, fools that they are. They came here, not a thought for how they'd find the prince they were seeking. They were lucky there were folk here who knew where a carrion rider could be found to send their message. And then they heard news it was nearby and the woman would have stayed put like any sensible person, but the brother wanted to see it. Soon enough he'd talked her round and off the pair of them went, not a care in the world or a wise thought in their heads, as far as I could see.'

'Right,' Eric said, startled by the sudden torrent of words. 'I see. But you ain't said where they went.'

'Oh, to Smiler's Fair, of course.'

*

The fair was only three hills over. If they'd flown a different way, they would have seen it from the air. As Rii winged towards it now, Eric felt a whole troupe of feelings battling in his chest.

He'd never thought to come back to Smiler's Fair, not after he'd been taken all the way to the ice at the top of the world. He never thought there'd *be* a fair to come back to after he'd learned of its burning. But here it was, a fragment of what it used to be and yet still exactly the same place: the Roads to Ruin leading inward and the cluster of tall buildings at its centre that must be the Blue Hall and the temple and all the places he knew as well as the shape of his own thumbs.

He let Rii land behind the hill, out of sight of the fair. Its people had always been a curious bunch and he didn't want them coming to poke and prod at her or the baby he left with her.

Besides, he wasn't too confident Rii wouldn't eat some of them. She seemed to be hungry all the time these days.

The walk to the gates was a long one, but he was glad of it. At the start he was shaking so hard his teeth were chattering, but he'd pulled himself together by the time he reached the Jorlith guards. Tall and stern-faced, they crossed their spears to stop him passing.

'Let me through,' Eric said.

'Your name for the list,' the guard replied.

'I don't need to go on no list. I'm Eric of the Fine Fellows, and this is my home.'

The one on the right checked his list and he must have found Eric's name on it somewhere because they moved their spears aside and let him through.

And then he was walking the streets of Smiler's Fair, which were every bit as muddy as he remembered. The houses that lined them were the same too, rickety and tall, but the wood was pale. Only here and there were dotted older, darker buildings, some still smeared with soot from the fire that had taken all the rest. The crowd was as varied as it had always been, but none of the faces were known to him. He felt as much a stranger here as he did in Ashfall.

A boy loitered in a doorway, lips painted and smiling at any man that passed. He looked so young, no beard on his face and his brown eyes wide and innocent. It was impossible to think that Eric had ever been that young, or that innocent. The boy must have seen him looking, because he turned that smile on Eric. He hadn't quite perfected it yet, and it looked more cheerful than alluring. Eric tipped him the wink but walked on. He wasn't here for that.

A cluster of acrobats ran past, sweat from their show smearing the silver paint on their bodies. They brushed against him, and it was only when he felt a hand ghosting against his hip that he remembered too late what other profession the Queen's Men enjoyed. By then his purse was gone and he felt a flash of anger at being taken for a cully. The anger faded into sadness as he realised that a cully was precisely what he was to them.

He walked past the standards of the Merry Cooks into streets where every other house had the smell of some different food wafting from it, and then into the territory of Lord Lust's Girls, who looked much brighter-eyed than once he'd known. But the bliss that had kept them docile no longer flowed from Mirror Town. Smiler's Fair might like to think it was always the same den of iniquity, but the world around it changed, and it couldn't help but change too.

And then he stopped in his tracks in front of a building that hadn't changed at all.

Madam Aeronwen's had been his home for nearly half his life. He knew every beam of it, every line of the painting of a pretty girl that swung above its door. He'd been there when some drunk cully knocked it from its joist and it had fallen and cracked in half. Madam Aeronwen had worked two days to put it back together again. She'd botched the job, and Eric could see the thin, jagged line where the two halves were joined.

There was the usual hubbub coming from inside. The voices mingled together, but he thought he recognised at least two of them. There was a deep rumble that could only be Aarad, the barman they'd always teased for his long thin neck and the incredible deep voice that somehow came out of it. And that high-pitched giggle, that had to be Kenric. Eric remembered how much the falseness of it used to annoy him. He remembered a time when Kenric had been the worst enemy he had.

The house had one glass window in front. It was Madam Aeronwen's pride, carefully wrapped in wool for every voyage. The panes were thick and grime-streaked, but Eric knew that if he looked through them, he'd see inside.

He didn't look. He stood right where he was, his hands clenching and unclenching at his sides. He didn't know what was stopping him. It wasn't like he'd look inside and instantly want to be back there, was it? And if they spotted him looking, so what? He had nothing to be ashamed of in the life he was living now. He was an admiral in the Ashane army! Kenric was like to piss his pants with envy if he learned that.

But he stayed just where he was as cullies came and went, a couple giving him a pitying look as if they thought him a cully himself, too shy to go and buy a first time with some girl or boy. After a while, he realised he was hearing raised voices not far off, mostly a babble but a few shouting, 'There they are! Kill the fucking mages!' and he felt nothing but relief as he took to his heels and ran towards the sound.

Smiler's Fair was as much of a maze as ever. He twisted and turned through narrow skyless streets, overhung with houses, and the noise of the crowd was first to his left and then to his right but never quite ahead of him. He thought he'd found the route at last as the shouts grew louder, only to skid to a halt at a dead end.

By the time he turned one final corner and tumbled into the right square, it was almost too late. There was a growing savagery to the roar of the crowd, people riling each other up to nastier and nastier things. It was a noise he'd seldom heard in Smiler's Fair. The fair was a place for villainy but not for rage. This was the sound of hatred brought from a battle half a world away.

There were dozens of people in the thick of it. Cullies, mostly, from what he could tell, Ashanemen and women with anger on their faces and blood in their eyes. A few of the fair's residents had joined in too, never ones to shy away from a rumble. It was a mess, and he wished now he'd brought Rii along with him. There was nothing good waiting for him in the heart of that crowd.

There were others here who could sort it out, though – or should, if they remembered their jobs. The Jorlith were meant to stop any violence happening that wasn't organised and gambled on. No one had thought to call them, or no one wanted to. But the bell was right there, hanging from a post in front of a ramshackle whorehouse, and he grabbed it and rang it with all the force he could.

Half the crowd turned to glare at him, which gave him a very nasty feeling. A few started walking his way, makeshift weapons still in their hands. He would have liked to run, but he kept ringing the bell. Prince Krishanjit had raised him up, but it wouldn't mean anything if he still acted low.

The crowd were paces from him when the Jorlith finally came. They sauntered into the square from three different roads as if they hadn't a care in the world. But their pace picked up when they saw the crowd and soon a shout went up of, 'The law! The law!' and the mob fled, throwing their weapons in the mud.

The Jorlith never even had to use their spears. They leaned against them and watched as everyone ran, then shook their heads and slipped away as quietly as they'd come. Eric had forgotten that was the way of it. There was certain wrongdoing the rulers of the fair liked to discourage, but no one was in the business of punishing it.

Only two people remained, lying in the centre of a trampled field. Eric could see their faces: dark as any mage's, and their hair black and tightly curled. He'd been right. It was them. But he wasn't too sure he'd come in time. There was blood on the man's white clothes, and neither he nor the woman seemed to be moving, though he heard a low moaning that was probably coming from one of them.

He had to pick his way through the litter of weapons and animal bones and shit and gambling chits and half-rotted food that had always made up the floor of Smiler's Fair. Halfway there he saw the woman sit up, cradling her head in her bound hands. After a moment, she turned to the man and roughly shook him until he woke up too.

They didn't notice Eric until he was standing right above them. The woman skidded backwards in the mud in alarm while the man stared wonderingly up at him. 'Another one with golden hair,' he said. 'How extraordinary!'

Eric touched it with his fingertips, suddenly self-conscious. He could feel his face heating, which was ridiculous. He was no blushing maid, but the man was terribly handsome: long-limbed and with a long thin face and a mobile mouth and an extraordinary bush of hair above his high forehead. Eric saw for the first time that the pair of them had had their legs too were roughly tied.

'If you plan to kill us, please kill us,' the woman said. She had the same leanness and the same handsomeness as the man. But her face was haughty where her brother's – Eric was sure they must be siblings – was only charmingly innocent.

'I ain't here to kill you,' he told her. 'I'm here to rescue you.'

'Why then, perhaps you might consider untying us.'

The ropes had tightened in the wet and mud and Eric's mutilated fingers struggled with them. It didn't help that the woman watched him as he fumbled, one eyebrow raised as if she was silently judging his performance and meant to give him detailed criticism afterwards.

When he'd finished, the man struggled to his feet and grasped Eric's face in his muddy hands. He smiled broadly and kissed Eric once on each cheek. 'Thank you, stranger. Indeed your land is a strange one, but la! It cannot be all bad if it has such men as you in it.'

'A horde of peasants attempted to burn us alive,' the woman said. 'A warm welcome, I suppose, but by no means a desirable one.'

'You're the ambassadors?'

'Yes. I am Renar the Fox, and this is my brother Lanalan.' Her expression was still disdainful. Eric began to think that might be how she always looked, and not a particular judgement on him.

'And you're really from the Eternal Empire of Mizhara?'

Her brother laughed. 'La! No, we worship no gods, and especially not She Whose Name I Will Not Speak.'

'We left gods behind with the war they brought,' the woman said. 'We are no empire now but only Ofiklanod, the Mortal Lands, where humanity rules without the crutch of any greater power.'

'But you came here looking for Prince Krishanjit, didn't you? Leastways that's what the carrion rider said what brought your message to Ashfall. And Krishanjit is Yron reborn. Didn't no one ever tell you that?'

The woman smiled, far more carefully than her brother. 'They did. And it seems that we have need of him.'

'I thought you said you'd thrown out all your gods.'

'Indeed we did and prospered for it. But it turns out there are some problems that only a god can solve. And indeed, some troubles that might afflict a god that we may perhaps be of some small assistance with. We hope for our sake that Prince Krishanjit will come to us. And we hope it also for his, if he plans to live out the year.'

6

Krish had heard tales of the great serpents of the Hisaka Sea that could swallow a man whole, but he'd never believed them. In his youth in the mountains even the sea itself had seemed an improbable thing. He'd followed his goats into a small valley once, and seen a lake that filled it from side to side and marvelled at how deep and dark the water was. When people had spoken of the sea, that lake had been what he pictured.

He believed the tales now. It had taken five men to carry the remains of the mammoth into the great hall. It would have taken far more if the corpse had been intact, but all that remained were the head, and one of its thick front legs, still oozing blood. Its body had been bitten clean through. There was no possible doubt how it had died. One of the serpent's teeth had been left behind in the mammoth's flesh, twice as long as its trunk.

The leader of the men who'd brought it walked forward to kneel at the foot of the dais. The sun streaming through the hall's high windows shone on his bloody hands and the bald circle of skin in the centre of his hair.

'You've seen this creature yourself?' Imesha asked.

'No, my lady. But . . .' He shrugged and the eyes of the court returned to the slaughtered mammoth.

'Are sea serpents common here?' Krish asked.

Imesha looked down her long nose at him to let him know that he'd said something foolish. Perhaps a prince of Ashanesland should already know the answer. 'My beloved husband caught one in his youth,' she said. 'Its skull used to hang above us, but I had it removed. It seemed to make my landborn uneasy.'

She laughed jaggedly. Everything about her was jagged, from

the sharpness of her cheekbones and the long thinness of her nose to the swift and unexpected way she had of moving. In the two days since he'd arrived at this shipfort, Krish had often found himself flinching away from her, when an elbow would suddenly dart out towards him or her long silver hair would flick against his shoulder as she turned her head.

'This mammoth, and what else?' she asked the man still kneeling at their feet.

'A boat bitten in half on Silverlake, and they say a child was taken from a caravan near the Salt Fringe, though others think it was a Wanderer that took the boy and threw his body in the water. But the garfish and the perch are all gone from the western waters, that's for sure.'

'That's true enough,' said an elderly man standing to Imesha's left. Krish thought he might be the Master Fisherman, or perhaps the Chief Netmaker. Whatever his job, he looked weighed down by the burden of it.

Imesha nodded. 'So the beast must be somewhere between Silverlake and the Meander. I suppose it came past the reefs on the spring tide and is trapped here with the neap.'

'That's not a small area,' Krish said. He'd studied maps of Fell's End before he came here. His father had told him he was being sent to oversee the investment of Lady Imesha as helpmeet to her four-year-old nephew, but Krish had understood the real purpose of the visit – and the trips to the Whitewood and Fort Daybreak that were due to follow. It was his chance to show himself to the lords who would one day be his vassals. To show himself and to prove himself. He'd read history books of his people on the long journey here, the story of the rulers who'd come before him. It wasn't an unbroken line. If the master of the Oak Wheel steered the nation poorly, he didn't steer for long.

'It's a small enough area to hide a creature so monstrously huge,' Imesha said. 'We'll find him easily enough. It's killing him that will be the problem.'

'But your husband managed it, didn't he?' Krish said.

'Indeed, and only at the cost of his right hand.'

Someone sniggered and Krish flushed.

'My husband was too bold. He took only three men. I won't be so reckless. Nish, you'll bring a dozen of the guard and make sure they're all armed with metal.'

The Master Fisherman – or perhaps Chief Netmaker – nodded sharply and strode from the hall, shouting orders the moment he was out of the door.

'You're going to hunt it yourself?' Krish asked. The Lady Imesha was older than his own mother. Her knuckles were swollen and red and he'd seen her massaging her knees when she sat, as if they pained her.

'I shall lead the hunt. The hunt is a shiplord's duty. If we don't keep our landborn safe, what use are we? The west lakes are only half a day's sailing from here. We should be back within two, Lord Heir. Will you stay until then? I'll hold the investment ceremony as soon as I return.'

It was said so casually, as if it was entirely taken for granted that he wouldn't join her. But she watched him slyly out of the corner of her eye and her red-knuckled fist was clenched on her lap. It was a test she expected him to fail.

He shook his head. 'I won't need to wait. I'll come with you.'

He was rewarded with a tightening around her eyes. 'No, I can't allow it.'

'Can't *allow* it?' He tried to make his smile into the shape that Dae Hyo's wore when he was at his most dangerous. It seemed to work.

'I mean to say, it's too dangerous for the Wheelheir. What would your father say to me if I let any harm come to you?'

'What would he say to *me* if I let my people face a danger I wouldn't? When I'm King I'll be lord to the shiplords, won't I? It will be my job to protect you the way you protect your landborn.'

'Protect us with your wisdom, not your body, Wheelheir. You could perhaps send your man to aid us, if you truly wish to help.'

She gestured at Dinesh, loitering at Krish's shoulder. He

suspected she meant the suggestion mockingly. Thin and dreamy-eyed, Dinesh looked ill-suited to fighting, but no one who'd been at the Battle of Mirror Town would have dismissed him so easily.

'I won't leave Lord Krish!' Dinesh said, his smile for once absent.

'You won't need to,' Krish said. 'We'll both go with Lady Imesha on the hunt.'

Her eyes quickly scanned the room as if she was looking for another excuse. Then she bent closer to him, speaking softly but fiercely. 'I beg you, Highness. You'll be a danger to yourself and your companions. My men will be more concerned with guarding you than taking down the beast – such is their loyalty to the Oak Wheel.'

'Dinesh will guard me. And I can protect myself.'

He brushed his hand against the knife that hung at his belt, but it only seemed to make her more doubtful. Here in Ashanesland a shipborn lord fought with sword in battle and twin tridents when he duelled.

She nodded with obvious reluctance. 'We'll hunt the serpent together, then. We leave at dawn tomorrow, and may the Five watch over us.'

*

Krish had seen the ocean before, all the way over on the other side of the land. Perhaps this was the same ocean that circled all the world. Lady Imesha had called these the west lakes but it looked more sea than lake. There was a great deal of water and the land only strips of long thin islands. It was easy to believe that monsters might lie beneath these choppy waves.

Dinesh sat in the bow of the boat, trailing his fingers in the water. He was humming to himself, a lullaby that Krish's own mother had sung to him when he was a boy. Perhaps he was lost in memories of his own. The soldiers were ranked two by two behind him, straining at the oars. Their weapons lay at their feet, carefully swaddled in oiled sailcloth. Krish had seen them as they were wrapped: spears and harpoons and three fine longbows. But he'd seen the remains of that mammoth too and imagined

the size of a beast that could prey on it. The morning was misty
and cold and it was easier to have doubts now than it had been
last night in the warmth of the shipfort. Easier but more futile.

Imesha stood in the front of the boat, balancing without effort
as it swayed in the waves. Her legs pressed against the huge bow
built into its prow while her hand shaded her eyes from the rising
sun as she scanned the water.

'How will we find it?' Krish asked.

His voice sounded loud in the quiet of the morning. There were
splashes in the water to his left as some hidden creatures fled.

Imesha frowned at him. 'By the birds. But not if you startle
them away, Lord Heir.'

Dinesh nodded with sudden enthusiasm. His bright eyes caught
Imesha's and Krish saw the uneasy way her own darted away.
There was something unsettling in the boy's gaze. Something too
much. 'Yes! I remember,' he whispered. 'The birds are the way.
They, they, they feed on the leavings. On the carrion. Who doesn't
like to have their food made for them? That's what he used to
say. My last master.'

'Yes.' Imesha looked at him with surprised approval. 'Indeed.
The birds will feed on the beast's leavings and a serpent of that
size will need to feed often.'

Krish looked around the broad water and broader sky. There
were birds enough in both. Nearby, a half-rotted log floated
tangled in reeds. A cormorant crouched on it, its wings spread
to bathe in sunlight. There were pink, stilt-legged birds further
off, a whole flock of them marching through the shallows in a
high-stepping walk that made him smile. And overhead solitary
hunters circled and circled and then dived, the lucky emerging
with wriggling silver fish speared on their beaks. Nothing about
any of it struck him as unusual.

Imesha nodded an answer to his unspoken thoughts. 'He's not
in these waters. We'll head eastward. A bird from the Saltshoal
landborn brought news of a child snatched as she swam. He's
most likely still in that region.'

The sun rose a handspan as they crossed the lake, and the

midges rose with it, floating above the water in dense clouds. They clogged Krish's throat and bit at his skin.

The next lake was smaller, its waters green and choked with algae. The weed slowed the rowers' oarstrokes and soon the smell of their sweat was battling with the stink of the stagnant water. There were no birds here, the splash of the oars the only sound breaking the silence, and Imesha smiled and said, 'He's near.'

It was midday when they reached the channel at the lake's far side. The sunlight glittered on the water to fox the eye but offered little warmth. At a signal from the Chief Netmaker the men shipped their oars and the boat glided onward, parting the tall rushes with its nose. Their long thin stems crowded round and their bulbous heads turned the sunlight into green dapples.

The boat began to slow and the Netmaker pointed at four of the men, two in front and two in the stern. They dipped their oars back in the water, so gently they parted it without a sound, and began to ease the boat forward again. There were crickets here sawing their legs, and the men's breathing was harsh, even those who no longer worked the oars. It was fear. Krish felt it too. They knew their prey was near.

There were birds here, though he couldn't see them. The cries were loud above them, a great cacophony of whistles and tweets and harsher barks. And then a moment's silence before the sound of something so large striking the water that wave after wave of aftershock rocked the boat and droplets of water splashed around them like rain.

Two men hurried forward to man the huge bow, while the rest readied their weapons. Dinesh had a whole armoury hung about him. The boy had gathered the weapons from the bodies of the fallen at Mirror Town, two short swords of good steel, a tribes-man's axe and a spear that must have come from the Moon Forest folk. He'd stolen armour too, ringed metal that ought to have weighed down his thin frame, but he was stronger than he looked. He tested the point of his spear with a thumb and smiled dreamily at the blood ruby that grew there.

Krish had been given his own spear. The wood of its shaft

had been worn smooth by many hands but it rested awkwardly in his. He remembered those long-ago lessons with Dae Hyo on the grassy plains, when his only friend had tried to teach him to be a warrior. He'd failed and Krish gently put the spear back down and drew his knife. It looked pitifully small, but it was the one weapon he'd even begun to master. And compared to the size of the creature that must have made that splash, even the soldiers' spears were little more than pins.

Krish could feel it in his bones as they drew nearer: some danger sense perhaps, developed over the last two perilous years of his life. The hair on his neck prickled and he had to wipe his palms on his trousers twice before his grip on the knife was firm.

The light faded as they moved on, not even patches of sky visible above. The midges crowded in close and below them a school of dull grey fish arrowed through the water. The school swam underneath the boat and then away, no doubt fleeing the thing they themselves approached.

Finally the light began to brighten, green-speckled at first and then the cheerful yellow of the sun as the reeds thinned around them so that they began to see the lake that lay ahead.

It was the largest they'd yet seen, so wide its far shore was nothing but a smudged line, faintly grey. The lake itself was a startling pale blue, no colour of water that Krish had ever seen. And everywhere in it there were pillars and arches and large misshapen reefs of pure white, sparkling in the sunlight. The side of their boat scraped against one as they finally left the reeds. Dinesh reached out to touch it before Krish could stop him, then brought his fingers to his lips.

'Salt!' he said, delighted.

The soldiers hissed him to silence, horrified as his words echoed across the gently ruffled waters of the lake. There was no sign of the monster that had disturbed them so enormously moments before. Krish could see only birds, a wild and colourful profusion of them clustered at the left-hand side of the lake. There was a stain in the water around them, darker than the pale blue. Krish thought it must be blood.

Five of the soldiers stood, spears poised, while their four fellows rowed on. Krish's throat felt salty-dry and he couldn't seem to swallow. The soldiers standing were as still as statues, but the rowers' hands shook on their oars. Imesha crouched in the bow, a short curved bow in her hand and an arrow nocked. 'Only the eyes and throat,' she said. 'Everywhere else is armoured. He's big but he's quick. A harpoon to hold him steady, and then the rest of you do your work. Be ready.'

The boat moved on, through the pillars of salt and beneath the great flock of birds. The birds cawed their displeasure and the smallest flew away. Others weren't to be discouraged. All around them they dived, necks out and beaks poised to pull scraps of flesh from the water. It was impossible to say what had died here, but it had been very large.

'Where is it, where is it, where the fuck is it?' one of the soldiers hissed to himself, on and on and on until a glare from Imesha silenced him. His lips continued moving, soundlessly repeating the words.

'I can feel her,' Dinesh whispered.

Krish could feel her too. It was like an itch somewhere inside his head, a soundless voice calling to him. If he heard her and Dinesh heard her – with Krish's rune tattooed on his face – there was little doubt what it meant. The serpent they hunted was one of Yron's creatures, left over from the war between the gods a thousand years ago. But Krish wasn't Yron, and the wordless murmur in his mind wasn't a friendly or a safe sound.

Dinesh didn't seem to share Krish's discomfort. His eyes were closed to slits and his head tipped back as if this contact with the thing below the water gave him pleasure. 'I can hear her.'

Imesha looked sharply at Dinesh. She opened her mouth, perhaps to silence him, hesitated and then said, 'Where is she?'

He pointed the tip of his sword to their left, where the waters darkened to blackness and the salt pillars disappeared. 'She's there. In the mud. She's sleeping.'

The men's eyes slid to and from each other, uneasy at this evidence of something unnatural in the strange, half-blood boy.

'And how might we rouse her?' Imesha asked Dinesh. 'Will the scent of food tempt her?'

Dinesh shook his head. 'She's, she's, she's full. She doesn't need to eat.'

'Even the fullest belly will find room for the choicest morsel, and our serpent has grown a taste for the flesh of man. She risked a journey into the shallows of Greenlake to feast on it.' She nodded at the backmost of her oarsmen. 'A little nearer, and then throw the bait.'

The boat glided through the screeching birds until the water beneath their prow grew dark. There was some sort of sinkhole here. The lakebed fell away sharply, the sides of the hole ragged. Thick-trunked trees clung to them, a drowned forest marching downward into darkness.

Imesha nodded and the rowers backed their oars as one retrieved a sack from beneath his seat. A rank-rotten stench rose from it and Krish gasped when the man drew out the first chunk of flesh and threw it on the waters. It was a human hand, a brass ring still on one of its fingers. It floated on the surface where it was thrown, bloated with rot, and another hand and then a leg followed it.

Imesha was watching him. 'No need to look so horrified,' she said. 'The man was dead already. A horse thief hanged for his crime. His body would have been thrown in the midden heap, but now it serves a better purpose.'

But it didn't seem to be serving any purpose at all. The dismembered corpse floated in the dark waters above the sinkhole, little wavelets rocking the rotting limbs. The birds circled overhead and some, more bold, flew towards the meat.

'Don't let them have it!' Imesha hissed.

One of her men drew back his arm to cast his spear, and in the moment before it left his hand, something struck the boat.

Krish felt the force of it jarring through his bones. His numbed fingers dropped the knife. He stared at it stupidly as it hung impossibly in front of his face, and then what had risen began to fall and boat and crew and weapons all tumbled back towards the water from which they'd been thrown.

There was no time to breathe before he was beneath the water. It was a bubble-filled thrashing chaos. Something struck his face – perhaps another man's arm – and a scratch opened in his cheek, stinging fiercely in the salt and bleeding red into the waters. His eyes were stinging too and he wanted more than anything to close them, but he had to find the surface. There was no air in his lungs. His throat was filled with salty water and to his left a dark shadow loomed. White teeth flashed inside what must have been its head and Krish saw sunlight at last, beneath his left knee, or perhaps above it. He tightened his chest against the terrible urge to breathe and dove towards it.

When his head broke the surface he could do nothing but gasp air. He'd never learned to swim well, but it was easy to float in this strange oily water. Through blurred eyes he saw figures all around doing the same as him, and further away a brown hump that might have been their boat, hull up to the sky.

Something bumped against his arm and floated past. It was a severed hand, its fingers clawed to grasp something that wasn't there. The shock had left him numb and he felt only a faint nausea at the sight of it. Only when the foot followed did he realise that they weren't the ones the soldiers had thrown into the water as bait. This corpse was fresh.

'Dinesh!' he shouted. 'Dinesh!'

A pause and then, 'Lord Krishanjit! You're alive!'

The shout came from ahead and he swam towards it, paddling awkwardly like a dog. He passed other ragged lumps of flesh and the floating hafts of three spears. One of Lady Imesha's soldiers reached out for him as he swam past but there was no strength in the hand that grasped Krish's arm and he ignored it.

His ribs were bruised and his head ached. Every stroke pulled at his shoulder and he knew that he was slowing. It felt as if something was dragging at him, pulling him downward. He looked into the water beneath him, but there was nothing to see, only blackness.

And then the blackness moved and he realised that it wasn't

water at all. Something monstrously huge was rushing up to meet him and he swam desperately away.

It was useless. The serpent was too large. Its scales glinted blue-green as it came where sunlight could reach it at last. He gasped as its bulk pushed him from the water, up and up until the lake was thirty paces below him, littered with corpses, and he was clinging to the monster's back.

It was the largest beast he'd ever seen. It dwarfed even Rii, who put shipforts in her shadow. Its body vibrated beneath him and he had to hook his nails beneath its scales to keep his place. The vibration rumbled on, as loud as a landslide, until it emerged from far above as a roar that set all the birds winging frantically away.

A man whimpered close by and Krish saw that he wasn't the only one left alive. At least half a dozen of Imesha's soldiers had survived the attack, and Imesha herself, clinging to the hull of their upturned boat. There was a flurry in the water, some desperate effort, and the boat was righted. The monster's head swung to watch as Imesha and her men dragged themselves out of the water.

'Lord, Lord, Lord Krish!' Dinesh shouted from a patch of reeds. Krish saw that he was bleeding, a dark stain in the water all around him. It didn't seem to trouble him. His expression was delighted as he stared at Krish splayed helpless on the monster's back.

Imesha had seen him too. He felt her eyes on him, a cold assessment. Then she gestured at her men. Krish yelled a wordless protest when he realised what she intended, but it was too late.

The men had been well drilled. The harpoon bow in the ship's prow took the strength of two to draw it. They pulled it swiftly into a tense arc while another fitted a harpoon to its thick string. A moment later the thing was loosed.

Krish flinched away as the massive shaft sped towards him, but the men's aim was true. The point found the monster's soft throat and buried itself deep. Then all Krish could do was cling to its back as it roared and tossed its head in anger. He heard splashes below and knew that the men must have once again been flung from their boat. It had been foolish of Imesha, an act of desperation. There was no way a vessel so small could hold a creature so vast.

The monster tossed its head, like a horse in its bridle, and the boat skipped and bounced over the water, dragged by the rope that bound it to the harpoon in the creature's neck. There was a cry, quickly ended, as the boat's keel struck one of the men in the water, and then with a last jerk the creature freed the harpoon from its neck and the boat was flung away to shatter into kindling against a reef of salt.

Now the monster had nothing but Krish to occupy it. If he leapt into the lake, it would hear him. Its tail stretched out behind it, thrashing through the water. It was as long again as its huge body and barbed on the end. One blow and Krish would be dead. He could see now that it wasn't truly a serpent. Stunted limbs lined its sides, wriggling in the water.

He forced himself to his feet. By some fluke, his knife had landed on the monster's back beside him. It looked absurdly small, not even long enough to pierce beneath the creature's heavy scales. It would be no more than a pinprick, but he stooped to pick it up.

The sun was bright overhead, burnishing the monster's scales to an iridescent shine. The shine was shadowed as the beast swung its head towards him. The head was small for its vast bulk, with round unblinking eyes and what seemed almost a smile on its closed lips. The lips opened, wide and wider still, and he saw the rows and rows of fangs inside, like mouths inside mouths and all of them moving to swallow him.

His knife felt loose in numb fingers and he made himself grip it tighter. Dae Hyo would want him to die with a weapon in his hand. The beast's head was inches from his own and saliva dripped from its hundred fangs. He found his eyes fixed on a droplet, watching it fall. His mind couldn't seem to stay still long enough to face its fear. He felt outside of his own body.

The beast snapped its jaw shut and he was flung back into the moment: every beat of his heart, every huff of breath through the monster's nostrils, the cries of the circling gulls all painfully loud.

Its long neck swivelled until its eyes were level with his. They were black and pitiless. The head moved closer still, the beast's blood-stinking breath washing warmly over him. He didn't know he'd reached out to touch it until he felt its scales beneath his fingers, as smooth and cold as ice.

Someone shouted. Probably Dinesh. Krish didn't hear the words. He heard *something*, though. It rang in his head, a word-less word that he knew was the voice of the beast. It struck him like a bell, resonating deeply in his bones and flesh, and he knew that this creature was his.

It wouldn't kill him. It would do whatever he asked of it. The power was immense, the moon's power that must have fashioned this thing so many centuries ago. The beast made a noise, a soft chirrup almost like a cat's. Its feelings pushed their way inside his head, larger than his own. They were simple and clear: hunger, curiosity, the savage need to hunt. And drowning them all in a growing wave, a wash of love for Krish. His eyes streamed with tears, overwhelmed by the force of it.

Krish looked down to see the litter of dismembered corpses in the water and half a dozen living people, every one staring at him. Dinesh's face was a brown blur, but Krish could see the white slash of his smile. He understood. He thought the others were beginning to. There was a dawning horror on their faces as they saw Yron for the first time.

But Krish couldn't rule if they knew him as Yron. He needed the power without the name. His knife was short, but it was sharp and it pierced the beast's dark eye with little effort. His arm followed it in, until he was elbow-deep in blood and ichor and finally he hit something vital.

The monster screamed, a high thin sound of agony and betrayal. Krish pressed deeper, his arm shoulder-deep inside it, and finally the scream stopped. The serpent gave a convulsive twitch and Krish flung himself from its back, leaving his knife behind as it thrashed and died.

★

The celebration was very different from his initial reception. The hall was still as gloomy but the faces were bright, burnished by drink and relief. He'd been drinking too, the dark strong ale they brewed in these parts. His first sip had tasted of marshwater, but now it slid down comfortably.

'The hero of the hour,' Lady Imesha said, topping up his cup. Her face would never be described as cheerful, but it had lost its previous sour cast.

'I was lucky,' Krish said, shrugging.

'Luck. Yes.' Her eyes, boring into his, were too knowing; but then she stretched her lips into a thin smile. 'Luck that saved my life.'

He felt a swell of affection for her. For everyone in the crowded hall: the men and women in rough linen carrying flagons and trays of food among the revellers; the revellers themselves, dancing a dance not unlike the one the villagers of his home had danced at midsummer while he'd sat on the verge and watched; the musicians, fingers plucking at strings as they grinned at their own skill. They were all *his* people.

His eyes felt heavy, lids drooping without his consent. His earlier terror had washed through and out of him and left a happy exhaustion behind. He didn't know what time it was. The hall had no windows. But it must be past midnight. Without a boat, they'd had to wait for a passing fisherman to find them, and it had been dark by the time they'd returned to the shipfort, the remaining guards too astonished by their own survival to mourn their lost comrades, singing and laughing too loudly the whole long journey home.

Krish rose, wobbling. The room was spinning. 'I think . . . I think I need to go to bed.'

Imesha held the jug of ale out to him, temptingly tipped. 'Are you sure, Wheelheir? The celebration's far from over.'

'They can enjoy themselves without me.' He didn't feel steady enough to attempt a bow, but he nodded his head graciously to her and walked from the dais towards the door at the far end of the hall.

'Lord Krish! Lord Krish!' Dinesh jogged towards him, more nimble than any of the other revellers. A foggy part of Krish's brain remembered that drink could no longer touch Dinesh. Krish had done that, when he'd ordered the rune tattooed onto his face.

But there were other pleasures Dinesh could still enjoy. Krish had seen women with their eyes lingering on the boy. Better fed and well-muscled from all his training, Dinesh cut a far more pleasing figure than he had when Krish first met him. And there'd be many here who wanted to be close to a man so close to Krish. Why shouldn't Dinesh take advantage of it?

'Stay!' Krish said, and pushed Dinesh back towards the crowd. 'Enjoy yourself. I can find my room on my own.'

He felt a little less confident of that once he'd left the hall. The corridors were dark, their walls decorated with the stuffed heads of improbably fierce fish. Had he seen that one before, the blue, beady-eyed creature with a foot-long nose? He thought he might have and turned left to walk past it, only to be confronted by a fish with a thousand spikes in its flesh that he was sure he'd never seen before.

He found his room at last at the end of a corridor lined with nets. His head had cleared a little by then, the spinning replaced by a growing pounding, and he longed for sleep. The room was in darkness. He fuzzily recalled that the bed was at its far end, beneath the shuttered window.

He saw the shadow move a moment before the blow struck him. It hit his chest with terrible force and flung him to the wooden floor. The pain as his head struck was sharp and sobering.

The shadow came for him again, resolving into the looming silhouette of a person. 'This is for Cwen!' it hissed as it reached down to touch his chest. He fumbled feebly for the assassin's hands, trying to push them away, but there was no strength in him. There was something *in* his chest. The attacker pressed down on it and the pain grew overwhelming. Total blackness took him, surging from behind his eyes.

When he blinked them open again, there was light. He could see his attacker, kneeling over him with a lamp beside her. It was a woman, huge and pale-skinned with a lumpy face smeared with blood. His blood.

He groaned and forced himself up onto his elbows. Every movement was agony. The woman could have stopped him. He was as weak as a newborn kid. But she seemed frozen, wide eyes staring at his chest.

He looked down and saw a knife, buried hilt-deep in his flesh. Now that he saw it he could feel it too, grating against his ribs where its point emerged from his back.

That didn't seem right. His fingers were numb but with an effort of will he clasped them around the hilt and pulled. Darkness came for him again, more briefly this time, and when it receded the knife was free, its blade shivering as his trembling hands pointed it towards the woman.

She backed away, her expression horrified. He looked at the knife and then at his own chest, the cloth of his tunic cut raggedly open and the cut beneath gaping. He could see something bulbous and blue-red throbbing inside the wound. He realised with cold horror that it was his heart. Blood seeped from him in pulses along with its beat.

The woman took a step towards him. Her fingers reached inside her jacket and emerged with another knife, short and serrated.

It didn't seem possible to stand, but he made himself do it. The blood spurted from his chest as he rose, spurted again and then stopped. He took a step forward, shocked to find it was steady. The pain was gone, or maybe too great to be understood, and he tightened his fingers round the hilt of the knife and pointed it at the woman.

'Who sent you?' he hissed.

She opened her mouth but didn't speak. Her own knife wavered and he knew that she was poised on the edge of a decision: flee or fight? He stepped forward again, showing her his teeth, and she dropped her knife and ran.

The moment she was gone he fell back to the floor. He landed near the bed this time and leaned back against it with a groan. The knife was tacky against his skin, coated in his own blood. He put it down and touched his chest instead.

It felt smooth. He looked down and saw no wound, only a thin red line in the brown of his skin, already fading.

7

It was the first time Dae Hyo had contrived to be alone since whatever had happened in the fields outside Mirror Town had happened. He and Yemisi hadn't spoken of it. They hadn't spoken of anything. When he'd sought her out she'd closed her door to him.

But the freed slaves had been as demanding as they always were, and Olufemi had suddenly seemed fonder of his company than she'd ever been before, fretfully demanding he update her each day on the training of the slaves. He supposed she might be bored. Her lover had returned to Ashanesland with Krish and her family weren't too fond of her. Even her monkey seemed to shun her these days. Perhaps Dae Hyo was the best she could manage for company, which he'd be the first to admit was a sad state of affairs.

Today though there'd been some trouble with the irrigation of the west fields that had drawn her, grumbling, away. Yesterday he'd sent his army in training to run the perimeter of Mirror Town and now half of them were prostrated with heatstroke and the rest pleasingly shy about asking him for any more instructions. It had been easy to take the journal from Olufemi's shelves and bring it here.

This primitive hut had once housed some wretched family of slaves. Now it was home only to cockroaches. One scuttled across the pages as he flicked through them. The parchment was so new it still smelled of cow. Olufemi's writing was on every page, long neat rows of letters he had no hope of reading and, scattered here and there, the shapes of runes, drawn, redrawn and drawn again until their final form had been copied neatly on its own page.

Some of them were beautifully complex. He decided he'd best leave those alone. From the little he'd picked up about the making of magic, a complex shape meant a deep magic, and who knew what damage he might do? No, he needed something simple and small.

He turned back to the start of the book, where Olufemi's researches had begun, and yes, here were much easier shapes. He frowned at them. They might do simple things, but he wasn't sure what those things were and even a simple knife could kill a man, if it slid between his ribs. Should he risk it?

For the first time, he regretted that men weren't made to learn to read. But the coward doesn't catch the boar and a chance like this might not come again for days. He settled on a rune with two circles, a spiral and a line between them. There was something pleasing in its shape – friendly somehow. It seemed a good choice.

His eyes travelled the curves of the rune without his leave, stuttering past the place where Olufemi's pen had slipped, leaving one of the circles imperfect. The ink had run a little in another, and he found his gaze lingering there too, trying in his mind to wash away the stain.

Time passed and he began to feel increasingly absurd. He tried to concentrate harder, but his mind resisted him like an unbroken horse, bucking out of his control to flash a sudden memory of Dae Yeon, a boyhood friend he hadn't thought of in more than a decade.

'Belbog's balls!' he snarled and stepped back.

He'd done it before. He *had* done it: Yemisi had been quite sure of it and he'd felt it too, the sensation of a power passing through him, not his to own but his to borrow. What had been different then?

He sat down to ponder it on the wobbly wooden stool that, along with a rush mattress, was all the furniture the hut held. It was a low-roofed, dismal place, made of a rough red brick. At least it was cool in the dizzying heat of a Mirror Town midday. He supposed it needed to be, when so many of the slaves had been stolen from northern lands. They'd have died if left unshaded from the sun, else he was quite sure the mages would happily have made them sleep on the bare dirt of the streets.

Without his asking it to, his mind returned to the rune. It was a very pleasing shape. Now he wasn't glaring at it on the page, he could see it whole. It made sense in some way he couldn't quite explain – the same way a word of nonsense sounded different from a word in an unknown tongue. The image sharpened slowly in his head, all the imperfections of the scrawl on the page erased.

Oh yes, of course. This was how he'd done it. By not trying to. A kind of watchful peace settled on him and he felt that power again, larger than he could possibly imagine and fine-grained enough to pour into the rune's delicate outline.

There was a moment of perfect balance, and then the power was gone.

He looked around the room, but nothing seemed changed. He knew it had worked. He was sure of it. Had he changed something invisible, something inside himself? Fear welled as it occurred to him that he might have twisted his spirit still more than the rune inked on his chest. Would he lose his hunger for food next? His thirst for water? His head felt hot with worry.

No. His head felt hot. His head – his hair – was on fire. The pain hit him all at once and he yelped and beat at his head until there was no more heat and only the unpleasant smell of singed hair filling the hut.

He stared at his reddened hands, started laughing and couldn't stop.

So, that was fire then. In the hours that followed he worked his way forward through the book and found water – a few rather disappointing droplets that were quickly absorbed into the dry earth floor – and then a brush of air so delicate he might have missed it if his focus on the runes hadn't honed his senses to sharpness.

He had the fourth rune ready in his mind when a banging on the door shattered his concentration. The door was thrust rudely open and Olufemi barged in, her brow stormy and her usually generous mouth a thin, displeased line.

Dae Hyo wasn't delighted either. He'd finally been getting the hang of it.

'What do you want?' he growled at the same time Olufemi snapped, 'What do you think you're doing?'

Olufemi shook her head, eyes closed as if the very sight of him pained her. 'Never mind. I know what you're doing, you fool. Or have you forgotten that the runes extract a price from their user?'

Truth be told, he *had* forgotten.

'I thought as much,' she said, studying his face. 'How do you think I found you?'

She gestured sharply and he knew he was meant to follow outside. There was a nasty sinking feeling in his stomach that was probably guilt. The aftermath of the Battle of Mirror Town wasn't something any man wanted to recreate.

But when they left the hut for the narrow alleyway outside, there was little to see. The huts, shabby as they were, were still whole, and the sky was blue and empty.

'Look down,' Olufemi said.

It took him a moment to notice the bird lying in the dust, a small blue-breasted thing. He thought it must be dead until it cheeped feebly and its wings twitched.

'Well, that's a small price.'

She huffed, exasperated, and stalked on. They passed a few more birds, struggling in the dust. He supposed it was a shame to have hurt things too small to eat.

At the end of the long thin alley they left the huts. And then he had to stop, because it hadn't been just a dozen birds or even a hundred. The whole square was littered with their bodies, all the same blue-breasted breed. The price of his magic must have caught a flock in flight, one of the vast migrations that sometimes passed high above the city.

'I didn't kill them,' he said. 'Maybe they just need a rest.'

Olufemi stooped, knees creaking, to pick one up. It looked quite pitiful in her hand, its small brown eyes rolling in terror. 'No,' she said. 'I don't think they'll recover. I believe they may have forgotten how to fly.'

'Oh.' Dae Hyo wondered if he ought to stamp on them, ending their little lives. It seemed a kindness, but then he imagined the squish of their bodies beneath his boot and shuddered.

'So you've discovered you can use the runes,' Olufemi said. 'Congratulations. So could any child who put in the effort. So did the madmen of the Bakari family, if you recall. It requires no skill, only a mind with enough emptiness in it.'

'I thought it was a thing only mages could do.'

'Why ever would you think that? Anyone could do it – if anyone were allowed. Or have you forgotten that Krishanjit forbade the use of the moon's power?'

'Belbog's balls, this was nothing!' Dae Hyo protested. 'A flicker of fire, nothing more.'

'And the birds that paid the price for it?'

'At least they weren't people.'

She stared at him until he dropped his eyes. 'No more. You know why your brother forbade it. And if this was the price you paid for so simple a magic, imagine what might be demanded for something greater? If you truly wish to master the runes, first understand them. Drawing them is the greater art. Study that if you're interested. The Great Library has books you might find helpful. I'd suggest you begin in the children's section.'

★

He went to Yemisi. He didn't mean to deepen the cut, but men weren't made to read and even if he had been, there was no hope he could decipher the swirling marks of the mage's tongue.

He found her at one of the roadside wine stalls. They'd all been thronged when he first came to the city, but they were quieter now and Yemisi was the only person sitting on the wooden benches that surrounded this one. There was no one at the stall itself and she reached across it to pull out a bottle for herself. No doubt the job had once belonged to a slave.

She was quite drunk already. That could be good or bad. Drink had sometimes filled him with good fellowship and at other times stirred him to an unwise fight. He never could tell which way it would go.

Yemisi frowned as she saw him approach, suggesting the less helpful of the outcomes, but after a moment the frown melted into a sloppy smile. 'Dae Hyo! You've been avoiding me!'

In fact it had been the other way around, but he didn't think it wise to remind her. 'Well, I'm here now and I need your help.'

She wobbled to her feet and flung an arm around him, breathing wine-scented breath into his face. The feel of her body against his stirred him, but the glazed look in her eyes was less attractive.

'I tell you what,' he said. 'Maybe I'll take you home and give you some bean tea. *Then* you can help me.'

★

Sobering her up took the best part of the morning, and while the day and her mood had darkened by the time he managed to tempt her to the library.

'I don't see why I should help you to become what *I* want to be,' she said as they pushed open the great rusty doors of the building. 'That hardly seems fair.'

'Because helping me helps you,' he explained. 'Olufemi said that understanding the runes is the true mastery, and you've done it once already.'

She harrumphed but followed him in. The library was a peculiar place. The mages of old had designed it to rotate on its base, and being inside made him feel a little sick. The musty smell of the air didn't help. It was huge too, rows and rows of shelves stacked with parchments and books. In some places there were slabs of stone or bricks carved with a script he didn't recognise.

'Well, this is ridiculous,' Yemisi said. 'Where are we supposed to start?'

'I thought you'd know.'

'I don't remember!' She shrugged away the hand he reached out for her and strode into the gloom between the shelves.

He trailed after her in silence, marvelling that there could be so much knowledge in the world. It didn't seem to be doing much good to anyone. He and Yemisi were the only people in the place, and from the dust that had settled over all the books and floated into the air in their wake, they'd been the first to visit this room in many weeks.

Apparently the books weren't much use to Yemisi either. She strode past them all with barely a glance. He would have suggested they give the search up as a bad job if the library hadn't been so pleasantly cool. He caught himself staring at Yemisi as she strode in front of him. The embroidered white cloth of her robe swayed tantalisingly against her, alternately hiding and revealing the shape of the body beneath. The gods had been unkind to make so unpleasant a woman so beautiful.

But even staring at Yemisi paled after a while. He was about to call the whole thing off when she gave a glad cry and pulled one of the books from the shelf. 'I knew it! I knew it was a real memory!' She grinned at Dae Hyo.

He studied the book, whose cover was dyed leather, a surprisingly bright green even though the parchment within was brown with age.

He reached for it, but she snatched it away from him and danced back, suddenly playful. 'Not yet. We're not in the right place.'

'But this is a library.'

'A library's for reading not for doing.'

'There'll be no doing. Olufemi told me I shouldn't use the runes, only learn them.'

'Who cares what Olufemi wants?'

'It's what Krish wants too.'

'Is it? Or is it just what Olufemi says Krish wants? Don't you think he'd want you to practise magic if he knew you had it?'

Dae Hyo wasn't sure Yemisi even remembered meeting Krish, but she had a point. 'Well,' he said. 'Perhaps I should practise a few easy runes. He'd want me to test what I can do.'

She grinned and grabbed his hand. Her firm grip dragged him from the dusty cool of the library to the dusty heat outside and onward through the city. She laughed unrepentantly at the curses and scowls as she barrelled past knots of mages at gaming tables and former slaves lounging at rest.

She brought him at last to the very edge of Mirror Town, where the sea wall guarded it from the waves. It hadn't done too good a job of it. The wall that was high and white and shining to the north of them had fallen into ruin here. Blocks of marble lay jumbled beneath a ragged base, like a vast staircase leading to the brilliant water below.

He thought the damage must be a result of the battle. The city had been more ruin than building in its aftermath. But when Yemisi took his hand to lead him scrambling down, he felt the coarse barnacles beneath his feet and the slipperiness of seaweed. The stone slabs had crumbled in places, leaving dark nooks and crannies in which crabs had made their homes. They scuttled away as he and Yemisi passed, retreating into shadows.

'What happened here?' he asked.

'It was a storm, two hundred years ago. It's not just people who excel at destruction. Nature has a talent for it too. The waves ate out the cliff beneath and a whole district sank beneath the sea along with the mansion of the Odegbames. It was said to be the fairest in the city. The storm took out our fort, too: the one they made when they still thought their enemies might sail the long way round to come for them.'

'That's a shame, but I can't use the runes to fix it. It would probably just knock down the next bit of wall.'

'Why would I want you to fix it?' She settled herself cross-legged on a stone slab at the very edge of the water. Little wavelets lapped against it and its surface was slimed and slippery.

He sighed when she gestured peremptorily for him to join her, then did as she wanted. The water looked temptingly cool beneath the relentless sun. The spray of the sea had misted Yemisi's face with fine droplets to join the sweat on her brow.

'We come here, my friends and I. Came here. I think of it and I think, oh yes, yesterday morning myself and Omolewa and Tolulope and Wura had a picnic here, and then I remember that they're all dead, or close enough to it that they can't bear the company of the young. Least of all my company – I remind them of everything they've lost.'

That was a wound he didn't know how to heal, so he nudged her with his shoulder and said, 'If you came here to be melancholy, we could have done that back in town with less walking.'

He could see that she wanted to cling on to her sadness, so he nudged her again until she huffed in indignation and pushed him away.

'So you don't want to rebuild what's broken,' he said. 'What magic did you have in mind?'

She smiled at last, pulling out the book she'd taken from the library and opening it on her lap. He saw pictures as she flicked through the pages, brightly coloured and simple.

'Is this meant for children?' he asked.

'From a time when even children could work the runes as easily as read. This was for their entertainment and education, games they could play that taught them the principles of being and becoming. Or so the writer says on the first page.'

'But you didn't use them when you were a child. You couldn't have. Krish wasn't in the world then and the moon and all his magics were dead.'

'No. My friends and I, we used to swim here, below the fallen wall. Look – can you see the buildings beneath the surface?'

He'd taken them for natural reefs. A dozen different species of plant had grown on them, and other odder things that looked like living rocks. Their fronds and tendrils drifted in the water until one of the many multicoloured fish swam by, and they withdrew shyly back into their stony carapaces.

'It must have been fun,' he said. He remembered his own childhood, swimming in the swift streams that flowed through the plains. The waters had been far colder there, clouded with mud, but it had been a joyful game.

She looked across the water, her own eyes misty with memories. 'It *was* fun. But I could never hold my breath long, so I never saw as much as the others. They used to laugh at me, and when I lost my temper they'd give me purple and rose starfish to make me smile. A few years later I found this book, and that was what set me on the path to study the runes. That's what Olufemi told me. No great purpose. Just the thought of how much more fun we all could have had, if we could have breathed beneath the waves.'

It made something inside him feel unexpectedly soft, that she wanted to recreate those precious childhood moments with him. Of course, he was her only possible choice for a companion, so he could hardly take it as a compliment.

'I tell you what, show me the rune and I'll see what I can do,' he said. He moved the book so that it was resting between them, one side on his lap and one on hers.

'There.' She pointed to the left of the page, at a mark he'd taken for a drawing of some seaweed. Its swirls were as tangled, but there was a sense to them he couldn't quite explain.

'And all I have to do is think it?'

'No, I think you must draw it on each of us as you put the power in it.'

'Draw with what?' There was nothing around but rock and barnacles and crumbled seashells.

'Oh.' She looked forlorn, like a child who'd bitten into a strawberry and found a maggot. Then her expression brightened and she leapt to her feet, nearly slipping from the rock as she leaned down to pick up one of the iridescent fragments of seashell.

'We can write with this!' she said, grazing the shell across her own palm to draw a thin line of blood.

It seemed ill-luck to do his marking in blood, but he couldn't think of a better plan so he took the shell from her. The rune came far more easily to his mind this time. He thought he might be learning the knack of it, like a swordsman whose muscles grew with practice.

The shell was a clumsy instrument, and the shape of the rune he carved into her was all wrong, lines where there should be curves and places where he was too tentative and left no mark at all. It didn't seem to matter, though. The true form of the rune, the one he held in his mind, understood what was meant. As he called the power into it he felt it flowing back out again, into the rune on her arm – and as the power grew, the lines filled in and the curves re-formed until the red marks on her skin were perfect.

He held the rune a moment longer and then released it, grinning. There was a pleasure in this he hadn't anticipated, not like the ecstasy of bliss or the fuzziness of drink but cleaner and sharper.

Yemisi smiled back at him. She opened her mouth to speak – and instead of words, water gushed out of it.

He laughed in shock, as if she might have done it as a joke. Then she coughed water again, fingers clawing at her own throat, and the horror of it struck him. He hit her hard between her shoulder blades as he'd once seen his cousin do when one of the elder mothers choked on a rabbit bone.

More water jetted from her. There didn't seem to be an end to it. She seemed to be breathing out water . . . and then all at once he understood: she *was*. The rune had done its work and turned her from an air breather into a water breather. And like a fish on land, she was drowning in air. She tried to cry out when he grabbed her around the waist, vomiting up more water, and then he spun and flung her in the sea before diving after her.

She flailed desperately in the water. Every instinct must be telling her to reach the surface, and he grabbed her round her ankle, expelled the air from his own lungs in a mess of bubbles, and pulled her down.

The salt water stung his eyes so that all he could see was a blur of brown and the roiling of her struggles. He tried to shout at her, to tell her to breathe, but all he did was swallow water and he knew that he'd have to surface soon himself or die.

The rune came into his mind, perfectly formed and urging him to fill itself with the moon's magic. But what if he was wrong? He could kill them both.

His chest tightened, desperate for air. His mind darkened as he resisted, slipping towards something that wasn't quite sleep. The rune's light shone in the darkness, but it was guttering, almost extinguished. The last of his strength could take him to the surface. He turned it inward instead, dragging power from the darkness and into the rune. There was no way to mark it on his body, not now. He pictured it instead, a pen of fire writing on his chest.

He felt a burn as if it was real, and then the magic was gone and the last of his strength with it. He opened his mouth, not meaning to, not really thinking at all, and the water rushed in.

The salt of it stung his tongue where he must have bitten it in his struggles. It rushed coldly past his throat and in its journey downward it somehow became warmth. He choked, tried to cough it out, and it slid up as easily as it had slid down. His chest loosened. The blackness left his mind, and when he blinked his eyes the sting of salt was gone and he could see everything around him.

Yemisi floated only a few paces in front of him. Her eyes were wide with wonder and she touched her own mouth as if she couldn't quite believe that it was filled with water.

Dae Hyo couldn't feel the water inside him either, no more than he could normally feel the air.

'It worked!' Yemisi said. Her words were clear, only the tone of them a little deepened by the sea they travelled so improbably through.

'And the price?' he asked, having learned his lesson from Olufemi.

She gestured all around and he saw the bright fish he'd noticed earlier, floating motionless in the water. They weren't dead. Their eyes blinked in bafflement as their fins flapped wildly to no purpose. If the birds that had fallen from the sky had forgotten how to fly, perhaps these fish had forgotten how to swim. It was a shame for them, but a bargain for everything he'd been given in exchange.

He and Yemisi were like young children at first, taking their first stumbling steps. Dae Hyo knew how to swim, but when he tried to bring his arms over his shoulders in the strokes that should have moved him forward, they pushed him downward instead and he felt the soft body of a sea slug squelch beneath his feet.

Yemisi laughed at him. She tried waggling her arms instead, but that only wobbled her backwards and forwards in the water. After that they stopped trying, delighting simply in the absurdity of it all, kicking and twisting around each other until, when they weren't thinking of it, their bodies decided on their own how to move. They found themselves making long undulating waves, a little like the movement the fish themselves seemed to have forgotten.

Their clothes tangled them, though, and Yemisi shrugged out of her embroidered robe. Some current snatched it away and Dae Hyo made himself watch the shapes it made as it floated out to sea.

'Take yours off then,' she said. 'I never knew the people of the plains were such prudes.'

He picked at the ties of his trousers, but the water had tightened the knot. After a few moments of his inept fumbling she tutted and helped him, her long thin fingers far more nimble.

It was a sort of agony to have her naked body so close – to feel her hands brushing against him. His cock wanted to rise to the occasion, and he turned his back on her as soon as the job was done and swam away until he'd contemplated enough slimy sea creatures for it to start behaving itself.

'Show me the drowned city then,' he said.

She led him into deeper water, where the light was blue and the fish still swam. A stripy, fronded thing drifted towards him, as complicated as a flower. He reached for it, but Yemisi pulled his hand away. 'Lion fish,' she said. 'Deadly poisonous.'

They swam past what might once have been a grand hall, its base lost in the shadows of the seabed. Now it was home to a thousand different living things, every shade of green and purple, and rocks shaped like stars or mazes or tiny rosebuds.

A shadow fell over them, and a moment later they were surrounded by a vast shoal, so many that the sea seemed suddenly more fish than water. Dae Hyo reached out to grasp a handful but they flitted away from him. Others tickled his feet and one slipped past his nose. For a moment he smelled it, not the briny stink he was used to but something far more delicate. A moment later they were gone, a cloud of life disappearing into the distance.

Further in, they swam past slave huts, little different from the ones he'd done his magic in. 'Did many die?' he asked, searching the ruins for skeletons.

Yemisi shook her head. 'The records say they had warning. They had time to flee, but not to take their possessions with them. My friends used to come back with trinkets sometimes, when they'd managed to dive deep enough.'

She plunged suddenly lower herself, kicking her feet to propel herself through the open doorway of a decaying hexagonal building. He followed her in, misjudging the motion and scraping his side against the doorway. His blood left a pretty brown trail in the water behind him.

It was far darker inside. He struggled to see anything until his eyes grew used to the gloom, and then he blinked around him in surprise. The place was filled with clothing: dresses and trousers and shirts all floating in the water, waving in its waves. The clothes were miraculously whole, despite their two centuries in water, and bright jewels glittered on collars and sandals.

'The Odegbames had a secret way to make cloth,' Yemisi said. 'It was a recipe in a book passed down from woman to niece. But the book was lost in the flood and now the clothes they made are a treasure that other families pass down mother to daughter and father to son. My mother gave me an Odegbame scarf when I was a girl, but when I looked it was no longer in my wardrobe. Perhaps I lost it in the years I can't remember.'

He took her hand. 'Maybe we can find the book here. You could make new—'

He broke off, clutching his head in pain as a massive noise crashed through them, so loud it rattled his bones. It came again and again and he realised that he recognised it. It was the ringing of bells.

'The tower bells!' Yemisi said, as if that should mean something to him, and swam frantically back towards the door.

He followed her out and up, almost to the surface, until he

could see what she meant. On the outer limit of the drowned buildings three towers rose from the wreckage, still improbably whole. The noise grew more unbearably loud as they drew nearer, but Yemisi didn't stop swimming until Dae Hyo could see the golden bells inside, swinging as they tolled.

'How can they be ringing?' he asked, and then realised there was a much more important question. 'Why are they ringing now?'

She reached for his hand, grasping it tightly enough to hurt. 'These are the warning towers the mages built. The bells were made with magic to ring if invaders came by sea. Another army's coming to take Mirror Town.'

8

The men had been lined up at the edge of the jetty, heavy chains binding them. The sky was piled with grey clouds, heavy with rain, and the crowd behind Krish was silent but heavy with something else, an unpleasant expectation that would soon be fulfilled.

The blood had been cleaned from the men's bodies but the marks of their torture remained. Krish had heard their screams during the night. The wounds were untended, the eye socket of one old man already festering, weeping a thick, noxious yellow fluid. A pimply youth's entire hand was black and stinking.

'Show your respect to the Wheelheir!' Imesha said, and one by one they fell or were pushed to their knees.

Krish scratched at the skin of his chest where the assassin's knife had slid in. There was no mark there, not even the faintest scar. He'd spent enough time staring at it in the mirror to be sure. But he felt a phantom itch all the same.

'Confess your crime,' Imesha said to the first of the kneeling men.

'I . . . I don't remember.'

The guard slapped him and Imesha snapped, 'You tried to kill the Wheelheir!'

His eyes were dazed as he blinked at her. The guard raised his hand to strike him again, and he croaked, 'I . . . yes . . . I did it. Whatever you say, I did it.'

'And you?' Imesha asked the next in line. 'Will you confess your crime?'

'I killed the Wheelheir!' he gabbled. 'I mean, I tried to kill him. I'm sorry. I'm so sorry.' His voice broke into rough, gulping sobs.

She asked each man in turn and got the same answer out of him. Krish found it less convincing every time, but tried not to show his doubt on his face. This performance was being put on for his benefit.

He wished it wasn't needed. He would never have told Imesha about the assassination attempt if he'd had the choice – but the fight had caused too much of a commotion and when guards had come running they'd seen blood all over his clothes. He'd had to give them an explanation. He'd claimed the knife grazed his ribs and told a fussing Dinesh the same thing. He didn't want to share what had really happened. He still couldn't comprehend it.

When the parade of confessions was done, Imesha turned to him. 'Will you pronounce the sentence, Lord Heir?'

There was no hope in the faces that turned to him. They knew they were doomed. The confessions they'd given hadn't been to avert death, only to bring it quicker.

He *could* spare them, though. He was sure they were innocent. His attacker had been a lone woman with the ugly pale skin of the Moon Forest. What could have brought her to conspire with these landborn Ashane? And why would any of these men want him dead?

But they'd been declared guilty. If he spared them, how many more would make attempts on his life, knowing there'd be no price to pay? His fingers rubbed at his chest again, at the place where there was no scar.

Besides, they were all crippled now. He'd grown up as poor as them. A man with no hand to fish or eyes to hunt wouldn't last long. He'd be a burden on his family – if he even survived the wounds whose festering stink was poisoning the air around them.

'The sentence is death,' Krish said, holding up his hand to stop Imesha interrupting. 'But let each of their families be given ten gold wheels. There's no reason they should starve because of their men's crimes.'

The men his words had murdered barely reacted – some of them seemed too far gone to understand – but there was a surprised murmur from the crowd. Imesha frowned fiercely, displeased but unable to say so.

'Then let the sea take them for their crimes,' she said and nodded at her guards.

Krish had thought they meant the heavy chains to drown them, but the guards took those off the men and replaced them with rope. Perhaps the metal was too precious to waste. Some of the condemned cried out in pain as their mutilated hands and feet were bound. One whimpered and begged for mercy. Krish could see that he'd pissed himself. But this wasn't such a terrible way to go. He'd heard that drowning was a little like falling asleep.

When they were ready, the guards looked back to Imesha for her leave and then kicked the unlucky first man into the sea. There was a splash and a muted cheer from the watchers. The smell of stagnant water washed over them as the first fat drops of rain fell. The water below the dock churned as the man writhed hopelessly in the water.

Then his screams began. Krish jumped, and Lady Imesha smiled. It was a slash across her face, cruelly amused. 'There are fish in this water that hunger for flesh. Human flesh pleases them as much as any other.'

She gestured to her men and the second man was thrown in and then the third. The screams were loud but soon ended. Krish hoped it meant their deaths were quick, but he feared it was because their lungs were filling with water as the fish ate them alive. He wanted more than anything to look away, but he made himself watch as every single man was thrown to the same fate.

★

The land and sea smeared into an unpretty brown-green smudge beneath them. It was nothing to get excited about, but Eric's passengers got excited all the same. In the few days they'd been with him he'd learned that they could find excitement in pretty much anything.

They'd made Rii land the first time they flew above a shipfort, thrilled by the sight of the mammoths drawing it. Renar had drawn a book of blank parchment from her satchel and begun a sketch of it in a cramped, fastidious hand. It had occurred to Eric halfway through that he was allowing possible enemies to make a record of Ashanesland's fortifications and he'd hurried them back into the air. But it soon became clear they didn't have any mischief in mind. She'd made the same careful notes at the sight of a peasant's wagon, a field of cows and a shipborn man ahunt with his hawk.

He didn't let them get a good look at Arwel. He took the boy aside whenever he needed to feed him and left him in Rii's care when he could. He didn't like the thought of Lanalan exclaiming over him as if he was another weird specimen and Renar making careful notes about it in her little book.

The way they carried on, it was no wonder it took them so long to travel from the border back to Ashfall. The marvel was that they'd made any progress at all. And then, just when the peak of the broken mountain around which the shipfort circled had been in sight, Rii swerved east, towards the sea. 'Lord Yron has need of us,' she'd said, and who was Eric to argue? And so here they were, retracing the route Eric had once ridden on the way to his very first meeting with Rii.

'Why, this must be what the plains of Ofzib were meant to be, if the water hadn't failed,' Lanalan shouted above the rushing of the wind. 'Do you not think, Renar? The channels everywhere through the dry earth are just like the rivers here. How marvellous.'

Eric didn't think it was marvellous at all. Smiler's Fair had never come this far east on its travels. The ground was too marshy to hold it and besides, everyone knew Fell's End was the very poorest of the Ashane shipforts. The whole place was more water than earth, and none of it very appealing: mud-brown and choked with weeds. They said its people lived off the worms and minnows they harvested from its lakes and made secret midnight sacrifices to the Lady, to spare them from the many diseases its unhealthy waters bred.

Rii circled a while, searching for a firm landing place, until finally she sighed mightily and settled on a small island, barely big enough to hold her and unpleasantly damp, to judge by the squelch she made as she landed. The shipfort was barely visible in the distance, only its turrets poking above the reeds of the marshland.

'How do you expect us to get there?' Eric asked her. 'Don't know about these two, but I can't swim. And anyway, the water's probably full of man-eating fish.'

'Indeed, I believe there are such fish in these waters,' Renar said, reaching into her bags for a large notebook, this one entirely filled with writing. 'This is Fell's End, is it not? A merchant who travelled here once told of the giant serpents that are the terror of its residents.'

'Do not trouble thyself, morsel,' Rii said. *'My lord hath marked my arrival. He will send boats for thee.'*

Eric didn't know how she could be so sure, but he wasn't about to argue. He could see she was in a bad mood from the low-set angle of her ears and the way she fidgeted in the mud and bit impatiently at the places it was drying in her fur.

'La! The wildlife here is most wonderfully ugly!' Lanalan exclaimed. He'd fallen to his knees, heedless of the muck, and was staring at a warty frog crouched beneath a fern.

His face was in perfect profile, backlit by the sun so the features were indistinct but the shape sharply outlined. It was a handsome face and his smile was both charmed and charming, as guileless as a child's. Once, it would have stirred Eric to more than idle interest. Now he looked at men and wondered what sort of a protector they'd make for Arwel. Sadly, on that front, the sister was a better bet than the brother.

'I hope our transport won't be long,' Renar said.

'How come you two was chosen to come?' he asked. 'You ain't rulers back home, or they'd never have sent you into danger. Who does rule you lot anyway?'

'A Triumvirate,' Renar told him. 'Of youth, parentage and wisdom, or so it is this grand-year. But 'twas not they who sent us. It was Bruyar, who sits above them all, or perhaps one should say beyond.'

'Bruyar's your king?'

'No, no,' Lanalan said. 'Almost the opposite.'

'But she's the one what sent you?'

'Bruyar is not a woman,' Renar said.

'All right, *he's* the one what sent you.'

'Nor a man neither.' Renar smiled thinly. 'I had heard that inters were unknown among the god-sick folk. It seems it's true.'

'Inter? Like a knife woman? Someone born with boy parts who had them taken off.'

Renar winced as if he was being indelicate. 'Inter remain as they were born. I suppose you would call them both man and woman, though they are better than either because of the balance they achieve.'

'Right. I see.' He didn't, but Renar didn't look inclined to explain much further. 'So this Bruyar, she – he—'

'We say "oms" and "omas",' Lanalan said kindly. 'Bruyar doubtless had *omas* own reasons for sending us, but *oms* didn't share them with us. Ain't that right, Renar?'

The expression on Renar's face suggested it wasn't as right as all that, but before she could answer, the sound of oars in water carried to them over the lake.

The boat that hove into view was a pretty thing, painted pink and with dainty white umbrellas on sticks to shade the rowers from rain or sun. They were all bent to their oars, but another man stood motionless in the prow. Eric was surprised to realise it was Lord Krishanjit himself, with that strange bodyguard of his crouched beside him.

'Sorry to come out of the blue, my lord,' Eric said, putting on his posh voice as he always did when talking to Krish. It was probably a wasted effort. Folk said the prince had been raised among the poorest of churls. But Eric had been taught to make an effort where nobs were concerned, especially those that might give him gold.

'I'm glad you're here,' Krishanjit said. 'Now get us away from this place.'

His strange silver eyes pinned Eric, and Eric didn't bother to argue that Rii was tired and could use some food before she flew again, great fat lump that she'd become. Eric wouldn't have turned down a bit of grub either, but he nodded and said, 'Ashfall?'

'No! No, not there. Not yet.'

'Where then, my lord?'

Krishanjit hesitated, as if he hadn't thought that far ahead. He looked ill at ease, his face drawn and his eyes restless. Eric wondered what could have happened to him in gloomy Fell's End.

Lanalan and Renar had been loitering at the back of the hillock staring at Lord Krishanjit, seemingly struck dumb at the sight of him – which was no mean feat for either of them. But now Lanalan strode forward, feet squelching through the mud, and bowed elaborately. 'La! Where are our manners? I am Lanalan the Thespian and this my sister is Renar the Fox and it's a pleasure – why, what am I saying? – an honour to meet you. And perhaps if you're open to suggestions you might take one from me. I've been praised quite widely for my discernment, as Renar can tell you.'

Renar looked as if she'd tell him no such thing, and Eric hid a smile.

'You . . . want to suggest somewhere to go?' Krish said cautiously, as if it had taken him a while to unpick Lanalan's meaning.

'My brother's being absurd,' Renar said. 'Of course we will follow you. Indeed 'tis why we came.'

'But the Five Stars! The home of gods who are no more than idols. Did you ever hear of such a thing? Of course we must visit.' Lanalan pouted like a small child. Eric had told him about the shipforts on the lakes as they flew over, and he'd pouted the same way when Eric explained they didn't have time to stop and visit them.

'The Five Stars.' Krish considered a moment, then nodded decisively. 'Yes. That's where we'll go.'

★

It was deep night by the time they arrived at North Star, the nearest fort on the Five Lakes. The mammoths were shaggy shadows and the guards who stopped them on the bridge from land to fort were sleepy-eyed – then wide-eyed and fumbling as they realised just who their guest was.

Krish let Eric do the talking. His was a face – open and cheerful – that people warmed to. 'Ain't no need to wake your lord,' he said. 'All we need right now is a bed and pillow. We can talk in the morning.'

It was an easy enough request, but the servants roused to deal with it made it seem as difficult as they could, fussing and whispering when they thought their guests were out of earshot. Krish had discovered that being powerful was far less simple than being poor. In his youth – less than three years past – he'd had to worry about food in his belly and hiding from his father's brutal right hand. Now there were people to agonise about finding silk sheets for his bed.

He was allowed to sleep at last on sheets that were icy against his skin, alone in a gilded room that would have fitted his entire village. His dreams were filled with blood and the feeling of his flesh knitting itself back together unnaturally fast. He woke with his hands clasped to the scarless flesh where the knife had sunk in. He wasn't afraid. It was strange to realise it. He'd woken in fear for so many years.

He knew what the day would hold for him. He'd had many days like it since he'd returned to Ashanesland. It would be filled with ceremony and flattery and utterly exhausting even though he'd spend most of it sitting on his arse. He didn't want that, he decided. Not for today. Not for this place.

Dinesh was outside his door as he'd expected, more watchful than ever since the attempt on Krish's life. Krish wasn't sure if he'd slept since it happened. His eyes were sunken with exhaustion and black-shadowed. He seemed to be keeping them open by sheer force of will, but he still smiled cheerfully at the sight of Krish.

There was a servant too, sitting cross-legged on the ground. She must have dozed off in the night, and she twitched and then scrambled to her feet when Krish nudged her.

'It's all right,' he said through her gabbled apologies. 'I don't need anything. I just want to visit the shrines.'

'Of course, yes, of course, Lord Heir. Lord Nalin will organise—'

'No,' he cut her off again. 'I want to visit them alone. I want . . . I want to visit them the way any landborn pilgrim would.'

It was clear she wished to argue with him, but his rank kept her silent. It had no such effect on the emissaries from the Eternal Empire when he told them the same thing.

'But we wished to see the shrines for ourselves!' Lanalan said. 'Why, it was the whole point of the visit.'

Renar eyed her brother askance, but added, 'I did feel perhaps it would be a chance to tell you the purpose of our embassy.'

'I'll tell him,' Eric said, winking at Krish with the eye the strangers couldn't see. 'Fill him in on everything you said.'

'I don't want to stand out,' Krish told them all. 'I'm an Ashane and Dinesh is close enough. We can travel as ordinary pilgrims. You'll draw attention.'

'*They* will,' Eric said, nodding at Lanalan and Renar. 'I'll just tell anyone what asks I'm a Worshipper of Smiler's Fair. The company sends out people to the shrines all the time.'

'Are you a Worshipper?' Krish asked.

'Not as such, but they ain't gonna know that. I've got the gift of the gab and I spent enough time in the temple to learn all about your— that is, the Ashane gods. Besides, I've been before. I can give you the guided tour.'

Krish had wanted to see the shrines alone – or at least with only Dinesh, which was as close to alone as he got these days. But it would be useful to hear what Eric had to say about the two strangers before he listened to what they said for themselves.

'Yes, that makes sense,' he said decisively. 'We shouldn't be gone too long, should we?'

'Back by dinner,' Eric said.

'Why, that's an age!' Lanalan exclaimed.

'It will give Eric time to fill me in on what you told him.'

Renar frowned. 'But what of what we didn't tell him?'

'Tell me at dinner,' Krish said, and turned his back on them before they could protest further.

★

The lake that North Star circled was an unwelcoming place. There was no greenery on its shore, only scattered rocks, shit-splattered by the gulls who made their home among them.

'The Lady guards the fort from a rough landing,' Eric said. 'She keeps the winds gentle, or so they claim. Madam Aeronwen said the place hits the rocks at least once a year, but they ain't gonna admit that to all and sundry. Gold from the pilgrims what pass by keeps the fort afloat, so to speak.'

Krish studied him as they walked. Olufemi had told him what Eric once did: that he'd sold his body to men in Smiler's Fair. Krish couldn't imagine what that would be like. He didn't like being touched without warning. He didn't much like being touched at all by people he didn't know. The idea of letting some stranger do . . . whatever they did with Eric repulsed him.

But despite the life Eric had led, there was something boyish and carefree about him. Especially now he was relaxing enough in Krish's presence to talk like a normal person and not put on the airs he seemed to think Krish wanted. And then there was the baby sleeping in a sling across his chest, wrapped so tight that only his silver eyes were visible, the mirror of Krish's own.

The baby wriggled and whimpered. Eric rocked him, murmuring gently, but it didn't seem to soothe him. 'He's hungry,' Eric said.

'Then feed him.'

'It ain't wise, my lord. Not with so many cullies around. They don't take kindly to him.'

It was true they no longer walked alone. Other pilgrims shared the path, landborn men and women who looked as if it had cost them their last coin to reach here. The shipborn probably came by carrion mount or horse, if they came at all. They had their own prow gods to pray to, who took exclusive care of them. Or they had, until Krish came. What did any of these gods mean, now he was here? But if that was a question in the minds of the pilgrims, it didn't show. They looked eager, despite their weariness.

'Surely they won't hurt a baby,' Krish said.

'I'll protect him!' Dinesh curled his hand around the scabbard of his sword.

Krish put his own hand over Dinesh's, stilling it. 'We don't want to draw attention.'

'It's all right. I'll give the boy a quick sip now – that'll keep him quiet.'

Krish watched, fascinated, as Eric wormed a finger beneath the blankets until the baby's mouth latched on to it. Eric winced, but only for a moment. He used his other hand to gently brush his baby's wispy grey hair beneath the swaddling cloth.

'He drinks blood?' Krish asked.

'One of yours, ain't he? You can't expect him to do what any ordinary baby would.' There was unusual hostility in Eric's voice.

'Yes, I suppose he is mine,' Krish said. 'Thank you for taking care of him.'

His words seemed to startle Eric and he lapsed into silence as they walked on. Soon they reached the foot of the lake and joined a wider and far busier track, curving away to right and left. Krish had studied his father's maps of the homeland to which he was a stranger. He knew the lakes were arranged in a rough ring, with the shrines of the prow gods at the centremost tip of each. This path ran between them, only a few miles in length. Pilgrims could come and make their devotions and leave, all within a day.

Did they find it disappointing when it was over? The first shrine was in sight now, a wooden sculpture of the Lady, who was said to rule over storms and rain and every other kind of weather. The statue was very tall – at least fifty hands – but roughly carved and ordinary. And yet, as they drew nearer, Krish saw that the bowl on the ground beside her feet was filled with coins. More were thrown in as the pilgrims filed past, some pausing to kneel at the Lady's feet until the annoyed rumble of the waiting crowd hurried them on.

Why do you still come? Krish would have liked to ask them.

What use are they to you when I'm *in the world?* But he couldn't give them whatever they'd come to ask for. He wasn't sure the Lady could either, and yet he still kept his own hearth god in his pouch and touched it sometimes when he needed luck. They said Yron had a sister once. Who's to say there weren't more gods somewhere, waiting to come back to life?

'Do you want to stop here, Lord?' Dinesh asked, but Krish shook his head. He hadn't come to see the Lady.

They walked on, a throng of pilgrims around them. Some glanced at Eric curiously, but he grinned merrily back and Krish kept his head lowered so they wouldn't see his eyes.

No one stopped at the next shrine.

'The Fierce Child,' Eric said. 'That one don't care about anyone but beasts.'

The statue didn't look fierce. He looked sad. He was smaller than the Lady and far more delicate, the boy's features and shaven head so perfectly carved that Krish could almost have taken them for real. The statue was seated, knees drawn up to his unnaturally thin chest and his chin resting on them. Only his hands hinted, thin-fingered and long-clawed, at what he might be. They rested loosely on the ground, yet the sculptor had somehow conveyed that they were in the process of moving. Of lashing out, Krish thought. And perhaps the expression on the statue's face wasn't sadness but simmering rage.

'Strange,' Eric said as they moved off. 'I never thought of it before, but he looks a bit like one of the worm men.'

'Or like me. Like Yron, I mean, like I was.'

'You know what, he does in a way! Like those rocks all across the high plain what some Wanderers told me of. They was all carved with Yron's face. By the Seonu, I suppose. Or the Yronim as they're now calling themselves.' He studied Krish and then said, far more hesitantly, 'Why did we come here? I don't mean to pry, only a boy don't do the trade I did without learning to read a man. And there's something more to this outing than getting away from our guests.'

He seemed earnest. Krish had one friend, and he was half a

world away. Eric was no Dae Hyo, but perhaps Krish could afford to trust him a little. Eric was father to one of the moon's servants. His son's fate rose or fell with Krish's own, and if Krish was sure of one thing, it was that Eric loved his son.

'You can call me Krish, if you like,' he said.

Eric laughed. 'Not if I want to dodge the gibbet. They'd have my guts for garlands.'

'When we're alone then.'

'All right . . . Krish. So why have we come?'

'My ma came here, before I was born. There, I mean.' He pointed ahead, to Lord Lust's shrine.

'Praying for some love, was she?' Eric's eyes scanned the length of the statue. It was twice as tall as him and entirely naked, its member as thick as its arm and standing out proudly from its red-painted body. Young women crowded around the shrine, and Krish wondered how many had come for the same reason as his mother.

'Not for a lover,' he said. 'For a child. My da . . . she never bore him one, and he was angry and so she came here to beg for what he wanted. On the way back she found me, and she took me home with her instead.'

'Did she know who you was?'

Krish nodded. 'And she hid me away in the mountains where she thought I'd be safe.'

They walked up to the shrine and Krish knelt for a while. Eric and Dinesh stood patiently behind, but he couldn't seem to find a prayer. He wanted many things, but he didn't think love was one of them, not that kind of love. He'd never seen it do any good.

Eric shifted on his feet and his face told Krish the question he wanted to ask. He could have guessed it anyway. He walked away from the path, until the three of them were alone in the waist-high grass. It brushed against their legs as they stood, moved by the uncertain winds that water always seemed to bring.

'I don't know where she is now,' he replied to Eric's unasked question. 'I don't even know if she's alive. She helped me flee when . . . when my father's men were hunting me. Not my da's men. My da was already dead.'

'Where, where, where did she run to?' Dinesh asked. He seemed as fascinated by the story as Eric. But then he found everything about Krish fascinating. His love was so total it sometimes felt stifling.

'To her sister's,' Krish said. 'Across the valley in another village.'

'But she didn't arrive?'

Krish's throat was suddenly thick with a grief he hadn't known he felt. He swallowed it down, turning from the others until he was sure his eyes were clear. 'No. I mean, I don't know.'

'But . . .' Eric looked at him, then quickly looked away. 'But you could find out, couldn't you? You're the Wheelheir. You could send a carrion rider to look for her. You could send a whole flock of them!'

'But what if she's dead?'

'Then you'd know. Knowing's always better, in my experience. It's the not knowing that eats away at you.'

Krish looked back, at the tall red figure and the women clustered around it. 'Except if she's dead then I'd know my father killed her. I'm not sure I could forgive him for that, and I have to forgive him, or the war starts up all over again. So I can't ever find out the truth.'

★

Lanalan was clearly drunk. *Everyone* was drunk on the vile wheat wine they brewed in these parts. It was possible Renar herself was also drunk, but she at least had retained her dignity.

She had wanted to travel, but it struck her now that she hadn't realised she might travel so *far*. To be so surrounded by these godlanders, with their limp hair and their small, mean features and their harsh voices, these things she'd expected. But the utter strangeness of it all came close to overwhelming her.

How her mother would have mocked. And Renar would have deserved it, for why had she not expected this? A gods-ridden land was bound to be as different from Ofiklanod as the society of apes from that of men.

They looked like apes indeed, chattering and laughing too loudly, flinging food down their necks and occasionally at each other. The room they were in was dark and dank. It was filled with smoke from a fire that barely warmed the chill air blowing in from the lake through cracks in the woodwork of the outer walls. It was both far too solid and not solid enough – and yet this, apparently, was the highest a person might aspire to here.

Far worse were the bowing and cringing, the deference to the sour old man seated at her right who was lord of this place. They treated him like a god to be worshipped, as if having actual gods wasn't enough for them and they must treat men as divinities too.

And as for the true god she'd travelled here to meet . . . She found it easy to bring his face to mind, although she generally had no memory for faces. It was his eyes, she supposed, moon-silver as the histories said. But he was just a man. Barely that: a boy still awkward in his newly tall body, hunching his shoulders when he felt himself watched. She couldn't imagine what Bruyar was going to make of him. But that wasn't her concern. If she brought him to Bruyar she got her reward and that was all she needed to care about.

Lanalan leaned towards her, slopping wine over the top of his cup. 'This is outstanding fun, Renar! Why, I can see a play already: *Travels Among the Savages.*' He probably meant that for a whisper, but his voice was far too loud and several of those nearest to them glared. No one liked to be called savage, least of all those who were.

The man at the head of the table, the lord called Nalin, turned to them. 'So you think we're savages, do you?' His reedy voice was toneless, but only a fool would have missed the anger in it.

Her sib was just such a fool. 'Savages only compared to ourselves, but then our society is so much more ancient than yours, for we remember when your people came to these lands. No doubt in time you might reach our own high level of civilisation.'

Even her sib could not be oblivious to the rage on Nalin's face now. 'Your *own* level of civilisation? We had quite enough of that in Mirror Town. Or have you not heard of the slaughter your people performed there, and the foul magics they used to do it? This hall was twice as full before we crossed the mountains.'

He swept his arm around, and Renar noted for the first time how many empty seats there were at the long tables. And more than that, how many incomplete men, missing eyes or arms or legs.

'You speak of those you call the mages,' she said carefully. 'They are not, in fact, our people.'

Her sib's expression had fallen at the evident hostility from Nalin but it quickly brightened again. 'Why, now I see! You blame us for their actions! No wonder that mob so very nearly killed us when we first arrived. But you see, the people of that city are exiles. They are anathema to us. They were driven from our land when we rejected all gods and the magics they brought with them.'

That at least seemed to cool some of the old man's anger. But Renar wasn't sure the cunning look that replaced it was to be preferred. 'So your people have no magic?'

'None at all!' Lanalan looked scandalised.

'And yet you beat us without seeming effort in the Fool's War.'

'Why, that was because—'

'But the more recent war ended in peace, or so I heard,' Renar interrupted. Nalin seemed like a man to whom the least possible information should be given, especially any he might take as a weakness to be exploited.

'Yes,' he said grudgingly. 'Our King chose to come to terms with . . . his son.'

'It must be hard,' she suggested, 'after so much blood was spilled. There must still be resentment.'

'Our King commands and we obey,' he said flatly.

'But you believe the war should have been prosecuted to its end?'

'I believe a man doesn't clasp a snake to his bosom and expect it not to bite. And why are you so very interested?'

'I'm afraid I'm quite incapable of being *un*interested. It's my nature and my work. I'm a . . .' She struggled to find a word for 'politician' and realised that the Ashane tongue had none. How curious. 'I'm a person who helps those who wish to rule.'

'A plotter, you mean?'

She smiled pleasantly. 'If you wish.'

'And is that why you speak our tongue so well? Because you've come to these lands to plot?'

For once her sib's intervention was welcome. 'No, no! 'Tis a fashion, you see, to learn outland languages. All the most well-favoured youth engage in it. As well as your tongue, 'tis not boastful to say I've mastered that of the tribesmen across the mountains and the denizens of the place you call—'

He might have gone on all night, but at that point the hall's doors were flung open and the prince and his escort walked in. They didn't seem to have washed since their outing. Indeed, they looked quite bedraggled and not in the slightest godly, and yet a wave of silence washed out from them like icy water, for it was certainly a very cold silence.

'They're here!' Her sib lurched to his feet. He must have been far drunker than she'd realised. He swayed from side to side until a frowning man at his left reached out to steady him, no doubt to prevent Lanalan toppling into his dinner.

If the prince was aware of the hostile silence around him, he didn't show it.

'Prince Krishanjit!' her sib slurred. 'You've come back to us at last. We've much to tell you!'

'Not here,' Renar hissed. 'Our message is for his ears alone.'

But her sib didn't hear, or chose not to. 'We've travelled half the world to find you and faced death itself,' he declaimed. 'And all because we have tidings that would rot like spoiled meat if given too much time.'

Renar knew the look on his face. It was the one he wore when he took to the stage: self-loving and oblivious to all around. A sense of impending doom swept over her, already unstoppable in the moment it was seen.

'What news is that?' Krishanjit asked.

'Why, of a weapon. A spear, or perhaps a hammer – no one seems quite sure. But that it exists, we know, and that it's being searched for as we speak.'

'Not *now*,' Renar hissed desperately.

'And why are they looking for the weapon?' Krish asked.

'La! Ain't it obvious?' Lanalan boomed, loud enough for the whole hall to hear. 'Because it's the only thing between the oceans that can put an end to a god.'

9

The high sea walls of Mirror Town towered above the city, offering a bird's view of all that lay beneath. In her youth, Olufemi had enjoyed walking here with her lovers and marvelling at the achievements of her people. Now half those achievements had been toppled into rubble and Olufemi was more concerned with watching her footing on the weather-roughened stones. This was the fifth day she'd walked here and she wasn't growing any fonder of the exercise.

And all because that fool Dae Hyo had heard bells ringing beneath the sea. Yemisi claimed to have heard them too, but Olufemi suspected the whole ill-considered outing had been her idea. All her wisdom seemed to have melted away with her years, and the mentor Olufemi had once respected had become a flighty youth who irritated her almost beyond endurance. To risk a use of the runes, all so the pair of them could frolic like children beneath the waves! Who was to say the ringing of the bells hadn't been a consequence of the magic itself?

Dae Hyo had posted guards all the same, to keep watch over the water. And Olufemi had found herself drawn here every day by a fearfulness that disgusted her. It was the battle, of course. Mirror Town's residents had been broken along with its buildings, and she didn't know how to mend herself.

As with many of her age, her eyes had grown stronger at seeing what was further away, and weaker at making out what was right beneath her nose. Fatinikun Ogunleye had written a metaphorical poem on the subject that Olufemi's tutors had once insisted on her memorising. But all she could see today was the endless ruffled blue of the sea.

She'd reached the stairs back down to the city streets when the cry rang out, more startled than afraid. It came from her left, one of the lookouts Dae Hyo posted.

Olufemi's running days were behind her. She hobbled as swiftly as she could towards the source of the alarm. She could see the woman who'd sounded it, a distant figure bent over one of the rune-marked telescopes that were scattered at uneven intervals along the white walls.

The woman turned to watch Olufemi approach. She was fair-haired and her pale skin had been burned a fiery red. She must have stood unsheltered under the sun since dawn, keeping her watch. But so it was with the freed slaves. They knew that Dae Hyo was Krishanjit's deputy, and their devotion to him knew no limits. The rune that had both freed and re-enslaved the woman was a dark swirl on her cheek.

'Ships,' she called when Olufemi was near enough to hear. 'There are ships! A fleet is coming.'

Olufemi found that, after all, she wasn't surprised. Recent experience had taught her to expect the worst.

*

The ships were close enough that their hulls could be seen, light wood against the dark sea, and their sails billowing white above. A former fisherman among the freed slaves told Dae Hyo they'd arrive with the sunset. If the winds had been with them it would have been far sooner, but Dae Hyo hardly felt lucky.

After the bells had rung beneath the waves, he'd set his strongest people to repairing the broken segments of sea wall and ordered the building of great catapults from plans he'd found in Turnabout. He'd asked the mages, useless for physical labour, to search for runes that could be used against a ship. He'd asked for every defence he could think of, and none of it was ready. He cursed the months he'd wasted since his brother's departure preparing for an attack by land. But how could he have known?

News of the fleet had spread to every corner of the city. He'd expected panic but only the freed slaves were running to do what they could. The mages hardly seemed to care. He saw a group sitting around a gaming table, calmly drinking wine as men and women ran past them towards the walls, buckling on armour.

'Get up!' he shouted at them. 'Go to the walls! We need everyone to guard them.'

One of the women shrugged as she refilled her goblet. 'Let them come. How much worse could it get?'

'You could be killed – you could all be killed!' he yelled, but she only shrugged again and he shook his head in disgust and ran on.

He would have liked to drink to help the time pass more quickly, or at least less clearly. It was probably lucky he couldn't. He had responsibilities and a thousand people who couldn't seem to make a single decision without him.

He soon reached the half-built fortifications he'd ordered of the broken wall. 'Leave it!' he shouted to the slaves gathered there. 'It's too late. Find caltrops and scatter them on the ground.'

'Poison,' a red-headed boy said, brighter than the rest. 'There's poison in the Chukwu Mansion. We can use it on the caltrops.'

'Do it,' Dae Hyo told them, and ran on. He found his best archers in their barracks and told them to dip their arrows in the same poison. The rocks that had been set aside to build the wall he ordered others to drag onto the battlements, and also vats of oil to drop on anyone who tried to scale them. He sent other runners north and south along the coast from the city, in case the fleet decided to beach elsewhere and make their attack by land.

But he knew what their best defence would be. Even Olufemi understood it had to be done. As the first stars scattered the dark blue sky, she met him on the battlements with the mages she'd gathered.

'Belbog's balls, is that all?' he said.

'You're lucky it's this many! They know the price they'll pay this time.'

'Don't they want to save their city?'

'By destroying it?' one of the gathered mages asked venomously.

Dae Hyo bristled but decided wisdom lay in silence, as the elder mothers had so frequently told him. They couldn't afford to lose the help of these few mages they had.

They could all see the approaching ships now. There were a very great many of them. Dae Hyo counted fifty-seven before he lost the reckoning and gave up. They were huge, bigger even than the sunken wrecks that had once carried his people to this shore. He hadn't known things so large could stay afloat. The mountains of sail above their decks ought surely to have toppled them and yet they stood tall and came relentlessly on. He shuddered to think how many fighting men each ship could hold.

'Who *are* they?' he asked.

Olufemi only shrugged.

'I tell you what, whoever they are, they'll fry as crisp as any man. You've made the runes?'

'I've tried. There hasn't been time to test them.'

'Battle's the only test that counts. Wait until they're close enough to see their passengers, and then burn them on the water. If any of them swim ashore my people will kill them before they can climb the walls.'

The wind was so light, the ships seemed barely to move. Dae Hyo wished it would blow more strongly. Waiting for battle had always been hard. Waiting for it sober made every part of him itch. But the ships were only a few hundred paces from the shore, the rising moon making their white sails shine. 'Nearly there,' he said tensely.

'No,' Olufemi said suddenly. 'Wait!'

'We can't wait. They're close enough. I can see the sailors hanging from the ropes.' They were silhouetted against the moon, scrambling up and down them like apes.

'Not them,' Olufemi said. Her voice was strangely thin. 'The woman in the front.'

'The figurehead?' The golden figure stood proud at the prow of the leading boat, leaning forward as if to urge the fleet on. It seemed almost to glow in the twilit gloom.

'She isn't a figurehead,' Olufemi said and now he recognised the unfamiliar note in her voice. It was fear.

'Attack!' he shouted. 'Burn them!'

Power gathered like a thundercloud as two dozen mages called it to the runes from some place beyond. Gouts of fire flew from the battlements towards the ship and the watching people of Mirror Town cheered. The flames fell on wooden decks, burning brightly for one glorious moment. And then, like a candle, each was snuffed out.

In the moment the fire died, he felt another power far greater than the one the mages had wielded. He felt it pulled not from some other place but from this one, from the air around them. From his own flesh. He shuddered in revulsion and turned to Olufemi.

'Mages of the sun,' she said, before he could ask. 'Those ships are filled with her servants.'

Beneath their hulls, the sea itself had frozen, each wave stilled, the white caps near the shore turned to white ice. And using the ice as their bridge, an army marched towards land. There were pale-skinned folk of the Moon Forest and broad-faced men of the Maeng and the Four Together. But it was the golden-skinned women who terrified him. The one who marched at their head seemed to burn with light and he felt the vast power flowing into her.

The power burst back out again in spears of light and he flung himself on Olufemi and pushed her to the ground.

Others were slower and he saw the spears pierce them and travel on, deeper into the city. One man looked down at the gaping hole in his own chest, soot-black and bloodless. He frowned as if he couldn't quite understand that he was looking at his own death. A moment later he'd fallen to the battlements, a crumpled heap of flesh. Others were dying all around, and those who hadn't died were fleeing.

'Get up!' Olufemi said, pushing weakly at his chest.

'How can we fight them?' he shouted above the screams.

'We can't.'

'Then what can—'

'We have to get away. We must warn Krishanjit. His death has come for him. His sister has returned.'

★

The slaves stayed on the walls where Dae Hyo had ordered them to make their stand. They stayed and died. He could hear their screams. He would have ordered them to run if he could, but there was no time and his own life to save.

Olufemi gasped for breath beside him as he fled, slower than he would have liked. He slipped an arm around her shoulders but she was too short and frail. All it seemed to do was weigh her down. He sighed and scooped her into his arms, ignoring her squawk of protest. Her bones felt too near the surface of her skin and as fragile as china. He squeezed her to him, afraid that if he dropped her she might break.

The streets he ran through were eerily calm, the mages still at their gaming tables. A spear of light shrieked down to pierce one of their grand mansions. It left a smoking ruin in its wake, but the mages only turned to watch with empty eyes and then bent back to their game.

He knew that look. He'd seen it in the eyes of his brother Dae, the few who'd survived the massacre and turned their backs on their people and walked away to become something else. It was the look of people without hope, and he despised it.

'We have to find Yemisi,' he said. He pictured her impaled by a burning spear, or crushed beneath the falling buildings, and his stomach heaved.

'No! Not now.' Olufemi squirmed impatiently in his arms. 'We have to tell Krishanjit. It's the only thing that matters.'

'I'm not carrying you all the way to Ashanesland.'

'The Graveyard, you fool! There's a device, a rune-thing. It was made to speak across great distances.'

'Then why—'

'Save your breath for running!'

The streets grew rougher as the assault continued, littered with rocks and a growing number of corpses. The ground was slippery too, improbably frosted with ice. The air had grown so cold he shivered as he ran.

His legs and his eyes were busy but his mind was free to turn and turn. Krish needed his help. Yemisi needed his help. The thoughts pounded through him in time with his strides. If he helped one he abandoned the other.

'Keep running!' Olufemi shouted, and he realised that he'd slowed without quite meaning to.

'We can't leave Yemisi,' he said. 'We have to find her.' He knew, without having to think about it, where she'd be. He could see the exact expression she would have made when she realised what was happening – and the purple stain on her lips of the wine she'd be drinking to drown out that knowledge.

Olufemi yelled in fury as he turned away from the road to the Graveyard and headed east instead, towards Yemisi's home. She beat feebly against his chest with her fists. 'Let me down, you cretin!'

He ignored her. This district was perilously close to the sea and there was destruction and death everywhere. Dae Hyo's fear grew with every step he took. He wasn't even sure he liked Yemisi, but it felt essential that he save her. She meant something to him, if not who she was then who she had been and who she could make herself again. If she could find a new purpose in life, then so could he.

The house to the left of hers was no more than dust. He sobbed and staggered on, hope draining away. Flames crackled nearby and smoke choked the air, but then he saw that for once luck had chosen his side. It was the mansion beside Yemisi's that was on fire. Her house was untouched.

'Only a fool would have stayed here!' Olufemi said, then sighed. 'Let's fetch her and be gone. We can't save Mirror Town, but Krishanjit might be able to save us.'

While she spoke, the ice had turned into snow, falling improbably on the dusty streets and quenching the fire that threatened to consume Yemisi's house once it was finished with its neighbour.

The door was unlocked. He set Olufemi down to open it, and

as he turned the handle, a spear of light shot past him to pierce the house behind. The shock of it propelled him forward and he stumbled over the doorstep and to his knees. The ice was here too, riming every wall and floor. Even the flagon of wine that Yemisi had been drinking was frozen over.

Yemisi was no longer sitting beside it. She stood shivering in the centre of the room, but not from cold. There was another woman beside her. Her golden glow shone brightly in the gloom. Beneath her feet, the ice had melted. Dae Hyo could feel the warmth of her from ten paces distant.

'Hyo of the Dae people and the mage Olufemi,' she said. 'I've been waiting for you.'

PART 2

The City Below

10

Krish's legs ached from the climb up the dead fire mountain. There was fresh spring grass everywhere, the colour of young life, and flowers beginning to unfurl their petals.

The slope smoothed as he neared the top, where no greenery grew and there was only the black ash of the mountain's last eruption. The skeletons of the man and woman who'd betrayed him on the day of his birth lay ahead, but they weren't why he'd come. According to Janiinna, burning rock had burst from mountains across Ashanesland at the climax of the last battle between sun and moon, ending the war and slaughtering her people. The crystalline soot crunched beneath his boots and reminded him of the price that others had once paid to side with him.

The blue waters of the lake surrounded the mountain, Ashfall floating on them like a turreted island, and all around, Ashanesland's gentle hills rolled towards the horizon. The mountains of his youth had been a far harsher landscape, but this was the true heart of the kingdom he'd one day inherit.

Rock scraped beneath heel behind him, and he turned to see the man from whom that inheritance would come striding up the winding path towards him.

'Wheelking,' Krish said, bowing.

'Oh, enough of that.' His father settled himself on a boulder at the rim of the crater and waved Krish to sit beside him.

Krish nodded, keeping his eyes on the landscape below.

'Are you ready for the voyage?' Nayan asked.

'Yes. Rii's been taking on supplies. We'll leave in the morning.'

'And I won't persuade you to take the carrion flock?'

Krish shook his head. 'Too visible.'

'And that great beast isn't?'

'Apparently there's a place she can land where she won't be seen.'

Nayan sighed. 'For a thousand years they kept their borders closed to us. They sold us spices and silks, but they hid everything that mattered from us. They hid even the true name of their land! And now they summon you with talk of a secret weapon.'

'Before she left, Renar told me they've agreed to our terms. They've promised to open their borders to our traders. That's good for Ashanesland, isn't it?'

'The goods they bring back will benefit the Kingdom, yes. And the knowledge they bring back will benefit our spies – if any of them live to return with goods or knowledge. What do we truly know of this Renar and this Lanalan?'

'Nothing,' Krish admitted. He'd spoken to them often enough in the weeks since they'd arrived, but learned only their language. Lanalan seemed too foolish to tell him anything important and Renar too wise.

'Do they even have the power to make the promises they've made?' his father asked. 'They've claimed no kingship – not even any lordship. Do we know they're any more than landborn aspirants, reaching far beyond their grasp?'

'I'm not worried they're less than they say. I'm worried they're more.'

'You think they suspect our trick?'

'No.' Krish considered whether he actually meant it. 'No, I don't. When Renar and Lanalan left yesterday I think they really expected me to come when I'm invited. I don't think it occurred to them I'd try to beat them back to that city of theirs, to Täm.'

'Maybe you shouldn't. Why not go when the formal welcome comes, when you'll be greeted like a prince rather than skulking in the shadows like a thief?'

Krish shook his head. 'They wouldn't have told me about that weapon unless they already had it. All that talk about needing me to heal their land's sickness . . . Actually, I think it might be true. Lanalan said it and he's a terrible liar. But there's more to it than that. Renar knew the weapon was bait, and you only use bait in traps.'

'Then don't go at all.'

Krish could have told his father what happened when the woman put a blade through his heart. It would have made him worry less. But a tiny part of Krish wondered if it was Nayan himself who'd sent the assassin and not some other shipborn lord. If he had, Ofiklanod might be safer for Krish than Ashanesland.

'I have to go,' he told his father. 'If there really *is* a weapon that can kill gods, the whole kingdom knows about it now. And I've enemies who'd like the sound of it. Half your lords want me dead. More, probably.'

'Probably.' His father sighed, leaning back on his hands to tip his face up to the sun. It shone harshly on the wrinkles of his thin, old skin. 'These arguments I've heard a dozen times, Krishanjit, and perhaps they're correct. Renar is a cunning one and she's left you with a choice between worse and worst. Just tell me truly, do you expect to return?'

Krish looked at his father. Behind him, the skeletons of the man and woman he'd tortured and killed hung against the sky. 'Do you want me to?' he asked.

His father paused long enough to make it clear it was a question he took seriously. Finally he nodded. 'I've brought you here now and named you my heir. I've tied your fate to mine and it's too late to untangle it.'

Krish nodded, accepting the cold reason, but then his father reached out to clasp his cheek in one palm. His skin was dry, scratchy against Krish's.

'You're a stranger to me,' he said. 'I don't love you. But if you return, I might learn how.'

★

Eric had been flying patrols when the message finally came. He called them patrols, though truthfully no one asked him to do it and there wasn't much to guard against here in the heart of Ashanesland. But he took any excuse he could to get away from

Ashfall. He felt safest with Arwel in his arms and the pair of them in the air.

Now they were nearly back. Rii's course took her above the carrion stables, where the great grey birds were climbing their wheel perches to fling themselves into the air for their morning patrol. They took one look at Rii and winged wide around her as she hissed her disdain.

'It's the best they can do,' Eric said. 'They ain't got your strength. You know, we could take a couple of 'em with us, if you don't fancy carrying the prince all that—'

'*The task is mine,*' she said and he sighed and didn't argue further.

He could see the prince and his bodyguard waiting considerately a little distance from the shipfort, so the mammoths that towed it wouldn't be upset by Rii's closeness. Eric heard them snort as she landed, stamping in their traces and being yelled at by the poor drovers tasked with keeping them in hand.

Eric bowed as he drew near the prince, seeing as how they were in public. 'Ready to head off?'

Krish nodded. 'And your son? You're sure you don't want to leave him behind?'

Eric clutched the swaddled bundle tighter against his chest. 'He ain't going nowhere but with me.'

It was a long boring day, flying over the green spring fields. The sun had fallen below the western mountains before they reached the limits of Ashanesland. Eric hadn't thought to be afraid before, but suddenly he remembered that he ought to be. He might be leaving nothing good behind, but that didn't mean he was heading anywhere better. They were flying into the unknown.

The Great Rift was a dark slash ahead, filled with nothing but shadows so late in the day. The one bridge over it glowed orange and Eric could see the stain on its northern border. At this distance it seemed no more than a shadow, but he knew what it was: the horde of people who'd come here over the last few weeks, waiting for the day the border would finally open.

They camped far from the crowd, at the edge of the rift, and at first light Rii took wing again and crossed the chasm that separated Ashanesland from what lay beyond. The ground beneath was brown and barren, unfarmed and uninhabited. Eric was almost disappointed. He'd expected something more dramatic. Then the dull brown changed suddenly beneath them to a deep, rich green.

Eric had heard from Lanalan how the sun's magic still kept Ofiklanod fertile, and Eric believed it – he knew better than anyone what Mizhara's power could do. But seeing it was still a shock: the trees and broad-leaved bushes and dots of colour that must be flowers stretching to the horizon. It was lusher even than central Ashanesland, where enough corn grew to feed the whole nation. Only here and there blots of a sickly purple slashed through the green – some unknown blight, or perhaps just another unknown plant.

Rii winged higher. The sky was empty of everything but red-winged hawks who gave their giant rival a wide berth, but Krish didn't want them seen from the ground. The long flight went on, and the grumbling of Eric's stomach told him it was time for lunch. They wouldn't be stopping, though. Not till they reached the right spot.

Ashanesland had far more folk in it than the Moon Forest, but it still held stretches of untamed woodland and fens and moors and other wild places. Here there were houses everywhere, sometimes gathered into clumps of villages and towns, and some-times on their own in neatly fenced-in fields. It didn't seem there was an inch of this place that wasn't claimed by someone.

He wondered who these people were who lived here. He'd met Lanalan and Renar, but two people were just two people – they might be normal or they might be so odd their own folk hardly knew what to make of them. He'd met Moon Forest folk who liked nothing better than to feast like Ashane shiplords and tribesmen who sang the sad laments of the Moon Forest. People were strange, but taken together you could get a sense of them.

Their land revealed something about the folk of Ofiklanod, he supposed. Ashanesland from the air was a mess of squiggles, meandering hedgerows and messy fields, like a quilt sewn by someone who'd been drinking Yeom vodka all day. This place was far more orderly, more like the bedding his careful mother had once made to sell.

'Is that it?' Krishanjit shouted to be heard above the piercing wind. His arm appeared beside Eric's head, pointing a little to the left of their direction of flight, where the land rose upward. Something very high seemed to hover above it, floating in the heat haze.

'Might be,' Eric said. 'Let's take a gander. You game, Rii?'

'*I do not like this place*,' she said. Still, she did as he asked, turning her head towards the distant, monumental thing. On the ground below, the neatly fenced fields ended with the same abruptness with which they'd begun, leaving nothing but grass. It moved in the wind so that its colour shifted beautifully from grey-blue to grey-green, and then a very bright emerald when it all leaned a certain way.

The looming form on the horizon grew slowly clearer, more impressive with every wingbeat. It was hundreds of paces tall and very narrow. When they flew to a place where the western mountains were lower and the sun could peep above them, the structure's top glittered brilliantly. It was a statue, the largest Eric had ever seen. Surely the largest that could ever have existed. Renar hadn't lied to them after all – they'd found the place where Rii could land.

'Who, who, who is she?' Dinesh said in wonder.

'*Ill-luck*,' Rii said and Eric agreed with her.

Soon the statue's face was clear: wide-nosed and high-cheeked and very like the Hunter – very like all the Servants, who he could see now had been made in her image. In her hand she held a giant spear made out of crystal. It shattered the sunlight shining through it into a thousand rays.

It must have been possible to see her for miles around, even for those glued to the ground. But there was nobody *to* see the statue, not a single human habitation they'd passed in all the acres and acres of untroubled grass.

'We'll land beside it,' Krish shouted.

'*Here, god-lord?*' Rii hissed.

'It's only a statue, ain't it?' Eric said to her. 'Must have stood here for a thousand years, since Mizhara herself ruled over these folk. And it ain't done nothing bad in all that time.'

He could tell she wasn't happy, but she tipped her wings and glided down.

As soon as she'd hit the ground, Dinesh slid from Rii's back to walk closer and gawp at the statue. Eric set Arwel in his cradle, then walked right up to the toe of her left foot, taller on its own than his head. The surface of the statue was slick and strangely warm, as if the sun was shining right on it. His flesh wanted to cringe away from it, but he made his hand stay resting casually there. It was nothing but a leftover from an ancient war.

'Renar told me their people rejected the worship of Mizhara,' Krish said. 'They changed the name of their country to help themselves forget her. They even changed their language so they wouldn't have any words that reminded them of her. That's why no one lives around this place. They think that living in the statue's shadow is terrible bad luck.'

'Then why didn't they just knock it down?'

'Maybe they couldn't.'

Eric didn't like the sound of that. The people who'd built that statue knew things the Ashane and the Moon Forest folk didn't. They'd already been in this land when the Ashane sailed to it across the broad ocean. Who knew what secrets they'd dug out from it and kept to themselves all these long years? And then there was magic, the runes Prince Krishanjit had woken up. This was their birthplace.

'Do you know the story of Jaspal the Raven?' Eric asked Krish. 'Lord Lust's girls was particular fond of it. How he was tricked into putting his head in the mountain lion's mouth.'

The prince smiled crookedly. 'But Jaspal makes it through, doesn't he? He tricks the lion into eating a stink-cap along with him, and the lion throws them both up.'

'That's true. But Jaspal always wins because he's half a god.

You're a god too, but me and my boy, we're only men – or close enough.'

'I won't make you stay here,' Krish said. 'Rii can take you back if you like. I can go on with just Dinesh. It will be easier for us to pass unobserved, anyway.'

'Don't be daft,' Eric said. 'You need me for your plan, don't you? And I won't let you down.' It was lions one way and jackals the other. If Eric had to choose, he'd stick with the one person who might be powerful enough to protect him.

I I

It was hard to judge the passage of days when you were kept in darkness. Olufemi counted meals instead. There had been thirty-two since she had been thrown into this cage with Yemisi and Dae Hyo. If they were fed twice a day, more than two weeks had passed, and fewer if they'd been given three meals a day. It was impossible to tell. She slept at random and unexpected intervals, sometimes lulled by the *click-click-click* of metal passing over metal that accompanied their motion, other times jerked awake when it stopped.

At first their passage had been smooth, eerily so, no lift and fall as if they were carried by men and no squeak of wheels as though draft animals pulled them. The last five meals were different. They'd been jiggled and bounced enough that Olufemi's back was covered in bruises and she'd become far more intimately familiar with the tribesman's body than she'd ever have chosen.

Just before their last meal, a storm had raised winds strong enough to blow aside the heavy cloth that covered their cage and she'd finally seen sky, precious after all this time even though it was dour with clouds. Rain had doused them and washed away the reek of vomit before the cover was replaced. Dae Hyo's stomach had proven to be distressingly delicate.

But since their last meal, they hadn't been moved. Could their journey finally be over? She'd given up on hope, which had only caused her pain in the early days of this dark journey. Now she felt only a weary resignation. Her shoulders and knees and hips all ached dully and her eyes had spent so long blinking at nothing that she'd begun to lose the memory of sight.

Her magic was entirely gone. Something in this cage prevented her mind from reaching for the moon's power. Dae Hyo told her it was the same for him. Olufemi had felt around the bars of the cage and found that they were scored with deep marks. It must be some great runic spell, knitted into the metal. She hadn't realised how used she'd grown to having her power in the months since it had awoken. Its absence felt like an unhealing wound.

Yemisi groaned and fidgeted. Her elbow dug into Olufemi, but she said nothing. They'd long ago run out of things to say to each other. The sun had them her prisoner and there was an end to any conversation.

At last, when she was at the borders of sleep, the cloth was snatched from above them. Hands grabbed her and pulled her from the cage, snapping something around her wrists. Ahead there was a golden light that wasn't the sun's. It fractured through tears of pain and resolved into a woman's face.

'I apologise,' Mizhara said, 'for your discomfort.'

It was so absurdly inadequate a response to their suffering that Olufemis choked a laugh. Mizhara frowned, before nodding curtly at the women who'd released them from their prison and walking away. Olufemi could see now that they were tribeswomen of the Four Together, wearing the blue-beaded shawls of unwed knife women.

She would have liked to reject their help, but her knees had lost their strength and the women had to slip their arms around her waist to help her walk. They were gentle about it, which only made Olufemi angrier. She saw that they were leading her towards a table laden with food, where Mizhara had already seated herself. 'I'd like to wash first,' she said, although her stomach felt hollow with hunger.

'Your smell doesn't offend me,' Mizhara said, as if offending her must surely be what Olufemi most cared about.

The women set Olufemi on a chair between Dae Hyo and Yemisi. Dae Hyo didn't wait to begin eating, stuffing food into his mouth with his hands. It was a simple meal: meats and berries and coarse bread. Not a feast for a goddess. The golden glow had faded, leaving only a glitter on their captor's skin. Her face was shockingly young and innocent.

'Mizhara,' Olufemi tried, and the woman looked up from the apple she'd been carefully slicing.

'Eat,' Mizhara said.

Olufemi wasn't in a cooperative mood, but there was a limit to how far she was willing to spite herself to make a point. She sliced her meat and took a delicate bite, determined at least not to show the same desperation as Dae Hyo. He'd slowed his ravenous eating at last and watched the goddess thoughtfully.

'You're the other one, then,' he said. 'Krish's sister.'

'The moon is my brother of spirit, yes, though not this time of flesh.'

Dae Hyo nodded, his mouth still filled with meat. 'Olufemi here brought Krish back. Who was it brought you?'

That golden face was hard to read, but Olufemi was sure she saw a moment of pure anger on it before calm blankness returned. 'I apologise that you were kept in such conditions,' she said. 'I wish I could have freed you sooner, but I'm sure you understand why your misuse of the runes must be contained.'

Olufemi looked down at the manacle on her wrist, carved with a complex, power-quelling rune. It was wooden, easy enough to make though impossible for her to remove. 'You could have put these on us at any time.'

Mizhara's eyes darted away from hers and Olufemi hid a smile. So. It had taken the goddess or her people that long to work out the form of the rune needed.

'I tell you what,' Dae Hyo said. 'I'm wondering why we're still alive.'

Olufemi winced at the bluntness of the question but wasn't altogether sorry it had been asked.

'I don't kill without reason,' Mizhara replied.

Yemisi looked up from her own slow but determined demolition of their meal. 'We're friends of your enemy. That's reason enough.'

'Perhaps among your people!' Anger flashed momentarily in

her golden eyes. 'I've no need to kill you. And killing needlessly is the province of monsters – such as those your master rules.'

'Krish isn't any more fond of monsters than the next man,' Dae Hyo protested. 'Well, except for that huge ugly bat, but she didn't leave him much choice. I've seen wives less fond of their husbands than she is of him.'

Mizhara leaned forward, elbow on the table. It was clear this information mattered to her. 'The monster Rii. She survived then?'

'She's hard to kill,' Olufemi said.

'And the man who fled us with her? I . . . I cannot recall his name.'

She wasn't a very good liar. 'Eric?' Olufemi said, and saw the goddess flinch.

'Yes. Yes, Eric.'

Olufemi shrugged. 'He's alive.'

She could see that her answer frustrated the goddess, and hid a smile.

'But not in Mirror Town,' Mizhara said.

'No.'

'He's—' Yemisi began, and ended on a yelp as Olufemi kicked her under the table.

'Yes?' Mizhara said, turning burnished eyes on her.

Yemisi shrugged. 'He's alive, as Olufemi says.'

Olufemi thought she could see Mizhara's teeth grinding. 'He's with my brother, then?'

Olufemi's mind was beginning to move again, like a rock gathering speed as it rolled downhill. 'Yes. But you didn't know it. Yet you knew where we were. You came right to us.'

'I have . . . ways of seeing.'

'Of seeing us, but not your brother. The moon is hidden from you.'

'It doesn't matter,' Mizhara said. 'I'll return to the land of my birth where my people await me. With their armies at my back, there'll be nowhere my brother can hide.'

'You're very sure your people want you back,' Dae Hyo said.

'You've been gone a thousand years – that's a long time to wait.'

'But I am their god,' Mizhara replied, as if that answered everything.

Olufemi noticed that Mizhara had started sounding far more human the moment the subject of Eric entered the conversation. She smiled. 'I suppose if you can't see your brother, you can't see the moon's servants either. Even the very youngest – the babies . . .'

Oh yes, that hit its mark. The mask was stripped entirely from the goddess's face now. It twisted into a mixture of fury and grief that Olufemi thought she understood. Eric hadn't been too forthcoming with information about the mother of his child, but Olufemi had wrestled it out of him. She smiled at Mizhara. 'His baby is thriving. Or rather I should say *your* baby.'

The goddess's chair fell back as she rose from the table. She towered above them, the golden glow of her face so bright that Olufemi had to squint her eyes against it, but she'd never looked more human. 'That monster isn't mine.'

Dae Hyo looked between them, fascinated. 'You're the babe's mother? I tell you what, I don't think much of a woman who throws her child away.'

'*I am not his mother!*' Mizhara roared.

It was an effort to stay calm in the face of her fury. 'Perhaps he never suckled at your breast, but he came from your body, didn't he?' Olufemi said. 'What other word would you use but "mother"?'

Mizhara was silent for a long moment as she struggled for control. Finally she breathed out once, sharply, and then again with deliberate slowness, and turned to one of the tribeswomen who served her. 'Get them out of my sight.'

★

They weren't brought to her again. But they weren't caged either. Dae Hyo was glad of that. A man didn't like to void his body in front of any woman, let alone one as prone to mockery as Yemisi. Olufemi had been scathing enough about his weak stomach; he could barely look Yemisi in the eye after their imprisonment together. She seemed to be avoiding him anyway, which he should have been grateful for but found that he wasn't. Nothing about their captivity was proving pleasant.

Still, at least in the cage there was a reason for their isolation. Outside it they were still being ignored but it was taking more visible effort. The knife women of the Four Together hastily averted their eyes whenever he met them and the Moon Forest folk kept the same careful distance they would from a plague carrier.

They didn't seem too concerned about hiding their numbers. But if he'd had an army this big, he wouldn't have done much to hide it either. Mizhara seemed to have swept the Moon Forest clean of people, and half the plains too. Maybe news of what happened in Mirror Town had helped win people to her cause. Dae Hyo loved his brother, but he couldn't say he'd fought very prettily.

He would have asked some of the Maeng what exactly they were doing here, but he knew he'd be wasting his time. He hadn't even been able to find out exactly where *here* was, though he knew it was nowhere he'd ever been before. The army marched day after day through rocky valleys between mountains unlike any he'd ever seen.

The shape of them couldn't be natural. Someone must have carved those thousands of rings around them, like huge, grassy stairways leading to their distant icy summits. Perhaps they'd been fields once, snatched from the wilderness, but the wilderness had reclaimed them. Roads ran through the valleys, fashioned from a stone as smooth and dark as flint, but they were cracked, more treacherous underfoot than the grass on either side.

'Do you recognise this place?' he asked Olufemi, in one of the rare moments they weren't being watched.

She swept her gaze over the stairway mountains. 'I don't know. I've never been here.'

'But you've been everywhere.'

'Yes. So if this is a place I don't recognise, it must be – I believe it can only be the Emiwinku Mountains, the haunted mountains that lie between the Silent Sands and the Eternal Empire.'

'There are spirits here?'

She shrugged. 'So the name suggests. I know no legends of this place, only that our people never came here.'

'But your people feared nothing in the days of their power. That's what Yemisi told me.'

She nodded.

'Then what did they fear here?'

'I don't know. And I very much wish I did.'

★

The days piled on top of each other, each no different than the last. They followed the broken roads winding between mountains, walking from sunset to sundown and sleeping in the soft, sweet-smelling grass. Hawks flew high overhead, circling in the wind, but Dae Hyo never saw them dive. Wildlife was sparse in these mountains and the hunting lean.

Conversation was scarce too. He couldn't seem to find a word to say to Olufemi that didn't send her into a fury, and Yemisi didn't care to speak to him at all. He found her eyes following him on occasion but when he caught her gaze she turned her back to him. He didn't think he'd said enough over the past weeks to so thoroughly offend her, but perhaps she'd begun to find his mere presence intolerable. The thought lowered his already low mood.

On the fifth day, he tried to run. He didn't think there was much hope of escape, and he was brought to ground by Jorlith warriors while still within sight of their camp, but he needed to make the effort. Captivity had begun to feel dangerously normal. He'd seen it before, among warriors taken in raids. You didn't have to treat them well. You just needed not to treat them badly and soon enough they lost the will to fight.

On the ninth day they came to the city. At first glance Dae Hyo took it for yet another mountain, bare of grass but cut into great circular steps like all the rest. Its symmetry was broken in only one place, where a river tumbled frothily from its peak to the rocky valley at its foot. Where the river cut through it the rock sparkled pink-gold in the sunlight and he saw that it was seamed with crystal.

As they drew nearer, he began to make out the buildings. They were perfectly smooth and even, undecorated but clearly very finely made, though to no pattern he'd ever seen before. Where normal buildings had four walls, these had six. They were stacked on top of each other as neat as a honeycomb. Only the size of them changed between levels: little bigger than a man at the mountain's foot and as large as palaces at its top.

He wasn't the only one who stopped to look. The whole loose column halted.

The oddest thing was how familiar the place seemed, though he was sure he'd never seen it before. 'I know!' he said, pleased at the sudden revelation. 'It's the game. The city looks like that game your people play. The boards are shaped like the city.'

'Night and Day, you mean!' Yemisi said. She turned to him with a delighted smile and then quickly looked away again as if she'd momentarily forgotten to find him irritating.

Olufemi looked thoughtful. 'I believe you may be right. We were always taught the game was ancient, but if this was its inspiration . . . I don't know what it means.'

Now their caravan had stopped, the sounds from the city were far clearer: the cawing and honking of birds, the barking of dogs and the growls and screams of other animals whose calls Dae Hyo didn't know. A loud splash drew his eyes to the tumbling river, where something huge dragged itself from the water. It shook itself mightily, then lay back to bask in the sun.

He frowned. That river really was very broad and very fast. And they seemed to have passed the apex of the mountain range. That torrent might run a very long way down.

He nudged Olufemi and whispered, 'You said Mizhara's people weren't very good at their runes? That their magic is weak?'

'It's more powerful than you can possibly imagine, but it isn't practised. The runes they used at Mirror Town might have taken them months to design. It's clear to me they had to learn them afresh, as I once did. But I at least have had the advantage—'

'Yes. So you're saying they won't be able to just . . .' He snapped his fingers, then had to wait until the few Moon Forest folk who'd turned to look at him looked away. 'They can't make it up as they go along. They can't *react*.'

'No, I suppose not. But since we have no magic at all, it hardly benefits us.'

He nodded his head towards the river that fell in giant waterfalls from each terrace of the city. 'If we jumped in that, we'd be moving too fast for them to stop us.'

'We'd be *dead*.'

'Maybe. But would our corpses be moving too fast for them to stop?'

'I'm old,' she said testily, 'I've little life left to lose. Why are you so ready to throw your years away?'

He opened his mouth to make some quick reply and then closed it again and thought a little longer. 'I tell you what, if you'd asked me that question three winters ago I'd have told you my life was worth as much to me as dung. Now I think I could find reasons . . .' His eyes flicked without his bidding to Yemisi. 'I could find a purpose again, enough of one to live to see grey in my hair. But these people mean to use me against Krish, and by Belbog's balls, I'd rather die than be used against my brother.'

'And so is youth squandered on the young. And what about you?' She turned sharply to Yemisi, who seemed startled by the attention.

'I don't know,' Yemisi said. 'I don't want to die. But I think if we stay here we'll be killed anyway, one day soon. Mizhara doesn't love us.'

Olufemi sighed. 'Well then. But we're too far away. If we ran now, they'd catch us before we reached the water. Half a plan, that's all you ever have, warrior.' She shook her head at him, then turned on her heel and marched determinedly towards Mizhara, gesturing them to follow.

Mizhara didn't seem pleased to see them but she stopped walking when Olufemi planted herself in her path.

'I'm surprised to see you so uninterested in the place of your birth,' Olufemi said.

The goddess looked baffled. Dae Hyo didn't blame her.

'Or one of your births, I should say,' Olufemi added. And then she laughed. Dae Hyo wasn't sure how she managed it, but she heaped a double load of contempt into that laugh. 'Oh, I see. You didn't know. Well, I suppose you didn't encourage your servants to remember the past too clearly. They might have remembered some uncomfortable things. And you . . . well, it seems you remember your previous lives in fragments – if at all.'

She must be guessing. She'd said nothing of this to Dae Hyo.

'I remember enough,' Mizhara said, which was as good as an admission that she remembered too little.

'But not your life here, it seems,' Olufemi said. 'Did you think that your birth in the Eternal Empire was your first? Ah, I can see you did. My people remember more. I've always believed that they brought you back quite deliberately, you know. Much as I did with your brother.'

The goddess studied her acutely, as if she sensed some trap in Olufemi's words.

Olufemis shrugged and turned her back, seemingly uncaring, and that seemed to decide things for Mizhara. 'We will scout the city,' she said.

The goddess's voice was quiet, but it carried to all her people and the long column began turning, wheeling to face the mountain city.

'Clever,' he whispered to Olufemi, who quelled him with a look.

He found his steps hesitating, though, as they neared the ancient city. He was close enough now that he could hear the rush of the waterfalls – almost close enough to flee. He should be running forward, but something held him back.

'It's . . . sick,' a Jorlith warrior said and yes, that seemed right. Something ailed the city.

A crow cawed from the crown of a stunted tree ahead. Its branches were full of them, claws clinging to its bare boughs. As

Mizhara's people walked closer – a smaller crowd of them now, many holding back – the crows' eyes turned to them. But their eyes were cloudy. They were all blind, and their feathers were draggled and torn.

A fox shuffled past, its once-red fur now mangy and streaked with white. In the distance, Dae Hyo saw the sea beast that had crawled to land from the river. It was five times the size of a man, but its flesh was deeply wrinkled and when it yawned he saw that what teeth remained were yellowed and blunt.

Time hadn't touched the city's stern grey houses, piled tier on tier to the mountain's summit, but it had raked its claws across all the beasts that now made them their home. And the plants too, he saw now, were withering on the vines that curled and climbed across the buildings.

'Well, don't stand there gawping like a pelican,' Olufemi hissed. 'This is our chance.'

She was right. The goddess's people were gawping too, and Mizhara herself couldn't seem to drag her eyes away from the city that might or might not once have been her home. The river was still more than fifty paces away, but as they used to say in Smiler's Fair, the untossed die will never show a six. This was their only chance.

He'd seen Olufemi's stiff-kneed walk. She'd never make it without him. She yelped when he picked her up and slung her over his shoulder, then grabbed Yemisi's hand and ran.

He tried to move as silently as a hunter, but his boots crunched the brittle plants and he'd only gone a few paces when the cry went up. After that he could only put his head down and force his legs to work their hardest. He pushed Yemisi in front of him so any arrow or spear would find him first. His back itched with the fear of them, but none came, only the pounding of feet close behind and growing closer.

Twenty paces from the river and his shadow stood out stark black ahead of him, outlined by a golden glow. Mizhara herself was in pursuit. But god or not, she'd never chased a hare across the silver grass of the plains. He ran as if he were still that boy, ran harder than he'd ever run before, and finally the torrent was in front of him, frothing fiercely white.

As the first droplets of water hit him, a hand grasped his shoulder. It burned his skin and he knew it was Mizhara's. The grip was firmer than steel. But Yemisi and Olufemi weren't yet caught. Their freedom lay in the river and with a mighty heave he tossed Olufemi in and pushed Yemisi after her.

Then he turned to face Mizhara's anger.

12

Krish hadn't realised how quickly he'd grown used to comfort. He'd once slept on the hard ground in a cold tent without complaint. But now nights on the grass in the sticky warmth of Ofiklanod left him aching and bad-tempered.

Nervous, too. On the first days of their trek from the great statue, they'd been walking through unfarmed scrubland and then meadows and forest dotted with only the occasional field. It had been easy to remain unseen. But the nearer they came to the city of Täm, the less wild land there was. The last three days had been spent entirely in habitation. The strange, polished amber roads were thick with people and Krish and Eric and Dinesh had been forced to make their slow way through the fields instead.

It was a rich land, hilly and bright. Flowers edged every orchard, and the orchards themselves were filled with extravagant large-leaved trees drooping with fruit. The sun was relentlessly bright and often the only shade came from the high marble arches that strode across the sky in every direction. Renar had told him they carried fresh water and the narrow boats that rode it. All he could see from the ground was white marble, and the occasional staircase leading up.

They slept their fourth night against one of the pillars whose foot rested in a cherry orchard. Krish woke to the feeling of eyes on him, and opened his own to see Eric squatting above him. The youth was an early riser. He held out a cup of water and a hunk of dry bread for Krish with a cheerful grin.

'I think we're nearly there,' Eric said, always ready to chatter the moment he woke. 'There's a whole flock of them bright pink birds circling up ahead. Didn't you notice? They're always about when there's a big crowd. I suppose they live off the scraps.'

Krish hadn't noticed, but it didn't surprise him that Eric had. Krish had learned not to underestimate him. Eric chattered so much it was easy to imagine he didn't also watch and listen.

The bread was stale but Krish ate it hungrily. His body might be impervious to death; it certainly felt hunger. At night, when sleep escaped him, he stared at the stars and waxing moon and wondered what would happen to him if he were trapped in a cave for a hundred years. Would he experience a hundred years of thirst and starvation, of terrible lonely boredom?

'I don't like it here,' Dinesh said suddenly, his words muffled by the dry bread in his mouth.

'I've been worse places,' Eric said. 'Least this is warm and the streets ain't knee-deep in shit.' He was feeding his baby as he spoke, holding a bleeding finger to Arwel's mouth.

Krish looked away. 'I don't like it here either,' he said, realising the truth in the saying of it. There was something in the air. His sister's presence – or maybe her absence, which was somehow equally large and oppressive.

Dinesh smiled, as if reassured that his feelings were shared. 'I'll protect you, Lord Krishanjit.'

'And who's gonna protect us?' Eric asked. He lifted his son to kiss him on his grey forehead, then began to carefully bind him in his swaddling clothes. The babe was too big for it, but it wouldn't do for him to be seen, not with his ash skin and his moon eyes. This was a land where people might remember what that meant.

It wouldn't do for Eric to be seen either. The agreement Krish had made with Renar would see the border to Ofiklanod opened soon, but it was too early for any outlander to have made it this far north – and no one was more obviously foreign than Eric, with his wheat-blond hair and milky skin.

So Eric became a leper. He was putting on his rags and hood now. It must be hot beneath them, but he never complained. The hood hid his fair hair. His skin wasn't so easily covered and he rubbed walnut oil into it each morning and then worked carefully, lip between his teeth as he glued flakes of sawdust across his cheeks and then brushed a red dye across them.

'Old beggar's trick,' he said, when he saw Krish looking. 'No one wants to stare too close at illness. Makes 'em feel they might be coming down themselves.'

'It's horrible,' Dinesh said.

'That's the idea.' Eric grinned and pulled the hood up, leaving his handiwork shadowed and somehow even nastier for it.

'You weren't a beggar though, were you?' Krish said.

Eric studied him, assessing, then shook his head. 'Nah, not except when I first pitched up at the fair. I was a sellcock mostly.'

Krish remembered the woman Dae Hyo had bought for him at the shabby house in Smiler's Fair, and the painted boys who'd been there too. Eric was very pretty. It wasn't a word Krish had thought of for men before, but it was the only one that fitted. If Krish had been as pretty, could he have taken the same work to escape his da, selling his body for coin? He didn't think so, but he wasn't sure if that made him stronger or weaker than Eric.

'It weren't terrible work,' Eric said. 'But I was getting too old for it. I ain't sorry I've had a change, though maybe this wouldn't have been the one I picked.' One hand plucked at the mutilated fingers of the other. It was a habit he often had when he was thinking.

'I used to think about running away to the fair sometimes,' Krish told him.

'And why didn't you then?'

Krish bent his head over his tea, letting the steam envelop him. 'I couldn't leave my ma. And I think . . . maybe I didn't have the courage.'

Eric laughed. 'Ain't never thought of myself as brave. I'm bold all right, but bravery's a whole other kettle full of sprats.'

Krish thought of Dae Hyo, flinging himself into every fight as if he hoped it might be his last. 'You flew a monster to battle from the other end of the world. That seems brave enough to me.'

'Or desperate.' Eric looked down at his son, muffled in his swaddling clothes. 'Truth be told, I ain't ever had too much choice in what I do.'

'But you chose to run away to Smiler's Fair.'

'And you didn't.' He tipped his head as he studied Krish's face. 'Is it true you grew up poor like me? A peasant in the mountains.'

'It's true.'

'And now you're a prince and a god. Life's peculiar, ain't it?'

'Oh, oh, oh!' Dinesh said, and for a moment Krish thought he had had a recollection of his own twisted childhood. But he was looking over Eric's head, pointing to the path snaking through the orchard behind him. 'Something's coming!'

The creature was hideous, an oily brown with stick-thin limbs and snapping jaws outside its mouth. Insect-like – but how could any insect be that huge, legs as long as a man's? Its head was on a level with Krish's heart.

Dinesh leapt in front of him, sword drawn. The creature reared to strike – and then jerked back, tottering on two many-jointed legs before falling back to all six. Krish realised its neck was circled by a thick leather collar as its master stepped forward, yanking on its chain to bring it to heel.

He was a tall man, bare-chested above the long embroidered skirt that all Ofiklanod men wore. Krish still found his own awkward, often tangling his feet when he walked. It nearly tripped him now as he backed away from the creature.

The creature's jaws snapped, a lurid green froth growing between them.

'Too many gnats in the orchards these days,' the man said in the harsh, clipped tongue of Ofiklanod. Using the books Renar gifted him, Krish had found it easy to master – as he did most languages – but hard to love.

'Please, sir, we were going on only,' Eric said haltingly. He was a fast learner, but not so fast as Krish.

The man's plump lips rounded into a disgusted moue. 'And diseased gnats, I see. Did you stray from the swarm? Best you return to it before I use my fly swatter.'

Dinesh still had his sword drawn, metal glinting in the sunlight. The man glanced at it, seeming more irked than afraid.

Krish rested his palm over Dinesh's fist, gently pushing the blade back towards its sheath. They weren't here to be noticed, and spilled blood always drew attention. Besides, fierce as his dreamy-faced bodyguard could be in a fight, Krish wasn't sure he was any match for the creature on the man's leash.

'We're going,' he said. 'Our apologies.'

The landowner watched them with dark hooded eyes all the way from his fields to the road that ran at one side of them.

'That went well, didn't it?' Eric said, when they were finally out of earshot.

Krish smiled ruefully.

'No, I ain't kidding,' Eric said. 'He chucked us off his land just like we was real locals. Never stopped to think we might not belong here. Or at least he thought we didn't belong in the right way.'

'That's true. Our disguises held.' Krish scanned the road ahead. It was a strange thing: as wide as ten men abreast and perfectly smooth as it dipped into the valley ahead and then rose to crest the hill beyond. The surface appeared varnished but what was beneath wasn't wood. It was yellow-orange and almost transparent, like very old glass.

All along its length were clots of people, some only couples, others dozens strong. 'We'll stay on the road from now on,' Krish decided. 'I think the city's close. If we can't fit in, we'd better find out before we arrive.'

They moved tentatively at first. Krish saw Dinesh casting constant worried glances around him and forced himself not to do the same. There were too many people to keep a close watch on any of them and trying only made them look suspicious.

But they weren't the only ones being cautious. The road was filled with frightened people, more and more as the day wore on, until there was no longer any way to avoid the crowd. By afternoon they were no more than one small part of it.

Krish was afraid to speak at first, worried their voices would betray them. But he heard accents around him far odder than theirs and some that didn't even sound like the language he'd learned from Renar. The faces were varied too, fat-lipped and thin, some with skin the same shade as his, others as dark as Olufemi, some hair in braids, some trimmed close to the scalp, some allowed to grow free. But every person on the road was sweating with exertion and the clothes they wore were threadbare and stained. These were poor and desperate people.

Renar had told them about the refugees fleeing to Täm from every region of Ofiklanod, but Krish hadn't been sure he could believe her. It seemed too convenient a story: a crop blight and a murrain that had left them destitute and a god who was the only one who could save them. It was clear now that she hadn't been lying about all of it.

And then at last, as the sun touched the horizon, they saw the city of Täm. It had been built on nine hills and they approached it from the brow of another. The strange amber road on which they'd travelled forked ahead and then forked again until it formed a web through the city and across its many bridges. The whole place was riven by chasms, visible even from this distance. Their darkness stood in contrast to the bright colours of the houses and the green of the many parks.

'We'll stop for the night,' Krish said. 'It'll be easier to find our way around in daylight.'

'And in the morning?' Eric asked.

'We all know what we need to do.'

*

Eric hadn't realised how much reassurance he took from the others' presence until they were gone. It was odd. He'd heard Prince Krishanjit described as cold, but that didn't seem right. There was a fire in him, he just kept it carefully guarded. Eric had met his type before, and when the fire was finally let out to rage, then you'd better watch out.

Except Eric was more sure than he could explain that Krish was on his side. He thought they understood each other, or at least were willing to accept the parts of each other they found strange. That was rare enough in Eric's experience. And a boy had to put his trust somewhere, especially when he had a babe to care about.

Not that Krishanjit seemed quite as ready to put his trust in Eric. Or at least, he didn't much seem to trust his ability to stick to the plan. They'd gone over it half a dozen times last night, just to be sure they knew their parts, and then Krish had made Eric speak it back to him, to prove he had it by heart.

It wasn't like it was complicated. Eric was to make his place with the poor of the city, and find out what they knew about this God Killer. The answer was probably nothing, but they had to cover every angle, and it wasn't like Renar had given them much to go on. She'd only talked about a person called Two Hands, who was thought to have been looking for the God Killer and was also among the lowest in the land. And Lanalan in a drunken moment had said there were rumours about some secret the poor were keeping, or some plot they were hatching, and together those were enough to be worth looking into.

Lanalan wasn't a subject Eric wanted to think about. The man wasn't exactly what you'd call sharp, but there was something about his smile – the easy friendliness of it, and the way his laugh seemed to invite the whole world to laugh along with him. Eric liked him, but he'd still used him to learn about Ofiklanod. That's what Krish had asked him to do, but it didn't make him feel any better about it. Shouldn't he have learned his lesson about taking advantage of people from Drut?

Eric stumbled as a small child pushed past him and he dragged his thoughts back to the plan. He understood why it called for Krishanjit to mix with the wealthy of the city while Eric hobnobbed with the scum. Eric knew more about how to handle cullies than the prince did, for all his poor childhood. But the end result still left Eric in the mud and noise.

There were too many bodies all heading towards the one gate, that was the problem. Eric could see it up ahead, an arch of the same amber as the road with a cluster of folk building up around it. He could see beyond it too. There were a dozen of those strange stripy horses they rode around here trotting towards the gate with military-looking types on their backs.

You didn't live in Smiler's Fair without learning what the start of trouble looked like. The city beyond the gate seemed prosperous and tranquil and the crowd heading towards it the exact opposite. It wasn't a surprise they weren't finding much of a welcome.

This was the moment when all his instincts told him to make himself scarce. There were other ways into the city. He looked down at his boy, still sleeping peacefully in his swaddling. Taking care of him was all that mattered.

Only taking care of him hadn't proven to be Eric's strongest game. And there was one person who *could* protect him, who'd been born to it in a way, and he'd told Eric to stick with this crowd and learn its secrets. He wouldn't learn anything if he ran now.

The stripy-horse riders fanned out on either side of the mob. They had weapons drawn, long cudgels with wicked-looking nails driven into them.

They could mean to herd the crowd or they could mean to ride it down. Their faces weren't giving anything away. Other cullies had noticed them too. The crowd started a restless shifting that Eric had seen before. It usually meant either a panicked flight or a riot, and neither was a good thing to get stuck in the middle of.

He found that he was on his tiptoes, rocking back and forth like a racer of the Four Together on the start line of the Spring Games. The riders were closing their noose around the crowd and the worried murmurings grew into a desperate, many-throated yell.

Arwel began to cry and Eric knew he'd been a fool. Of course he should have taken him out of this. But there was no leaving now.

The world paused, like a rope-walker in the middle of his passage, caught between falling one way or the other. And then the stripy horses stopped, the riders yelling and holding their cudgels high but not swinging them. And somehow the crowd seemed to understand its danger and step back from the brink. The yelling dropped down to a murmur and Eric found himself not in a stampede but just a crowd of uneasy people being herded wherever the horsemen chose.

They took them first through the gates of the city. He would have liked a chance to have a gander at the place, but it was hard to get a view when he was surrounded by so many people, and most taller than him. Unwashed too and pressing in tight, so the smell of it was every bit as bad as Smiler's Fair.

It was a long march. Arwel was grizzling by the end of it and the sound pulled at Eric's gut something chronic, but there was no way he could take him out and feed him here. He stroked Arwel's cheek and let him cry and wished for it all to be done.

And then at last there was grass beneath his feet and the press of filthy bodies around him eased. The long walk was finally over.

'The poor of the park,' Renar had called the folk making their way to Täm in droves. Eric had thought it was nothing but a phrase, the way the King's Men were also known as the Kenners, which, if there was a reason for it, no one could remember it. But Renar had meant it as it sounded. They really had been herded into a park, though not much of one.

The ground was grassy, stretching out for acres either side, and there were scrubby flowers here and there, but all of it had already felt the tread of many feet. No doubt they hadn't been the first lot to be herded here, and Eric couldn't help but wonder what had happened to those who came before.

It was a big enough place that the crowd could spread out into little groups, probably those that had come to the city together. It left Eric isolated, but he wasn't going to learn anything useful sitting on his tod. Still, he took advantage of the isolation to unwrap Arwel and let the babe suckle on his finger. The feel of it gave him the usual peaceful thrill, as his life passed into his boy's.

The sun had already set, but the light of it lingered in the sky, and he got his first real sense of the city. It seemed a pleasant open place, spread out on tall hills – Lanalan had told him they were the subject of some famous poem he'd insisted on reciting after Eric had done too good a job of seeming interested. The houses weren't tall, nothing like the towering mansions of Mirror Town, not even as high as the wooden makeshifts of Smiler's Fair.

He felt eyes on him, in that shivery way between his shoulders, and looked left to see a group of a dozen or so cullies staring his way. It wasn't necessarily a friendly look, but it was at least an opening and Arwel had finished suckling. Eric wrapped him up tight again and walked over to the strangers.

They definitely didn't look friendly, though not exactly threatening either. Some of them shuffled away as Eric drew near, as if he was the one who could be a danger. Only one of them stepped forward, puffing out his chest as he stood in Eric's path.

'Sorry. Sorry, friend,' Eric stammered, finding it hard to hang on to the harsh words of their tongue in the heat of the moment. 'I not harm. I just want mouth move.' No, that wasn't right. 'Talk. Talk. I just want talk.'

'Chatter, is it? We don't choose to chatter with the likes of you.'

Eric remembered his disguise a little too late, the sores on his face. He'd tried to make them look like relics of a long-gone carrion fever infection, but maybe that wasn't known here and they took it for something they might all catch themselves.

'It not dangerous,' he told them, touching the sores lightly so as not to risk brushing them off. 'It long ago past, not now. I not sick now.'

The man laughed. 'You think I'm an idiot? You think I don't know a beggar's tricks, or what you're hiding beneath that cloak? I painted on a wound or two in my day, to waken pity and win myself some cubes. We know what you're covering up. You've got the warp.'

'I don't understand,' Eric said, but the man was already backing away.

'You can't sit with us. If you're wanting for company, I saw a group of your kind over yonder by the wasp-leaf tree. Best you go and sit yourself with them.'

Eric supposed he meant the tree with yellow leaves that twirled prettily when a breeze hit them. There *was* a group sitting around it, a couple of dozen strong, and then a clear ring of space around them. In his experience, only two things led a person to give another such a wide berth: fear or disease.

That was the group he belonged with, right enough. He didn't know how much they might be able to tell him about this weapon the prince was after, poor and outcast as they were. But then again, in his experience it was often those ignored by the rest who heard the most.

He sat a little outside the ring, head down and eyes averted. It wouldn't do to stare and he didn't want anyone staring at him too closely either. But after a moment he felt a tug on his arm and arses shuffled over on the grass to make room for him.

'Thank you,' he said, smiling cautiously. He flicked his eyes up briefly and saw that it was a grey-haired man who'd helped him, stooped at the shoulder though he didn't look old.

'You're not from the south,' the man said.

'North,' Eric said.

'Ah, so it's spread there too.'

Others in the group turned to look at Eric. It was dark in the park now, the moon behind clouds and only scattered lamps here and there among the crowd. The figures all around him were in deep shadow, but there was something . . . wrong about them. Not an illness like the one he was faking. Something worse.

He clutched Arwel tighter against his chest, but that only served to draw attention.

'The child too?' a woman asked. 'Well, that's a shame. But leastways he was born. My sister's son killed her in the bearing and himself too.'

She leaned towards him and he saw her face for the first time. The left half of it looked fine enough, but the right side was a horror. The lower lip was twisted down and her teeth pushed out over it, long and sharp like a beast's. Her ear was like a beast's too, furred and pointed.

'The warp', that's what the man had said. Now Eric thought

of it, Lanalan had mentioned it too, but he'd seemed only to be talking about crops: a blight that caused famine and was driving farmers from their homes.

He could see it on the others too now. The boy to his left had an insect-like hardness to the skin of his hands. Another woman had the nub of a third arm growing from her shoulder. Eric saw its tiny fingers grasping at air and shuddered, then pulled his hood tighter over his own face. He didn't fit in here quite as well as he'd expected.

'No need to hide, cousin,' a young woman said. 'You've got nothing that will shock us.' She had her arms bare, the fur covering each one thick and silver.

'I shame,' Eric mumbled and several around the circle nodded. There were more people covered here than not.

Two Hands is a hero to the poor, that's what Renar had told them. And if anyone needed a hero it was these people. It occurred to him for the first time that this was what that daft name must mean – not that the man had two hands like any person, but two extra like the poor girl opposite him.

Still, it wasn't a topic he could slip subtly into conversation. Especially when he could only make himself understood about as well as a five-year-old. Or maybe he could use that. If he said something these people didn't take kindly to, he could just pretend he hadn't meant to say what he had.

The conversation had broken up into little groups around him. He joined the nearest, two women with their deformities hidden, and the man with the fur and teeth. They were talking about cubes, which he knew meant money in these parts, and where to get them. He wasn't quite clear if the methods they had in mind were begging or theft or maybe even honest work but it wasn't a topic that was of much use to him. He had a supply of cubes of his own squirrelled away in Arwel's swaddling.

'I have question,' he said, when there was a brief lull.

'You won't know if we have the answer until you ask it,' the fatter of the two women said.

He smiled reflexively, then remembered it would be hidden by his hood. 'Good. Thank you. It is, I hear . . .' What was the word for rumours? 'I hear story-talk about person who help.'

'And what is this story,' the other woman said, very slowly. He suspected she'd decided he was slow in the head, which worked well enough.

'About a person who help. Person name Two Hands.'

If he'd been hoping for a dramatic reaction, he would have been disappointed. The two women shook their heads and the fur-man shrugged. 'I've heard the name,' he said. 'People of Täm have it in their mouths, but there's no rich high-hill type would be any help to the likes of us.'

And that seemed to be that. It was full dark now, and the two women took some odd contraption from their backs. He'd thought the people hunched, but he saw now that they'd been carrying things that looked like fans but folded out into long tubes. They pushed blankets into them and then crawled in to sleep, neat as you like.

Eric had no such comfort with him, but he laid out his own blanket on the ground and made a nest in it for Arwel to snuggle into his chest. He'd find out more in the morning. This lot couldn't be the only ones with the warp. They talked about it as if it was everywhere in the south of the country. And the poor of the park had been a problem for a while now, according to Renar. Some of the unlucky sods must have been here for months. They'd know what was what.

He was ready to lie himself down and call it a day when he felt a tap on his shoulder. The man smiled shyly when Eric turned to him.

'You were asking about Two Hands?' he said. 'She's no high-hiller. They say she's in the City Below. The City can't cure the warp, so best give up that hope, but they say that she has secret knowledge deeper than the City's. They say she'll sell it for a price.'

He nodded once firmly and then slunk away. It was the furthest Eric had got so far. He'd think about it more when he wasn't so bloody tired. He laid himself down, Arwel snuggled warmly into his neck, and fell asleep as soon as his eyes were shut.

★

It wasn't a sound that woke him. He gasped as he jolted up-right, Arwel clutched to his chest, some animal instinct in him roused – the sense that lets prey know when the predators are closing in. Around him the rest remained sleeping, dark forms just visible in the first glimmer of dawn. And other figures were visible too, ringing their group and walking closer.

He'd been around thieves long enough to know the look of people trying to be sneaky. But these weren't thieves. What was here that anyone would want to steal?

Arwel sensed his tension. He wriggled in Eric's arms and griz-zled, the sound loud in the sleeping silence. The nearest figure turned its head, looking for the source, and Eric knew he had to move now or lose the chance.

He didn't dare stand. The sky was lightening by the minute and he'd be outlined against it for them all to see. He crawled instead, belly as low to the ground as Arwel allowed, one hand cupped gently around his babe's mouth to muffle any cries. Arwel's breath was warm and moist against his palm, still calm but quickening. He was almost awake.

The tree ahead wasn't large. Its lowest branch jutted out at the height of Eric's shoulder, but he had to stand to reach it, gut clenched in fear, and then it was a mad scramble to pull himself up, twigs snapping and leaves rustling all around. Arwel must have been scratched. He started bawling – and the men chose that moment to attack.

Eric kept his head down, body curled around Arwel in the scant cover of the leaves. He only saw what happened in flashes and heard it in desperate screams, broken off by the horrible meaty thump of a cudgel. People died, he was sure of it, but that didn't seem to be the purpose. The men had brought ropes and they roughly bound the men and women and children they'd beaten into unconsciousness.

The thugs outnumbered their victims and any who tried to put up a fight were beaten into submission. The men were quick and efficient but they weren't silent, yet no one came to help. There was a tense, watching feeling as they slung the poor cullies over their shoulders and slunk away into the night, leaving only trampled mud, scraps of clothing and splashes of blood behind.

There was a shocked quiet after they left. And then the sun rose a little higher and the cheerful multicoloured birds began their morning chatter. As if the birdsong was their alarm, the poor of the park rose too, and soon enough it was like nothing had happened. Eric slunk down from the tree to find that the surrounding groups were already beginning to edge into the space the brutal kidnapping had left behind, heads carefully averted from the evidence of what had happened there.

Eric sat at the base of the tree, Arwel cradled against his chest, and wondered what he was supposed to do next.

13

Renar thought how strange it was that Ofiklanod looked so foreign to her eyes after a bare few months among the god-sick peoples. The canal racer was in the final stretch of its journey, borne by brisk winds down the Grassleap Canal towards Täm. The outskirts of the city surrounded them, and the many low, neat, brightly coloured houses were a sharp contrast to the imposing mass of Ashfall and the restless slap of the waves against its hull.

Here it was all so orderly and still: neat slick roads running in a web between neatly trimmed gardens, and bridges taking them across the place of which they did not speak. Ashfall had been ringed by water, but the only water here was high above, contained in the walled canals. Even the people seemed strange to her: too tall, their movements graceful like dancers'.

But perhaps it was just lack of sleep. Her nights had been troubled in the last weeks. Her sib had asked her why she rolled and mumbled in her bed and she had lied to him because she couldn't tell the truth. She had been dreaming of Mizhara. There had been a time when twins who dreamed of gods were taken to the fields and buried alive under ten yards of soil. The world was more civilised now, but such things were still not said aloud.

The Mizhara in her dreams had seemed little like the one she'd heard whispered of in disreputable eateries and wineries frequented by the Xilabi. Her dream Mizhara had been slight and gentle-faced, and her expression as she'd looked at Renar had been tender. That had been the most terrifying aspect of the dream, the moment that had wrenched her from sleep with a gasp: the love she'd seen in the god's eyes. And worse, the love her dream self had felt for the god.

Well, that was something she most certainly would not be sharing with Bruyar when she saw *omas*. And Bruyar must be her first visit after the canal racer docked at the pillar on Seventh Hill. The Remembrancer would already know of their return. *Oms* had informants in every town and Renar didn't fool herself that she'd been able to identify more than a third of them.

The boat rocked as Lanalan joined her in its prow. He'd been unable to visit his favourite hair-tailor during their long journey and it had grown wild and free, framing his long face. It reminded her of how he'd looked as a boy, when he'd cared only for what his sib thought and nothing for the opinion of others. But those days were long past.

'La! 'Tis good to be back, is it not?' he said, shading his eyes to gaze out over the city. Her sib was normally as easy to read as a playbill, but today his expression didn't match his words. There was an apprehension in his eyes she didn't understand but certainly shared. The question of how good it was to be home remained to be answered.

★

The Mortals carried out their business in the Jemod, high and forbidding and dark on the peak of the First Hill. Many of their homes clustered about it, equally grim and dark, but Bruyar saw no such need to signal *omas* devotion to the order *oms* ran. *Omas* home was on the high and lush Fourth Hill, and it had never wanted for either ornament or luxury.

The house had always been huge, a hundred paper panels used to make its walls. But when last Renar had seen it, it had at least been tasteful. Now every wall had been printed with pictures of insects. The fashion for panelling this year was small tessellations, but Bruyar clearly cared nothing for that. The nearest wing held a painting of a bug so huge it occupied eight panels. It could only be custom work. Of course it was; Bruyar would never stint. When *oms* made a mistake, *oms* made a grand one.

'For the love of all,' Renar said to the man approaching her in long strides across the grass, 'what was Bruyar thinking?'

'And a happy return to you too,' Jonul said sharply. His tone was often sharp, though his body was rounded and solid and strong, like a weathered boulder.

He led her to the door and through, between the huge mandibles of the giant bug.

'The Fox doesn't like your taste,' he said, when they finally reached Bruyar. *Oms* sat in an inner courtyard fringed by palms and cooled by the spray of a fish-mouthed fountain.

'Do you not?' Bruyar asked. *Oms* mopped sweat from *omas* brow, hot despite the fountain. Everything about Bruyar seemed soft and generous: large belly, rounded breasts, a wide mouth and a mass of curled brown hair, piled beneath a green scarf. A child of three, perhaps Bruyar's, perhaps a niece, toddled at *omas* feet. It was only when one's eyes drifted to *omas* arms, the stumps where *omas* hands had once been, that the illusion of joyful domesticity was shattered and one remembered who *oms* truly was.

But Bruyar preferred that people pretend to forget.

'Your walls are hideous,' Renar said. 'Truly, you want people to look on your home and feel disgust?'

Bruyar seemed more amused than offended. 'You don't recognise the work of Kakad the Alert? He made the puppets for the production of *The Termites of Terror* that has been so admired.'

'The audience screamed and half of them fled,' Renar said. 'I know – I was among them.'

Bruyar laughed. 'Well, indeed, but a strong effect is better than a tepid one, my darling. And you know how my taste is admired. Next month a hundred homes will be so decorated and mine will not be such a sensation. But of course, you are not here to speak of that. A most happy return, Renar. A most happy return indeed, for how better to come back than in triumph. And your trip was a triumph, was it not?'

Omas gaze was piercing and it made Renar uneasy, though in truth she had nothing to be ashamed of in her report. 'It was a success,' she said. 'The prince has sworn to journey to our lands before the solstice, if only we show willing by opening our borders to the god-sick traders.'

'Yes, yes, and such terms have been supported by the Mortal Council, though not easily, even with my voice to lift them. You could not have made an easier bargain, my fox?'

'I made the best I could. The prince is not as unripe as he seems, though he's more sharp than sweet. And as I've told you often, the best bargains are those where each party believes themselves to have bested the other. Let Prince Krishanjit think he's triumphed over us. Let him watch the hand that holds the trade deals and the sanctuary for refugees, while our other hand plays its trick.'

Bruyar laughed, holding *omas* belly to still its jiggling like a player in the lesser theatres. 'You think there's to be a trick, and one I haven't told you? Dearest, you're far too sly.'

''Tis my greatest weakness,' Renar agreed, and didn't add that it was also most often the reason for her employment. 'So, shall I begin preparations for the prince's visit?'

'No need for now – I shall make all the arrangements that are required. It's been a trying time for you, I have no doubt. Rest. Recuperate. When I have need of you again, I'll call on you.'

'And my payment?'

Bruyar's smile was as warm and loving and unyielding as ever. 'When the prince is here.'

★

Renar's mind was uneasy the whole of the walk back to her far more humble home on Sixth Hill, Fourth Quarter. There had been something in Bruyar's tone, something in the whole situation that told her there were currents pulling at events below the ones she could see. She despised not knowing. It was her job to be informed – and especially to be informed of Bruyar's needs. But something smelled rotten in the meat of the matter and it troubled her that she didn't know what.

What *did* the Mortals want with the moon reborn? It was the question she had carefully not asked herself before and tried not to ask herself now, but there it was, lingering in the corners of her mind.

In her experience there were two solutions to unwanted

thoughts: sleep or work. Since she was now approaching her house, and exhausted from her journey and her meeting with Bruyar, she would choose the former.

Her garden was gated, but the gate had been left open, no doubt by the porters who'd delivered her baggage. It sat where they had discarded it, piled untidily outside her door. The star-flowers she'd planted at midwinter should have been blooming, but they'd been left unwatered for weeks and were withered into dust. The panels of her house had at least been changed, but the pretty blue flower print she'd ordered was nowhere to be seen, and the building was pale brown all over, the colour of undyed paper. Her servant Podio had clearly bought the cheapest available in the city and pocketed the difference.

And there was the man himself, lounging untidily in one of the amber chairs she reserved for her more important visitors.

'Oh,' he said. 'You're back.'

'As is my luggage. But I see it still languishes on the doorstep. Put it away, would you? And fetch me some water. I mean to bathe and sleep out the heat.'

He sighed loudly, waiting just long enough before moving to signal his annoyance at the demand. Such was the price of playing at politics in the riven city. An obsequious servant suggested a woman who thought too highly of herself, who might perhaps consider herself above others, and that would never do. Though Renar had more than once wondered if she'd travelled too far in the opposite direction when she hired Podio.

Still, the inside of her house remained much as she'd left it, cluttered with unwanted gifts and piled high with books, so at least he hadn't resorted to theft. Her bed was unmade, but the sheets had been clean enough when she left and she shucked off her robes and fell back on the goose-feather mattress with a sigh of relief.

★

She woke to a scratching on the door of her room and the setting sun shining through a hole in the paper that Podio hadn't seen fit to repair.

Her visitor didn't wait for her invitation to enter. She had a rebuke ready until she saw who it was and frowned. 'He can't have got himself in trouble already?' she said. 'We haven't been back a day!'

Seividan shrugged his constantly slumped shoulders. 'He has. But wasn't that why you sent me to watch over him?'

She'd appointed Seividan her sib's hidden shadow near two years ago. She was impressed that he'd resumed the task before their return had even been announced. She should probably increase his pay.

'So what has he done?' she asked.

'Nothing yet. It's what he may do I thought would bother you. He's announced he's to perform an "extempore" on the subject of your recent travels at the Establishment of Ladöfik the Amiable. It's expected to draw quite a crowd.'

'How? No one should know of our travels, let alone that we've returned!'

'Renar, really. This city is full of people who know things they shouldn't. It's why we both thrive here.'

She couldn't argue with that. No doubt people did know too much already. But there was a lot more Lanalan could tell them that Bruyar would prefer to keep hidden. Lanalan could speak of the God Killer. She briefly considered leaving him to make the noose for his own neck, but it wouldn't do. Knowing Bruyar, there was every chance that noose would be made to fit two.

'Ladöfik's Establishment?' she asked.

He nodded.

'Then I suppose you'd best lead the way.'

★

The city was dyed ember-red by the setting sun as Seividan led her to the winery. Renar felt a twinge of unease as they circled the bottom of Sixth Hill and came to Flad Park. It was a scrubby stretch of ground whose low brick walls were crumbling into disrepair and whose flowers were barely venturing above ground, despite the approach of summer.

She'd come here often during the run-up to the Triumvir

elections, looking for cheap muscle to hire. But in the year since, while she'd been in Bruyar's employ, the numbers of poor camped in the park had multiplied beyond belief, thousands where before there had been a bare hundred.

'Must we really go this way?' she asked. 'Their mood seems sour.'

'If you want to be there in time for the performance, we must. Your sib had a head start.'

Carriages were scarce in this neighbourhood, where so few could afford them, and they were forced to labour back up the next hill, past the meagre cubes of the lowest householders until the mansions all around were of a better quality. And then down again, the lowest they'd yet been, into a valley so deep the sun barely touched it; outsiders called it the City Between, neither high nor low but utterly disreputable. Ahead of them lay the most disreputable place of all: the Establishment of Ladöfik the Amiable, a sprawling structure that looked to be made of a hundred long, narrow corridors twining over and around each other.

'Your sib has terrible taste,' Seividan grumbled.

'He has exquisite taste, at least where fashion is concerned. If he's chosen to perform here it must be where the cream of Tämish society come. It would be just like them to choose a place so ill-favoured. No doubt they find it delightfully daring.'

She was quickly proven right. Inside they found silk-skirted merchants rubbing shoulders with the poor of the park and some figures high up in politics who might have thought better than to be seen here. The interior was as confusing as it had looked from the exterior. It had been designed to be nothing but dark corners and hidden little rooms where business could be conducted in private. Seividan led her towards one of the larger of these, with a fine view of the central bar. She knew that was where Lanalan would perform: where he was the most visible.

And here he was now, dressed already in the finely embroidered fashion he favoured when he wasn't on the road. A cheer rose from his cronies as he jumped on one of the tables. A servingman – perhaps Ladöfik himself – frowned but said nothing. It was clear how much custom Lanalan had brought to the Establishment. The place was thronged with his friends, all of them sipping tall glasses of the most expensive cane wine.

Lanalan bowed once and then again when he was applauded, and then a third time smiling delightedly, milking the goodwill of the room dry. Perhaps that was wise. Renar had heard his poetry before. The reception was unlikely to be quite so rapturous once the recital was over.

'My friends, my friends,' he said at last, his eyes sweeping the room but missing Renar and Seividan in their dark corner. 'La, 'tis a delight to be back among you after my long and painful absence.'

That brought a cheer. A dozen or so of his closest companions – the vainest youth of Täm – raised their glasses and then flung their contents on the floor. She'd heard it was a rural thanksgiving ritual that had lately become fashionable after the idle rich of Täm had decided to find it enchanting.

The chief server, who almost certainly *was* Ladöfik, gestured at a young inter to mop up the mess. But he didn't complain, probably counting the cubes they'd pay to replace that wasted wine.

'My talents alas are small, my voice unsweet, but I hope you'll lend me your ears to hear a short and humble tale of my travels,' her sib continued.

There were confusing cries of both 'no' and 'yes' from those responding to different elements of the statement.

'An extempore, my friends, by Lanalan of the Roaches, upon the subject of my recent travels.'

'Here it comes,' Renar whispered to Seividan. 'If I kick your ankle it means we need to stop him.'

'How?'

'I don't know – use the considerable skills for which I hired you. Start a fight. I imagine most people here would find that more entertaining than my sib's extempore.'

'My friends, let me set the scene,' Lanalan said, throwing out his arms expansively. 'Let me paint with words upon the blank white paper of your minds.'

'Blank is right,' Seividan muttered and Renar pinched his arm to silence him.

'La, the sun was high in the sky, glowering over the wastelands like the stern eye of a farmer over his errant sheep,' Lanalan continued. 'The fields were filled with crops, like a basin at a feast for the wealthy. The Bitter Canal ran overhead . . .'

'Like a snake that had swallowed a rat that was in the midst of a long-running battle with his inter sib?' Seividan whispered. 'Isn't this supposed to at least rhyme?'

Renar sighed. 'It's the fashion apparently.'

There was a great deal more scenery. Renar had drained her drink to its bottom before Lanalan had moved their travels beyond the borders of Ofiklanod, and even his friends were beginning to talk among themselves.

Her sib was no poet, but he was a man who loved attention. He felt it wander from him and finally began to drive his story towards its destination.

'This is it,' Renar said to Seividan. 'This is where the fool will say what shouldn't be said.'

'And what exactly shouldn't be said?'

'Anything about how we drew the prince here.'

'And then at last we reached our destination, a brown land of brown fields,' Lanalan proclaimed, having apparently run out of similes at last. 'And that was where I met him.'

Renar clasped Seividan's arm in warning and she felt his muscles tense.

'His hair was pale as the wheat in summer, his skin the colour of pearl.'

Seividan looked at Renar, but she shook her head: not yet.

'His mouth smiled and the smile was as warm as the waters of the Tuigahon, his lips as ripe as peaches and my own stomach swelled within me, growing to the size of the Tuigahon itself.'

'Is . . . is that the prince he's speaking of?' Seividan whispered.

Renar rolled her eyes. 'No, not the prince. The prince is dark of skin and hair, and I couldn't name one time I saw him smile. I should have known. The fool isn't here to spill secrets. He's in love.'

'With a sour-milk man of the god-sick?' Seividan sounded scandalised.

Renar shrugged. 'No one has ever claimed my sib to be wise. But this presents no danger to anyone but himself.'

They listened a little longer, as Lanalan went on to describe the white-skinned boy – Eruk, had he been called? – and his many physical perfections. 'At least love improves his poetry,' Seividan muttered, leaning back at last when it became clear that Lanalan intended to speak of nothing but his infatuation. 'So tell me, what is he like, this prince?' He lowered his voice. 'This god?'

Renar hesitated but there seemed no need for secrecy. Bruyar had already sent the canal racers to the border to open it to the god-sick traders, as had been agreed. And the Mortals would make the announcement tomorrow that the moon reborn would be returning to the sun's lands. The news would be old by the time Seividan could spread it.

'The prince is . . .' She laughed. 'Imagine a man the opposite of my sib in every way, and that is the prince: a listener, a thinker, a planner. His people don't love him, for all that his father has named him heir to the Ashaneslands. The moon is considered ill-luck there too. They have gods of their own and don't want another.'

Seividan frowned. 'If the prince hopes to find the welcome here he didn't in his home, he's bound for disappointment.'

'Perhaps he hopes that peace with us will raise his value at home.'

'He's brave, I'll give him that. I wouldn't come here if I were him.'

His words hit her exactly where all her doubts sat. The prince had struck her as clever precisely because he was cautious. And in her experience caution and bravery seldom walked hand in hand.

She might have asked her sib about it, but it was clear he'd only paid attention to one man on their trip. It galled her that she hadn't noticed that either. It wasn't as if he'd been subtle about it. She remembered now how he'd burbled on about the boy while she'd attempted to ignore him.

'Bright eyes locked onto mine as my words spilled like nectar in his ears,' he was saying now. 'And eager as any bee he hoarded them, writing them down for safekeeping. La, dare I hope it was near his heart he planned to keep them safe?'

Seividan was right, love did improve his poetry. His tale moved on, but the words stuck like a burr in her mind. 'Writing them down for safekeeping.' Why would the boy have wanted a record of her sib's words? He hadn't struck her as returning Lanalan's affections.

At last, at long last, the recitation drew to a close. 'Wait here!' she snapped at Seividan and rose to intercept Lanalan before he could make his way to his cheering friends.

'Why, Renar, you came!' His smile was as broad and sincere as ever.

'Tell me,' she said. 'What precisely did you and this boy Eruk speak of?'

'Eric. His name is Eric.' He looked offended. 'Were you not listening? I told you, we spoke of the stars, and history on its long march, and the beautiful birds of the air.'

He pulled against her arm, keen to get to his friends. She held him fast. 'Not the poem. The plain truth. What was the boy so keen to find out from you?'

'Why, nothing of import. He only wanted to know of my life here. I told you at the time how fascinating he found me. Where we lived, what we ate, when we rose. He told me he wanted to know all there was to know about me, to feel as if he'd grown up by my side.'

She released him. The shadow of unease that had hung over her since her return had resolved at last into a recognisable form and she very much wished it hadn't.

Her sib was absolutely and visibly guileless. That was why she'd brought him, something in the nature of a living disguise.

She'd never thought that his innocence might be used against her. That his very innocence would allow him to reveal far too much without even realising it.

All the details of an unremarkable life in Ofiklanod. All the details of a daily routine, the meals eaten in the morning and at sunset, the layout of the streets of Täm, the places to buy and to be seen. All the details a person could use to slip into the land and move about unseen – if that person's skin was dark. If he could learn their tongue with ease as the prince had, choosing to speak it with her every day before their departure. A courtesy, he'd said, and she'd thought him vain enough to want to show off his talent and then thought no more about it.

The prince was very much like her: cautious and watchful. He'd watched and listened and drawn the conclusion – as any thinking person must – that there was more to her invitation than she was revealing to him.

And then the prince had done precisely what she would have done, if she'd been him. He'd sent them on their way with the promise that all they'd come for had been agreed. And, probably hours after they'd left, he'd set off for Ofiklanod himself. It was easy to guess how he'd travelled: on that great flying monster of his, far outpacing her canal racer.

She'd been a fool, and Bruyar would kill her if *oms* ever learned of it. The prince was already here, making his own search for the God Killer. And the only way Renar could save her own skin was if she found him before the Mortals did.

14

The Great Rift lay ahead, a chasm a mile wide and a mile deep that none had been permitted to cross in a thousand years. Now the land in front was dark with the crowd waiting to finally make that journey. Horses were pressed cheek to cheek and merchants squeezed themselves between them in their eagerness to be the first across. But the bridge that crossed the Rift was sideless. However eager Alfreda felt, she'd not risk the first rush across. It was a very long way to fall if anything went wrong.

The horse she'd found to replace Edred wasn't a patch on him. He was an ugly light brown and as lazy as a slug. But he liked the crowd no more than she did and plodded happily away from the road when she pulled his reins. The instant she let him, he dropped his head to crop the living grass still growing in ragged patches. Marvan dozed on the bench beside her and she didn't bother waking him. Algar had known to be silent when she needed it. Marvan never did.

Ofiklanod lay ahead. That's what she'd learned to call it. Other Wanderers had traded with it when they still thought its name was the Eternal Empire, but her family never had. The people there were known to be uninterested in metal goods. It was one of the very few things that *had* been known about them.

That had all changed in the weeks since the Wheelheir had received his invitation. Books on the Ofiklander language had been copied and passed around once news of the border opening spread. And other news had spread with it, less openly but just as widely: a revelation that the Ofiklanden ambassador had made during a feast at North Star. Marvan's mother had passed it on to them on one of her rare visits to their secret chamber in Fell's End. She'd told them about the weapon called the God Killer.

Marvan hadn't complained when she told him they needed to go to Ofiklanod to hunt for the weapon themselves. He'd been in an odd mood since they left his mother. Alfreda wondered if he'd really expected her to take them in. Perhaps he'd hoped the opposite. It was easier to hate people who did you wrong, and Marvan hated his family more than anyone she'd ever met.

But Imesha had done everything for her son a mother could be expected to. She'd taken him and Alfreda in and hidden them from the prince when they'd asked. And after Alfreda had tried to murder Krishanjit, Imesha had hidden that too. She'd sacrificed her own people to spare them. And yet none of it seemed to have been done out of love. Marvan and his mother hadn't even embraced when he left. It wasn't hard to understand why he'd grown up so twisted.

He twitched awake now at the excited screams of children hidden in some wagon nearby.

'Are we ready?' he asked, looking at the crowd.

A group so large was like a living creature. As Alfreda saw movement on the bridge's far end, she felt it give a collective in-breath of expectation. The breath out was a roar as those near the front realised the way was clear.

Despite their distance from the road, Alfreda had to fight not to be caught up in the first eager stampede. Their horse, for all his idleness, raised his head and whinnied with foal-like enthusiasm. The wave of motion washed over them and she pulled on his reins and held him still against the tug of that human tide.

When it went wrong, it happened very quickly. One moment the crowd was eager and jostling but happy. The next a horse brought too close to another bit its flank, the second horse reared and the chaos spread with lethal speed, a riptide pulling a score of wagons towards the bridge's edge.

At the far edge of the bridge, figures milled. Alfreda thought they might be trying to shut the gate they'd only just opened, but it was futile. People screamed as they were trampled beneath the hooves of the onrushing wagons and Alfreda turned their own wagon away, towards a small deep pool she'd seen on her ride up. There'd be no crossing today.

★

She woke the next morning to a clear, overbright day and silence. The grass around them was trampled into mud but the wagons that had made the many ruts were gone. She shaded her eyes to scan the land ahead.

It wasn't entirely empty. Others had made the same decision as her and waited for a quieter crossing. Their tents lay scattered across the slate-grey ground but no people were in sight. It seemed she was the first to rise. Birds flew high above, ragged scraps of brown in the blue sky, and the hissing of the turbulent river far below was the only sound to break the silence.

She stopped a moment to enjoy the solitude. She wasn't sure when she'd find it again once she'd crossed the border. But too soon other figures began to spill from their tents. Their noise disturbed Marvan and he emerged from the wagon too, yawning hugely.

Their horse was even more shy to move today. She knew why. The smell of blood drifted towards her on the dry wind as they set off. Soon she saw the first corpse, arms splayed and face a bloody mash. The third was a child and she looked away, drawing the wagon in a wide circle around the bloodstain.

She kept the wagon in the bridge's centre even now. The wind was strong and she knew there were many more bodies far below. The fisherfolk who scrabbled for a living downriver would find their water polluted for weeks to come, but the ugly knife-fish would grow fat on the carrion feast.

The horse's hooves made a hollow sound as they struck the bridge, not dull like wood or ringing like metal but something halfway in between. A part of her longed to stop and study the amber surface, unmarked by time or the thousands who'd so recently crossed it. But she had a purpose more important than that. She refused to fail again.

The far side of the bridge grew clearer only slowly, heat haze blurring the outline of its brown cliffs and crooked, low-limbed trees. Soon they were close enough to see the people waiting. Alfreda had expected them to resemble the dark-skinned, curly-haired mages who'd fled the Eternal Empire when that was still its name. But this was a far more varied crowd: some with broad, flat noses and loose curls of auburn hair, others with jet-black skin and fine-boned faces who looked too like the image of the god Yron carved into the rocks of the high plains.

The faces shared one thing, though: an expression of distrust. They stood strung across the broad earth road that led from the bridge's end, widely enough spaced that she could have ridden between them. But that didn't seem wise.

One of the waiting people was dressed all in black, loose robes that flapped in the wind to briefly outline the breasts beneath and a black veil that obscured every detail of the face except the dark pits of her eyes. 'Your business here?' she asked, in the harsh language of Ofiklanod.

Alfreda had managed to learn enough of the language to understand the question. She'd had little else to do except study it in the time she and Marvan had needed to stay hidden from the Oak Wheel's spies. But her voice didn't want to emerge in front of these strangers. She shrugged and held out her hands in apparent helplessness.

Silence stretched for a long moment, broken only by the piping calls of the birds.

'Why, they don't even have the manners to learn our language,' one of the men said at last, shaking his head. 'Five thousand questioned, and not a bare dozen that could reply.'

''Tis better so.' The movement of the dark-clothed woman's mouth shifted the veil over her face so that the arch of her cheekbone was momentarily revealed. 'The less we understand them, the less they can sicken us with their own illness. Let this one pass – she seems simple to me.'

As the woman lifted her arm to wave them through, Alfreda saw that she was handless, her arm ending in a metal-capped stump. When she gestured her companions back with her other arm, it revealed a stump in place of a hand there too.

The wretched horse seemed as fascinated by the woman as Alfreda was repelled. He turned his head to watch her, chewing at the bit in anger when Alfreda yanked the reins to pull him on. She felt the urge to turn herself. She could feel that cold dark gaze follow her, prickling the skin of her neck, all the way through the border gate.

★

Beyond the borderlands, Ofiklanod was far greener than Alfreda could have guessed. The part of Ashanesland that led here was arid, parched by the heat of the southern sun. The sun beat just as strongly here, but the land teemed with life. She saw trees with broad and shiny leaves and others with heart-shaped foliage so dark it was almost black. She loathed the sight of them. They could only be the work of magic.

Signs of the others who'd passed here were everywhere. Gnawed bones and orange peel and the sloppy remains of a bowl of porridge had been thrown carelessly on the side of the road. But the road itself was unmarked, despite the thousands of hooves that must have trodden it. It was that same orange material as the bridge, and maybe she *would* study it when she had the chance. Algar would have wanted her to.

The silver track of a river wound through the high grass ahead. Its banks would make the best campsite, but others would have reached the same conclusion. She didn't want company and she steered away from the road before they'd quite descended the long slope into the valley. She had to dismount, pulling out a knife to hack through the vegetation at one point, but beyond lay a small clearing, hemmed in by saw-leaved trees.

'Do you think we'll find rabbits here?' Marvan asked. 'Our stores are growing low.'

She shrugged. 'Lay out snares and see.'

They didn't have rabbits, but the snare caught a strange, gangly-limbed creature with a head almost like a cat's and fox-red fur. Marvan wrinkled his nose at it, but when Alfreda had skinned and roasted it, they both enjoyed the taste of its flesh. It was sweet, as if the creature lived on ripe berries.

Afterwards, Marvan went on a different sort of hunt. Night fell fast in these southern lands and the fire's flames, almost translucent against the bright sunlight, were richly orange against the surrounding darkness when Marvan stepped back out of it. He looked like an ancestor spirit of the tribes, his dark clothes and dark skin barely discernible, only the whites of his eyes and his drawn knife glinting.

'Did you find anyone?' she asked.

'Yes. I would have chosen the black-veiled one – the one they call a Mortal, some kind of priest, but . . .'

He didn't need to say it. She was a woman, and Marvan preferred men.

'Who then?' she asked.

'An old man, grey in his hair. He looked like he'd been at the job a while and when I followed him I found he lived alone.'

'Isolated?'

Marvan grinned. 'That too.'

It wasn't easy navigating the steep slope by moonlight, but it was full tonight and bright enough to show them the trees and the jagged silhouettes of thorn bushes. The ground was clearer, just low grass and flowers she didn't see but smelled as they were crushed beneath her boot heels.

Marvan moved far more silently than she, a duellist's grace about him. She made twigs crack under her feet and branches snap as she eased them aside. There was no other human sound in the night save hers, only the thousand busy hums and chitters of nocturnal insects.

The house was visible first as an absence of stars, a square of blank nothing. As they drew nearer, the moonlight revealed its pale walls.

'They make their houses out of paper,' Marvan whispered. 'A knife can cut through it.' He knelt and demonstrated, his blade parting the material with no visible effort.

It was utterly dark inside, but not entirely silent. Alfreda heard the rasping breath of a man sleeping. She paused, allowing her mind to build a picture out of sound that it couldn't out of light. The man was to her left, but he wasn't alone. *Two* people were breathing. She tapped Marvan's shoulder and held up two fingers.

He nodded, tapping her chest and pointing right and then his and pointing left, dividing the job between them. His knife widened the hole in the wall until it was a doorway they could both walk through. Moonlight followed them and Alfreda saw that this room was empty. Their prey lay ahead, beyond where the frame of a door was barely visible in the paper wall. She fumbled for a handle that didn't seem to be there.

Marvan moved her gently aside and pressed his hands against the doorway, pushing the door sideways rather than out. It made a faintly audible hiss, but the quality of the breathing didn't change, only growing louder as they walked in to stand above the sleepers.

It had taken her a while to learn the exact place and force needed to knock a person out and leave them living. She looked at Marvan, crouched above his own victim, and waited for his nod before striking. The crack of her rock-filled fist against her victim's jaw was loud, but Marvan had done his job and there was no one left conscious to hear it. They waited a moment to be sure, then Marvan drew out his tinderbox and lit the lamp that sat by the bedside.

In its gentle light she saw that one man was young and one old, but similar enough in features that she guessed they were relatives, not lovers. Although who knew how they did things here? She'd heard rumours the mages lay cousin with cousin, and these were the folk from whom the mages had sprung.

Her own victim had been the older man. Marvan glanced at his face and then back to the young man above whom he knelt, drawing the blade of his knife across his throat in one quick slash. Blood surged out, soaking the paper floor and speckling Marvan's face. He licked it from his lips and wiped his hands on the man's sleeping robe before turning back to Alfreda.

'Take him to the other room?' she asked.

'No, we'll do it here. You tie him up so he can see his friend. It might loosen his tongue. Although hopefully not too much.' Marvan licked his lips again, though no blood remained on them. 'We wouldn't want him to oblige too soon.'

It didn't take long. The man was brittle, like steel quenched too quickly, and he snapped at the first pressure. Marvan had only started on his chest when he begged to tell them everything he knew.

'How long have you lived here?' Alfreda asked. She'd found it hard to speak to their victims at first, the same doubts she'd always held freezing her. But what did it matter what they thought of her? They wouldn't be thinking it long.

The man didn't answer and she thought that perhaps her accent was too rough, but when Marvan slid the knife down his belly towards his groin, he screeched, 'Ten years! Ten!'

'Always so near to the bridge?' Marvan pressed.

He nodded frantically. 'Yes, yes, always.'

Marvan rocked back on his heels, running his fingers along the blade of his knife and flicking the blood away to show the metal still keen beneath. Alfreda knew that he didn't care about the answer any more than she did. But he'd taught her that it was best to ask simple questions first. Let the victim grow used to answering, and then ask what you really wanted to know.

'Where did you live before?' she asked.

'In . . . in Makat,' the old man said.

'And what did you do there?'

'I farmed stib bugs. Two nests of them and one of sof beetles.'

Alfreda had no idea what he was talking about, but she nodded. He was starting to offer information unasked for. That was good. It was probably time for the real questions.

Marvan must have decided the same thing. 'What do you know about the God Killer?' he asked.

'Don't lie to us,' Alfreda said sternly. 'We'll know if you lie.'

'But I don't . . . I've never heard of it. We don't use that word here!'

It took her a moment to realise the word he meant was 'god'.

Marvan didn't wait before using his knife and there was a brief interval of sobbing before the man sniffed back the snot and blood and babbled, 'Please, please, I don't know, I'm only a farmer.'

'Then who would know?' Alfreda said. 'The black-robed people? The priests?'

Marvan frowned at her and she bit her lip, annoyed with herself. It was no good telling them what you wanted to hear; they'd just say it back to you. Pain made people do exactly what you wanted – or what they thought you wanted.

'Yes,' the man said desperately. 'The Mortals, yes, they'd know.'

But thanks to her stupidity, they couldn't trust his answer now. She'd have to try a different hammer. 'This thing we want, the God Killer, it's a thing of magic, of the runes.'

The man winced at the words and shook his head. 'I know nothing about that, nothing – I promise! My uncle went to the City Below to cure his fever but I'd never truck with it. Never!'

'But if you know nothing, what use are you to us?' Marvan asked silkily.

The man sobbed some more, uselessly. Alfreda thought they might already have found out the little he had to tell. But then his eyes brightened with desperate hope.

'Vien,' he said. 'That's where you want to go. That place is sick with the . . . with *her* power. If it's a, a rune-thing, they might know about it there.'

'Ah,' Marvan said. 'Vien, you said? And is that it? Is that all you know?'

'I swear, I swear, that's all. There's no more.'

The man had only a moment for terror as Marvan's knife slashed across his throat. It was unlike him not to savour the kill, to let his victim spend a little time in the knowledge of what was coming. But they had a scent, however weak, and they needed to follow it. They wouldn't be alone in hunting the God Killer and they had to make sure they reached it first.

15

Olufemi thought this place might be the ugliest she'd ever seen. The sun was bright, but the jagged hills and aging woodland seemed gloomy nonetheless. The trees looked weary, draped in shrouds of moss, their pine needles browning or already on the ground. Patches of the forest had been killed by strangling vines, whose triple-petalled flowers hung heavy with pollen over the wooden corpses. She caught glimpses of beasts, too, their bodies twisted into shapes that she couldn't believe were natural, even here. But what did she know? Her ancestral lands were far stranger to her than any Ashane shipfort.

In places the forest gave way to open ground, piled with slag heaps or cloven by the deep, dark cuts of the mines themselves. The mountain settlements of Ashanesland had something of the same look, but they at least had the pristine white of the high peaks as a backdrop. Here the hills marched endlessly into the distance and there was nothing beautiful to be seen in any direction.

'Can't we rest?' Yemisi asked – whinged, really. She'd been discontented ever since they'd parted ways from Dae Hyo so spectacularly. Olufemi hadn't even thought she liked the crude tribesman, but she seemed to blame Olufemi for leaving him behind.

'A little further,' Olufemi told her.

'Are you sure we aren't travelling in circles?'

'Quite sure.'

But despite her words she glanced around for some landmark, any indication that they were making progress. There was none. The slag heaps were all slumped identically, the trees all equally

old. Even the sun provided scant guidance this far south. Only
at its nadir and zenith did she know where east and west lay.
They were trying to head north, whenever they could be sure
where north was. She had to warn Krishanjit about what was
coming for him. She'd seen no maps, but it was obvious how far
south they'd come. The journey to Ashanesland wouldn't be short.

'We'll stop there for the night,' she decided. Ahead was a small
town cramped between high slag heaps.

'Will they have an inn?'

'If they don't, someone will house us. We have the money to
make it worth their while.'

They'd stolen it from a grand house they'd found deserted a
few days back. She wasn't proud of it, but they'd fled Mizhara's
people with nothing but their tattered robes. Now they wore the
clothing of local people, also looted from the empty mansion.
She hadn't known it, but Olufemi's trousers and vest seemed to
mark her as some sort of noble. It had made it easier to pass
unquestioned, which was just as well. She knew nothing of these
people, their customs or their beliefs. She'd thought she'd at least
be able to speak their language, but the first time she'd tried the
tongue of Mirror Town, the language of these people's ancestors,
they'd looked at her with bafflement and growing distrust. Now
she and Yemisi pretended to be mutes. Their money did all the
talking they needed.

As they drew nearer, she saw that the town did indeed possess
an inn, a wide building whose walls were decorated with a recur-
ring pattern of trefoil leaves. Many houses had the same
decoration and she wondered what it meant. These were the sun's
lands and she'd expected Mizhara's face to be everywhere, but
neither sun nor moon appeared on any house she'd seen.

A man rushed out to greet them before they could reach the
door. He smiled obsequiously, no doubt noticing the quality of
their clothes, far better than his own plain cotton skirt. He said
a few words that Olufemi had picked up enough of the tongue
to recognise as an offer of food.

She pointed to her mouth and ears and shook her head. After

a little further mime and, more importantly, the flashing of the orange cubes these people used as coin, he seemed to understand. The room he led them to was plain but clearly the largest of the house. On her previous travels she'd often been relegated to the meanest accommodation on offer, all that her purse could afford. Here they were far better treated. It would be easy to forget they were fugitives. But she was always conscious of the army at their back.

A servant brought them water to bathe and quickly backed out. Of course, in these houses you were never truly alone. The paper walls stopped no sound and the murmur of voices surrounded them. She thought she detected a panicked note, and she heard doors hiss open more than once and footsteps on the ground outside.

It wasn't the first time their coming had provoked an uneasy reaction and Olufemi would have dearly liked to know why. What was it these people felt they had to hide from others? Did they know something of the sun's return?

Still, the chance to wash was welcome. She quickly stripped herself, then ran a cooling cloth along her sweat-stained limbs, swiping with rough speed between her legs. She looked up to find Yemisi watching her and felt herself blush. Yemisi made an unexpectedly attractive young woman, lush-featured and with the flush of health and youth in her cheeks.

But Yemisi was looking at her with more repulsion than lust, and Olufemi was done with love. She'd said goodbye to it when Vordanna chose to travel with her god rather than stay with Olufemi. Besides, they had far more urgent matters to worry about. 'Quickly,' she whispered. 'Get the rune before they come back. They're bound to offer us food soon.'

The rune-marked parchment was buried at the bottom of Yemisi's pack. She pulled out clothes and packs of travel food and the coloured pebbles she collected for no reason Olufemi could fathom, throwing everything in a careless heap so unlike the fussy neatness of the woman she'd once been. Olufemi often wondered if *this* Yemisi would ever again become *that* Yemisi. Or would the different experiences of her relived youth turn her into someone else entirely? In another time, before Yron, before everything had changed, Olufemi might have cared enough to make a study of it.

'Do we really need to do this every day?' Yemisi asked, glancing furtively around the room. 'What if they see the light?'

'Then they'll think it's a lantern,' Olufemi hissed. 'Hush now, I need to concentrate.'

In truth, she barely did. This rune she knew so well, she could have summoned it in the heat of battle or in the depth of sleep. Her mind held it so easily, it might have carved out its own shape for itself there: Säday, the glyph of joy, woven through Häwt, the eye, and bound together with the glyph of fire, Yey. It was the simplest of spells and one of the most ancient, meant only to point the user's mind towards the sun. Once the priests of Mizhara had used it in their worship.

Its shape perfect and whole in her mind, she summoned Yron's power into it. She let herself have a moment of hope that the rune might remain powerless, that something might have happened in the weeks since their escape, that Krishanjit might have learned of his sister's return and somehow defeated her without Olufemi's aid. But her head filled with the same knowledge it always did, a sense of Mizhara rising in the west, where the sun that was merely her symbol was currently setting.

'So Mizhara is still following us,' Yemisi said.

'Yes. But perhaps we're a little further away from her.'

'And a little further away from Dae Hyo. If he's still alive.'

'It was his decision to push us into the river without him! He hardly gave us any choice about it.'

'I know.' Yemisi curled one of her braids around her thumb. 'I don't understand why he did it.'

Olufemi stared at her, astonished. 'Because the fool was in love with you.'

'Don't be ridiculous, he didn't even like me and I couldn't abide him. He might have wanted somewhere warm for his cock, but that's no reason to offer your life for someone else's.'

'Yemisi,' Olufemi said with heavy patience, 'what that man felt for you was more than lust. I think perhaps he felt a kinship with you, since you'd both lost something so important. And now I've spent more time than I ever intended contemplating the feelings of that savage, so could we perhaps talk about something of real importance?'

'I don't know why we're going to Krishanjit anyway,' Yemisi said stubbornly.

'Because he needs to be warned that his sister has returned,' Olufemi said, exasperated.

'So they can fight the war again? I may have forgotten a lot, Olufemi, but even I remember what the war between sun and moon did the last time. It tore up half the world. I don't know why we're running towards it rather than away from it.'

'Because it's my fault. Because I did this!' Olufemi shouted.

'Olufemi!' Yemisi hissed, and Olufemi realised what she'd done, that her words would have sounded throughout the whole paper house.

'We have to try to stop the war,' Olufemi whispered fiercely. 'There has to be a way. *This* Yron and *this* Mizhara have no reason to hate each other. War isn't inevitable. It can't be.'

Yemisi, as stubborn as a sulky child, looked like she meant to argue further, but then she stopped and sniffed. 'Do you smell smoke?'

Within moments there was a choking cloud of it. Flames crackled, and Olufemi saw their orange glow through the paper walls. The heat was already unbearable and her body rose and ripped open the door before her mind had decided what to do.

It was a mistake. The instant the door was open, a gout of flame leapt through, burning the hairs on her head and snatching the air from her lungs. She tried to suck in a breath to replace it and drew in agonising heat instead. It was so intense it seemed to eat away at her thoughts, leaving a terrifying blackness behind. She felt her limbs loosening, weakening – and then hands were in her armpits dragging her backwards. They stumbled through a wall that tore around them, then charged through another.

Finally they were in the open air, still smoke-clogged. Olufemi had just enough left in her to stumble a few paces further until the smoke was gone and she could gasp clean air into her lungs with agonised relief.

'They tried to kill us,' she said, her voice croaky and disbelieving.

'I don't think so,' Yemisi said. 'It wasn't just our house. Look.'

There were flames to left and right, flames in every direction. People stood in scattered clumps, watching as their houses burned – as their entire town was reduced to cinders.

But the people didn't look surprised. They barely seemed upset and not one of them was streaked with cinders and marked with burns as she and Yemisi were. Several of the people had possessions piled at their feet, as if they'd emptied their houses before the fire started.

'They did this themselves,' Olufemi said. 'There was something here they didn't want us to find.'

'As if we cared,' Yemisi said glumly. 'They could have been fucking their own pigs for all it mattered to us.'

And yet the people had been scared enough to burn it all, just on the chance that their visitors might prove curious. Olufemi wondered what they were hiding that could possibly be so important to them.

★

The question kept gnawing at her through four trudging days of rain and Yemisi's constant complaints as they walked between village after village that seemed innocent of everything except excessive dullness. But how could that innocence be trusted? The folk of the first village could easily have sent warning ahead of them, down secret paths she didn't know.

She'd begun to realise that this province – Nesevadan, they seemed to call it – was far richer than it at first appeared. Its ugly slag heaps and dangerous mine shafts spoiled its face but had made its fortune. No one here seemed hungry or wanting in any way. And for every nothing town filled with the simple houses of labourers and farmers there were half a dozen mansions of extraordinary size.

Another such mansion lay ahead of them now. The path leading to it was surprisingly narrow, as if its owner didn't much care for visitors, and Olufemi caught only glimpses of its white walls through the tightly packed pine trees. Their needles crunched beneath her heels, releasing a resinous smell that made her nose itch. The rain had slackened, but droplets ran down the mossy trunks in runnels and the muddy earth sucked at their feet.

'There was an inn in that town,' Yemisi said.

'There was,' Olufemi agreed. She'd found the easiest way to deal with Yemisi's discontent was not to argue with her. That often robbed her of more complaints, but not today.

'I don't see why we're going here,' she said.

Olufemi couldn't answer that. She wasn't entirely sure herself. It was only that the question raised in that burned village had yet to be answered, and everyone they met looked at them with fear and distrust in their eyes. She knew there were parts of the world, many of them, in which strangers were distrusted. But *fear*? What did they think an old woman and her servant could possibly do to them?

And then there was last night. Yemisi thought it happened because Olufemi was tired, and she *was* – even her bones were exhausted. But when she'd reached for power to fill the runes, there'd been nothing. Nothing at all. And the night before that, when the power had come, it had come sluggishly, as if fighting its way through some barrier that Olufemi couldn't see.

There was something else too, a discomfort she couldn't name. It felt like an itch inside her head. She couldn't shake the feeling that the land itself wanted her gone.

This house, out of the way as it was, might not be expecting their visit. Its owners might not have hidden whatever it was they had to hide. And Olufemi was increasingly sure she needed to know what that was.

'And there it is now, the plainest house I've yet seen. Fascinating,' Yemisi said with heavy sarcasm. 'I suppose it was worth the long, wet, uphill walk.'

After the last bend, the mansion finally lay in unobstructed sight, a huge structure that must hold a hundred or more rooms, sprawling outward rather than upward, in these people's style. And Yemisi was right: each wall was a plain and unadorned white.

'Well, at least they look as if they might have a comfortable bed and warm water to wash off all the cold,' Yemisi said, but Olufemi grabbed her arm when she made to walk forward.

'These people like patterns. We've seen it everywhere we've gone. And the bigger the house, the brighter the patterns.'

Yemisi shrugged. 'Maybe this woman likes white.'

'But look *how* very white they are. There's not a stain on them.'

Yemisi's character might have been transformed by the magic that had robbed her of her years and the knowledge that came with them, but her intelligence was undimmed. The sour set of her sweet face shifted into something more interested. 'She changed them before we could arrive. Probably when word that we were coming reached her.'

'Yes. Yes, I think that's what happened.'

'We should turn back. The last time they thought we'd seen too much, they tried to burn us alive.'

'We could. But Yemisi, haven't you felt it?'

She expected a denial, but Yemisi hesitated, and then nodded. 'Yes, I've felt it. There's something wrong. Something . . . I don't know. Something in the air. In the spirit of the place. But that isn't our problem. We're just passing through.'

'What if it is our problem? This was Mizhara's land. What if this is a part of her power we know nothing about?'

'So what do we do?'

'I . . . I don't know.'

'Then let's watch. Quiet mouths and open ears learn most.'

It was something Yemisi – the old Yemisi, the querulous teacher – had said to Olufemi often. The old Yemisi would have been full of ideas about what they faced, but she'd been killed by the very power her own research had helped to waken.

The forest provided good cover. Their dark clothes blended with the shadows so completely they could barely see each other.

No one from the house would make them out, and Olufemi sank down onto a fallen log, grimacing as the cold dampness instantly soaked through her trousers.

They didn't have to wait long. They'd barely had time for Yemisi to sigh twice more before they saw the first woman approaching the house at a run. Soon after, a man came to the door, perhaps the owner, and the two spoke in high, anxious voices. A succession of visitors followed, and after the third a party emerged from the house, congregated in an agitated knot for a brief while and then headed leftward, towards the densest area of forest, on the flank of a hill so high it strained to be a mountain.

There was, now Olufemi looked, a narrow path there, a pale grey cut through the muddy brown of the forest floor. The people didn't take it, though. They hovered at its start for a short while and then turned back towards the house, their distant faces more relaxed.

'What are they up to?' Yemisi whispered.

'Look at the path,' Olufemi said.

Yemisi blinked uncomprehendingly for a few moments before her eyes widened. 'It's gone – they've hidden it!'

'Yes. I wonder where it leads.'

But they couldn't risk finding out immediately. As the hours wore on, more visitors came to and from the house, some carrying away boxes whose contents she couldn't guess, others going in and not leaving. Olufemi saw the glint of weapons from many.

Finally, when she'd begun to think they'd be forced to move on with their questions unanswered, the last visitor departed and no more came. The sun hovered just above the treetops, edging towards a bank of clouds. She gambled that the gloom would hide them as they crept through the verge of the trees and towards the path that these people were clearly so keen for them not to find.

They'd done a good job of hiding it. Even knowing where to look, it took her and Yemisi a frustratingly long time before they stumbled over the grey rock of it. They'd never have found it if they hadn't known it was there.

The path took them upward only a short way, and then veered left, skirting the lower stretches of the hill, where the trees were so ancient that half of them listed perilously to one side and the rest stretched high into the now twilit sky.

After a mile or so the path opened onto a broad meadow, ringed by rocks painted red and green and blue in sequence. Olufemi paused beneath the trees, afraid that others had been left here to ambush them. There was no human sound, though, nothing but the senseless twitter of birds and the occasional rustle of the shy creatures that made their home beneath the trees.

At first she took the structure in the clearing's centre for a sculpture: wooden, intricate and more than fifty paces tall. But as she and Yemisi inched closer, she saw that it was made from three living trees, their trunks and many limbs trained into unnatural shapes over what must have been many years. Leaves still grew thickly on them, some rusty-red and hand-shaped, others a lurid, speckled green and the rest narrow and so delicate they were almost translucent, their veins like yellow-green threads running through them. It was very dark beneath those branches.

'Don't they fear the moon's servants?' Olufemi asked.

'Perhaps they think Mizhara will protect them,' Yemisi answered.

'Perhaps they're right,' Olufemi said gloomily.

But though this had the feel of a sacred place, she didn't believe it was the sun's. It didn't feel like the moon's either. The senses she'd honed over her years working with the runes twitched with unease at the feeling of something foreign – something *wrong*.

'Well,' Yemisi said, 'shall we go in?' But she waited for Olufemi to precede her.

Olufemi felt a great reluctance to do so. Nothing in her wanted to be near this place, but she made herself step forward and push aside the branches so they could peer inside.

It *was* a temple, that much was clear. Low wooden benches stood in lines before three statues, each taller than her. One had the body of a man carved from a rich, dark stone, the other a woman's body moulded from what she thought might be clay.

The third seemed female, until she looked more closely and saw that it had a penis dangling above the folds of its vagina. It had been fashioned from the strange amber material the Ofiklanders used to make their roads and their weapons. But the figures weren't human. The man had the head of a bird with a crown of brightly coloured feathers. The woman's head was an insect's and the third had the head of a coyote.

'Are they gods?' Yemisi asked.

'So I would imagine. But not any I've seen before, not in all my years as a Worshipper of Smiler's Fair.'

'Not Mizhara, though. She isn't here.'

'No, not her.'

There was a rustling among the leaves and Olufemi tensed, knowing that escape was impossible if the people of the town had come for them. But it wasn't anything human that emerged from between the leaves.

The coyote came first, nosing forward to stand before the statue in its image, and then the birds, bright-feathered, waddling to stand beside it. The coyote should have eaten the birds. The birds should never have come so close to it, but the animals stood peacefully before the foreign gods. And then the coyote bowed down onto its front legs, the birds bobbed their heads, and Olufemi couldn't bear to be in that place any longer. Its strangeness squeezed the air from her lungs.

'What was that?' Yemisi asked, her young face drawn and sweat beading on her brow.

'Something new. A new power that's neither sun nor moon.'

'What does that mean for us? For them?'

Olufemi saw movement on the ground before the temple. A column of ants, thickly black, marched inside. She didn't need to see to know where they'd end up: at the foot of the insect-headed god. 'I don't know. But I don't believe it can mean anything good.'

16

From above, the city of Täm seemed broken. Krish stood in the prow of the barge and looked down the hundred paces from the aqueduct to the city's lacquered streets and the two hundred paces further to the bottom of the fissures that divided them. The rifts were everywhere, as if the foundation of the city were made of mud that cracked as it dried.

According to Renar, that was exactly what had happened. A thousand years ago, when the people of Ofiklanod had rejected their past and its god, they'd buried her city and built a new one on top of it. But over the years, what was buried had started to be revealed. Now a thousand bridges crossed chasms whose depths revealed tantalising glimpses of what lay beneath.

Another barge glided towards theirs, its sides painted with white feathers and a swan's head on its prow. It seemed to be a pleasure craft. Two ranks of polemen sweated as they worked, but there was a table laden with food on its deck – a dressed swan as its centrepiece – and the passengers all held glasses filled with brightly coloured liquid.

The city looked broken, yet still more whole and healthy than either of the two he'd visited before. Smiler's Fair had been a home to crime and corruption. Mirror Town crawled with slaves and seemed aged to the point of decrepitude. The crowds who walked Täm's lacquered streets walked with purpose and what looked like pleasure.

There was something odd about their behaviour, though. Whenever the people came to a bridge over one of the deep chasms, they turned their heads away. It was subtle. Krish didn't think they even realised they were doing it. But they refused to see the ancient ruins on which their own city had been built. It was the same with their language, according to Renar. At the end of the war between sun and moon, they'd thrown out their old tongue and created another to replace it. 'The gods were in the words,' Renar had said. 'It was the only way to rid ourselves of them entirely.'

Krish wasn't sure he could blame them. The society that had been built on the ruins of the old seemed better in so many ways, perhaps the best he'd yet encountered. Living without gods had freed them in some way. But now the gods had returned – *he'd* returned – and the people of Ofiklanod didn't even have the words to discuss it.

Or most of them didn't. Krish's hunt for the God Killer had seemed doomed when he started it. It was hard to discuss something that people didn't even want to admit existed. But the people of Täm did have one quality they shared with the folk of Smiler's Fair. They loved to gossip. And eventually he'd heard about Mamma Kaaziad and where he could find her.

'Close now,' Dinesh said. He stood tall and muscular in the rear of the boat, bare-chested in the bright sunlight. It startled Krish to realise how much the boy had changed. In fact, 'boy' no longer seemed the right word for him. His body had the sturdy strength of a man – a warrior. Only his face remained as unlined as a child's.

Unlined, but not unmarked. The ink of the rune had faded a little over the months but it was still clear and readable on Dinesh's cheek. They'd covered it with a dressing and told anyone who asked that it was an infected insect bite.

Krish thought that wasn't too far from the truth. What the rune had done to Dinesh was a sort of infection. Maybe the changes in his own body were the same, like the carrion fever that left its survivors permanently scarred. Except the changes in Krish hadn't made him weaker. They'd made him stronger.

It was strange to feel so vulnerable and invulnerable all at once. Their disguise was as thin as the walls of the Ofiklanod houses. Their skin was near enough in colour to pass, but he and Dinesh had been forced to shave their heads to hide the straightness of their hair. They'd said it was the fashion in their far southern village and no one had questioned them. And no one had yet questioned the thin veil Krish tied over his eyes 'to shield them from the sun'. But all it would take was one person to doubt, to look and see the moon-silver of his pupils . . .

Yet Krish felt more secure than he ever had. His entire childhood he'd been weak. He'd lived every day in fear of the man he thought was his father. And lately he'd lived in fear of the man who truly had fathered him. Death had seemed a near neighbour. But not any more. Now there was perhaps only one thing in the world that could hurt him. And if he could find it, and then break it for ever – if he could do that, he'd be a god indeed.

While Krish pondered, Dinesh poled the barge on, and soon there was a park beneath them. The long marble legs of the aqueduct were planted in grass and its shadow fell across the ragged flowerbeds and even more ragged crowds. There must be thousands below, insect-small from this distance.

'The poor of the parks,' Dinesh said. 'They've, they've, they've been coming to the city for years now. The crops failed and they came for food and work.'

Even from this height, Krish could see how thin those people were. 'But they found neither.'

'Täm takes shipments of maize from four provinces, meat from Vien and fish from Ofzib. Five to ten ships every day of maize—'

'I know.' Krish had learned that cutting through Dinesh was the only way to stop him. He seemed to have a mind for facts. He remembered anything he was told and everything he read. He'd devoured the books Renar had brought with her and the others they'd bought since their arrival in Täm. It was thanks to him they'd managed to find their way so easily in the city: the map he'd seen once guided them every day. But it made for very boring conversations.

'I, I, I'm sorry,' Dinesh said. He couldn't bear any hint of criticism from Krish. It seemed to physically pain him.

'It's all right. You did nothing wrong. But I know. I know the warp has meant not enough grain and not enough meat, even for those who were here already. And the city isn't a place of work for people who can't read or write.'

And he'd sent Eric to live among that desperate mob. It had seemed like a good plan before he saw them. Now he wasn't so sure. They'd arranged a drop-off point for messages, a fountain near a park where anyone could pass unnoticed. But there'd been no word from Eric since their parting, although he'd sent Dinesh to check every day. In his next message, Krish would tell Eric to give up his half of the search and come and stay with them.

It was as if, Krish realised, the stronger he became, the more fragile everyone around him seemed. And Eric had a child.

'They're moving,' Dinesh said. 'The poor of the park. They've seen something.'

Below there was a surge in the crowd, bodies pushing forward. Many faces were upturned, dark brown ovals. Krish thought for a frightened instant that they were looking at him, until he heard yells from the barge in front, the pleasure craft.

'Away, away!' someone shouted, and the poling of the men in its bows sped up.

Krish could see the danger. This section of the aqueduct was an entry point for travellers, a place where two spiralling stairs led down from either side to the ground. Those stairs were already thick with bodies. The legs of the aqueduct were long but pitted with age and people were climbing them too. A woman screamed and fell, but it didn't stop those behind her from clawing their way higher.

'What do they want?' Dinesh asked.

'I don't know.' Krish wasn't sure *they* knew. It seemed the travellers on the swan barge had incited them somehow. Perhaps they were rich folk whose wealth felt like an insult to the very poorest. Perhaps they were rulers whose rule had led to this. Whatever had set it off, Krish didn't think it had a purpose now, beyond anger and desperation. He'd had enough experience of crowds over the last two years. They weren't wise.

The first few people reached the top of the stair. They were a pitiful sight, their cheeks sunken with hunger and their bellies swollen with disease. It was a wonder they'd had the strength to climb. Some of them clutched bundles in their arms, and when they reached the water's edge, they held these out towards the passengers on the pleasure barge. They were babies: thin and twisted, their skin pocked with scars. The babies didn't make a sound and Krish realised that they were already dead.

He dropped his eyes to the water, unable to watch. The little rucks against the side of their barge rose higher as Dinesh speeded up. The pathetic form of one of the babies floated past him in the water, the rags of its swaddling falling away. Krish watched it pitch and sway in the current until the aqueduct turned a corner and the desperate crowd was lost to sight.

The folk of Ofiklanod might not want gods, but perhaps they needed them. He'd seen the power of the runes. And yes, there was a price, but to save these desperate people, wasn't it worth paying? What was the point of him, if it wasn't for this?

The canal opened up beyond the bend, and the colour of the water changed from a clear turquoise to a much darker blue. Dinesh paddled through a stream of bubbles with no sign of fish, and Krish recalled that this portion of the waterway was known as Corpse Lake. It was said that many once rich and famous folk lay beneath its waters, weighted down with stones. The bubbles came from the decay of their flesh and anyone who drank from fountains downstream of the lake risked sickness and death.

The swan craft had pulled several boat lengths ahead of them, but now it was forced to slow by an even larger vessel. The polemen stood on the flanks of both boats and shouted abuse at each other, but it was clear which boat would have its way. The newcomer was high-sided and unbeautiful, its blunt towers covered in a deep purple lacquer.

'That's it,' Dinesh said. 'That's her ship.'

Krish's loose skirt was sweat-soaked where he'd sat on it. He tugged it, trying to ease the discomfort, but it only moved the chafing to his thighs.

'Those are the right clothes,' Dinesh said. 'You look as a man should.'

Krish laughed tensely. 'And how should a man look?'

'I read *The Nature of a Man* by Sipon the Younger that Renar gave us. Men like jewels and bright colours, so that skirt is very fitting. And men like food a lot, so you should eat anything she gives.'

'It must be nice to be so sure of how a man's meant to behave.'

'Whatever's right and proper, you'll always be that,' Dinesh said earnestly.

If the gossip they'd heard was true, the owner of that boat dealt in forbidden things. Krish needed the plans to a place that the people of Täm liked to pretend didn't exist. If anyone could supply them, it would be this woman. *If* she had them. And if she could be made to trust Krish enough to sell them.

The sides of the boat loomed darkly above them as Dinesh poled closer. The faces peering down at them didn't look welcoming and there was no ladder visible. The prow of their boat bumped against the lacquered wood and set them bobbing so that Krish struggled to stand, unsteady on his feet.

The men above continued to watch, unmoving, and he cupped his hands around his mouth to shout, 'Please, we need to come aboard. We want to do business.'

After a moment there was a clatter and a rough rope ladder unfolded, stopping inches from his head.

The climb looked precarious and there was no way to secure their boat. It seemed the invitation was only for him.

'Don't, don't, don't go alone,' Dinesh said. 'It's not safe.'

'It's all right,' Krish told him. 'They won't hurt me.' They *can't* hurt me, was what he meant. But Dinesh kept secrets badly and Krish's new invulnerability was more powerful the less it was known. Besides, it felt . . . private.

'You're only guessing the God Killer is in the Garden,' Dinesh said stubbornly. 'No one told us that.'

'If I was hiding it, that's where I'd put it. The Mortals have got to be the ones who have it – they were the ones who invited me here. But you've seen how full of gossip this place is. Someone would have heard something if they kept it in their mansion. It's in the Garden, I'm sure of it.'

'But the Garden is *your* place.'

'Yes. So no one would suspect it's there. And the Mortals are in charge of guarding the entrance. It's perfect for them.'

He didn't give Dinesh the chance to argue further. The fibrous rope chafed at his hands as he pulled himself up, but the movement itself came easy. There was new strength in his limbs and it felt good to test it. It occurred to him that he hadn't coughed in months. His chest filled easily with breath these days.

The men above made no move to help, even when he reached the guard rail of the boat and was forced to climb over it in an undignified scramble.

'Come,' one of the men said, expressionless, and turned to walk away as the others flanked Krish. Neither carried visible weapons but he knew he was being guarded. There'd be another body in Corpse Lake if he did anything wrong.

The ship was very different above than it had seemed from the water. The lacquered purple of the deck was strewn with rugs and vases and lamps that the polemen had to skip nimbly around as they moved from side to side of the boat to keep it on course.

Below decks was even more cluttered. There was barely room to move through all the chairs and candlesticks and small, ornate tables and statuettes and crystal goblets and a thousand other knick-knacks piled carelessly on top of each other. Krish saw yellow and red beadwork that Dae Hyo had once explained to him was the work of the Four Together, and carved birds and animals that made their home in the Moon Forest. Tucked in one corner, there was a small figurine of a laughing, sly-faced man who could only be the Smiler.

'You like my collection then,' a woman said. Krish saw that there was a small space in the heart of it all, piled with rugs, and an even smaller woman sitting on top of them.

She was darker than most Ofiklanders, her skin a beautiful

blue-black. Her age was utterly unknowable, though the look in her eyes as she watched him wasn't young.

'Your collection's very large,' Krish said. 'And . . . from many places.'

'You recognised some of my finest, I see.' Her gaze swept the room, seeming to catch on the same objects his own had.

'Yes.' He swallowed, knowing he was about to take a great risk. 'I've seen them in the lands they came from.'

'Ha! A traveller from the god-sick lands – I knew it! I watched you as you came up.' She gestured to a strange contraption, a square of glass at the end of a long tube that twisted twice and then led to the boat's side. 'I saw your servant pole you up, and I said to my people, I said, "That one's not what he's pretending to be. Let him in to see me." And I was right! But you've come far in a very short time. The border only opened days ago. I didn't think Täm had seen your kind yet.'

'I'm a fast traveller,' Krish said.

'Well, traveller, you have good eyes. Good eyes, though you keep them covered and I won't ask you why. My greatest treasures are from the god-sick lands.' She leaned forward in her enthusiasm, half-toppling the rugs she sat on and ending tilted at a precarious angle she didn't seem to notice.

'But I thought that wasn't allowed.' He nodded at the sculpture of the Smiler.

'Ah.' She reached out a short, stub-nailed finger to tap him on the arm. 'You're new to Täm. Soon you'll learn that the way we *say* things are done here, and the way they *are* done, is as wide as the rift between Seventh Hill and Orchid Park. We scorn gods, then crawl to the City Below to take the god-given cure that lies there. "They died," we say, if we're asked where our uncle or cousin or brother is. "So very sad." And all along we know they're drawing breath on the hidden streets beneath us. But you didn't come to buy back what my people bought from your kin, I think. So what brings you to Mamma Kaaziad?'

'I need . . . something different.'

She leapt to her feet, tottering on the half-spilled pile of rugs.

'Oh, oh, oh! I see. A bad thing. A forbidden thing. But what could be forbidden in the god-sick lands that can be found here?'

'A map.' He drew a breath, then made himself go on. 'A map of the Garden of Yron.'

Her eyes widened, flashing briefly white in the darkness. She didn't look so friendly now. 'That? *That* is what you want? And why would you think I had such a map?'

'Because I think you like to own things other people are afraid of.'

Her lips moved silently, her hands clenching and unclenching, wringing each other and then gesturing sharply. She seemed to be having a heated conversation with herself.

'I can pay,' he said. 'I've got many things from Ashanesland, from the god-sick lands. Things I don't think you've got here.'

She shook her head. 'Well – and I'd like those things no doubt – but are they worth my life? Are they worth that?'

'I don't understand. Is the map dangerous?'

She studied him, narrow-eyed and untrusting. 'Could you be so naive? Perhaps, perhaps. You're a stranger here. The map, no. To own it? Yes, very dangerous indeed. Deadly, should the Mortals learn of it. You know who they are, I think, yes? They guard against gods and they guard the Garden against intruders.'

'So you do have it then.'

'Did you not hear me? The map is a ruling of death to anyone who owns it.'

And now he knew that she did. And Corpse Lake waited outside. He wondered if he could drown, or if his lungs would fill with water and he'd lie trapped beneath the surface, endlessly choking and stubbornly alive.

'If I take it,' he said, 'then you won't own it any longer. The crime won't be yours.'

'But it's precious. Unique! Why would I give away the most singular piece in my collection?'

Her reasoning was so circular it left him feeling dizzy. But maybe there was a way to cut through. 'A loan then. I'll give you what I've got and you'll lend me the map, not for long, just for a few days. And then when I give it back you'll have the map and the things I've given you.'

'If you give it back. *If* you give it back. You mean to go into the Garden, I think. For why else would you want the loan of a map?'

He nodded. There seemed no point denying it.

'Then I will never get the map back. The Garden is full of his god-power still. The map will lie there with your body and only the birds will own it.'

The huge cabin felt too close around him. He knew he'd only leave it with the map, or chained and weighted down with rocks.

He felt something inside him reaching out to her: a sense beyond sound or hearing. He hadn't known he had it in him, but he knew its power. He saw every part of her, the tiny walled particles that made her flesh and the impossible tangle of her thoughts.

It didn't take much, just a tweak here and there, to make her want what he wanted. He barely had to change anything at all. And in the moment his aim was achieved the sense was gone and he was back inside his skin again, just Krish, desperate and afraid.

'Give me the map and I'll go to the Garden and I *will* come back,' he said. 'And when I do, I'll bring you something from the Garden. Something no one else in Täm will ever have.'

'Ah.' She sank back onto her pile of rugs, as if all the strength had gone out of her. 'A relic from the Garden. A god-touched thing. And on this I have your vow?'

'Yes. I swear. I'll bring you a relic and I'll bring you back the map.'

'*If* you return,' she said again, but he could see that the tiny change he'd worked inside her had been enough. It was obvious in the glitter of her eyes and the nervous twitching of her fingers. 'Yes. This is a bargain I'll make, and I'll give you this advice for free, since it seems it's now in my interest. The Mortals will kill you for entering the Garden, it's true. But that won't be your greatest danger. Watch the flowers and the trees, godlander. Watch the statues and the fountains, for they'll be watching back.'

★

It took Eric a while to find the Path of No Return. It wasn't that Täm was a particularly confusing city. It was a well-organised place, its roads long and broad, its lawns short and all its many flowerbeds without weeds. That was the trouble. When a boy didn't want to be noticed, a well-organised city was the worst possible place to be.

He hadn't stayed in the park after the thugs came. What if they came back? He couldn't count on his luck a second time. He might take a gamble or two for himself, but never for his boy.

But if the parks were dangerous, the city streets weren't exactly hospitable. After learning about the warp, he'd taken off his fake sores, darkened his face with nut oil and covered himself with a hood and veil and plenty of dust, hoping to be taken for a traveller. It had got him no more than the odd glance on the streets at night when he did all his moving, but he couldn't risk anyone looking closer during the day. He slept huddled behind bushes in neat gardens and moved on quick-sharp whenever Arwel cried for food.

It had taken him days to work his way round to the right place, though at least the hills on which the city sat made for good guides. First Hill was easy enough to recognise, topped as it was by the great grim house where the Mortals lived. The Fourth Hill held the city's largest mansions and most lavish gardens. It lay to his left and the flat, low Fifth Hill to his right. He even had a map to guide him, bought from a street vendor that morning after he realised he'd walked a complete circuit of the Ninth Hill without even noticing.

But the map only showed half the city, the half that sat in the light of day. There was another city Eric caught glimpses of every time he looked down from one of the thousand of bridges into the shadows below. It was the ancient city on top of which they'd built the younger Täm.

Eric had tried asking Lanalan about his country's history. Krish had wanted to know and besides, Eric had been curious. All those years he'd been hearing of the Eternal Empire as the source of spices and silk and not a single shred of information more. And now it turned out they'd been lying even about their name. Ofiklañod was an interesting little riddle, but Lanalan hadn't seemed much interested in puzzling it out. He didn't care about the past. It seemed like the whole bloody country wanted to forget it – and in Täm they'd literally buried it.

Eventually Eric had managed to winkle a few facts out of Lanalan. He heard that before Täm was first built, its makers had caused a great mudslide from the mountains whose wooded slopes loomed over its westward side. But in Eric's experience, buried things had a nasty habit of uncovering themselves.

The sides of the fissures that criss-crossed Täm were honeycombed with holes, the windows and doors of the lost city. Eric had noticed the way the people of Täm seemed to look away from the ruins below them, mock-casual as if it was just an accident they never saw the foundations on which their city was built. But Eric had stared, fascinated. He'd seen glints of gold and precious metal, carvings of unknown creatures and the outlines of devices, huge and still half-covered by mud, whose purpose he couldn't guess. And moving in and out of the buildings or standing beside the carvings, there were people: the Xilabi, the exiled citizens of the City Below who tonight he meant to join.

If he could find a way down. All he knew was that across the whole breadth of Täm, with all its many fissures, there was only one way to cross between the twin cities. Then again, why would they need more? It was a journey that was only ever made once, and in one direction.

Finally, after he'd snaked his way past Second Hill, he saw it: a path that started out stone-flagged and turned to hard-packed earth as it led downward, beneath a high-arched bridge. Eric paused at the point where stone turned to earth and took one last look at Täm, a city he barely knew, and the sun, which he'd no doubt miss a lot more. He thought for one last time about going to Krish and Dinesh rather than down here.

But every time he'd tried to find them he'd felt a prickle in his neck, the fear that he was being followed. If he let anyone know the Wheelheir was here, it was all over.

Besides, he'd been given a job and he thought this was the place he could do it. And . . . well, he wasn't going to hope too much, but what if what they said about the City Below really was true? What if simply being in it could cure any ailment, even bring the dying back from the brink of death? There must be a reason some of the sick chose to take the one-way trip, disowned by all their relatives, outcast for ever from the life they'd known. What if the City Below could cure his son, and make him just like any other baby?

He'd been told there'd be people at the bottom of the path, but they surprised him all the same, like shadows come to life, their dark robes hiding them until he was right by them.

They seemed almost as startled by him as he was by them. They stared at each other in mutual surprise before Eric said, 'Down. I want go down.'

'Down, stranger?' the nearest asked. It was a woman's voice, though her face remained obscure behind its dark veil.

'To City Below.'

They shifted uneasily, their robes rustling. 'And what ails you?' a second asked. 'Is it the warp?' Eric could feel eyes behind the veil trying to pierce his own disguise.

'No,' he said hurriedly. 'Not me. Not me. Boy.'

This was the moment. His hand shook as he pulled the swaddling back from Arwel's face. The greyness *could* look like a sickness. It had to, or else this would all go wrong and . . . He pressed his other hand against the knife he'd hidden beneath his robes. He'd never been trained to use it, but for Arwel he'd try.

He couldn't see the frowns of the robed guards beneath their veils, but he sensed it in the woman's voice. 'This is no illness I've ever seen. What is it?'

'Don't know,' Eric told her. 'Don't know. No one know. Must make safe. Must make safe son.'

The woman's stance didn't soften exactly. She didn't seem a person with much softness in her. But she relaxed, and he thought he must have convinced her.

'If you go, you may never return,' a man said. He clearly took Eric for slow-witted, as most people here seemed to.

'I know. Better live there not die here.'

'You know about the mark you'll bear? And the boy too?'

He hadn't heard of any mark, but it was too late to go back now. He nodded and hoped it wouldn't hurt too much. Some of the boys in Madam Aeronwen's had liked to get tattoos. They'd boasted of the pain they'd had to endure for them, which Eric always thought was daft. Why take pain you didn't need?

'Your hand,' the man said, sounding bored, as if the whole thing had suddenly become routine.

Eric held out his left, which only lacked for the one finger, and tried not to let it tremble. His skin was brown-stained from the nut oil and the man frowned but didn't question it. He snapped his fingers and one of the silent guards brought him over a bowl. It seemed to glow queerly as she carried it and when it was put down, Eric saw that it carried a strange bright golden liquid that glolopped about as if it had a mind of its own.

It looked like liquid metal, only there was no heat off it. The man dipped a brush in it and before Eric had a chance to snatch back his hand, he'd daubed a quick blob on its back with half a dozen lines coming out of it. A sun, Eric realised – or a child's drawing of one. Another daub of paint and there was one on Arwel, just a dot and two smudges that took up almost all of his small hand.

The liquid wasn't painful. It didn't sting or even burn, just sort of ached. It was dry within moments and then a moment later it seemed to just . . . sink into his skin, so the skin itself took on the colour, as if it was a peculiar birthmark. 'Is done?' Eric asked. 'We go?'

'You *must* go now,' the woman said. She waved the stump of her hand towards the path leading down. 'You are no longer of the World Above and the sun's light will never again shine on you.'

Eric looked up for one last glance at it, but the day was late and the sun was no longer visible. He didn't suppose it mattered.

He'd turned his back on the sun's people once before and it had worked out all right for him.

The path narrowed as it descended. Its sides were formed from mud that had worn away into strange globules and tubes leading nowhere. It made a cracked mosaic beneath his feet. Then, without him quite noticing the change, he realised that he was walking on a true mosaic, the fragments of rock and crystal not dulled by time. Mud walls still loomed on either side, and he couldn't figure out the pattern on which he trod until one huge golden eye stared up at him and he saw the snarl of white teeth. A lion maybe, or a panther. Nothing friendly.

It was eerily silent down here. Lanalan had told him that thousands of people lived below. But as the path broadened until he could see the mosaic creature's entire paw, he remained alone. Far above, the pale blue sky was split in two by the length of a bridge – perhaps one that he'd crossed himself. The path had bottomed out and now he was walking along one of the many gullies that divided Täm. Except, he realised, he was no longer *in* Täm. The fissures in the City Above were the streets of the City Below.

This one ended a hundred paces ahead at a small doorway. Above it the mud bulged outward so it was impossible to see what building it was part of. There was light inside, but no other sign he should enter.

He expected something grand inside, or at least surprising. A room made entirely out of diamonds or a chamber a thousand paces high paved with bones. But it was only a hallway, little different from those of Ashfall, though here the walls were smooth stone. He followed it inward, ignoring two doors along the way. Ahead he could hear the low murmur of voices.

The last door opened and then he had the grand hall he'd imagined. He could have stood on his own shoulders, and three more Erics on top of that, and none of them could have touched the ceiling. The whole huge place was lit, glowing gently golden with no visible source.

Despite its size, the room was packed. The people whispered to each other as they watched him, their dark skin wan from lack of sunlight and their expressions grave. In the centre there were five high-backed chairs, the only furniture. The occupants wore the robes of Ofiklander women, and it took Eric a moment to realise that two of them were men. They all had the look of people used to giving commands and seeing them obeyed.

'Welcome to the City Below,' said a woman in golden robes.

'Welcome to your new life, the life reborn.' That was a green-robed man.

'There is no disease here, nor injury. No want, no hunger and no grief.' That was the other man. Eric's head flicked between them as they spoke until he realised it made him seem a right cully and kept it pointed forward. It hardly mattered who said what when they clearly spoke with one voice:

'Here there is only one law: violence above, peace below.'

'Do what you will, but never harm another.'

'One law and one punishment for breaking it: death.'

'Here all are wanted and all belong.'

'We are the Five Matriarchs and these are our families.'

'All must belong to one. And you . . .' And here for the first time, there was a hesitation. He felt them studying him, perhaps a touch of uncertainty before the woman finished – it was the golden-robed woman speaking – 'You must remove your hood. Here there is nothing to hide.'

He hesitated, but he could hardly refuse, not in a room full of them. And besides, they were bound to see his true face sooner or later.

They didn't react to it instantly. The light in here was diffuse, like sunlight through fog, and perhaps at first he looked as he'd meant to: like a dark-skinned man of this land. But after a moment, a confused murmuring began.

'You are . . .' The man trailed into silence.

'I am not Ofiklander,' Eric said. 'I am outsider.'

That led to a flurry of whispering between the robed people. They didn't look so leaderly now, more like a bunch of hawkers who'd been caught flatfooted by an offer they didn't understand and couldn't figure out if it benefitted them.

Well, in for a feather, in for an anchor. They'd said there was no death here, and nothing to fear. And maybe, maybe even a cure. 'It my baby. My baby not good, not safe,' he said, and pulled back the swaddling cloth.

The gasps this time were more open.

'A child of the moon,' someone said, not one of the leaders but someone in the crowd. The words echoed in the high hall and left a deep silence behind.

'Please,' Eric begged, not having to put on an act, meaning the word more than he ever had. 'Don't hurt. Just baby.'

Arwel chose that moment to stir, wriggling and fussing in Eric's arms. He let out the small whimper that always came before a whole load of shrieking if Eric didn't feed him.

Eric felt something break in the crowd, an easing of tension. People were smiling at him now – at Arwel – and he realised for the first time that there were no other babies in the huge crowd.

The woman who'd first spoken to him looked at Arwel with a tenderness he wouldn't have thought her capable of. Then she looked back at him and held out her open hand. There were five pebbles of different shades cupped in her palm. 'Your baby will be safe. You will be safe. You'll both have a family here. All you must do is choose it.' She closed her fist around the pebbles and held it out to him.

He stepped forward but hesitated to reach for the pebbles. He didn't like making a choice he didn't understand.

'Choose, stranger,' the woman said. 'None can live here who don't belong to the Five Families. It's not just our law, but your safety. Those without family have no light, and those without light die in the shadows.'

Her hand was swollen a little with the pebbles inside it. They all felt the same beneath his fingers as he reached into her palm until his finger rubbed against a slight flaw on one smooth surface. He hooked that one out and showed it to the company: a grey pebble flecked with shards of crystal.

The woman smiled warmly. 'A fine choice, stranger no longer. What's your name?'

'Eric.'

She rose from her chair to slip her arms around him, hugging him to the soft give of her chest. 'Welcome to my family, Eric Ikuesan.'

★

Her family, as it turned out, were mushroom farmers. They showed him the fields before they showed him his room. Their crop grew in what had once been the sewers of the buried city. The soil was probably rich with ancient shit, and the round brick tunnels were like the guts that had squeezed the shit out. It was dark and gloomy and nothing like the grand palaces he'd pictured for himself before he came here.

'You eat?' he asked, looking at the grey-brown fungus clustered in one corner of a field.

'We eat a few,' said the grey-haired old woman who seemed to have appointed herself his guide. Over the course of their walk here they'd shed people until only she and a large-eared young lad remained.

'You eat few, why grow many?' Eric asked. The red spots on the white caps of the nearest mushrooms looked like the symptom of some lethal disease.

'We sell them to the World Above,' the woman said.

'They fetch a good price,' the boy added. 'More cubes than I ever saw in my life.'

The old woman touched the sunburst on her hand, still as bright as his own despite the years she'd spent down here. 'This here isn't the mark of an exile. We're outlaws, godlander – outside its protection. Or its restraints. Above any can hurt us if they choose and suffer no consequence, so it's safest to stay below.'

The boy stooped to pick some mushrooms, slender and silver. He swallowed three and offered the rest to Eric and the old woman. She ate them without question and Eric shrugged and popped his own into his mouth, wincing at the bitter taste and woody texture. 'We farm,' he said. 'What rest do?'

'Why, their affairs are their own,' the woman said.

'And here?' Eric pushed. 'Many thing hidden here. No one dig or sell?'

The old woman squinted at him, suddenly suspicious. 'Is that why you came below, stranger? Are you like her, come to poke and pillage and not to join?'

'Like who?'

'Two Hands,' she said, and his face must have looked convincingly blank because she relaxed and added, 'But she works alone, that one, without family or ties. Hardly a person has even spoken to her.'

'Buying relics is forbidden,' the boy told him.

'And that's another family's business,' the woman added. 'Not our concern.'

It seemed very little was their concern and Eric was beginning to understand why. Her voice was slurred and her eyes glazed, hooded as if she was on the edge of sleep, though she kept on walking. His own brain felt mushy and the grey gloom of the tunnels began to shimmer with light.

He didn't like it, not one bit. It was too much like the drink the Servants had given him, to get him in the mood for rutting. He didn't feel in control and he'd had enough of that to last a lifetime.

The boy turned towards him, and Eric saw the trail of a thick white scar poking up beneath his collar. 'This,' Eric said, making the shape of the sounds with care. 'This why you come here?' He rested his finger on the scar.

The boy looked confused. 'What? Oh, that – it was so long ago now. Sometimes I forget it's there. I was a fool for fighting when I lived above. That's from the one I lost. The cut festered and they told me the rot was too deep. The fever was burning me up and I knew I'd die.'

'So you come here.'

'No, I never would have come. It's wrong to be here, don't you know? We left the sun's worship behind for a reason.'

Eric frowned, trying to figure out if the lad was making no

sense or if it was just his mushy brain that was making no sense of him. 'So why are you here?'

'He passed out from the fever,' the old woman said. 'Just hours left when his mother brought him down. She couldn't watch him die.'

'She saved you,' Eric said.

'She condemned me.'

They reached his room at last, little more than a hollow in the wall of one of the many tunnels with four beds stacked on poles one on top of the other. He climbed a rickety ladder into the topmost, and rolled onto his back. Arwel was cradled in his left arm, a warm comfort against his chest. The old woman wandered off and the young lad stood beneath him a while, staring into nothing, then fell asleep on the floor.

There'd been people working the mushroom fields but there were far more here, standing around in a dreaming silence, or talking or eating – food more appetising than mushrooms, thank the gods – or lying on their bunks themselves, sleeping. There was a life of idleness to be had here for a boy if he chose it, and no one to force him to do differently. He supposed it made sense. All the life these people had was stolen from death. Why should they waste a moment of it in pursuits that didn't please them?

He shouldn't be wasting his time either, but he'd been running for days and finally he felt – well, not safe. He'd never be cully enough to be that trusting. But safer than he'd been in a while. Sleep took him without asking, or maybe it was the mushrooms that slammed the shutters over his mind.

When he woke, it was to the sound of music. It was so deep and loud the bed beneath his cheek seemed to vibrate with it and the rock walls of their tunnels resonated to the same tune. Though tune didn't seem exactly the right word. There was no melody you could hum and the deep chords clashed horribly, jarring up his spine and through his brain.

He rolled upright in his bed to see many others doing the same.

'What is it?' he called down to the man in the bunk beneath, visible only as a pair of knobbly knees hanging over its side.

'Only the City,' the man said. The knees and the spindly legs beneath them pulled back into the bed and a moment later, the man was snoring.

Everyone was returning to sleep, though the music hadn't faded. It went on and on, each note rattling Eric's teeth and shaking dust from the ceiling.

It was so loud, it was hard to find its source. It seemed to be coming from everywhere. But when Eric walked to the far end of the tunnel and turned his face leftward he could feel it, a pressure against his skin that was more than just sound. He'd been around enough of it to recognise it. There was magic in this noise. Arwel cooed, as if the sound pleased him.

Once Eric had sensed the magic, he could follow it. It drew him deeper into the City than he'd yet gone, out of the sewers and into mansions grand enough they must once have been homes of the wealthy. The mud had been mostly cleared here and he saw that the mansions were slowly being picked apart, gold leaf scraped from the frames of long-faded paintings and jewels prised from ornate metalwork. One wall was a mosaic, images of men and women long dead, but their eyes were all blank holes. On the table beside them he saw a neat pile of pearls.

As he drew close, the music became unbearably loud. It felt as if it might rattle his bones apart. And then, abruptly, it stopped. He staggered forward a few paces until he was in the doorway of a pillared hall. There were people here, many with their hands over their ears and more crowded around some vast device at its centre. It seemed to be a collection of pipes, some the width of his thumb, others wider than his body and one so large it could have swallowed a horse sideways. He could see the largest still vibrating and knew this must have been the source of the music. And here the golden light that filled the City wasn't dim. It blazed from something at the centre of the pipes. He walked forward without really thinking, only wanting to understand what it was.

He got four paces before a hand was pressed against his chest by a woman with a bush of tight-curled silver hair and an expression like a hungry guard dog. Others saw him and clustered about her until a wall of people blocked him from the huge device. The air seemed heavy with the threat of violence, but he remembered the Matriarch's words, *peace below*, and stood his ground.

'What's your business here, stranger?' the woman asked. Her voice was croaky, as if overused. He guessed she'd been shouting above the deafening music only moments before.

'I hear sound,' he said. 'We all hear sound.'

'It's stopped now,' a thin-faced man told him. 'You can return to your sleep.'

Eric shifted, trying to see over the man's shoulder.

The man's expression darkened. 'Who sent you here, outlander? Was it Two Hands?'

This mysterious Two Hands again, and this time Eric couldn't look as if he'd never heard the name. It occurred to him that the law might forbid violence here, but the only witnesses to it were him and the ones who'd do it. He'd never met a law that someone wasn't willing to break if it suited them.

He smiled, shrugged and stepped back. 'Just here to look,' he told them. 'I go back to bed now.'

He didn't sleep, though. He lay on his back, Arwel cradled against his chest, and thought and thought. Because one thing seemed clear: the City Below was waking up. The machines that looked so familiar, the same runes on them he'd seen carved into cogs and wheels in the frozen far north, were starting to work again after a millennium of silence. And as far as he knew, there was only one thing that could wake them.

Somewhere in the world, Mizhara had returned. His mission was more vital than it had ever been and it wasn't any longer just about the prince. If he wanted to protect his son, the God Killer needed to be found.

17

At the river rapids, Dae Hyo saw his sixth chance to escape. The guard around him was tight these days, two burly Rhinnanish men walking to each side of him and willowy Servants of Mizhara in front and behind. They were there even when he slept – they had been ever since he'd slipped through their fingers in the rockfall two days back and made it almost to the treeline before they'd brought him down.

But here seemed hopeful. The rush of the water would drown any voices that called for help, and the sun's army was strung out, struggling through the wind and rain in individual misery. Even his own guards weren't paying him much attention. They mustn't think he could hope to flee here, where the ground sucked at your feet and mud would drag him down before they could.

He didn't mean to run over the ground though. He'd been watching the river. The currents were wild. Even so strong a swimmer as he couldn't hope to survive them, but the surface of the water was clogged with tree trunks. He'd seen the same thing in Ashanesland and he knew that above them somewhere in the mountains men must be felling the trees and sending them downstream for others to cut into logs.

But here, at this broad river bend, the trunks had become stuck. They'd break apart eventually, propelled by the fearsome force of the river, but for a brief moment there was a path across the water.

The fourth time Dae Hyo had tried to escape, they'd caught him before he'd made it twenty paces. He'd thought about it afterwards, in the sleepless nights of captivity, and realised that he'd given himself away. He'd tensed, breath shortening as he readied himself for his escape. Not this time. A man could learn from his mistakes. He walked as casually and calmly as anyone could through sucking mud and tried to steer his path near to the water without seeming to.

When he was close enough to the river to feel its freezing spray on his face, he knew it was time. He didn't give himself a chance to think about it. Between one step and the next he made his decision and flung himself towards the water.

The guards were quicker than he'd hoped. The man to his left spun and grabbed for him, but Dae Hyo's clothes were slick with rain and he lost his grip. The man between him and the water was clumsier, his lunge turning into a stagger that planted him face-first in the mud, and then Dae Hyo was past them both and leaping from the riverbank onto the first log.

He hadn't thought how slippery they'd be. His feet skidded on the soggy moss and it was either fall into the rapids or leap forward onto the next log, which was as moss-slimed as the first. He staggered along its length, arms held out to either side for balance like an acrobat of Smiler's Fair.

The roaring of the water filled his ears. He didn't dare look behind him to see his pursuit. He knew it must be there; the rough jostling of the tree trunks wasn't all from the water. But if he looked away for a moment, it would be the end of him. The logs were eager to buck him off and he wondered if this had truly been a wise choice.

Ahead he could see a place where the logs had been pushed so tight together they were like a shipfort floor, with not a drop of water between them. He clenched his teeth against their frozen chattering and made towards it, making himself think before he placed his feet although his shoulders prickled with the knowledge of the enemies behind him. He knew an arrow might come for him at any time.

But no arrow came and now he was on the mat of trunks. He let himself run faster here. He was halfway across the river and escape suddenly seemed possible.

He was three trees from the end when the river changed its

mind. He felt a pressure beneath his feet, as if the river shrugged, and the trunks split apart to reveal the frothing white water beneath. Others clashed against each other like battering rams. He didn't see the one that struck him until it was too late. It took him in the chest, throwing him into the water.

The cold shocked the air out of him, as icy as the first flow from the peaks. It numbed his feet and hands in moments so that it felt like they too were made of wood as he tried desperately to swim to safety.

The trees were all around. He saw one coming and tried to veer from its path but the trunk was far too long. Instead he was forced to gasp and dive, knowing that if it struck him it would be the end. He had to get out of the water. But every time he reached for purchase his freezing fingers slipped against the slick moss and all he could do was kick and kick to keep his head above water and spin helplessly in the churning current.

The world showed itself to him in brief dizzying glimpses. A moment of a vast trunk bearing down on him – until the fickle waters dragged him out of its path. Another moment when the wood all seemed to clear and he saw his pursuers at last, one of them caught in the moment of tumbling into the river, arms flailing desperately. Then that too was gone and it was just white water and wood and no way out of it. His gut was full of the gritty water he swallowed every time a wave washed over him.

And then, when he was all but done for, he saw the shore. It was only paces away. Somehow, through no effort of his own, he'd worked his way out of the logjam. His arms and legs were so weak he could barely make them move. All he could do was keep his head high and kick feebly onward, hands reaching, reaching, until what was beneath them was mud and not water and he pulled himself hand over hand onto the bank.

He knew he had to get up. He'd been followed. This desperate chase was only the first stage of his escape. But he lay on his back with his eyes closed, grateful only to be alive.

When he opened them he saw a ring of faces peering down

at him, impassive and golden-skinned. He groaned in despair. How? How had they followed him across so fast and stayed so calm? But when two of them dragged him to his feet, he realised that they hadn't crossed at all. Mizhara's army were all around, sullen eyes judging him. He must have made it no further than the midpoint of the river, and all his desperate struggles had only brought him back to the bank from which he'd started.

★

They let him dry himself and change his clothes before Mizhara led him away. He supposed he should be grateful, but it was hard to feel much gladness with those miserable faces surrounding him. The goddess's face didn't show much of anything, but there was a coldness in the way she gestured him to follow and then turned away without speaking.

They hadn't been happy the last five times he'd tried to run either, but this felt different. Mizhara strode ahead, not looking back, not checking that he was following. There were no guards and it seemed a far better opportunity to run than any he'd had previously, but he didn't take it. His bruises throbbed and he was still racked with shivers from the cold water.

They walked through the gloomy pines, needles mushy under-foot though the rain had stopped at last. He didn't know where she was taking him but he began to wonder if it was somewhere she meant to bring him back from. Had he tried her patience once too often? She seemed the kind of woman who'd want to do her killing in private.

When at last she turned to face him, there was no weapon in her hand. There was nothing to indicate why they'd stopped in this particular small clearing. It had nothing to recommend it but a pair of hollow logs, and Dae Hyo sank gratefully onto the knobbled top of one.

She perched opposite him, spine upright and as dainty as a shipborn lady. She looked young in the grey light, not much like a god at all.

'Five of my people died chasing you down today,' she said.

No wonder they'd had such an angry look about them. 'I'm

sorry,' he told her, which was reasonably true. 'I didn't mean for them to be hurt.'

'*You* nearly died. It was foolhardy to enter the water.'

'I tell you what, I don't like to point fingers, but it's your fault I had to take the risk. If you'd guard me less well, I could try to run in easier places.'

She answered him with silence. After a while it felt awkward to stare at her, and he looked around, but there was nothing much to see. The trees were all the same: tall and broad with thin green needles. Tracks passed through the mud all around them: the little tridents that birds left when they walked. He couldn't hear their song, only the occasional throaty calling of frogs.

Every so often a big drop of water would find its way down from the treetops and fall on the logs, and once on Mizhara's long golden hair. She probably could have commanded the water to stay away from her, but it didn't seem to occur to her. Or maybe it was against the rules. Like all her people she seemed very keen on following rules. Gods made rules but he didn't see any reason they should feel bound by them.

'You're very loyal to my brother,' she said at last. 'You risk your life to go to him.'

'He's my friend.'

'Gods have no friends.'

'That's a sad thing to say. I'll not claim Krish is good at friendship. Truth to tell, he still has some work to do before he's learned how to treat a man as his brother. But if he can do it, so can you.'

She clenched one of the hands that rested against her thighs and he was glad he'd finally managed to say something to move her, even if it was to anger. It made her seem like a person he could deal with. And he didn't think she'd kill him while she was angry. She'd think it beneath her to let herself be ruled by any feeling so human.

'I want no friends,' she told him. 'My love can't be given to one. It's meant for the many.'

'Well, that seems even sadder. Loving everyone's like loving no one at all, if it all feels the same.'

'You loved the woman Yemisi, I think. You sacrificed your chance at escape for her.'

He shrugged carefully. Her words felt like they had a trap in them. 'I barely know her. My uncle always said you can't love a person you haven't seen snow and harvest with.'

'And yet you love her. But she doesn't love you. I watched you both together. She wouldn't have made the sacrifice for you that you did for her.'

That stung, he had to admit it, though he couldn't see why he'd want Yemisi's love. She had no respect for him, and respect was the ground cloth of love. That was something else his mother's brother had been very firm in telling him.

'So there's to be no friends for you,' he said, 'and no husband either. That leaves only family. But here you are trying to kill your brother, who's never done a single wrong to you. Why do you hate him? You've never even met. I can understand men who've been with Krish wanting him dead. He's a problem-causer. But you? You're trying to kill him because of something another man did a thousand years ago.'

'Yron is Yron – the years count for nothing. You have no idea of the evil he did. He twisted nature to his bidding, and people to his pleasing. He cares nothing for anyone else, only his own desires. He had to be stopped. He would have remade the whole world if I'd let him.'

'But Krish hasn't done any of those things, not yet,' Dae Hyo said. 'Maybe he's learned his lesson from the last time. You'll never find out if you kill him, and what will happen then? You'll just come back in another thousand years and do it all over again. I don't much see the point of it.'

She rose and he thought that he might have finally said too much. But she only shook her head once, sharply, as if to dismiss all he'd said. 'You can't understand. You don't remember. Dae Hyo, I don't want to kill you. But if you try to escape again, I must. You've led too many of my people to their deaths.'

'Then let me go.'

'No. I know where my brother is now. His . . . his lackey entered the city of my birth and in the heart of my power he couldn't hide from me. This army is now marching to war. Give me your word you won't run again until we're in sight of my brother, and I'll give you your freedom among my people until then.'

And if I won't give it? But he didn't need to ask. She wore a sword slung at her side as if she knew how to use it. And there was a hardness to her, for all her gentle face and slender limbs. She was very certain she knew what was right. In his experience, those were the people who found it easiest to do what was wrong.

Still, he hesitated. He'd vowed to be Krish's brother, and a brother would warn him what was coming. But he'd tried six times now, hadn't he? And he was more use to Krish alive than dead, a spy inside the enemy camp. Yes, that was the truth of it. The vow she asked for could serve Krish as much as her.

'All right then,' he said. 'My word on it. I won't try to run again.'

★

As it turned out, having the run of the camp wasn't much different from being in a cage if nobody would speak to you. Faces turned from Dae Hyo as he approached, while eyes bored into his back as he retreated.

Still, there was one group he kept finding himself drawn back to, despite the cold faces they showed him. They were tribespeople – tribes*women*, every single one of them. He recognised beadwork of the Four Together, Maeng leather and Chun snow-flake embroidery. There was more of that than anything.

He thought if he hovered long enough they might eventually tire of pretending he didn't exist, but they proved more stubborn than that. On the day they finally left the endless drab forest, he decided he'd have to take matters into his own hands. A man could go mad if he spent too much time alone.

As usual when the sun was close to done for the day, they formed a neat little camp within the camp, tents circled around cooking fires and one large bonfire in the centre, where they gathered. Dae Hyo joined them there. He sat beside three of the older women, whom he judged less likely to start a fight with him. Every tribeswoman he'd seen carried a weapon, for all that they were women and should have been above such things.

The three he'd sat beside didn't reach for their axes, but they hardly looked thrilled. Up close he could see that they were knife women, Chun all three of them. He'd heard what the tribe had done to their women when they'd turned themselves into the Brotherband. He was surprised any had survived.

'I tell you what,' he said, nodding at the pot steaming on their fire. 'That smells good. Those Moon Forest folk don't know how to spice their food. Far too much sweet-bark to hide the rankness of the meat.'

The oldest of the women turned to him. Her face sagged like a scenthound's and she looked angry, although not necessarily with him. 'You're not welcome here,' she said.

Dae Hyo shrugged. 'I'm not welcome anywhere. So I might as well be here.'

They watched him eat the rest of his meal in silence. He couldn't honestly call it a success, but many a fine hunt started with a poor trail.

★

He sat and ate beside them for three more nights without anyone saying another word to him. When they finally did, it wasn't a friendly one.

The group he'd chosen that night was a large one, three elder mothers and a dozen or so younger knife women sharing a roasting antelope between them. They didn't offer Dae Hyo any, but did nothing to stop him tearing off a strip of the fatty belly flesh for himself. Its greasy juices were smeared across half his face when one of the elder mothers turned to him.

'You're Dae, aren't you?' she said.

He nodded, hastening to swallow his last mouthful.

'The Brotherband killed the Dae, and yet here you are, the moon's follower. What kind of man are you?'

'Krish didn't rule the Brotherband,' he told her. 'He didn't . . . he didn't choose for them to do what they did. He didn't choose to be the moon and he doesn't want war. Yet here you are bringing it. What kind of woman are *you*?'

'There's always war when the sun and moon are reborn,' one of the younger women said. 'That's what she told us. All that's left is to choose sides, and I won't choose the side that killed my mother and my cousins.'

Dae Hyo picked at the rune-marked shackle that still circled his wrist. 'They killed my mother and cousins too. And my sisters and all my people. I'll be honest, I wanted revenge. But the Chun are gone, the Brotherband are dead. Why make more brotherless women and sisterless men?'

They had nothing more to say to him that night. But the next morning when he woke it was to find three of the younger women standing over him. One of them offered him her arm to drag him to his feet and the other gave him a bow and a quiver of arrows fletched with red and yellow feather.

'You ate our kill yesterday,' the prettiest said. 'You can hunt for your supper with the rest of us.'

He ran his hand along the smooth hickory-wood curve of the bow. It had been finely made, but then the women wore the blue beadwork of the Dokgo, and the Dokgo were known as excellent crafters. Excellent crafters and untrustworthy traders, but was it even true any more? The Fourteen Tribes were now eleven and only the grass of the plains remained unchanged.

The meadowland that they'd travelled yesterday had given way to a broad, marshy valley. Fat waterbirds waddled in its streams and were easy prey for arrows. The hunters of the Sisterband downed a dozen or so before the rest grew wise, but the birds wouldn't be enough to feed an army. For that they needed larger game.

A promising-looking herd of such beasts grazed in the distance. They looked a little like deer, but as Dae Hyo and the other hunters crept closer through the chest-high grass, he saw that their horns weren't branched but straight, twisted into long, pointed spirals that could probably gut a man.

'Stringy eating,' a silver-haired woman said.

'Better than no eating at all,' Dae Hyo told her.

Their leader seemed to agree. She split them into pairs, sending them out to circle the herd, and Dae Hyo found himself with the same silver-haired woman. Her face looked young, despite the hair, and the embroidery on her jerkin marked her as Chun.

'I don't trust you,' she whispered, as their path took them closer to their prey.

He shrugged. 'Then trust my hunger. I can't live on air any more than the rest of you.'

There was a fine drizzle. The grass was beaded with droplets of water and their clothes were soon soaked, but the dampness brought no chill. The sun had grown fiercer as they descended from the mountains, and even hidden behind clouds it sucked out sweat to join the rain on his face. He wasn't sure he liked this land. It couldn't seem to make up its mind what it was.

'Here,' the Chun hunter said, when they reached a pile of mossy boulders half-hidden in the grass. She crouched behind them, bow strung but undrawn. Dae Hyo saw no reason not to join her. It was as good a hide as any. If these hunters knew their business, the herd would be driven within fifty paces of them and they'd be able to take down a good half a dozen as they stampeded.

'So,' he said, when the silence had dragged on long enough to be more uncomfortable than the damp. 'You know my name. It's only fair you tell me yours.'

The face she turned to him wasn't friendly. 'Chun Jimin.'

'That's a pretty name.'

'I don't want your compliments.'

Now she was looking at him with open contempt. It would have been sensible to let the conversation die, but Dae Hyo was more hungry for talk than food, and her voice reminded him of the plains. It had been a long time since he's seen the grass of his home. The grass here was the wrong shade of green, its seedheads too large and bright.

'You're a long way from home,' he said to her. 'Why leave it all behind for a god who isn't ours?'

'So says the man who followed the moon.'

'The moon means nothing to me. Krish is my friend.'

'Then perhaps Mizhara is mine.'

He would have said that Mizhara claimed to want no friends, but in that instant the horns sounded and the hunt was on at last.

The herd sensed the threat. Dae Hyo barely had his bowstring drawn before the stampede began, a sudden pounding of hooves and panicked bellows. Grass that had been peacefully grazed moments before was trampled underfoot and the smell of the herd washed over him all at once, musk and shit and a scent that said prey to the deepest animal parts of him.

The scent and the sight and the noise woke a memory in him, as sharp as a sword and misty as a dream. It came from his deep childhood when he'd barely had words to put names to what he saw. He was high up, so high he must have been sitting on his uncle's shoulders, and all about him sat the men of the tribe on the women's ponies and the distant thunder of the deer herd coming.

The memory was lost to him as quickly as it came. He returned to the present to the feeling of tears on his cheeks and Jimin shouting, 'Loose, you fool.'

The herd was almost on them. He felt the wind of their coming on his face. It had been far too many years since he'd hunted as one of a tribe, but he found he hadn't forgotten how to do it. He made the mass of animals resolve into individuals and then chose one and sent an arrow into its flank. More arrows were ready, stuck into the ground in front of him, and he loosed another and another without seeing whether they found their marks.

The herd knew its danger. They were a hundred paces away and their panicked white-rimmed eyes were on Dae Hyo. They could have trampled him if they chose. For a throat-drying moment he thought they would. But grass-eaters were cowards and instead they split like a stream around the rocks and galloped past to either side of him and Jimin.

He had time for four more shots. He could hardly miss with so much animal flesh all around, but the herd thundered on and it was only when it had gone past that he saw two straight-horned deer lying motionless on the muddy, trampled grass and a large striped bullock still twitching.

Dae Hyo drew his knife and slit the bullock's throat, leaning hard against its legs to stop their thrashing as it died. There was meat enough on here for a feast, though others would have to help him carry it.

'Jimin, I need . . .' he began, but the words died on his lips as he turned to her. Her bow was still in her hands, an arrow nocked and pointed at him. She was twenty paces from him. She could draw and loose before he reached her.

'I tell you what,' he said, and realised that in truth he hadn't a single thought of what he wanted to tell her. Her face was red with fury.

'Your people killed my husband,' she said. 'Little Cousin was a friend to all, but they cut him down in the desert and left his body for the vultures.'

He had no words for her, so he nodded and hoped that would be enough.

'Is that all?' she asked. There were flecks of spittle at the side of her mouth as she spoke. 'Won't you even say sorry?'

His words came at last. 'If I told you I was sorry, you'd kill me. And if I told you it wasn't me who killed your husband, you'd kill me too.'

'You're dying either way, moon warrior. Say what you like.'

His skin prickled with fear. He knew she meant it. He would have meant it too, if he'd had one of his tribe's murderers at arrow's end. But she was letting him talk and he might as well try to talk her out of it. He wanted to live. He hadn't truly known he did until this moment. He wanted to see Yemisi's face again.

'If you kill me,' he said, testing out each word in his mind as he shaped it, 'then you'll kill the only man who can stop this war.'

'What makes you think I want to stop it?'

'You've seen war. Only a fool who's seen it wants more of it, and I don't think you're a fool.'

He couldn't tell if she was more or less angry, but she was still listening. And he found that he liked what he was saying. It surprised him to realise he meant it.

'You can't stop it,' she said. 'No one can. It happens every time they come, doesn't it? And every time, the rest of us die. But the sun always wins, and it wasn't the sun's men who killed my husband. So I'll side with her.'

'I *will* stop it, or die trying. I swear it on Belbog's blood.'

'How?'

And there was the question. Because his tribe had died in the first true battle of this war, and he'd killed a woman in the second. Now he'd met the Sisterband and the soft-voiced sun servants and the sun herself, grave and thoughtful. The prospect of winning the war was no more appealing than the horror of losing it.

'I'll talk to Krish,' he said. 'He'll listen to me. Well, probably. And definitely more than he'd ever listen to any of you.'

She looked more sad than disbelieving. 'Maybe you mean that, moon man, but we're leaves and they're the wind – they'll blow us where they will. And they want to fight. They were born to it, to be each other's worst enemy. The sun and the moon have nowhere that they meet. Every child knows that.'

Her shoulders tensed as the bowstring tautened and he knew that he was moments from death. She didn't even seem angry any more. An angry person could be calmed, but she was only determined.

'I'm where they meet,' he said, his throat so tight the words came out thin and strained. 'The sun and the moon meet in me.'

It was absurd. He knew it in the moment he said it. He didn't seem to have control of his mouth any more, the fear moving it all on its own. It was useless anyway. He saw the narrowing of her eyes, the bunch of her muscles beneath her shirt. And he saw the moment her finger released the bowstring.

His mind leapt with the arrow, emptying and filling all at once. The rune formed whole and without understanding. He reached for the power to fill it, knowing already that the fingers of his mind would grasp at nothing. But to his shock, the power came, sudden and bright and burning, and then the arrow was burning too, faster than natural flame. When it left the bow it was wood, and when it struck his chest it was ash: a long thin stick of it that the wind shredded and blew away as a thousand embers.

'How . . . ?' Jimin said. 'How did you . . . ?'

'The runes,' Dae Hyo told her, fumbling his own way to understanding. 'I used the sun's runes.'

18

Alfreda saw the tip of one vane on the horizon. She watched it sink out of sight to be replaced by another. As their wagon drew nearer, the windmill's whole form became clear, first all four vanes at once, spinning with a speed too great for the gentle wind, and then the precarious base, at least a hundred paces high and only gently flared so that it seemed impossible it could support the weight of those vast vanes.

Scores more windmills were scattered across the landscape ahead of them. All seemed identical, their bases made of some matt white material, perhaps ceramic, and their vanes of the same translucent orange substance as the bridge across the Great Rift. They were beautiful in their elegant simplicity.

'What's the point of them?' Marvan asked.

'What's the point of any windmill?'

'To grind grain. But do you see a millstone? And where's the corn?'

He was right. Now they were closer to the first windmill she could see no entrance, nothing but smooth ceramic that, when she circled the wagon round the base, proved to be entirely seamless. And there were no crops in sight, only endless, lush rolling meadows and herds of cattle dotted on them, grazing on the rich grass.

'It's fascinating,' she said.

Marvan raised his eyes skyward. 'You mustn't take one apart to study it.'

'I amn't planning to.'

'You were. But I doubt it can be done, and even if it could, that's hardly the point. Our friend told us true. Look there on the vanes, do you see it?'

A rayed sun had somehow been etched into the material, or perhaps moulded from it. It glowed a brilliant yellow when the light of the sun itself shone through.

'Mizhara's symbol,' she said. 'They work by magic.' It had been a long and boring journey to get here, through the dull farmland of the province called Makat, but for the first time she thought it might have been worthwhile.

'I doubt the windmills can be used as a weapon, however,' Marvan said. 'The God Killer must be elsewhere.'

It was strange to Alfreda how easy conversation was between them. It was as easy as it had ever been with Algar, though she felt nothing of the love for him she'd felt for her brother. He wasn't a man she could imagine loving – it would be like falling for a rock or a tree. Something utterly unable to return your feelings. Or, no, these days it would feel more like loving her own hand. In some way she couldn't explain, Marvan had soldered his life to hers. He'd become a part of her and she couldn't imagine continuing now without him. Her revenge would be incomplete in his absence.

'You should question some people,' Alfreda told him. 'Not that sort of questioning. Just conversation. Everyone we've met so far's been ready enough to tell us whatever we want. In that valley – do you see? It looks like a town.'

The windmills were so large, they distorted all perspective. The town had seemed a mere hour's ride away, but it drew closer far more slowly than she'd anticipated. And when the lacquered road curved close to a field grazed by cattle, she stopped again to stare.

They were cows, that much was clear, with reddish-brown hair, shaggy over their eyes, curved horns, drooping udders and placid, idiot eyes – but they were vastly bigger than any cow Alfreda had ever seen. The largest of them would have overtopped a mammoth.

'By the gods,' Marvan said, 'I wouldn't like to step in one of *their* shits. And there's milk enough in those teats to feed that town for a week.'

Alfreda heard the clop of hooves behind them a moment before a young voice said, 'They're not for sale,' and she turned to see a horse approaching – piebald and entirely normal in size – with a girl on its back halfway to womanhood.

'Oh,' the girl said when she saw them. 'You're godlanders! Your faces are so pale – you look quite horrible. Or maybe just as if you're sick. Were you admiring our cows? They're the pride of Vien.'

'They're remarkable,' Marvan said, smiling the friendly smile that often put strangers on edge. It didn't seem to trouble this girl. She had the most trusting face Alfreda had ever seen, a mouth that looked like it was always waiting to smile beneath hair tamed into neat rows across her scalp and braided with silver beads.

'It's the windfarms that do it, you know,' the girl said, 'though no one knows how. In the time before that we don't speak of, there was some magic put in them. Siamo says that the magic wasn't meant for cattle, that the sun meant it for something else, and that's why it's failing now. Our herd are healthy but Kamalelit lost ten of his and his field touches on to ours, so Siamo says it can only be a matter of time—'

'Siamo?' Marvan asked.

'My father,' the girl explained, without pausing to draw breath. 'But Prasic, who's my joiner, says Siamo's just being contrary, because Siamo's always contrary and why *wouldn't* the windfarms have been made to make the cattle fat and fertile when they do it so well. And people needed to eat, even then, so there's no reason at all our cattle will sicken with the blight when they haven't yet. Hello! I'm Nabofik, Nabofik the Oldest, they call me now, but not for long, because that's a boring name. One day I'll be Nabofik the Politician – no, that's boring too. Nabofik the Wise. Or maybe Nabofik the Wealthy. That would be good, wouldn't it?'

'And we're Marvan and Alfreda, strangers in your land,' Marvan said, the moment there was pause enough to say it.

'I know!' Nabofik grinned widely, then pulled the reins to guide her horse away. She'd trotted to the bottom of the hill before she turned to look back at them. 'Well, what are you waiting for? You have to come and meet my parents – they'll be so excited to see some godlanders. The whole town will. We've all been wondering when the first would arrive, ever since the Remembrancer's proclamation arrived by canal racer. But hurry up, or we'll be too late for supper.'

Marvan looked to Alfreda, his brow raised in question. She shrugged and shook their horse's reins, sending their cart after the girl.

★

The town was larger than it had seemed from a distance, its scale distorted by the huge windmills and oversized cattle. The girl had spoken of a blight and Alfreda could see it now. Some of the cattle didn't graze but stood gently swaying, their eyes milky and their flanks mottled with a strange purple infection. It afflicted some of the fields too, eating away at the grass.

The town was clearly a prosperous place, though, the houses large and brightly painted, each a different, startling colour: fuchsia and emerald and scarlet. Like the road, they'd also been lacquered with some translucent substance and they shone in the sun like jewels.

The inhabitants must have seen them approaching. Many emerged from their homes to watch them pass and Nabofik called out a cheerful greeting to everyone. Her openness reminded Alfreda a little of Cwen, but she was sure Cwen had never been so carefree, not even as a child. There was a spark of joy in Nabofik bright enough to lighten any gloom.

Nabofik's friendliness wasn't matched by that of the townsfolk. Their stares weren't hostile but some were shocked and some frightened. Their eyes seemed drawn to Alfreda especially and she tried to imagine how strange she must appear to them: so pale, and with eyes a washed-out blue, not the rich brown of theirs. This was a land that had never known outsiders and she doubted any of those who'd crossed the bridge had come in this direction. They'd have been making for the city of Täm and the wealthy central provinces. She wondered if she even appeared human to the townsfolk, when the only people they'd ever seen were so different.

Nabofik led them towards the largest mansion, which had been built in a crescent to encircle a garden of roses arranged as a simple maze. The girl flung herself from her horse before the flowers could be trampled beneath its hooves.

'You don't have any children in your wagon, do you?' she asked.

Marvan smiled with an irony the girl couldn't have understood. 'We're not the parenting kind.'

'Oh, that's a shame. I hoped you'd have a girl–child. My parents wanted a girl-child – I did too, I wanted a girl sib more than anything. But they're all boys.'

It took Alfreda a moment to realise what she meant: that Nabofik wasn't female, but one of those people they called inter, who seemed to be both male and female. It seemed obvious now, in the broad set of her shoulders and the lines of her face that were a little too firm for a girl, too soft for a boy. But then with Alfreda's own muscles and height she was probably taken for inter by these people herself. And of course Nabofik wasn't *she,* or *he.* Nabofik was *oms* and *omas.* It fascinated Alfreda how awkward it felt to think in another language, like wielding tools that had been made for hands of a different shape.

'Prasic! Siamo! Komot! Come and see who I've brought!' Nabofik shouted, turning her head – turning *omas* head – to the house.

The door opened and three people seemed to tumble out all at once, the fattest of them throwing his arms around Nabofik and the other two squinting up at Alfreda and Marvan.

'Nabofik, Nabofik, Nabofik.' The fat man, probably *omas* father Siamo, had an absurdly high voice, as squeaky as a young child's.

'Pappa!' Nabofik yelled. 'Look what I've brought us!'

He peered at Marvan and Alfreda over *omas* shoulder, his benign expression unaltered. 'Godlanders! What a welcome surprise. What a *very* welcome surprise indeed!'

'They're to be our guests,' Nabofik said, with the certainty of a person seldom denied their desires.

'*Are* they?' *omas* father said, and for a moment Alfreda thought they'd be turned away, as of course they should be, as any sensible person would turn away strangers coming to their door. But then he added, 'How *wonderful*,' and suddenly they were being ushered inside and offered a fruit so highly spiced it burned her throat, and given a liquid to drink equally spicy that did nothing to soothe it.

Komot, the mother, was as thin as Siamo was fat and quiet where he was expansive, but seemed equally pleased to welcome Alfreda and Marvan to their home. She silently served their food and smiled if she caught their eye. Only Nabofik's inter parent, Prasic, seemed to have any caution, asking quick, probing questions whenever *omas* talkative child and jovial husband left an opening.

'Blacksmiths?' Prasic asked, the word sounding rusty with disuse, though it was in the Ofiklander tongue.

'Indeed,' Marvan said. 'Not myself, of course – I've not the skill or the strength, but my . . .' He stumbled a moment, obviously reaching for the Ofiklander word for 'wife' and failing to find it.

'Your female spouse,' Siamo supplied.

'Yes. Alfreda is the finest smith you'll ever meet.'

Four sets of eyes turned to her and for a moment she felt that well-known pressure to speak, to say something, and the equally familiar absence of any words. But Marvan shifted noisily in his seat and the family looked away.

'A blacksmith,' Nabofik said. 'That's a metalworker, isn't it?'

'Right again.' Marvan's smile was looking stretched by now, the fine wrinkles around his eyes deepening with strain. He was very good at seeming an ordinary man, but like any performance it wearied him.

'It's a lost skill among us, alas – at least here in the southern provinces,' Siamo said.

'You don't work metal?'

'We don't need to!' Siamo laughed and reached for the hilt of the weapon hanging at his waist. Marvan tensed, every muscle in his body preparing to do what he did best. But Siamo merely held out the blade hilt-first towards him. Alfreda saw that it was made of the same strange, translucent amber material as the vanes of their windmills.

'Glass?' Marvan asked, running his thumb along its edge. It looked blunt, but left a thin line across his skin that quickly beaded with blood.

Glass would shatter at the first blow, Alfreda thought as Siamo laughed and turned to his spouses and his child to say, 'Shall we show them?' a note of innocent mischief in his voice. Nobofik grinned and nodded and Siamo jumped to his feet and gestured them to the door.

Alfreda had expected another garden at the back of the house, but there was only grass, and on it three ugly earth mounds, conical and taller than the house itself.

'They're . . . very striking,' Marvan said.

Siamo guffawed and said, 'Step closer.'

Alfreda took two paces before she looked down and leapt back with a gasp. There were beetles everywhere, crawling all over the grass – and they were massively, horribly large. One of them had begun to crawl up her britches and she flicked it from her with a shaking hand.

'Don't worry, they won't hurt you,' Nabofik said. 'Well, they might bite – I've got a scar on my ankle that's longer than my finger – but if you stay still they'll get bored and move on.'

'The magic here makes them grow?' Marvan asked. He'd frozen in place as Nabofik suggested and his voice affected nonchalance, but Alfreda wasn't fooled. When he'd been a child, his brother had tormented him by hiding spiders in his bed. She could almost pity him, if she didn't know what he'd done to his brother in return.

'Yes! Exactly that,' Siamo said. 'I knew it would, even though they laughed at me when I said it.'

'And these . . .' Marvan swallowed thickly as one of the

hand-length, termite-like creatures crawled across his chest. 'They make the substance you use to make weapons.'

'Weapons and much else,' Prasic said. There was an edge to *omas* voice missing from Siamo's, the suggestion that this was as much warning as information. *Oms* wanted them to know *omas* land's power and perhaps to fear it, and Alfreda was suitably impressed. With such a material a great deal could be achieved and at far less cost than the one their people paid for drawing metal from the ground.

'We'll have our first collection next month,' Siamo said, 'and then let people talk of Vien as a backwater! We'll be the wealthiest province in Ofiklanod.'

They seemed wealthy enough already to Alfreda. When she and Marvan would have returned to their wagon, Siamo insisted they stay in the house instead. A whole wing was reserved for visitors, though she couldn't imagine it saw very many. There was a frozen sort of tranquillity to this province that she wasn't sure if she liked or hated. It felt as unchanging as granite, not a place where new things often came.

Other Ofiklanders made their walls of paper. These seemed to be fashioned from that same material the insects made, but opaque where the weapons and windmills were translucent. She examined the joins and saw that the structure was a frame into which square panels slotted and could easily be removed. That was probably how they allowed the cleansing sun to shine through when they wanted. The panels gave little more privacy than paper, but the illusion of it was enough to free her words.

'Is this a good idea?' she whispered to Marvan.

'Well, it's not a bad one. Our hosts are clearly notable people in these parts. They may know something. And if not, they may know others who could be useful to us.'

She felt a swell of gratitude for how completely her quest had become his own. Marvan killed for pleasure, not for purpose, yet he'd turned his skill to her use without complaint. There were moments when she felt guilt for joining him, moments when she saw Marvan through Algar's horrified eyes or with Cwen's unwavering judgement. But they'd both left her and Marvan was all she had left.

At supper he mentioned the God Killer, casually as if it was gossip they'd heard on their journey, but he got the same blank looks in return that they'd had before. So when Siamo asked what they planned to do during their stay, Marvan said, 'To meet people, to find customers for our business. Though it seems that smithing might not be as popular here as we'd hoped.'

'Nonsense – everyone will be intrigued!' Siamo insisted. 'We'll throw a star dance for you, won't we, Prasic? People will come from miles to attend; we're famous for the quality of our hosting, though perhaps that's not for me to say.'

The only one whose smile was wider than Marvan's was Nabofik's.

★

The dance was held at midnight, where musicians played stringed instruments that Alfreda had never seen before. Some had bellies as round as a pregnant mare's and others were long, thin and played with a long, thin bow, but together they produced a melody so complex her mind constantly tried to unknot it.

As the music played the guests drank palm wine, glass after glass of it, until the talk was loud enough to drown out the tune. Siamo had planted lanterns between the roses of his garden, but their flames were dying now. She saw Marvan with his arm around a black-clad figure, leading him through the growing gloom. It was the local Mortal whom Siamo had proudly introduced to them. Marvan couldn't mean to kill him, could he? The partygoers were drunk, but not so far gone they wouldn't remember Marvan leaving with the murdered man.

She slipped away after them, shoulders hunched in a way Algar had once teased her about. *It doesn't make you any smaller, Freda,* he'd said. *It only makes you look like you're off to do something disreputable.* But if anyone at the party thought so, they weren't concerned enough to follow her.

She'd thought Marvan might lead the Mortal to their wagon, but the pair were weaving down the road instead, Marvan's slurred words blending with the harsher laughter of the Mortal. Marvan's drunkenness was probably feigned, but his companion's was real enough. Alfreda could smell the wine on his breath when she moved to flank him.

'My darling,' Marvan said when she frowned warningly at him. 'My friend Vatom here has something interesting to show me.'

'Interesting?' The Mortal giggled and Alfreda wondered just how young the face was beneath that black cloth mask. 'The books of Bakan the Bald are interesting. This is . . . it's . . .'

'It's going to help us find that weapon we misplaced,' Marvan said, winking at her behind Vatom's back.

'Your spear, yes. Tell me about it.'

Alfreda grimaced but Marvan said smoothly, 'It's old, very old. A family heirloom.'

'Some of your godland metalwork?'

'No,' Marvan said, 'it hails from these parts.'

Vatom staggered to a halt, half-tipping until Marvan pulled him upright and they stood in a swaying line. It took Alfreda a moment to realise they were facing a building. Its walls were so darkly stained, only the absence of stars marked out its shape against the night sky. The Mortal swayed into forward motion again, leading them both to the blacker blackness that was the front door.

Once inside, he fumbled a while at the wall until there was a spark and a lantern flared orange. It revealed a room far different from what Alfreda had expected. The gloom of the house's exterior wasn't reproduced here. The floor was carpeted in furs and the walls hung with silks in stark, bright colours. Cushions lay scattered everywhere and a young girl lounged in them until she saw them enter.

She leapt to her feet as her gaze flicked between Vatom and his visitors. With her large eyes and larger ears she looked like a mouse panicked by the approach of a cat.

'Fetch drinks,' Vatom said.

When her mouth opened, the stub of a tongue wriggled in its back and she made a noise that might have been agreement. She scurried to bring a flask of some strong-smelling stuff that Marvan only pretended to drink and Alfreda sipped gingerly. It burned with a heat that was only partly alcohol.

'So, this help you can give us . . . ?' Marvan asked.

'Power,' Vatom said. 'Magic. All these years it wasn't working, and now it is. I can't show them, the cattle, the, the . . .' He gestured clumsily outwards and Alfreda thought he meant the people of his town, or perhaps his whole country. 'But you, you outlanders know gods and don't fear them.'

'You've been doing moon magic?' Marvan asked, but Vatom pressed the stump of his hand against his lips to silence him. The Mortal was sweating beneath his robes. It plastered the material of his veil to his face and Alfreda began to make out the features beneath. She thought he might be a handsome man. The thin cloth caught against generous lips as he spoke.

'Not moon magic, no. No moon for us. No sun.' He surged to his feet with the abruptness of the very drunk and staggered across the room. When they didn't immediately follow he peered back at them, frowning. 'You won't see it sitting there.'

He led them unsteadily through a room that seemed designed for eating, or perhaps sleep. Bedding and half-filled plates were scattered all around it. And then a final corridor brought them to a place unlike anywhere else in the dark-walled house.

This chamber alone was perfectly neat. It reminded Alfreda of idolators' huts she'd visited in villages scattered through the Moon Forest. It was certainly a place of worship. The folk had liked to burn spice-flower seeds to honour the Hunter, and here there was a bowl of milk with a golden swirl that might have been honey.

Behind the bowl stood three statues. They'd been carved nude and she saw that one was male, one female and one must be inter – though she'd never seen an inter Ofiklander unclothed. Their bodies were human but the heads were those of animals: a bird, an insect and a doglike beast she didn't recognise.

'I see,' Marvan said. 'It's your gods who'll help us. I don't mean to be rude, friend, but we've gods enough of our own.'

'They can't be gods. No gods are allowed in Ofiklanod,' Alfreda said, pleased to find that Vatom's drunkenness had freed her tongue.

'But you are god-people, you paper-skins. I thought you'd understand – I trusted you!' Vatom's hidden eyes burned into hers.

Marvan slung an arm around his shoulder, casually drawing him back from Alfreda, though she hardly felt threatened by him. She could have snapped him in half with her hands. 'You *can* trust us,' Marvan said soothingly. 'It's only that we *do* know the ways of gods, and in our experience they're slow to answer the requests of mortals, and when they do it's seldom in a helpful way.'

Vatom shrugged Marvan's arm away, but he no longer seemed angry. 'But the moon has magic, doesn't he? The moon and sun broke the world between them.'

'So these gods are servants of the sun?' Marvan gestured at the trio of statuettes.

'Oh no. No, no. We'll have no truck with the sun – nor with the moon. We found another way. Here, take these.' Vatom gestured at three thin reeds lying in a basket beside the altar and then called, 'Come here! Come here at once!' and his tongueless servant scurried back into the room.

'They're pipes,' Marvan said, dubious. 'Are these gods of yours fond of music?'

'It's their language.' Vatom's attention was no longer on them. His head was bent over a parchment thickly marked with a notation Alfreda didn't recognise. His handless arms struggled clumsily to unroll it until he found the section he was searching for.

'I knew it!' he said. 'I knew the summoning had been composed. A tune to direct your feet onto their true path. Now then, how does that sound?'

'It sounds like the very thing we need,' Marvan said, but Alfreda could tell his enthusiasm was feigned.

Vatom seemed oblivious. 'It is! It is! And all you need do is play . . . let me see. High-high-low-high for me, low-low-low-low for you and low-high-low-high for you. And the rhythm must be . . . ah yes.' His stump tapped against the rug: two long beats, one short and another long.

'You want us to play these?' Marvan held out the reed flute.

'Of course! How else can the power be called? Blow and cover both holes for the low note and neither for the high.'

Marvan gave an experimental blow and the sound that emerged was surprisingly pure and sweet.

'Exactly! But it must be all at once and in time. I'll beat out the rhythm for you.'

'And what will happen then? Will a golden light appear to illuminate our way?'

Vatom's frown wrinkled the material of his veil. 'No, no, not so . . . It's just – it's a feeling. Or so I've been told. A knowledge that wasn't there before.'

'You've never used this power yourself?' Marvan asked. 'I thought you said it had been proven to work?'

'The power *is* there – others have told me so. But I haven't been able, I couldn't – I'm all alone here, can't you see! Posted all these leagues from the Cinderlands. I couldn't do it until you came along!'

Marvan's hand was creeping towards the knife at his belt and Alfreda could see from his face that the blood fever was rising in him, but it wouldn't be wise. They'd have to kill the servant too, for all that she was voiceless, and then who else could be accused of the murders but them? She put her own pipe to her lips and blew a note loud enough to wrench Marvan's gaze from the Mortal.

'Yes, yes – but not alone!' Vatom's tone was again that of an enthusiastic teacher. 'All three of us at once, and on my mark – one, two, three. Now play!'

The first note sounded from the three pipes, an unpleasant disharmony that had the hairs on Alfreda's neck bristling. Then the second note came, somehow equally discordant and yet almost harmonious. With the third the disparate notes seemed to weave and bind together, and when the fourth played the vibration that began at her lips seemed to shiver into every part of her. She stopped her breath but the tune rang on, repeating its four strange chords over and over until both she and Marvan dropped their pipes and put their hands over their ears to mute the overwhelming sound.

Vatom's face moved beneath his veil, his mouth shifting the cloth in what might have been a scream, or perhaps a question. It was inaudible. His servant had curled herself in a ball, tears streaming from her eyes. The tears were bloody and Alfreda saw that she'd bitten through her lip.

And then, as if brought into being and woven from the sound itself, an image formed. It was nowhere that Alfreda recognised, a dense moist tangle of greenery clinging to the slopes of a soot-black conical peak. The image was so clear the leaves seemed to shake and she felt the touch of an unreal wind on her face and the grip of a moist heat on her body.

A moment later it was gone and the note with it. It left a profound silence behind, quickly filled with the sobs of Vatom's servant and Vatom's own terrified gasps.

'Well,' Marvan said, with a levity she could see he didn't feel, 'it appears your magic is more powerful than I believed. I apologise for my doubts.'

The veil across Vatom's mouth trembled with his breaths but no sound came from him except a thin, panicked whine.

'We'll need your help just one last time,' Marvan continued when it was clear the Mortal didn't mean to speak. 'The land your gods showed us – can you tell us where it is?'

'How?' Vatom said at last. 'How did that happen?'

Marvan frowned. 'Your gods, of course.'

'Never . . . never . . . it has never been like that. No one has ever reported such power! What did you do?'

'We did nothing, friend, except what you told us. Now will you answer my question?' There was a sharp edge to Marvan's voice.

Vatom bowed his head as he rocked and moaned. His servant eyed her master, her face a mask of fear, and then ran from the room.

'I suppose we could ask around,' Marvan said. 'We can hope that someone recognises the description.'

Alfreda nodded. They needed to leave and quickly. Vatom's mood was poised to shift again, she could sense it, but she didn't know which extreme it might lurch towards next. And the feeling of that alien magic hung in the air, like the stillness before a violent storm.

They were almost at the door when the servant hurried back into the room. She called out in her strange, rattling way, and Alfreda saw that the girl had brought a map of Ofiklanod, almost as large as she was tall. She put it down on the floor and moved to stand at its bottom tip, where the country ended in a gulf of sea and then a great island off it. Her finger shook as she pointed to the island, where Alfreda could see a conical mountain marked.

'There?' Marvan asked and the girl nodded, eyes darting between them and her still incoherent master.

'So,' he said to Alfreda. 'It seems we'll be travelling south.'

They didn't return to the mansion. They didn't want to be within sight when Vatom regained his senses. Who knew what he'd tell anyone about them?

*

The night-dark landscape flitted by, barely a sliver of moon to illuminate it. Huge shadows loomed to their left and then their right, but it was impossible to tell if they were windmills or more cattle, and the rattle of the wagon's wheels over the lacquered road muffled any betraying noise. They wouldn't have dared to make this journey on the potholed and perilous paths of the Moon Forest, but the folk of Ofiklanod kept their ways well. There was little for Alfreda to do but hold the reins and let the horse have his head.

She was in a daze, half-sleeping as Marvan snored beside her, when she heard a sound from the wagon's back that could only be something moving. Marvan woke as she pulled his belt knife from its sheath and flung open the canvass covering of their home.

The darkness inside was almost total, but the intruder made

no effort to stay hidden. Alfreda heard the scuffle as feet knocked against their pickle jar and then a voice said, 'Oh, I'm sorry – only I really need to make water.'

'Nabofik?' she said, startled into speech. 'What are you doing here?'

The inter youth moved forward until moonlight outlined *omas* rounded cheek. 'I'm travelling with you.'

'Really? You weren't invited.' There was more amusement than threat in Marvan's voice.

'But I want to see the world outside Ofiklanod,' *oms* said, 'and only you can take me there.'

'We're travelling south, not north,' Marvan told *oms*.

'Oh.' *Oms* bit *omas* lip and then shrugged and sat between the two of them, a tight squeeze that left *omas* warm skin pressed up all along Alfreda's left side. She shivered at the contact. No one had touched her so intimately since Cwen.

'We can't take you home,' Alfreda said, surprised to find her tongue loose around the youngster. But there was something about *omas* face, even shadowed by night, that was so open – as fearless as Jinn had once been when he'd looked at her. 'If you know a town along the way, we can give you coin to find a ride back to your parents,' she added.

Nabofik grinned and Alfreda stopped herself from twitching away as *oms* slung an arm around each of their shoulders. 'There's no need for that. How far south are you going?'

'All the way,' Marvan said.

'I've never been all the way south. I've been to Täm, of course, but so has everyone. And I've been to Kanad too, but that wasn't at all interesting. I'll come with you.'

Marvan's eyes met Alfreda's across their passenger's head. They didn't need to speak for her to know what he was thinking. If they sent Nabofik back unwilling, what might *oms* say about them? What might *oms* find out from Vatom once the Mortal had been given time to recover?

'Well, what do you say?' Nabofik asked. 'Shall we have an adventure together?'

They could kill *omas*, of course. She saw Marvan's hand reach for the knife that was no longer at his belt, but it was without his usual eagerness. Nabofik was too much a child for there to be any pleasure in slaughtering *omas*. And Alfreda felt the warmth of *omas* arm, warding against the growing chill of the night, and knew that she wouldn't let *omas* die.

'Go back to sleep then,' she told Nabofik. 'We've a long way yet to go.'

19

The City Below was alive. Eric could feel its pulse, a throb of magic that haunted his sleep. He woke on his narrow bunk in his windowless underground room, feeling unrested and uneasy. It was the sun's power, there was no doubt about it.

He'd asked about it, as subtly as he could, and learned it was a recent thing. There were folk here who remembered a time before, when the City had been quiet and dark. Back then the only light had come from the sun images owned by every family. Theirs sat at the centre of their eating hall, but someone had covered it in gauze, obscuring the features. That was bloody typical of this lot. The whole buried city was Mizhara's place. It was her lingering power that had cured their illnesses, but they'd rather die than admit it. He'd never even heard anyone here say her name.

They wanted even less to talk about what the growth of her power here meant, but Eric couldn't afford to ignore it. When Krish had come, the old runes had woken up. And now the sun's city was doing the same. Mizhara must be back. It was the only thing that made sense.

'Going to the fields?' a soft voice said from the bunk below him. It was that young lad, Koten. The room was dimly lit and Koten's eyes looked huge in the darkness, their blackness swallowing up the rest. He was as high as a floating hawk and enjoying every second of it.

'I go work,' he said, though Koten was no longer listening, lost in his happy dreams.

It had taken Eric two days to learn the way from his room to the nearest mushroom field, twisting through the round, wet tunnels of the sewers. As he walked, the brick floor gave way to softer earth and the ceiling rose, but only a little. The weak golden glow of Mizhara's light was the same here as everywhere; or everywhere that was claimed by members of one of the Five Families. It was some consequence of her magic he didn't understand. They said anyone adopted into her families got the protection of her image, even if the family's blood didn't run in their veins.

The soft brown earth filled him with a weird, disgusted sort of fondness. It was very like the shit-and-mud soup that Smiler's Fair had left behind at the end of each of its stops. He must have travelled thousands of miles in his years with the fair, but the distance he'd travelled after he left it felt far longer, and not just measured in miles.

The mushrooms didn't fill him with the same fondness. Their flesh was too giving against his fingers as he plucked them one by one and placed them carefully in separate pockets of the sack they'd given him on his second day.

Others worked the fields beside him, but there was no conversation to be had. He watched the old woman to his left pluck two fleshy yellow mushrooms. She put one in her sack and kept the other in her hand, nibbling on it as she worked. It must have been some different variety from the one the boy had taken. Where his eyes had been black and glazed, hers were nothing but whites. They darted everywhere, like a cornered hound's.

Didn't look much fun to Eric, but who was he to judge? He reckoned some of his pastimes wouldn't much appeal to the old lady either. Still, he followed her path as it veered from the centre of the field. The outer edges were where *they* always came.

After a while the woman wandered back to the centre, but Eric stayed where he was. He'd stopped pretending to work. No point, with no one watching. He fed Arwel instead, breaking up one of the food mushrooms into small chunks. They were the only thing Eric had ever managed to make him eat besides blood. He supposed that must mean they were the moon's, not that these folk would admit it – any more than they'd admit to living with the sun's blessing. They were a rum bunch.

But then Arwel wasn't precisely normal either, and he was growing like a weed. When Eric let him on the ground he'd sit himself up on his bottom, and lately he'd started trying to walk, though he generally made a pig's ear of it and Eric had to wipe his tears when he toppled. Sometimes he seemed exactly like an ordinary baby, despite his grey skin and black-and-silver eyes.

Then there were the other times. Like when he'd be crying and Krish would walk past and he'd stop straight away, his gaze fixed on the prince, more intent than any baby should be. When Krish spoke, Eric could swear that Arwel understood him. The Wheelheir had mentioned the mammoths outside Ashfall one time and Arwel had turned around and stared straight at them.

Sometimes Eric wondered if Arwel truly belonged to him. He was the babe's dad, but Krish was his god. Arwel had been *made* to serve him. And it didn't make Eric love him less – he didn't think there was anything that could – but it made something ache inside him.

'But you're a good boy, ain't you?' Eric said to him, even though right now he was being anything but. He'd decided he'd had enough of the mushroom and when Eric tried to press one last bit on him he tore it from Eric's fingers and flung it away as if the very idea of it disgusted him. His little face wrinkled up in a frown and Eric couldn't stop himself from smiling.

He made to wipe Arwel's mouth, and stopped with the hem of his tunic halfway there when the thing he'd been waiting for finally came, announcing itself with a rusty clank.

He thought it must have been made in imitation of a man. It certainly walked on two legs, and the snake-like cables hanging from its shoulders might have been meant for arms. It was hard to say what it had been made from, covered as it was in filth. Fungus grew in bulbous protrusions all over it. But there was a gleam beneath that might have been metal and in its head shone two bright red jewels for eyes. Eric couldn't guess what it had been made *for*, but he was sure of two things: the sun's magic had made it and the sun's magic had woken it.

It never did anything but walk, staggering from one end of the field to the other and into one of the long dark tunnels that were everywhere in this part of the City Below. The other workers ignored it. He heard it had first appeared more than a month ago and done the precise same thing in this field every day. Eric had kept his distance and watched the first two times it came, afraid to seem too interested. But today he tied Arwel back into his sling and fell into step behind it.

A few eyes tracked him but no one tried to stop him, and hadn't they told him there were no rules here? The thing itself seemed oblivious, lurching onward with its feet leaving deep imprints in the mud of the mushroom field. It crunched through a patch of the grey-green fungus and spores rose in a choking cloud all around.

When it reached the end of the field, Eric followed it into the tunnel. The same dull yellow light was all around, like sunlight at the end of a long and lazy summer day. The tunnel wound confusingly through the guts of the buried city, but the thing seemed to know where it was going. As Eric slogged through millennium-old filth, it turned right into a broad corridor faced with verdigrised copper and then right again, into a narrow but high-roofed room.

There it finally stopped, its cable arms drooping and all light dying from its jewelled eyes. Eric couldn't for the life of him see what had drawn it to this room. He thought the place had been used for sleeping. There was a rectangular imprint on the lacquered floor where a bed might once have rested, though it was long gone. The device didn't seem to need it anyway. It was sleeping standing up.

Eric walked right up to it, thinking that might spur it into action again, but it remained motionless as he reached out a tentative hand to scrape away the muck on its chest. As he'd thought, it was metal beneath, though not one he recognised: too light to be gold and with a peculiar pinkish tint. As he scraped further, he began to uncover engravings on the metal and he grinned as they came clear.

Runes, just like he'd figured. They looked just like the ones he'd seen on the great machine in Salvation. He hooked his nails beneath the panel, trying to prise it free, but it didn't want to come. His nail tore raggedly instead and he yelled and sucked the welling blood in his mouth before remembering there was someone who'd like it more and offering his finger to Arwel. His little mouth latched on and the sharp pulling pain of the suckling had just begun when Eric heard the footstep behind him.

It was a woman, or at least he thought it was. It was hard to tell beneath those enveloping black robes. Her face was veiled like those who'd marked him and sent him down. She was dressed as a Mortal, but when she took a step towards him, she held out her hands, black-gloved and whole.

'Two Hands!' he said, suddenly understanding the name.

The veil shifted in the shape of a smile. 'You have interesting interests, outlander.' There was something familiar about her voice. He'd heard it before, as sure as sheep were sheared. Weirdest of all, she was speaking the tongue of the Moon Forest.

She ran her gloved fingers over the engraving on the thing's chest, tracing out each mark in turn.

'The runes,' he guessed. 'You know them, don't you?'

She did something he couldn't follow, a quick movement of her fingers against some hidden mechanism, and the thing's eyes glowed back to life. 'Yes, I understand them. And what did you hope to find here?'

'I don't rightly know.'

'Is that so, Eric of the Fine Fellows?'

He stepped hurriedly back, clasping Arwel to him. So they did know each other; but he still couldn't put a name to her. She had him at a disadvantage, and he guessed she was enjoying it. 'What did *you* hope to find here?' he asked.

Her veil shifted again in the suggestion of a smile. 'You. Come with me now. Come,' she repeated as he hesitated. 'Or would you like me to tell your new family who you truly are – and who you truly serve?'

★

She led him back through a mushroom field, not the one he'd worked but hardly any different. The strange device clanked after them, eyes aglow, and this time the farmers all turned to watch. He heard some of them mutter as she passed.

'Don't seem to care for you too much,' he said. He couldn't tell if their expressions were more fearful or hostile, but they weren't friendly.

'I am a stranger here like yourself,' she said, 'and without family.'

'I thought that weren't allowed. They told me that when I come here.'

'They also told you there are no rules below,' she said, which was such a good point it shut him up until they were out of the mushroom field and winding their way through another of the gut-like passages.

'Yeah,' he said as it occurred to him, 'but you need a family for the sun's light to shine on you underground. Without the light down here the worm men'll eat you.'

She stopped and turned to him. He could feel the touch of her hidden eyes, and the moment when they slid over Arwel. 'But the worm men are a threat no more. The last generation of Yron's servants lost their taste for flesh on the day that the first of his new servants was born.'

That kept him quiet and worried until they reached her destination, a courtyard that must once have been open to the sun, but was now roofed by mud. Four trees stood in its four corners, long dead, their wood the colour of ash, and a fountain sat in its centre. A fish-headed device stood on its lip, mouth slowly opening and shutting in a silent gape from which no water came. Snakes writhed at its feet in an endless circuit round what must once have been a cooling pool. Their metal scales scraped against the marble and their movements were jerky, as if each flex and bend took a lot of effort. There were runes inscribed on them too.

'All right, listen,' he said. 'Enough fun and games. You know me. And I know I know you. So why don't you tell me who you are?'

'I am a seeker, much like yourself.'

'And what are you seeking?'

'The same as you.' She reached out a hand to touch the writhing snakes in their bowl, the metal scales hissing against the fabric of her glove. 'The power that slept here for a thousand years has begun to wake.'

Eric watched the mechanical snakes crawling on their circuit. It was easier than looking at the blank black material over her face. 'You know I'm with Prince Krishanjit, don't you?'

'I know you arrived in his party, but separated from it when you reached Täm.'

'So you reckon I'm here on his business.'

'The sun *is* his concern – or she should be.'

'Krish don't like magic.'

Her expression was unreadable beneath its veil, but he felt her sudden interest in the way she shifted towards him. 'Does he not?'

'Not after the Battle of Mirror Town. He forbade anyone to use the runes. Said the cost was too high.'

'So there is some wisdom in him.'

And something about the way she said it, some shift of tone or the weariness beneath it, finally told him who she was.

'Oh. Oh, it's you. Bloody hell, did you follow me here?'

She laughed as she drew off her veil. Her golden face was just as he remembered it – beautiful and ancient, despite its apparent youth. But for the first time he saw that she'd been made in the fashion of a woman of these lands. That curly hair, the wide nose and generous lips – she could have passed for an Ofiklander, if it weren't for the colour of her skin. No wonder she'd taken on the disguise of a Mortal.

'No, Eric,' the Hunter said, 'I did not follow you here. We both came, I believe, for the same purpose.'

'But . . .' He had so many questions, he didn't quite know where to start with them. He settled for, 'How did you get here?'

'By a shorter road than yours.' Her face had looked briefly human in its laughter. Now it settled back into its more familiar stern lines. She gestured behind her. 'Come – sit. We have much to discuss.'

There was a table to one side of the fountain, ornate metal rusted to a skeleton of its original form. Two chairs were beside it and she pulled one out for him. It looked just as decayed as the table and he sat gingerly, but it bore his weight. She took a seat opposite him, her long legs stretching out until her foot was beside his.

'Would you like to eat?' she asked.

It was a daft question in this empty, ancient room, but it was obvious she'd say whatever she wanted to say in her own sweet time. 'A drink would go down a treat,' he told her. 'I'm parched.'

She nodded and turned from him to the metal man, speaking a fluid stream of words. They sounded a little like the mages' tongue he'd heard in Mirror Town, but all twisted out of shape.

The thing seemed to understand. It jerked back into motion, creaking with each step as it moved to a doorless cupboard on the far side of the room, and pulled out a bottle from its top shelf.

'Do not fear,' she said. 'It has not decayed there for a thousand years. I brought it myself.'

He accepted a glass when the thing offered it to him, his hand cringing away from its strange, metallic skin. His first tentative sip revealed it to be some sort of whisky. It burned as it went down, and he was careful not to drink too much. A boy knew when he needed to keep his wits about him.

'What do you know of the Mortals?' she asked when she'd drained her own glass.

'They're the priests here, ain't they? Or I suppose the opposite of a priest, whatever that is. They hate all gods and they'll kill you for worshipping them.'

She nodded, resting her hand against her own goblet, but not raising it to drink. 'The first of them were priests of Mizhara in the Age of Chaos, when the war with Yron had just ended and this nation faced what it had done in her name, and the price it had paid to do it. They turned against her priests and killed them, but one saw a way to escape, to become a leader of this new age as she'd been a leader of the one she now understood was departed for ever. She amputated her own hands – or perhaps they were cut off by the mob, none can now remember. And she said that with the sacrifice of her hands she foreswore all use of the runes, any touch of magic or worship of gods. And she and the Mortals who followed her swore they would never again allow runes to be used or gods to be worshipped.'

Eric tipped the dregs of his drink to one side. He could see fragments of fungus floating in it, fallen from the device's skin. 'But you used the runes,' he said. 'You brought that thing alive.'

She shook her head. 'No, I merely knew how to command the eroagba, the metal man. The power was already in him – but only when Mizhara returned to this world did he awake.'

He'd suspected it, but hearing it confirmed still gave him a horrible jolt. 'Is she really back? Have you seen her?'

Her smile was too twisted to be happy. 'I saw her birth. Had you stayed in Salvation a few moments longer, you might have seen it too, though I think you were wise to flee when you did. I was only able to escape because of a brief weakness in the moment of her rebirth. She would not otherwise have suffered me to live.'

'Well, fair's fair. You did kill her the last time.'

'I did.' She looked down at the liquid in her goblet, golden eyes shaded. 'I did. And I will stop her again, if fate permits.'

'You're here for the God Killer. Now I think about it, that's what the rumours said Two Hands was after. That's why I came here to talk to you, without knowing who you really was. You've been hunting for it down here. But don't you know where it is? Ain't that what you used to kill her the first time?'

'No. Do you think Mizhara and Yron need a weapon to do harm to each other? It is not so. They each contain within themselves the seeds of their own destruction, and of their sibling's. The God Killer was made by humans for their own use.'

'But *you* killed Mizhara and you ain't her, or Yron.'

'Mizhara loved me once, and so she gave a large part of her power to me, and it was that I used to kill her. Love is a giving away of the self. Perhaps that is why Yron was always the weaker. He loved too freely. But the love I had is spent. I could not kill her now, not without the weapon we both seek.'

'You ain't found it, though, have you?'

'With your help, I can.'

'But it ain't just a weapon that can kill Mizhara, is it? It's a weapon for killing gods, and Krish is a god too. You never liked the moon no more than you liked the sun. Don't treat me like a cully. I'd be an idiot to help you find it. Krish don't even know his sister's back. All he wants with the God Killer is to stop other people using it on him.'

Her eyes were on Arwel now, where Eric least liked them. 'And what is your loyalty to the moon?'

'You know the answer – you're looking at him. Krish is the only one can keep my son safe. It was your lot tried to kill him. It was . . . it was Drut.'

'Drut. The wife you left for dead.'

He didn't like to be reminded of that. He'd spent a good few months trying not to think about those last moments with her, the awful betrayal in her eyes that he knew he'd earned every drop of. But now it was out there he had to know. 'Did she . . . did she die then? Did you see her before you went?'

'I saw her. And no, she is not dead. It is Mizhara who wants your child dead, Eric, it is true. But the moon is the reason for it. With neither sun nor moon in this world, your son could live in peace. He might perhaps even change to become what he should have been, an ordinary child of man and woman.'

She wasn't lying, he could tell. And it was horribly tempting. But Krish had been kind to him. Eric pictured him: that thin distrustful face, and the watchful eyes. It was the face of the poor peasant boy he'd so recently been. Krish hadn't asked to be a god, had he? Of course, maybe the new Mizhara hadn't chosen to be a god either, but Eric had never met her. If someone had to die to stop the war that was coming, it was going to have to be her.

'I won't kill Krish,' he said firmly. 'And I won't let you take the God Killer to do it yourself.'

She sighed and shut her eyes and he wondered if that was it, if the conversation was over. But then she said, 'Very well. Do you trust me, Eric?'

'What kind of question is that?'

'An honest one. Do you trust my word?'

It was ridiculous, but, 'I do.'

'Then I give you my word that, should we find the God Killer, I will not use it to kill your Lord Krishanjit, nor pass it to any other to do the same.'

There had to be some clever trick in the words, but he couldn't see it. 'Why do you need me anyway?' he asked. 'I've only just come here. I can't find my way back to bed, let alone to the God Killer.'

She rose, murmuring to the metal man until the light in its eyes died once more. 'Because I know where it is. But the weapon is magically locked away, and I do not possess the key.'

'And I do?'

She rested her hand against Arwel's cheek, so gentle Eric couldn't take exception to it. 'You do. The lock was made to be opened only if servants of Yron and Mizhara were in agreement – only if both had come to believe that their master and mistress must be stopped. To open it requires both a servant of the sun and a servant of the moon. That is why I have been waiting for you, Eric. That is why we must work together, or not at all.'

★

She took him deep, deep down. Even when the City Below had been a city above, he reckoned this place must have been buried. The corridors they walked were tiled or painted, and then bare but smooth and finally rough-walled and no more than tunnels through bare rock.

She seemed to know where she was going. The pale sun glow of the upper city faded, but she handed him a lamp to light his way and strode on ahead as if she didn't need it. And finally, when the air was beginning to feel both too thick and too thin, they came to a door.

There was no handle that he could see, only a golden disc in its centre inlaid with an obsidian rune with a handprint to either side of it.

'You tried kicking it down?' he asked.

'It cannot be broken, only opened. Your son can do what needs to be done.'

Arwel's hand looked absurdly small when Eric pressed it against the disk. It only filled the palm of the handprint and he wondered if this could work. But when the Hunter put her hand against the other side, the rune between them glowed brighter and brighter until his eyes watered from it. He felt something lick at the edges of his mind, a fragment of a memory that wasn't his, and then the rune had burned its way out and left a plain wooden handle in its place.

The Hunter hesitated. He didn't like to think what could make a person like her afraid. But he'd learned it was better to see the worst than dread it, and he reached for the handle himself. The door swung silently open and a yellow-gold light shone through. He covered his eyes at the brightness, momentarily struck blind.

When he could see again, he saw a city. It spread out beneath them, brilliant daylight reflecting from the gold-leafed surface of its towers and sparkling in its thousand fountains. The door had brought them out high up, perhaps at the highest point of the whole place. The wind whispered past, filled with the smell of spices whose taste he'd never known. It was the only sound. The whole place was eerily quiet and he realised that in all the great expanse below, he couldn't see a single person.

'Where *is* this?' he asked.

When the Hunter answered, her voice was choked with some strong emotion. 'The City Below in its time of glory, the place they once called Alangba Itunse, the home of lizards, and later Dara Ilu, the most beautiful of all cities.'

The buildings were all perfectly proportioned, both delicate and sturdy, pleasing to the eye in a way Eric couldn't fully explain. 'But how is it here? Or . . . or are we there?'

'It is an illusion, of course. The runes we woke created it.'

Now she'd said it, he could sense the power thrumming through the broad, tree-lined streets below, tugging the hairs on his arms upright. 'What are we supposed to do with it?'

'We are supposed to know where to go,' she said.

'Do you?'

'I believe I do. I believe we are to go to the house of those who created the God Killer.'

'And you know where that is?' The city spread below them was vast. It must have been home to a thousand thousand people, though not one of them trod the empty streets of this illusion.

'I can find it,' she said.

'You got a map?'

'I have no need of it. Dara Ilu was once my home.'

She strode along the path that led down from their hill. Eric followed, forcing himself not to look back. He suspected that if he did, the door they'd come through would be gone.

Her face was turned from him, drinking in the sight of a city she couldn't have seen in a millennium. He wondered what she felt.

'It *is* beautiful,' he said to her as they passed a square filled with statues of birds, their bodies made of wood and their wings lacquered in shades of blue and green that reminded him of the sea on the shores of distant Mirror Town. 'And the power – that's what cures the cullies who come to the City Below, ain't it? Don't seem to me like everything the gods do is evil.'

'No,' she said. 'The trap must be baited with cheese if the mouse is to venture inside. The gods offer much that we desire, and only ask us everything in return.'

He heard the sound of metal clinking and stepped aside as some strange long device trundled past, like a carriage without a horse, its wheels carved with runes. 'But Krish ain't Yron,' he said. 'The gods are reborn, ain't they? They're new people and every person is different. You've lived a thousand years with cullies like us. You know that better than me. And Krish don't want war. I don't reckon he even wants power. I think . . . I think he just wants to be left alone.'

She sighed. 'So did Yron in days gone by. And Mizhara desired health and prosperity for her people. They desire peace but they were made for war, and war will always come from them.'

Eric remembered Mirror Town. He remembered searching through the hospital tents and then searching through the bodies, and not finding what he was looking for. The battle had done for Lahiru and it hadn't even left Eric a corpse to bury. And he wasn't still the same boy who'd loved him but it didn't seem right that Lahiru wasn't in the world any more. It didn't really seem possible.

The streets around them narrowed, turning from broad avenues to winding lanes with a thin line of blue above them. From above he'd seen only the golden roofs, but here even the walls were faced with the metal, diamonds sparkling round the rims of the windows and doors in a display of extravagance that would have shamed even the great houses of Mirror Town.

'The folk what made the weapon had a few coin to spare, didn't they?' he said. 'Madam Aeronwen would have called this vulgar, and she had a pisspot lined with pearls.'

'These are the homes of the priests,' she told him.

She strode forward with confidence, though the houses all looked the same to him, left, right and right again until she stood before a diamond-rimmed door like all the rest. He reached out his hand to open it, but she laid hers on top of his. It startled him with its heat, or maybe its cold. The feeling was so intense it was hard to tell.

'Have a care, Eric. There may be traps inside. I will go first.'

He stepped back and let her push the door open.

A waft of cool air came out to greet them and with it the smell of nutmeg and freshly baked bread. There was a feeling in the air: the sense of living things. Unlike the rest of this deserted city, which had the lonely emptiness of a graveyard, this house felt inhabited. The Hunter stepped in, while he waited outside, stomach rumbling with the smell of food.

'Eric,' she said at last, 'please . . . please enter. I think we are both required.'

There was so much fear in her voice, going inside was the last thing he wanted. But he needed her if he and Arwel were ever going to get out of here. There was no way he'd find the path on his own. And even if he did, would the doorway open for only one of them?

As soon as he crossed the threshold, he saw her. It wasn't possible. He knew it wasn't. He'd left Drut bleeding on the white ice of Salvation. But here she was, beautiful golden face just as he remembered, staring back at him more calmly than he could understand. And she didn't look once at their son – didn't even seem to notice him, cuddled tight in Eric's arms.

The Hunter stood to her side, frozen.

'Do you see her too?' he asked.

'I see . . . I see Mizhara.'

The person, or illusion, or whatever she was, stepped back and beckoned them deeper into the room. There was a rug on the floor showing a tree with seven branches and a different fruit on each branch. It was soft beneath Eric's feet as he stepped forward. In each corner of the room a metal man stood. They were a bit like the one that had served him his drink, only these weren't broken and half-rotted away. They'd been polished to a fine shine and someone had put blank obsidian masks over their heads, where a person's face would be. They gave Eric the shivers.

'This is a test,' the Hunter said.

'You have to answer one question, Eric. Answer it truthfully and you can pass.' Drut's voice was soft and sad as if he'd disappointed her but she was willing to give him a second chance. It couldn't be her. The last time they'd been together she'd been half out of her mind.

'Did she just tell you to answer a question?' he asked the Hunter.

She nodded. 'And answer it truthfully.'

'What if the truth ain't what she wants to hear?'

'I always want the truth from you, husband,' Drut said, and Eric flinched. He hadn't precisely been honest with her in the time they'd been together.

'I won't lie to you no more,' Eric told her. 'I never meant to hurt you.'

Drut smiled, so affectionate it made him ashamed. 'Then tell me – do you love me, or hate me?'

He didn't hate her. He didn't and he never had. He just hadn't felt for her what he'd let her think he did. But there were different kinds of love, weren't there? He might be a molly who couldn't care for a woman the way a normal man could, but he was a father and she was the mother of his baby. 'I love you,' he said, just as the Hunter whispered, 'I hate you,' and in the moment they'd finished speaking the vision of Drut was gone and the metal men at each corner of the room jerked into life.

The nearest metal man raised its arm, sun glinting on golden cogs as they turned, and Eric saw that there was a sword in it. He yelled and dodged aside as the blade came slicing down towards his head. He didn't have a weapon, but there was a knife on the table left over from some ancient meal. He grabbed it in sweat-slickened palms and slashed out wildly.

The blade did nothing, bouncing from the arm and leaving not a scratch behind. The things both turned, slow but relentless, and began to follow him as he flung himself as far from them as he could, which wasn't far at all. The room they'd trapped them in was small, and where the door had been now there was only a blank wall.

The Hunter faced two metal men of her own. They raised their creaking arms in unison and she moved in a blur of inhuman speed that took her from between the creatures and let their blades strike each other.

At least that seemed to do them some harm. Eric tried the trick himself, luring them in and flinging himself aside. But he was too slow, and two deep cuts opened on his arms, accompanied by the rusty creak of metal.

The sound – it nagged at him as the metal men's weapons

rose and fell while sweat slicked his body and he felt his strength begin to fade with frightening speed. But then he twigged: the metal men *creaked*, like they were half-broken. And they moved awkwardly too, their motions jerky.

This was an illusion. Of course it was. And the metal men fighting them were a thousand years old. They couldn't be in much better nick than the fungus-encrusted thing that had served his drink. He stopped trying to hit their smooth metal chests and aimed for the joints instead, where rust and wear must make them weak. Another strike, another dodge, another wound – and then at last his knife dug deep, between the joint of metal wrist and metal hand, and the hand fell free.

While he stopped to stare at the fallen hand, astonished it had worked, the other metal man was on him. Eric managed to twist away from one blow so only the flat of the blade hit him, knocking him back and savagely bruising his cheek. And then the blade rose again and he had no more strength to avoid it. He raised his knife weakly and stared into the jewel-red eyes.

The eyes dimmed as a sword – one of *their* swords, wrenched from a severed hand – swung and took its head from its shoulder. It took only a few moments more for the fight to end. The Hunter moved with all the speed and grace he remembered, and when she took the last metal head from the last metal shoulders, everything changed.

The head landed on the ground, not ringing on tiles but softly on a mud-caked floor, cushioned by fungus. They were right back where they'd started, in a rocky tunnel with a dying lamp.

'What happened?' Eric asked. He looked at his arms, hoping his injuries had also been an illusion, but the deep gashes were still seeping blood.

'We failed the last test,' the Hunter said.

'One of us lied?'

'Or both of us did.'

'So it was all for nothing.'

'No. Now we have defeated the guardians, the way is clear.' She stepped aside and he saw that behind her the door hung open.

'So we can just go in? Get the God Killer.'

She nodded, staring into the darkness beyond the door.

He didn't want to step into that darkness. On the other hand, he didn't want *her* to step in and claim the weapon first. He trusted her not to lie to him, but he didn't believe she'd told him the whole truth. People got wily as they aged, and she was older than anyone who'd ever been.

When he stepped through the doorway, he felt the space before he saw it, a sense of openness, of a ceiling high above and distant walls. The dim light of the lamp did little to illuminate it. The chamber revealed itself a little at a time as he walked through.

It was circular, its roof a sphere, though the apex was far too distant to see. Like some of the houses of Mirror Town it was faced with mosaic, but these seemed made of some harder material than stone or glass. Though this room must have been here, sealed, for a thousand years, there wasn't a sign of age or decay on any of it. The mosaic's bright colours shone in the torchlight, but he couldn't make any sense of them. They were a great scrambled mess, green mixed in with red and purple and umber and many other colours he hadn't learned to name.

It was almost painful to look at, like staring at the sun. And besides, it didn't seem the weapon was hung on the walls. He guessed it would be in the centre of the hall, beneath the peak of the dome.

The floor was smoothed rock with a dusting of grit. He had to watch his feet as he walked. He'd gone a good long way before he looked up and saw the plinth. It was just where he'd thought it would be, in the middle of the great chamber and carved from a white-gold marble.

The Hunter must have caught sight of it at the same time and they walked to it together.

'That's not the God Killer, is it?' Eric asked. 'That big lump of marble.'

But he already knew the answer. The Hunter ran her fingers over the centre of the plinth, where there was a deep depression in the marble. It was clear it had been made to hold something, a rod, perhaps, or a spear. But whatever it had been made to hold was gone.

'Someone has taken it,' the Hunter said. 'Someone else has the God Killer.'

20

'Hold still,' Olufemi said, grasping Yemisi's arm.

'I'm cold,' Yemisi complained, 'and it's wet.'

The mine *was* both cold and damp. Ill-lit too, as they'd only thought to bring one lamp and it was near to extinction. But the pursuit they'd expected to shake by hiding underground had proven far too persistent.

'Hold still,' Olufemi said again and this time Yemisi obeyed her.

There was a moment of quiet, filled only by a distant almost musical dripping. But soon another percussive sound joined it: echoing footsteps on rock.

'Maybe they aren't following us,' Yemisi said. 'Maybe they never were. We've never seen them, have we?'

They hadn't. But ever since that day at the woodland shrine to unknown gods, Olufemi had sensed them as she'd sensed the wrongness in the air of that place. She'd known that somewhere, an unwanted attention had focused on her, and over the following week she'd sensed it drawing closer. Someone knew about their visit to the shrine and wanted them dead before they could tell of what they'd seen.

She reached for the runes, as she'd done a dozen times before. And as had happened every previous time, the shape of them twisted in her mind and an unheard note rang out between her ears, so powerfully distracting it shattered her concentration. But for once, the force opposing her felt not entirely immovable. She sensed a weakness in it, a fading out of its influence ahead.

'We go deeper,' she told Yemisi.

Yemisi made one of her many sour faces, but she didn't

disagree. The footsteps behind them were louder now. They were very close.

After fifty paces, their lamp spluttered and died, but they weren't left in total darkness. A blue moss clung to the walls in ragged patches and glowed with a sickly light. There were insects too, as there were everywhere in this land. But these were misshapen, antennae too long and too many and their eyes smooth where they should be many-faceted, gleaming like drops of oil in the pale blue light.

Or perhaps the insects weren't misshapen; perhaps they were merely newly shaped. It was a thought that had been growing in Olufemi's mind over the course of their flight, as she'd seen more and more of this blight over the land. The more she saw of it, the more purposeful it seemed. Something was being torn down, but something else was being built.

'When can we stop?' Yemisi asked. 'I can't hear them any more.'

The footsteps had faded along with the nagging presence of their pursuers in Olufemi's mind. The light was fading too, the patches of glowing moss growing more and more sparse as they walked on. As they walked *upward*. Her legs ached, old joints resenting the additional exertion.

She felt a tug in the empty place inside her mind that she kept to build the runes. When she reached for them this time they came more easily: Yaq for clarity and Häwt for eye, which combined should allow her to see in this darkness. She held them for a moment in her mind, a perfect form, and then they twisted to escape her grasp and she let them go. The floor was smooth enough here: they didn't need light. And she had no wish to pay the moon's price for unnecessary magic. Yemisi was a daily reminder of how high that price could be.

There was another presence too. Olufemi sensed them sliding through the bones of the earth: Yron's servants, the worm men. But they weren't her enemy and she saw only the distant gleam of their eyes, quickly retreating.

'I can't see anything,' Yemisi complained.

'Then put your hand against the wall.' The floor beneath

their feet was rougher now, unpolished by years of human footsteps as their entryway had been. Olufemi stumbled but didn't let it slow her. She yearned for what lay ahead, a thing that had been denied her for weeks now and whose absence had gnawed at her in a way she hadn't quite noticed until it promised to return.

'Oh, there's light!' Yemisi exclaimed. 'This *is* the way out.'

It took several twists and turns and a long hard climb before the cave mouth itself became visible: a ragged circle of light in the darkness. They stumbled out, onto a ledge halfway up a small slope of scree.

The instant they emerged, Olufemi knew why the runes had returned to her. Only a hundred paces ahead of them lay a border, as clearly marked as a line on a map. For those hundred paces the ground was rock and scrub, malformed plants growing over the detritus of mining that covered much of this area.

Beyond, the earth was in riotous bloom. Olufemi couldn't call it a meadow, though she saw the green of grass among the rainbow of colours. But no meadow had ever been so filled with flowers, climbing over and twining around each other in their quest to turn their blossoms sunward.

Whatever had warped the plants and beasts behind them was absent here. But the fields ahead, bursting with life, were as unnatural in their own way. Olufemi touched the runes for comfort as they crossed the border into this new strangeness.

★

It had been late morning when they emerged from the mine. Travelling here was slow, with the ground so densely covered. At first they'd made some effort to avoid the most flamboyant of the flowers, but there were simply too many of them. And when Olufemi looked behind them she saw no trail. The plants had sprung back up again as if they'd never known human feet.

It was late afternoon by the time they found their first sign of habitation. What had been a wild profusion became orderly rows, the blooms no longer jumbled together but separated by type and colour into neat fields. The house was beyond the last of them, a plain white structure, entirely square. She supposed ornament would have been superfluous here.

The final field was the largest. She thought it a vineyard at first, until they were walking between its furrows and she saw that the plants clinging to the ranks of canes were roses. The smell of them was overpoweringly sweet.

When she and Yemisi came to the house, they found it deserted. It seemed to have been a hasty departure. As they wandered the empty rooms, they found a dinner half-eaten on silver plates, the food crawling with maggots. And then they left the house through its back door and realised there'd been no departure at all.

'Oh,' Yemisi said. 'Oh, that's horrible.'

Whatever had happened hadn't been recent. The blood that had spewed from mouths and noses to stain the floor was black and the corpses rotting. Insects swarmed, dismantling what little remained of their flesh.

'We should leave,' Olufemi said.

Yemisi nodded, a hand clutched over her mouth and nose. They didn't stop to loot the dead.

They walked onward more cautiously, hiding between the rose vines where they could, but they found no living people, only more empty farms. Some of them held corpses; others were entirely deserted. The buzz of the feasting insects was everywhere and Olufemi could smell the stench of it even when they were in the flower-filled fields.

'Is it them? Did they follow us across the border?' Yemisi asked.

'Don't be ridiculous, these people have been dead far too long. And I'm not certain they died by violence.'

'How else?'

'Disease.'

Yemisi shuddered. 'A disease that kills so fast? And everyone at once? Olufemi, let's not go near the houses any more.'

Olufemi didn't disagree. They stayed in the fields, where the cloying smell of the flowers was preferable to the alternative. The blooms invaded even her dreams, a meadow through which she ran and ran but never fast enough, though she didn't know what was chasing her, or why she feared it so much. It was the same the next two nights, though each time she sensed that her pursuer was coming closer. In the days, though, they saw no one. Only the endless fields.

On the third day, the fields began to dissolve into wildness. The same plants grew, but no longer in orderly ranks. Walking became difficult, with tangles of roots snagging their feet and thorny branches catching at their clothes. They were often forced to backtrack.

'We shouldn't have come here,' Yemisi said when they found their path blocked by a fallen tree.

It was about as useless a statement as any that could be made, and Olufemi chose to ignore it. The tree had a silver trunk and its leaves were a bright burnished copper. It was very beautiful. All the trees and shrubs and plants here were beautiful, but the profusion turned the beauty into something almost ugly. It was all too much.

After the tree their path led them down, towards a stream gurgling over rounded rocks. They stooped to drink gratefully and refilled their flasks. But the water did nothing for the hollow in Olufemi's stomach. They'd eaten the last of their food yesterday. There was fruit hanging from many of the trees and berries on the bushes, but they hadn't dared taste them. Their bright colours seemed too deceptively inviting.

At the other side of the stream the slope rose steeply and Olufemi was forced to accept Yemisi's help as she tried to scramble up. At times like these, Olufemi found it hard not to resent Yemisi's youth, for all that it had cost her. She seemed barely to have suffered from the exertion of their travels despite her many complaints. Olufemi felt every day of it in the dull ache of her joints.

Yet something seemed to be drawing her on. She'd only slowly become aware of it, this unseen tug in her gut. She'd dismissed it at first as a yearning to be home. But now it flared into life far stronger than before. It was magic: the moon's magic.

'Do you . . . do you feel it?' Yemisi asked. She'd stopped at the top of the rise and was peering ahead, shading her eyes from the midday sun. 'There. I think it's coming from there.'

The blur on the horizon was hard to make out at first, but as they drew nearer it became clear what it was: a vast wall, stretching from horizon to horizon.

'Oh no. We'll have to go around it,' Yemisi said.

'No,' Olufemi told her. 'I felt the power too – and that's its source. We need to look closer.'

Could Krishanjit have come to Ofiklanod? But the power didn't feel like his, not as she'd last known him. It was far more ancient and . . . less human somehow. This was a god without the clothing of a man.

The sun had travelled to the horizon by the time they approached the wall. Up close, she could see that it had once been made of a soft red brick. It stretched three times a woman's height to be topped with spikes of crystal. The spikes remained in some places, glowing red in the setting sun, but in most the brick wall was half crumbled, sometimes gone entirely. Where brick had crumbled, the wall had been rebuilt in stone. Patchwork, it still looked too sheer to climb.

But by some coincidence – or perhaps by no coincidence at all – Olufemi and Yemisi had emerged before the wall's ancient gates. A carving topped them, long since worn away. Only the eyes remained, gleaming silver.

'I know where this is!' Yemisi said. 'I read about it when . . . when I was young the first time. This is the Garden of Yron. The ancient mages built it to contain him, but the moon's power can't truly be imprisoned and he escaped.'

Olufemi stepped closer, close enough to touch the wall. The brick was cool beneath her fingers, despite the sunlight that had beaten on it all day. The surface was rough and grooved. She brushed aside brick dust and saw that it had been carved with a complex inter-linking of runes.

'What are they?' Yemisi asked.

Olufemi followed the carving round. It was faded in places, crumbled away entirely in others. 'Here is Kat, flesh.' She ran her fingers round the curved shape of it and felt the power grow in her mind, sparkling bright and then fading as she moved on. 'Täyt, voice, and Yax, weakness. But here is strength too, Yae. And Yu and Yar and Yagh and Gäml and Hoy. I believe all the glyphs are here, bound somehow.'

'Do you think it stretches all the way around the walls?'

'It must. A working of enormous power. But such would be required to hold the moon in check.'

'But why—' Yemisi said, just as Olufemi realised that she could hear footsteps behind her, the swish of legs striding through grass.

She spun, clasping Yemisi's arm to silence her, but she could see that it was already too late. The newcomers were mere paces behind them. If Olufemi hadn't been so absorbed in the study of the walls, she would have heard them sooner. But this had always been her greatest fault: too focused on the rock to see the spider beneath it.

There were a dozen or so of them, most in the long skirts of Ofiklanod men, with weapons hung at their sides and a long thin leather shield strapped to one arm. The figure in front was different. Olufemi couldn't say whether it was man or woman, swaddled as it was in black robes and a black veil. The figure gestured at the men behind to stop and Olufemi saw that its arm – that each arm – ended in a sealed stump.

'You are strangers here?' the newcomer said. He was almost certainly male, to judge by the depth of his voice.

Yemisi nodded before Olufemi could stop her. The man had spoken Ashane: a language no one in this land should know. But the man had spoken it in the expectation that they'd understand.

'I did not know,' he said, 'that travellers had come here yet, so far south.'

There were Ashane in this land besides them? Olufemi couldn't imagine how it had happened, but a woman who is drowning takes the rope that's thrown her. 'We travelled fast,' she lied.

'Ah yes. But, forgive me, you are not of the northlands, are you? I believe you are – please, please forgive me – I believe you are exiles of Nkankan-lati-Ohunkohun.'

'We're from Mirror Town,' Yemisi said, which was usefully neither a lie nor a confirmation, but the veiled man nodded anyway.

'And you, I think, you understand the runes.'

They'd been caught staring at them and talking about them and Olufemi couldn't know how much had been overheard or understood. A lie was too dangerous. 'We have a passing knowledge, yes.'

The veil shifted in what was unmistakeably a smile. 'You do. You do. Good. Good good good. But how rude of me, to leave you standing. Come, come with me, I can offer food, drink. You must be weary after your long travels. A bed too if you need it. Everything you could want.'

Surrounded as he was by armed men, it wasn't an offer they could refuse. They walked with him through flowered fields and around the high walls as he asked question after question: about Mirror Town today, about its history, about the runes. There was no reason to be suspicious of his curiosity, but Olufemi's instinct for distrust had kept her alive all these years and she didn't intend to abandon it here of all places. She answered as sparingly as she could, which was still more revealingly than she would have chosen.

She would have liked to ask questions of her own, but how to do it without revealing the extent of her own ignorance? She and Yemisi should have known far more than they did, if they'd entered the country from the north, as she'd gleaned that he believed. So far all she'd truly learned was his name: Rorön.

'And did you find the country much changed on your travels?' he asked, as they entered the outskirts of a small settlement. It seemed a temporary affair, half composed of tents and half of simple white paper cubes. 'Nkankan-lati-Ohunkohun – forgive me, I mean to say Mirror City – was that its name?'

'Mirror Town,' Yemisi said.

'Ah yes, Mirror Town. It is much unlike our cities, I think?'

'It's made of rock, not paper,' Olufemi said. 'But as for how things have changed, I couldn't say. I wasn't alive when the exile happened.'

'Of course! A foolish question, I'm sorry. Ah, but we're here, and the food and drink I promised can finally be had. Excuse me a moment, if you will, and I will send for it.'

He bustled towards the middle tent, robes swishing, and the guards dispersed. It left Olufemi feeling a little less threatened but no less observed. Curious faces turned their way all over the camp and she sensed hidden eyes peering from behind tent flaps.

'This isn't good,' Yemisi whispered. 'Or is it? They seem not to mind that we're here.'

'It appears they've opened their borders, although why . . . Could Krishanjit have arranged it? There's far too much we don't understand. And—'

But Rorön was back already. 'In here!' he said. 'It's not a feast, I fear, but good food, food and drink for the thirsty. Come.' He beckoned them inside one of the larger tents, where a meal that looked very much like a feast to Olufemi had been laid out. Cushions were piled around it. 'Sit! Eat!' he said.

Yemisi obeyed instantly, not even pausing to wash her hands before she stuffed her mouth with fruit. Juices dribbled down her chin and she wiped them with her sleeve. Olufemi blushed for her but the veiled man didn't seem to notice. He'd turned to welcome more people into the tent, each of them also swathed in black robes.

The smell of the food was pungent and oddly familiar. The same spices were used in Mirror Town, perhaps the very same dishes served. Olufemi helped herself to a sliver of honey-smeared meat and the taste of it was like home. A painful wave of longing washed over her.

'Palm wine too,' the man said and gestured for a servant to fill her cup.

It wouldn't be wise to let the drink overtake her, not here, but no water was on offer and she was too parched to refuse. She sipped cautiously as the other robed figures arranged themselves around the rug. A servant knelt beside each of them, carving the food they gestured to with handless arms and delicately lifting the pieces beneath their masters' veils. It was an unsettling process to watch, like babies being fed, but here the power lay with the most seemingly helpless. When one of the servants opened her mouth to yawn, the root of a severed tongue wriggled in its back.

Olufemi looked away. 'May we be introduced?' she asked Rorön, nodding towards the other robed figures.

'Of course, yes, how very rude. We are the Mortal Council of the South.'

Her expression must have been betrayingly blank, because his smile widened as if her ignorance pleased him.

'You have not heard the Mortal name? No, no, of course – why ever should you? Well then, we are guardians of the Ofiklanod way,' he said. 'We keep our people true to the path we set after the war between those whose names we do not speak. In short, we guard against gods and the love of gods.'

'And what do you do if you find any?' Yemisi asked.

He laughed. 'Why, we chastise those who've fallen to their worship and advise them to change their path.'

Olufemi remembered the village that had tried to burn them alive and thought she finally understood why they'd acted as they had. It hadn't been fear of them but of these veiled god-hunters that had driven them to attempted murder.

'We came here from the north and saw you not,' a woman to her left said. Her accent as she spoke Ashane was far thicker than Rorön's. 'Which way did you come?'

'From the south, I think,' Olufemi said. 'I'm afraid we've been lost and wandering.'

It seemed a good excuse but at her words there was a sudden tense stillness and she remembered the houses full of corpses. How could they not have seen them if they'd passed through those fields? And why would they not mention them?

Only the truth would seem innocent. 'There were bodies there. Many of them. Do you know what happened to them?' she asked.

Did you kill them? was the obvious, unvoiced question. She wished she could see their faces. The woman who replied in her thick accent gave nothing away. 'A disease. A plague.'

'A vicious one to leave none living,' Olufemi said, or tried to say, but the words came out jumbled. She tried to say them again and only managed a quiet hum. Her vision had begun to blur and her head drooped helplessly towards her chest.

'Do you feel unwell?' the woman asked, and then something more, but Olufemi couldn't hear it. There was a fever in her blood, burning all thought out of her head, and she groaned and fell back against the cushion, surrendering to the darkness.

21

Krish had decided to go on the day of the burning, when all of Täm's residents returned to their homes – even many of the Mortals charged with guarding the Garden. It was a slim hope that they'd leave the place entirely untended, but they couldn't afford to wait longer.

It was a long way from their small hostel in the city to the Garden on its outskirts and they set out with the dawn. Their path took them through the streets of the Third Hill, flanked by high-walled houses painted with flowers and fruits. The inhabitants stood idle as their servants filed in and out of their homes, bringing their possessions to a safe distance in their low-hedged gardens. Krish saw chairs carved from a red wood polished to a shine and lacquered boards for eating and many cages holding pet insects, the cages and the insects equally bejewelled.

The owners had leisure to gossip but Krish only caught snatches of their conversation as he passed. It was all about the poor of the parks. Beneath the easy movements of a routine task carried out without much thought there was an undercurrent of fear. Disease had entered the city with the refugees and everyone was waiting for the moment it would spread beyond the parks.

Below the Third Hill lay the Gulch, a deep ravine where the City Above came closest to the City Below. The closeness pleased no one and here the people were far poorer, though still able to cling on to the status of a standing home. The houses themselves were blank squares of paper, clustered together like cells in a honeycomb. Their inhabitants seemed bee-like too, busy and angry as they moved their few possessions to waiting carts. The houses here were clustered too closely for it to be safe to remain nearby and a steady stream of carts rattled over the narrow streets and upward to safer ones.

The Gulch was long and the houses grew shabbier as it progressed. Some had tears in their sides with more paper patched over them. The paper panels too were being carefully removed and stacked on carts alongside their owners' possessions. Paper was cheap in Ofiklanod, but not cheap enough for these people to waste. Some of them paused to stare at Krish and Dinesh and he realised that here, even their plain clothes marked them as too rich. They lowered their heads and hurried on.

Finally the Gulch sloped upward and the houses thinned out as the mud of the street gave way to scrubby grass. There was no clear border to Fotil Park. Its margins were marked only by the thickening grass beneath their feet.

The poor of the parks seemed every bit the mob that the rest of the city considered them. There were no houses to evacuate here and few possessions to preserve. Home was no more than a folded tube of paper, carried on its owner's back, and the people all looked strangely hunched as they stood in groups and talked.

It was angry talk. Krish didn't blame them. They'd fled here from plague and famine expecting help and found only rejection.

As Krish and Dinesh emerged from the park, the burning began. He'd read about it in the books that Renar had given him: a cleansing of the city by fire and then sunlight so the worm men couldn't come. But it wasn't the way he'd imagined it. It was no orderly process, with every fire lit at some prearranged signal. He supposed to them it was as ordinary and necessary as pissing.

The fires started one by one, flares of light brief but bright across the city, and then a puff of silvery smoke in the sky. The first fires seemed to spark the rest and soon there were scores of flames, then hundreds. The houses on the street they were walking were lit too, torches touched to the paper walls. The flames caught quickly, racing outward as the paper curled and flaked into ash.

Now the city was united, low red embers in some places and dancing flames in others, but everywhere on fire. It was a cleaner death than the one Smiler's Fair had suffered, what felt like a very long time ago. The Fair had begun to rise again and so would Täm, though far more quickly. Rolls of paper leaned beside each pile of possessions, ready to be put into place once the wind had cleared the cinders.

He was startled to realise that he liked Ofiklanod. He'd circled the world and seen deserts and mountains but never once found a place he felt he belonged. He shouldn't belong here either, but something deep inside him felt he did. There was a comfort he didn't quite understand in the strange greens and purples of the grass. In the very shape of the hills. A part of him he didn't want to acknowledge recognised this as the land of his birth.

The burning had left ash in the air, weightless and pale, but Täm was already rebuilding itself. As they reached the outskirts of the city, paper walls were slotted into frames and possessions carried back into houses. Maybe that was the other reason he felt so comfortable here. Ofiklanod, alone among the nations he'd visited, had access to its past but had chosen to forget it.

Finally they left Täm behind altogether. Most of the city had no clear limits, just roads leading into fields with building clustered around them – except in this one place. Here the streets themselves ended, orange lacquer giving way abruptly to grass. And there were no fields, just a large meadow and, at its far end, a wall.

Krish stared at the green tops of the trees he could see beyond the wall. 'I don't know why the Mortals didn't just destroy the place a thousand years ago when they buried the City Below.'

Dinesh grinned, delighted to have information to share. 'It's said they've been trying to destroy it for a thousand years, but the wood won't burn or be cut. And when the, the, the grass is cut it grows back straight away. The Garden is full of mysteries.'

'But you remember the map?' They hadn't dared carry it with them. If they were caught without it they could claim to be lost or foolish adventurers. With it there'd be no excuses to make.

Dinesh tapped a hand against his forehead. 'Yes, my prince, I remember it.'

The entrance to the Garden lay to their west, guarded even today. But the map had shown another way in, a river that flowed through the Garden north to south. They walked its banks now, thickly clustered with flowers. Their destination lay ahead: an arch in the brickwork of the great wall that allowed the river to flow through.

'Oh,' Dinesh said, 'there's no gap at the top. I, I, I thought there'd be a gap.'

Krish had hoped so too, but the river must be in full spate and its waters filled the arch. 'We'll just have to dive under,' he said.

Dinesh turned to stare at him, alarmed. 'But you can't swim.'

'Then you'll have to help me.'

The river was icy-cold when they plunged into it, despite the rising heat of the day. It shocked the breath out of Krish's body, and he had a moment of mindless panic before his feet found the muddy bottom and he raised his head above the water and gasped. His linen skirt swirled heavily around his legs.

Dinesh floated on his back beside him, eyes closed as he raised his face to the sun. There was a childlike happiness about him in that moment. Krish wondered if this was how he'd played in the swampy rivers of his homeland before he'd grown old enough to be put to work as a slave.

'How thick are the walls?' Krish asked.

'The map didn't say. I'm sorry.'

Watching the water rush beneath that arch filled Krish with dread. He tried to remind himself that he could no longer be hurt but it didn't much help. He could still imagine drowning, the terror of it. And what if that was a way he *could* be harmed? What if only other people couldn't hurt him?

'Take my hand,' Dinesh said.

His fingers felt hard against Krish's, still scarred and calloused from his years of labour. There was a surprising strength in him too. He always seemed so vulnerable, so in need of care. But here Dinesh would have to look after Krish and Krish would have to let him.

'Just kick with your, your, your legs,' Dinesh said. 'Up and down, you see.' He demonstrated, splashing muddy water over them both.

Krish had to swallow hard before he could reply. 'I'll try.'

'It's all right,' Dinesh said and then with sudden fierceness, 'I would never let anything happen to you.'

'Let's do it then,' Krish said, and sucked as much air as he could into his lungs before he could change his mind.

It took everything he had to force his head under the water. He'd meant to keep his eyes open, but the water stung sharply and all he could do was squeeze them shut, squeeze his mouth shut, and kick his legs as Dinesh had shown him.

It didn't feel as if he was moving. He opened his eyes a moment but all he could see was brown and bubbles and he no longer felt certain which way was up. Panic seized him then and his kicks became desperate, thrashing. His only anchor was Dinesh's hand and he clung to that and hoped it would be enough to save him.

His chest burned with the need to draw breath. He resisted and resisted until he couldn't resist any longer and in the moment his mouth gasped open his head broke through the water. He drew in a lungful half of air and half of water, convulsing with coughs as Dinesh doggedly dragged him to shore.

After that he could only lie on the shore on his back until the shivering and the mind-silencing panic had gone. When he finally opened his eyes, it was to Dinesh sitting above him, gazing down at him with smiling eyes.

'I told you I'd take care of you, my prince,' he said.

'And you did.' Krish forced himself to sit upright and look around.

He'd expected something odder. All the books they could find had spoken of the Garden of Yron as a place of mystery and paradox and danger, but they seemed to have emerged at one edge of a simple orchard. The trees were in fruit, knotty branches weighed down by clusters of red-skinned apples.

'The map called this Bim Bomen, the skeleton orchard,' Dinesh said.

'And which way should we go?'

'Through it.'

They were forced to stoop below the branches of the low trees. The smell of overripe apples grew strong as their feet crunched on fallen fruit and wasps clustered to feed where they'd trodden. A little further in and something different crunched underfoot, harder and more brittle. White fragments were visible beneath the grass and Krish realised what they were walking on.

The whole place was carpeted with bones, some little more than meal and some far more intact. Beside one dark-trunked tree, a skeleton hand clasped the remains of a still-rotting apple, and Krish was glad he hadn't tried to eat the fruit. It seemed they weren't the only ones who'd entered the Garden by this route, but many had made it no further.

After the orchard came a pond fringed with lilies. Stepping stones led across it from the orchard to a crumbling brick path at the other end, but Dinesh shook his head as Krish made to cross. When they walked around it, he saw dark shapes moving beneath the still water, far larger than the pond should have been able to hold.

The brick path was lined with drooping willows whose leaves murmured in the wind. Catkins draped the path and a dense, musky smell wafted from them. The more Krish smelled it, the more certain he became that there were words in the murmur of the leaves. If he could just stop – if he could walk closer – he might be able to understand them. But Dinesh led him on to walk through a garden of sculptures.

'Oh,' Dinesh said. 'They're, they're, they're fucking.'

The sculptures weren't all human, but every one of them was engaged in some act of love. Lion-faced men had been carved gently caressing the bodies of wolf-headed women and a beautiful young man crouched on all fours as a thick-bodied woman rutted behind him with a rod strapped to her hips. Elsewhere the statues fucked in groups, or gave themselves pleasure while creepers twined all around the silver-flecked stone.

There was something about the sculptures that invited

inspection. Krish felt as if they *wanted* to be watched. And he felt something else too: a sense of familiarity, as if he'd been here before. No, more than that. As if he'd been here often.

When Dinesh told him to take the left-hand path at the end of the sculptures, Krish was already turning in that direction. 'My herb garden,' he said, before they walked into it.

The herbs had overgrown their neat rows, meeting and melting into a mass of different greens and browns and purples. Or perhaps they'd always been that way. He recognised rosemary and thyme and the smell of wild garlic but others were entirely foreign, although when he looked at them, he could precisely conjure up their taste.

They stopped to rest in a meadow ringed with benches carved from amber. The orange glowed warmly in the midday sun, lace-winged dragonflies trapped inside it, and Krish was surprised to realise how long they'd been walking. With the realisation came a sudden thirst. There was a well at the centre of the meadow with a wooden bucket swinging above it. It was untouched by rot and he wondered if it was the Mortals who'd placed it there. It seemed impossible it could have stayed whole for a thousand years, but this was a place of impossible things.

'I'll get water,' Dinesh said, but Krish shook his head. It would be too easy to become used to having a servant. And he could never let himself forget that Dinesh hadn't chosen this service.

The well was deep. The winch's rope was nearly at its end before he heard the splash of bucket hitting water. He pulled the lever to wind it up again, but something resisted him, although the rope was passing cleanly through its drum. He tugged on it one last time, then leaned over the lip of the well to see if something had snagged it below.

There was nothing: only the wide circle of water, the narrower circle of the bucket's rim still beneath its surface, and in the very centre the reflected circle of his own face, made silvery by the water. He tugged on the rope again and ripples spread from the bucket. They shook the reflection, so that the face seemed to move and come alive.

As Krish watched, mesmerised, the face smiled. 'Ah, so that's who I'll become,' it said. It spoke the language of the mages.

'Yron,' Krish said.

The face smiled. It was long and thin, high-cheekboned. Krish had seen it before, carved into the rocks of the high plains.

'Are you here?' Krish asked. 'Or am I there? Or then?'

'Yes,' Yron replied. His face was clearer now. He was only a little older than Krish, but he looked far merrier.

'I don't know what I'm doing,' Krish told him. 'I didn't ask to be you.'

Yron's grin widened. 'Neither did I, yet here we are. They build these walls around us and never call them a prison. But they don't understand that the walls enclose the world and the only freedom is inside them.'

'But how can I—' Krish said, and then he felt a touch against his back and looked round to see Dinesh. When he looked back in the water, only his own face stared back, and the bucket began to lift as soon as he pulled its rope.

'Were you talking to someone?' Dinesh asked.

'Only myself,' Krish told him.

They set off again as soon as they'd drunk the surprisingly sweet-tasting water. Dinesh didn't need to direct Krish any more. He turned left past palm trees filled with long-necked pink birds and threaded a path through a foul-smelling marsh whose waters sparkled in a thousand rainbow colours.

'We're nearly there,' Dinesh said at last, and Krish had known that too. The centre of the Garden was a copse, the trees so dense that little sunlight penetrated between them and no plants grew in the bare earth between their feet. The trees themselves were all the same, the silvery trunks of birches with dark silver leaves and roots that rose above the ground to tangle with each other.

They had to watch their feet as they walked, and only the sudden and jarring sound of voices warned them that they'd reached their destination at last.

Krish pulled Dinesh down to hide in the lee of one of the thick roots. The Mortals were less than twenty paces from them, and twenty paces beyond that was the building they'd come here to find.

Building didn't seem quite the right word for it, though. It hadn't been made; it had grown, its walls formed of the trees around them, branches twisted together to make beams and tall ferns forming its walls. The trees here weren't the same silver as the rest of the copse. They seemed diseased, blotches of a sickly-looking orange on their trunks. And the ferns were overgrown with another plant, three-leafed, that seemed intent on strangling them.

It was impossible to tell the place's size from this one wall and the map had given no plan of the place, only its location. Krish felt oddly reluctant to enter it, but they had no choice.

The Mortals didn't seem to be taking their watch duty very seriously. Perhaps they thought the Garden on its own was guard enough against unwelcome visitors. They stood in the shadow of the building for a short while, talking idly about the latest crop of palm hearts from Bundanik and the recent high price of Makat's shellack. After a while, a voice called to them from somewhere out of sight and they sauntered idly towards it, still discussing crops and markets.

'How do we get in?' Dinesh asked when it was safe to speak.

'Through the walls, maybe.' Krish's skin rebelled against the thought of touching those weed-choked ferns, but when his hands brushed them, the strangling grip of the vines loosened and the ferns moved easily aside. Beyond was a room, its floor of roots and its roof more branches. The walls were ornately carved with scenes of writhing bodies not unlike the statues they'd seen earlier. When he touched them, he realised they too were living wood. But there was some sickness in them. He could feel it throbbing through his fingers like a fever.

There was no sound of voices nearby and he wondered if the Mortals feared to enter this place that was so strongly his. There were signs of habitation, though. In the next room there were two beds, plain wooden frames with hard mattresses that had clearly been brought from outside. They couldn't weigh much, but the floor had buckled beneath them as if their presence somehow offended it.

In the next room there was a dining table and cupboards filled with the wooden boards the Ofiklanders used as plates. There was dust on all the surfaces. It must have been some time since anyone had eaten here. Vines had grown from the walls to twine around the table's legs, the same three-leaved plant that strangled the ferns of the outer wall.

After a few more rooms, equally plain, he lost all sense of where they were or how far they'd come. The map had called this place Binäl, the heart and soul, and marked it with the slope-roofed symbol for a house. People lived here now, but it didn't seem a place intended as a home. It felt . . . larger than that. Or more powerful. Krish couldn't find the right word in his mind.

The deeper they moved, the more strongly Krish felt *his* presence: Yron, the god who both was and wasn't him. But alongside that feeling, opposed to it, was something else, something far more hostile. He thought it must be the God Killer. It prickled the hairs on his arms and churned the food in his gut.

'I, I, I don't like this place,' Dinesh said. 'There's something evil here.'

Evil didn't seem quite the right word for it. It felt no more evil than a flash flood or a plague that wiped out a town. The rooms grew darker as they moved inward, a gloomy blue as if the whole place lay deep underwater. It felt airless and Krish found his breath quickening as he walked on. Dinesh rested his hand on Krish's shoulder, as if he was afraid of being separated.

Krish's eyes lost their focus as he stared at the dark blue blankness, and in the absence of patterns his mind began to imagine them, forming shapes out of the thick shadows. The shapes began to move as he hesitated in a doorway, unsure if he should turn left or right. Dark blots seemed to skitter over the blue walls.

And then, all at once, he realised that they *were* moving, that the walls were swarming with dark shapes, more and more of them with every moment that passed.

'What—' Dinesh said, as Krish shouted, 'Out, out now!'

He turned back to the door from which they'd entered, but it had no handle on the inside.

'What *are* they?' Krish asked as the first of the creatures skittered from the walls onto the floor.

'Coal roaches,' Dinesh gasped. 'Their bite . . . you mustn't let them bite you.'

Krish could see them clearly now, each as big as his palm, long-legged and shiny-carapaced, a green-black sheen on them that was almost beautiful. They looked lumbering, like the knife-blade beetles that the youths of Ofiklanod kept as pets, but when they moved it was with startling speed. One lifted its shiny cara-pace and he saw that it hid wings, red on their underside with a pattern like a three-leafed clover. There was a sound in the room, high and strange.

'I can't get through!' Dinesh said. He was digging at the walls with his knife, but the blade barely scratched the ancient wood.

The insects were within paces of them now.

'No, no, no, no, no!' Dinesh yelled. He scratched desperately at the wall with his hands, tearing off his own nails and leaving bloody streaks across the brown.

The roaches' song rose to the pitch of a scream and Krish saw their mandibles all twitch and turn towards Dinesh. 'Get away from the wall!' Krish shouted.

Dinesh obeyed without hesitation, slipping back a moment before the insects fell on the bloodstains he'd left behind, their jaws working on the wood with a soft, horrible sucking sound.

'They eat blood!' Dinesh's voice shook and his eyes were wild with panic, though Krish knew it wasn't himself he was afraid for.

'More blood,' Krish said. 'We need more blood.' He grabbed Dinesh's hand, its ragged nails as sharp as blades, and scratched them harshly across the flesh of his inner arm.

Blood welled and the roaches twitched and turned to him, screaming their hunger. He flung himself away from them and at the wall, smearing his arm against it. It left a swathe of blood behind, but not enough.

'We need more!' he said.

Dinesh finally seemed to understand. He turned his knife on his own wrist, opening the vein and letting the blood spill to form a darker stain beside the one Krish had left. It put his arm far too close to the swarming roaches. They chittered and turned to him and Krish yanked him back with an arm across his chest so that only the roaches' twitching antennae brushed his skin before they returned to the wall, chewing and chewing.

But the blood wasn't just on the wall. It was on them too. It was dripping out of them, and the roaches could smell it. Some stayed where they were, but others screamed and scurried towards them. The walls were thick with their bodies. They crunched beneath Krish's boots. He could already feel three climbing up beneath his skirt, their spindly legs a horrible soft scratching against him.

They had no more time. They had to get out before they were overwhelmed, before the insects drank the blood that was freely flowing and then tore through their skin to drink the rest. Krish could see the serrations on their legs and their bladed jaws. It wouldn't take them long.

He couldn't see the wall any longer, only the roaches' shimmering green-black bodies. Revulsion held him frozen but he pushed through it and flung himself at the wall with all his strength, at the centre of the bloodstain where the insects had been feasting.

It was far more solid than he'd hoped. The impact bruised his shoulder and the wall resisted. The insects were already on him. He felt the pinpricks of a hundred tiny feet against his skin and something in his head shifted, or connected. He *willed* the wood to give, ordered it, and suddenly the wall parted with a wet sound and he was through, dragging Dinesh behind him.

The roaches scuttled to follow. But as they passed through the hole a substance dripped on them from the broken wood, sticky like sap. The roaches hissed as it landed and the room filled with a nasty, charred-flesh stink. As Krish sank to the floor, too weak with the aftermath of terror to move, the roaches curled into balls. Soon the sap had sealed the hole itself and no more roaches came.

Dinesh sank to the floor beside him. He seemed unharmed, but it was too dark to see if the insects had touched him. 'Are you hurt?' Krish asked. 'Were you bitten?'

Dinesh laughed a little too long, the laugh of a person not quit in control of themselves. It was the most normal Krish had ever heard him sound. 'No bites,' he said. 'When the coal roach bites you, first you have the pain, then you froth at the mouth. And then you die.'

The room they'd spilled out into was different from the rest. It was larger, almost the size of the great hall in Ashfall, and its walls had been draped with hangings. It was too dark to make them out, but Krish thought they showed human figures. Or . . . Perhaps not fully human. Lost in the shadows near the ceiling, their heads seemed misshapen. Bestial. And there was far more of the three-leafed vine in here, smothering the floor. The wood beneath it felt rotten, giving spongily as they walked across it.

'Is, is, is it safe to carry on?' Dinesh asked. 'There could be more.'

'We're nearly there. We're nearly at the centre.' Krish could feel it. Something had happened to him in the room with the roaches. His mind had touched the living heart of this place. He knew now that it had been made not from the bound-together branches of many trees but from just one, larger and more ancient than any he'd ever seen. The tree was his, or at least the moon's. It wouldn't harm him. It would protect him if it could, although it had been gravely wounded.

'It's this way,' Krish said, leading Dinesh to the far end of the hall, where three monumental statues loomed. Their heads too were lost in shadows but Krish felt them watching and unfriendly. He thought they were the same figures as those in the hangings. There were altars in front of them and signs that sacrifices had been made, the remains of burnt offerings. They must be the figures of gods, though not any that Krish recognised. Maybe Eric would know them. He'd told Krish about the hall of the

Worshippers in Smiler's Fair and the many gods who lived there. Krish had never known there could be so many.

The door in the far wall lay in the darker-on-dark shadow of the statues. Krish flinched from touching even that, but he made himself turn the handle. He knew their destination lay beyond.

The room they entered was far smaller, and almost totally dark. It took him a moment to realise there was someone in it and a moment more to realise that he knew her.

'Renar?' he said. 'What . . . what are you doing here?'

She shifted forward until he could make out the arched bridge of her nose and the oiled gleam of her cheeks. 'I'm sorry,' she said. 'I knew you'd come here. I knew you were looking for it, and I found out that this is where they keep it.'

'The God Killer?' Dinesh asked.

'I'm sorry,' Renar said again. She stepped towards Krish, just one step, and then her arm stabbed forward. He felt the impact before he saw what made it: a spear of pure crystal that flared brilliantly with golden light as it struck. He felt the moment that it pierced his heart. His hands fumbled for it, sliding against the slick surface as he tried to pull it out. But there was no strength in him, and then there was no feeling at all. And last of all there was darkness.

PART 3

The Three Beyond

22

Ofzib was quite the ugliest place Marvan had ever seen, and he'd once lived in Smiler's Fair, whose streets ran daily with shit. There were none of the elegant paper houses here that they'd seen in other parts of Ofiklanod. The buildings were rough brick things, each with a broad slot in its roof running north to south, so that the sun would shine through on its daily course and cleanse the ground beneath. He wondered what they did when it rained. Suffer, probably.

It didn't seem as if it rained here often. The streets were mostly earth that rose everywhere in clouds of choking dust so that the sky seemed yellow with it. There was none of the improbable profusion of greenery that characterised the rest of Ofiklanod. As he and Alfreda and Nabofik had travelled here by canal racer, high above the countryside, he'd watched the land beneath change from fruitful fields to an unlovely, scrubby desert.

There was only one trade here, and that was trade. Most of the ramshackle brick buildings were warehouses, and the docks were thronged with high-masted sailing vessels and the sleeker racers that came here on three different canals. It was clear a great deal of wealth passed through this port, though little of it seemed to stop here.

It was a town full of strangers, exactly the sort of place that made for a happy hunting ground, if one enjoyed the sort of game that Marvan did. But Alfreda had told him he mustn't. They were here only to find a ship to take them to the Cinderlands.

He'd held out for ten days while the need rose stronger and stronger until it was all he could think of. He didn't like to disobey Alfreda. The moment he'd looked into her furious eyes he'd

known he wanted her to be the master of him. His murderous
hunger was refined through her rage and each kill was made the
more satisfying. But a man could only wait so long. And with
that air-headed young inter Nabofik constantly present, he didn't
even have the freedom to talk as he wished. It had grown so that
his skin felt too tight to contain him.

Now he had his prey in sight. The man was young and fit and
enough of a challenge to make it interesting. There had been a time
when Marvan preferred to kill in a fair fight. Alfreda had taught
him caution, and now he found he preferred the thrill of the hunt.

They were near the water, walking one street back from the
docks. The smell was noisome. The clean salt tang of the sea was
buried beneath the stink of unfresh fish and unwashed people.
There were many of them about and Marvan was far from the
palest. The colour of the Ofiklanders ranged from a glossy near-
black to an elder-tree brown. With Marvan's head shaven to hide
his straight hair, he didn't stand out.

His prey certainly hadn't noticed him. The man had come in
on the last ship to dock. Marvan had picked him out immediately.
He couldn't say precisely what had made him so sure that this
was the one. It wasn't the face, broad and unremarkable. It was
probably something about the walk, the cocky sway of the man's
hips and the way he ploughed straight on and expected others
to move out of his way. The arrogance of it pulled at Marvan,
demanding answer.

He'd yet to decide where the killing would take place. Most
of the warehouses were guarded, the stock within too valuable
to leave unattended. And those that were empty might be filled
any moment by one of the incoming ships. At least the yells of
the sailors, the creak of the ropes and the angry calls of the gulls
would mask any sound Marvan was likely to make. But he could
hardly draw his knives in the open.

At the far end of the docks, he finally found his place. This
was where the fishermen had their berths and the cheapest
whorehouses were found. Half a lifetime in Smiler's Fair had
taught Marvan to recognise them. They were shabby buildings

with shabbier men and women loitering outside them, bodies quite ruined by their trade and yet still enough to tempt company-starved sailors inside.

The area was also home to fishmongers, who filleted and gutted the catch before it was sent on. Marvan saw whole buildings dedicated to the process, long lines of men and women at tables with gutting knives in hand and a bucket of newly caught fish at their side. Young children ran back and forth to replenish the buckets when the fish ran low, adding to the clamour and confusion of the place. The smell of it was like a physical presence in the street, crouching over everything. It would hide the more delicate smell of blood. And who would notice a few more guts among the piles?

All he needed was a private corner and a way to lure his prey in. The former seemed easy enough to obtain. At the end of the butchering line there were crates heaped with ice in which the gutted fish were placed. Any fool could see ice wasn't plentiful in this place, at this time of year. An ice house would be needed to store it. He found its location by watching where the young children went to replenish the supply.

Then the only problem was how to tempt his prey to the killing ground. He could hardly claim it was the entrance to a whorehouse. The man looked dim-witted, but not that dim.

But then again, a sailor's money was limited and the offer of a bargain turned many a man into a fool. Marvan hurried his step, until he was close enough to grasp the sailor's arm. His hand was shaken off, but the man turned to face him.

'You want a woman?' Marvan asked.

The man eyed him up and down suspiciously, but Marvan had always had a talent for seeming trustworthy, at least to those who didn't look too deeply into his eyes. The sailor relaxed and flicked his fingers in what Marvan had learned was the Ofiklander gesture meaning 'no'. He said something too quickly for Marvan to understand. It seemed like a question, and Marvan nodded.

'How much?' the man asked.

Marvan had no idea how much would be reasonable for

whatever the man had requested. He barely understood the currency here. He held up three fingers and smiled, hoping the man would draw his own conclusions about how much exactly that meant.

It appeared to work. When he beckoned, the man followed. Marvan led him towards a small alley at the back of the fisher-men's warehouse, where the ice house was. It was a squat building made of what appeared to be baked mud. It too was open at both ends but the entrances were low so that only the dawning and setting sun would shine through, too feeble to melt the ice. Clever, as many of the Ofiklanders' devices were.

The man was starting to look dubious. Marvan's gut clenched. He couldn't risk his victim escaping, not now when he was so very near and the hunger was building to its peak. He edged round until, without the man quite noticing, Marvan was standing behind him. And when a flicker of unease crossed his face, Marvan swung his fist in the hardest punch he knew.

It wasn't enough. The sailor was stronger than Marvan could have guessed. He fell, but only to one knee. A moment later he was standing again. Marvan lowered his head and charged him like a bull, knocking them both onto the pile of ice. It crunched wetly as their feet slid on the fish guts that littered the small clear area of floor. The stench of it was all around, overlaying the unnameable smell of the ice itself.

It was a vicious fight. The sailor had a knife and he stuck it deep in the fleshy part of Marvan's thigh, and then scraped it against his ribs as he tried for his heart. But Marvan was sober and the man wasn't, and Marvan's appetite had gone too long unsated. It wouldn't be denied now. At the cost of a nail he wrested the knife from the man's hand.

The fight was won then, although the sailor didn't seem to know it. He flailed at Marvan with his fists and tried to twist out of the lock Marvan had him in, sprawled across his body with his legs wrapped around the sailor's. His knife hand was free. He could finish it, but not quite yet. He needed a moment to enjoy the anticipation of the death to come. Saliva flooded his mouth and he smiled.

The sailor saw what was coming for him. He found a last desperate strength, as men often did when facing death. The end of the fight was a messy scramble, Marvan forcing the knife towards the sailor's throat and the sailor kicking and wriggling and doing everything he could to spoil the enjoyment of the moment. When the knife was finally pressed against the thick, throbbing vein in his neck, the sailor's knee hit a lucky angle, striking Marvan between the legs. He convulsed with a screaming gasp and the blade went in jaggedly, cutting out a lump of flesh along with the vein.

The blood pulsed warmly on Marvan, a sharp contrast to the chill of the ice beneath. Some landed in his open, panting mouth, the rest all over his clothes. He rolled onto his back, shut his eyes and tried to absorb the kill, to find the peace that always came in the moments following a hunt.

A noise interrupted him, the crunch of a footstep on ice. His eyes snapped open and he scrambled to his feet.

It was Nabofik. Of course it was Nabofik, who must always be where *oms* wasn't wanted. *Oms* stopped and stared, dark eyes wide. The scene around Marvan could hardly have been more incriminating. The red of the blood made a pretty stain on the ice, and the man's corpse was right there if the blood weren't evidence enough of what had occurred. It was splattered over Marvan too. The knife was still in his hand.

He could kill *omas*. That was his first instinct. But he didn't enjoy the killing of children and he was sure Alfreda would be furious with him. She seemed to have taken a liking to the young inter. *Omas* eyes kept tracking from him to the corpse and back to him again. *Omas* mouth was open as if *oms* knew *oms* needed to say something but had unexpectedly run out of words. It was the first time Nabofik had ever been truly silent and he wished he could enjoy it more.

'He attacked me,' Marvan said. 'I had to defend myself.'

Nabofik frowned. 'But I saw you following him. You were the one who led him in here.'

'I . . . I did. He was a man who once did me a great wrong and I'm afraid I took the opportunity to be revenged on him.'

Nabofik shuffled backwards, perhaps hoping he wouldn't notice if *oms* did it slowly enough. But he couldn't let *omas* through the door unless he was sure *oms* believed him. The inter yelped as he grabbed *omas* arm, and he slapped a hand over *omas* mouth, making shushing noises until Nabofik stopped wriggling and he could see that *oms* had understood.

'Are you going to kill me?' Nabofik whispered. He'd kept his hand close enough to *omas* mouth that he could feel the breath of *omas* words over his palm.

'I haven't decided.' He twisted the pair of them until he stood between her and the entrance, then released her arm. 'I should.'

'But you don't want to.'

He shrugged. 'It would give me no pleasure.'

The young inter's eyes were dragged back to the body on the ice. It was beginning to stink – or perhaps that was just the fish guts. 'Did . . . did that give you pleasure? Is that why you killed him? I haven't heard of people who enjoy killing other people, but Father always said that some people enjoy the slaughtering of the cows too much. He said people like that shouldn't be . . . I mean, he said . . .'

'He said that people like that shouldn't be trusted?' Marvan suggested, and the dark maroon stain of *omas* blush confirmed his guess. 'We shouldn't be trusted, your father is right.'

'Does Alfreda know?'

'She knows.'

'And she doesn't care?'

Marvan shook the knife, flicking droplets of blood from its blade, then knelt to scoop a handful of ice to clean it. The initial rush of joy that followed a killing had passed, and left the usual emptiness in its wake. He found that the thought of killing again so soon filled him with disgust. 'Alfreda accepts that this is how I am.'

'So you've tried to change? To . . . to not enjoy killing people?'

It wasn't a question he'd ever been asked before. Most of those in a position to ask it died before they could. It troubled him. *Had* he ever tried to stop? 'I always knew that killing gave me pleasure,' he told Nabofik. 'Life would have been safer for me if that weren't so, but none of us choose how we're made, and we can each only live according to our natures.'

'Oh,' *oms* said. 'That's very sad for you. It's hard to be different. They say that in the ancient times before the New Stability, inters like me were very rare. People killed or shunned us, because they thought we were an aberration, a leftover piece of . . . of her magic. But then the Mortals announced the Threefold Way and everyone understood that we're actually the best and most important, because we're the balance. It must be like that with you.'

It didn't seem the slightest bit similar to him, but he nodded.

'I'm so glad you told me,' *oms* said, and unexpectedly flung *omas* arms around him, pressing *omas* face against his bare, gore-smeared chest.

He rested his hands awkwardly against *omas* shoulders, the knife still in his right. Nabofik seemed to have forgotten the fear that he might kill *omas*. The face resting against his skin showed nothing but affection. He felt something bright and intense inside him, a gift she'd given without even knowing it. For so many years he'd believed that his nature was *wrong*, misshapen into something that the world could never permit. But now Nabofik had shown him that this wasn't so. *Omas* arms around him and the warmth of *omas* body pressed to his were like a promise. They told him he was as worthy of acceptance as any other man.

He realised that he felt something with *omas* that he'd only ever felt twice before: once with Nethmi and then again and far more strongly with Alfreda. In some way he didn't understand, and as infuriating as Nabofik was, they belonged together.

Oms pulled away suddenly, laughing and wiping at *omas* face when *oms* saw how it had smeared the blood on his chest. 'La, in all the excitement I forgot why I came to find you in the first place, and Alfreda said it was urgent. She's found us a ship! Talk in the town is that there's a large party of Mortals coming from Täm and all in need of transport. A dozen ships are sailing and there are a hundred crates travelling with them in which we can hide. We've found a way to the Cinderlands.'

★

Olufemi woke to the knowledge that she'd slept for a very long time. Her head felt thick and her thoughts sluggish. When she opened her eyes, the light speared painfully into them and shattered into fragments through her tears. She shut them again and tried to take stock of herself.

Had she been ill? Every part of her felt weak and her throat was as dry as the Silent Sands. She searched her memory and found a long darkness filled only with the sounds of . . . she couldn't say. A great deal of shouting and clatter and also the sensation of swaying. They had been travelling.

Slowly a little more of her memory returned, the time just before the illness must have struck. She and Yemisi had been eating a meal with the robed Mortals. And then the time before that, when they'd travelled through the flower fields and the houses – yes, the houses of the dead.

Her eyes snapped open with fear this time and she pushed herself to sit against the head of the bed. She was naked beneath a thin sheet and as she inspected herself, she gusted a sigh of relief. Her skin was unbroken, marked only by the lines of age. There were no signs of disease on her, none of the horrible changes that had marked the corpses they'd found.

But if she hadn't been ill, why had she been unconscious for days, possibly longer? And if she'd been travelling all that time, where was she now?

There was a bed beside hers with Yemisi in it, the sheet flung off her and her naked form glistening in the light of the lamps that lined the walls. The beds were large and luxurious, with high wooden headboards carved with flowers, yet even they were dwarfed by the size of the room. It was larger by far than the great feasting hall of Ashfall.

Olufemi rose from the bed, clutching the sheet around her. The floor was tiled but warm beneath her feet, the air dry and very hot. It didn't feel like the air of Ofiklanod.

She found clothes that seemed meant for her draped over the back of a tall chair. This too was carved with flowers and glossy with oil. It seemed old. Everything in this place did, even the dress. The material was clean but had the fine thinness of something worn away by years of use.

She went to the door at the far side of the room and wasn't surprised to find it locked. Yemisi woke as Olufemi rattled the handle, trying vainly to force it open.

'Where are we?' Yemisi asked, sitting up in bed. Her nakedness was distracting, alluring and disturbing all at once.

'I don't know,' Olufemi told her. 'Perhaps you'd care to help me find out.'

Yemisi rolled her eyes at Olufemi's sharp tone but slipped out of bed. The dress they'd left for her was sewn with tiny buttons in swirls and spirals that might have meant something, or might not. But on the walls, Olufemi saw marks that definitely had meaning. There were runes painted in a narrow panel all around them.

They looked like the marks she'd seen on the walls around the Garden of Yron. This was a prison and those were another of its locks. She reached for her magic and found her mind hitting something invisible and utterly impenetrable. The runes were too complex for her to unravel at first sight but their purpose was clear. This was a room intended to hold mages.

It was old work, from the age of Mizhara. She was sure of it, even though the colour looked as fresh as if it had been painted yesterday. She rubbed a hand against the wall, but when the paint flaked there was only more paint beneath it. It had seeped *into* the walls. She guessed that it must run all the way through, the runes as much a part of the structure as whatever stone the building had been carved from.

There was little else in the room: their two grand beds, a water closet and, in one corner, a stack of manuscripts. She felt a faint stirring of hope. This wasn't the place you put people you meant to kill.

'Oh, oh!' Yemisi called. 'Olufemi, come and see.'

She was standing by one of the room's windows, small and barred, looking out. Olufemi very much wanted to know where they'd been brought and yet she found her footsteps dragging, as if she already knew she wouldn't care for the answer.

Outside was a desolation: a desert made of rock, not sand, and barren of any life. Not a single speck of green interrupted the grey and black – only veins of red snaking down from the conical mountain that oversaw it all.

No, there was something else. In the distance she could see long strokes of white against the rock. Their form was impossible to make out but Olufemi was suddenly certain that they too were runes. She thought perhaps they were the same as those written on the surface of the Rune Waste.

'Where are we?' Yemisi asked again. With the irritating resiliency of youth, she appeared to have already recovered from their long sleep. She was grime-smeared, hollow-cheeked and stinking but her smile was carefree.

Olufemi studied the barren landscape and the rivers of red. 'I think this must be the island in the far south. I saw that fire mountain marked on a map. There are none on the mainland.'

'How did we get here?'

'I don't know. But I believe we've been abducted. Drugged and then brought here while we slept.'

'But why?'

Olufemi shrugged. 'Hopefully we will find out after we've had a chance to eat and wash.'

*

The sun travelled half the sky before anyone came. Yemisi spent most of her time staring through the window at the unforgiving landscape. Olufemi still found herself repelled by it, and the clear blue dome of sky above it, hazy with the fumes that rose from the fire mountain.

She turned to the books instead. They were ancient, and a spark of interest lit inside her at the thought that they might be works on rune magic, older than any she'd found in Mirror Town. But they were merely ledgers, recordings of crops and money spent and goods delivered to people a millennium dead. In the absence of anything more interesting, she read them anyway, slowly building a picture in her mind of who these people must have been: the farmer who always charged less when he sold to the poor; the miller who doubled her prices when corn was scarce.

She could have studied the runes instead. She knew it would be a better use of her time. But it pained her to look at them and feel nothing. When she tried to hold the shape of one in her mind, it faded into mist and she blinked back tears, turning her head so Yemisi wouldn't see.

She was reading the accounts of a cow farmer when the door finally opened.

Two women entered. They were dressed in light white robes, not the usual enveloping black of the Mortals, but their hands had been amputated, the stumps startlingly visible, scarred and purple.

'You've been summoned,' the younger said.

'By who?' Olufemi asked.

They only gestured at her sharply to move. When she approached the door, she saw that the Mortals hadn't come alone. Behind them clustered a score of guards, armed and keen-eyed. They were hardly needed. Where could she and Yemisi run in this barren and isolated land?

They walked in silence, the only noise the crunch of rock fragments beneath their feet. The sun hurt her eyes and she looked instead at the red rivers that threaded through the landscape. One lay ahead, bridged by a solid arch of black rock. In places the river piled itself upward and hardened into blackness and Olufemi realised that the red river was itself rock, melted by some power beyond imagining.

At the height of the bridge, the heat from below was almost too much to bear. Sweat evaporated in the moment it formed and her breath seared her lungs. The sea lay to their left, creeping up and down a beach of black sand. There was a long jetty where the ship that must have brought them was docked. She wondered where they'd found the wood to build it. Nothing grew or lived here.

They seemed to be going nowhere. Once they'd put the sea and the fire mountain at their backs the horizon was a straight line ahead. But they were climbing, subtly yet steadily, and she soon realised that the horizon was drawing closer.

At the cliff edge she stopped, startled into stillness by the view below. The cliff stood thousands of paces above a valley that was as verdant as the surrounding land was harsh. Different greens swirled and mixed on the steep curve down, and in the flat of the valley itself there were patches of violet and yellow. A river wriggled through its centre, and far away the valley climbed and ended in a sheer, white-faced cliff.

A path led downward in a series of sharp switchbacks. The drop from its side was terrifying, but the path itself was broad and faced with rock. There were wheel tracks on it, and it was clear it was well travelled.

'This shouldn't be here,' Yemisi muttered and Olufemi understood precisely what she meant.

There was . . . something in the air. It prickled the hairs along her forearms and seemed to hum silently in her ears. It wasn't rune magic, but it felt like magic all the same. It pressed against her in a way that felt threatening one moment and comforting the next.

It almost seemed to be seeping from the plants themselves. When she studied them more closely, she wondered if perhaps it was. Many were alien but some were familiar, though she'd never seen them in such profusion. They were the same intruders that had smothered the flower fields where the corpse houses were. Every leaf she saw was tripled and she remembered the shrine in the woods and knew that it meant something.

A forest lay ahead, vastly trunked trees with flowers in their shadows, and a man waited at the point where the path plunged into darkness, watching them.

His handless arms marked him as another Mortal, though he was dressed in a long skirt patterned with the same three-leafed plants that grew all around them. He smiled as they approached and she recognised the long, sardonic face whose outline she'd glimpsed beneath a veil.

'I'm glad to see you're awake,' Rorön said.

'If you were so keen for us to visit here,' she said, 'an invitation would have sufficed.'

He laughed. He seemed in a fine humour. 'An invitation might have been refused. And you are a person of great interest to us, Olufemi. I hope we can be friends.' She noticed that his speech was far less mannered, now he wasn't trying to deceive them. *If* he wasn't still trying to deceive them.

'Friends?' Yemisi's voice was high and incredulous. 'You abducted us!'

'I might put it another way: I was most careful to transport you through a troubled land in safety. But come, I can see you're weary and hungry and no doubt those account for your ill mood.' For a moment something dangerous flashed in his eyes, a hint of what might happen to them if they chose not to be his friends.

To their left, a paved path led to a clearing shaded by a structure of steel and wood, plain but beautifully proportioned with a pointed roof and simple wooden seats in its shade. The metal seemed newly forged, not a speck of rust on it, and the wood varnished just days ago. She suspected that the forest all around was recent too. It had sent tendrils of vine to creep towards the margins of the building with the eagerness of young growth.

Inside, plates were stacked in a pyramid, overflowing with meats and vegetables, but the smell of them was subtly wrong. There was a bluish tint to some of the meat, a yellowish one to many of the vegetables. Olufemi's stomach was empty, but it rebelled at the thought of putting any of this inside it. Yemisi as usual sat before she was asked and began to stuff her mouth with food. She paused as she first tasted it, frowning, but then gobbled on.

'It isn't poisonous,' Rorön said, taking a delicate bite of the nearest meat himself. He seemed adept at holding the fork between his wrists without servants to wait on him.

'So you led us to believe before,' Olufemi said coldly. 'No doubt the poison was already in our cups.'

'Now, now. Not poison – merely a gentle sleeping agent. But

there's none of that here. We want you awake. Yes, very much so. So don't be put off by the flavour. It will be unlike anything you have tasted before. But novelty is one of the joys of life, is it not? A woman who's travelled quite as extensively as you must surely agree.'

She sat but didn't eat and he smiled wryly as her gaze remained on him.

'You know a great deal about me,' she said.

'Not so much as I'd like. We have spies, of course, as all nations do. We know more of what's occurred in the god-sick lands than you might suspect. Gold will move many a mouth. But Nkankan-lati-Ohunkohun? That has always been closed to us. And we have many questions.'

'You've done very little to incline me to answer them.'

'And here I thought you might have appreciated our hospitality. But I don't require your cooperation, mage. I'm sure your young friend knows a great deal too that would be of interest. And I'm quite certain she can be persuaded to talk.' He nodded at Yemisi. His expression was still benign, but Olufemi understood what he was saying and knew that he was right. It would take very little to make Yemisi talk.

'What is it you want to know?' she asked.

'About the gods, the sun and the moon,' he said.

'You should know more about them than I. You live in the land of their birth.'

'La, I had forgotten you understood so little about us. How *did* you come into our lands so ignorant? No, don't answer. That's a tale for another time. Let me tell you then: our people foreswore all gods when they saw what destruction their coming had brought. And as I told you, we the Mortals' – he held up his mutilated arms, as if they were some badge of office – 'we took the task of keeping all gods and their worship from the land. Our people granted us the power that the priests once held. And here, to worship gods is death.'

'If you forbid gods, why should you want to know about them?'

He shrugged and smiled. She was growing to hate his smiles.

'And what precisely would you like to know about Mizhara and Yron?'

'Everything,' he said. 'We want to know everything.'

'Will you answer our questions in return?'

'Perhaps.'

'Then tell us about the other gods,' Yemisi said, before Olufemi could speak. 'The beast-headed gods that the people worship in secret.'

'If it's in secret, why would you think that we know of it? We who shun all gods.' But Rorön's expression was ironic, as if they were sharing a joke.

Big bets were better than small ones: it was a principle Olufemi's wastrel grand-cousin Obiswe had taught her. 'It's you,' she said. 'This worship of the new gods. It's not taking place behind the backs of the Mortals. You've known about it all along.' She studied his face and saw the confirmation she wanted. 'You encouraged it. So the guardians against religion have become its peddlers.'

'You're close,' he said. 'You're at the edge of it.'

'But why? You don't need more power – you told us you have it all already. You rule without gods. You had no need to invent them.'

'You lived without gods too,' he said. 'Our exiled mages. We thought of you, you know. Did you ever wonder? Nine times down the centuries, the Mortal Council debated whether to hire outland killers to finish you all off for good. I've read the records. And every time it was decided against. The justifications were reasonable enough: that you represented no more threat, that any contact with the outside world was more dangerous to us than you could be.

'But I don't think that was the full truth. I think in some secret part of them, my predecessors wondered if you could be working to bring the old gods back. I think at least some among them might have wanted that. Our founders were mages too, after all. Our history tells us that they cut off their own hands when they saw the great harm their magic had done and swore to keep all magic from the world in future. But what else would a mage say and do, who didn't want to follow your ancestors into exile?'

There was a brief silence between them, filled by the chatter of the forest. The birdsong was foreign to her, more complex and melodic than any she'd heard before. Speckled red and white faces peered from the branches of a nearby fruit tree, but it was impossible to tell if the song was theirs.

'There will always be gods in the world,' he said. 'People want them and people find ways to have what they want. And those who control the gods control it all. *If* they can control the gods.'

Olufemi took a yellow fruit from the table and turned it round and round in her fingers. The pale flesh bruised and a smell came from it that wasn't unpleasant, but foreign. 'So you want to control the gods. Many have tried.' She smiled bitterly. 'Many foolish people have tried. It never ends well.'

'But before there have only been two gods. Two is a bad number, we learned that here a millennium ago. With two there must always be opposition and war. That's why we have come to the value three. A stool that stands on three legs is balanced. Our land is ruled by a Triumvirate, our people marry in threes.'

'And now there are three new gods,' she said, realising it all at once. 'You mean to make them real. To warp the shape of the runes for three instead of two. It can't be done. The runes show what they show.'

'You might be right,' he said, 'if the runes were the only way to understand the world. But there are others, other languages of life with other patterns in them. We've found one that suits us, and for three hundred years we've sought to make it flesh. Now with your help we may finally succeed.'

'Only a fool makes the same mistake twice,' Olufemi said. 'I'll never help you.'

He smiled as he stood and gestured for the guards to take them away. 'Never is a very long time. You should know that better than most.'

*

Alfreda narrowed her eyes as she watched Marvan and Nabofik approach along the boardwalk. Something had changed between them, though she couldn't tell what. And were those spots of blood on Marvan's chest and Nabofik's cheek? But they both smiled when they drew near and she didn't have time to worry about it. If they didn't stow away soon, they might lose their chance.

Of all the places they'd visited in Ofiklanod, she liked this one the least. People on the streets spoke of the selfishness of the water-wealthy with bitterness and of Täm with outright hatred. This was a resentful place. Even the seabirds circling above the docks had an undernourished and vicious look about them.

The docks were crowded, filled with rough sailors and well-dressed merchants. But the place wasn't so crowded that she didn't draw glances, even with her broad sunhat pulled down to shade her face. She doubted any other outsiders had made it this far south.

'So, I hear you have us a ship,' Marvan said, his eyes scanning the forest of sails in the harbour.

Alfreda pointed at a pile of wooden crates beside one of the largest ships. It was a smaller pile than when she'd last seen it. The loading had already begun. A rank of cranes lined the dock, their shadows criss-crossing the people below and their beams creaking as they swung their heavy loads from shore to ship.

'La, you want us to hide in a wooden box?' Nabofik frowned, more in puzzlement than unhappiness. Everything was an adventure to *omas*.

'It's not a terrible plan,' Marvan said. 'It's unlikely they'll search the crates. But how do we enter them? And can we be sure that they're cargo for a Cinderlands-bound ship?'

Alfreda nodded. Sometimes her silence crippled her, but it had taught her useful skills. She was an expert at going unremarked and she'd heard enough to understand what was happening here. The Mortals were coming from Täm and they'd commandeered every ship they could. Black-robed figures were scattered over the docks, accompanied by their tongueless servants.

There were children with them too and carts full of possessions. The conversations she'd heard among the merchants and
sailors were about a great conference the leader of the Mortals
had called. But this didn't look like a gathering for a conference.
It looked like an evacuation, and Alfreda wondered what they
were fleeing.

It didn't really matter. The strange musical magic had told her
to go to the Cinderlands, and the nearer she drew there the more
she believed it. She felt something pulling her forward. It was
like an ache in her chest that eased whenever she made a move
that took her closer to their destination. She hadn't asked Marvan
if he felt it too, but she thought he might. He seemed more eager
to reach the Cinderlands than she could explain. The death of
the moon was her quest, not his.

'Well?' Marvan asked. 'How can we get aboard?'

Alfreda gestured them both to follow. The crate she'd chosen
was at the bottom of a stack lined up crookedly with one of the
dockside brick warehouses. The crates above had been placed
carelessly to form a corridor between the side of the bottom crate
and the building. It was as near to unobserved as they could
hope to be.

'A good spot,' Marvan said. He grabbed Nabofik and pulled
omas into the space before *omas* cautious peering about could
attract any attention.

'But how can we get inside?' Nabofik asked.

As a blacksmith, Alfreda had made far finer locks than the one
that secured this crate. They were inside within moments.
She closed the hatch behind them just as the crate gave a massive
jolt. It flung Nabofik into a pile of linens as the crate was lifted,
swinging wildly, into the air.

Nothing inside was fixed down. A table tumbled from one end
to the other, cracking two of its legs and missing Marvan's head
by a hair's width. Alfreda grabbed a stone pedestal as it flew past,
crying out as it wrenched the muscles of her arm.

The swaying finally eased as the crate found its balance. Alfreda
kept to her knees and crawled carefully towards Marvan, hoping

the shift of her weight wouldn't set everything askew again. Nabofik made to follow but Alfreda waved *omas* back. In the far corner the inter might act as a counterbalance.

'Not your best plan,' Marvan gritted as she reached him. The muscles of his bare arm were knotted with the strain of holding the crate's hatch closed. She placed her own hands above his and dug her nails in.

'We'll be aboard soon,' she told him.

But it was a long, tense wait before the crane finally began to lower its load. The rocking motion made the food sit uneasily in her stomach and she wondered how bad the voyage could be. The sea inside the harbour was as still as a pond, but there'd been storms since they came to Ofiklanod. Wind and rain would hit far harder on the open sea.

It didn't matter. She was more confident in her decisions than she'd ever been. She could feel her destination drawing her onward across the water and she knew she'd reach the place where she was meant to go.

The crate was still now, only jolted now and then as other cargo was placed around it. They must be in the ship's hold. Nabofik seemed to have forgotten *omas* fear. *Oms* was sifting excitedly through the contents of the crate, picking out chairs and cloths and cutlery as if preparing to furnish them a new home. Marvan, more sensibly, was piling the contents of the crate on one side, clearing an area of floor for Nabofik to set up their makeshift house.

Alfreda felt a confidence about them too, a certainty that they were meant to be beside her. There was an empty space where Algar had once been. She'd thought that Cwen might fill it, but Cwen had been taken from her. For months, that absence had ached coldly every moment she was awake. Now it was gone and the relief was almost greater than she could bear.

Slow hours passed waiting for the last of the cargo to be stowed. At times they heard nothing but the slapping of the waves against the ship's sides. At others sailors shouted and ropes creaked as yet more crates were lowered into the hold. The sound of the boxes falling into place echoed hollowly, and the air began to feel thin, as if it had to pass too many barriers before reaching them. Sweat beaded on Alfreda's forehead and under her arms.

'I'm going out,' she told Marvan. 'I'll see if there's a better place for us to stay.'

He frowned. 'It's too early, surely? We should wait for night to fall when most of the men will be in their hammocks.'

But she couldn't wait. A heat that might have been fear was building in her and suddenly she was desperate for fresh air. She'd never had the chance to lock the hatch and it opened easily at her push – only to stop a mere inch later.

'What's the matter?' Nabofik asked. *Oms* was at Alfreda's elbow, peering interestedly at the narrow gap.

Alfreda rattled the hatch, but there was no working it loose. 'It's nothing. Just another crate too close to this one. We'll have to cut another way out.'

Marvan brandished the knife he wore at his hip. 'Lucky we come prepared.'

'Don't be an idiot – that will do nothing but blunt the blade.' Alfreda didn't know why she was angry. She didn't understand the harsh, snapping tone of her own voice. But panic was growing inside her, a desperate need to be out of this small space.

She pulled out the tools she always took with her and chose a saw with a deep-toothed edge. It was the work of only a few moments to cut a window in the far wall of the crate, but all that lay beyond was another crate. She was a fool to have hoped otherwise. Of course the hold was fully loaded. The sailors would waste no space when they had so much to carry.

'Oh,' Nabofik said, when *oms* saw what Alfreda had found. 'Why, then I suppose there's no choice but to burrow our way out through those other boxes.'

Marvan had already had the same idea. He used his knife despite Alfreda's warning to hack away at the other crate. The blade rang against metal, and again when he wormed it between slats on a different face of the crate.

Alfreda could see her own panic beginning to grow on his

face. He took the saw from her numb fingers. As she watched, he sawed a hole in their crate's roof and another when all he found was stone. Then he went to work on each wall. There was no point. She knew with sick certainty that they'd put themselves inside a prison. There'd be no escape for them during this voyage, and they'd brought no food or drink with them into the crate.

She didn't know how far these Cinderlands were. But if the journey was longer than a few days, they wouldn't live to see them.

23

Renar felt hollow. The Mortal she'd bribed to allow her entry into the Garden stared in horror as she ran past. It wasn't until she flung herself into the bushes by the side of the road, retching, that she realised why. Her robes were drenched with blood. She waded into the filthy water of the ditch, swirling her robes through it and scrubbing at her skin with her own nails, but the stains remained, brown and incriminating. Her fingers found gobbets of blood in her hair and she scrubbed and scrubbed at her braids until her hair tore free of them.

It had to be done. It *had* to be done, and if she'd not been the one to do it, her own blood might have been washing away in rusty clouds in the ditchwater. But her own hypocrisy had been laid horribly bare to her. She'd ordered deaths before, hired assassins to do the politically necessary. She'd never imagined the act of murder itself to be so brutal. His *eyes* as she'd stabbed him, illuminated by the golden light of the God Killer. She only had to shut her own to see them now.

Suddenly and startlingly, she wanted her mother. But her mother was dead, or should be, and she found herself yearning for Lanalan instead. It was absurd. What could that fool possibly say to comfort her, even if she could risk telling him the truth? Yet she found her feet leading her to his home on the Fifth Hill.

There was a strange atmosphere in the city. She'd often noticed it after a burning. Perhaps it was an awareness of change, or at least the possibility of it, though every house was put back where it came from, all possessions carefully replaced. But the look of the places was different. The fashion had changed, as fashion did, and Bruyar had once again proven to be ahead of it. The houses of the wealthy were covered in images of insects.

It was hideous. Termites crawled up the side of one red-walled mansion while beetles lumbered around another. Stib bugs and sof bugs adorned one she knew had been paid for with the wealth their secretions produced. And the home of Leplekan the Generous, who must always go one better than anyone else, crawled with maggots and the flies that hatched from them. *Would maggots grow in the decaying flesh of a god?* But she mustn't think of that.

Lanalan was leaving as she arrived, red-skirted and white-faced for some role he'd no doubt told her about. He took one look at her and immediately turned around, ushering her into his home.

'Renar, for the love of all, what's happened? Are you hurt?' There seemed genuine concern on his face as he led her to his resting room, but then again he was an actor.

'I'm unhurt,' she said. 'An accident with wine, nothing more.'

'La! Were you bathing in it? Wait there, I've clothes you can change into. Why, it wouldn't do for my sib to be seen so bedraggled in public. What would people say?'

He returned a moment later with a fresh outfit, far more ornate than she would have chosen, seed pearls sewn in lines down its arms. Still, she slipped into it gratefully while he politely turned his back. It was strange to see him do it. As children they'd frolicked innocently naked together. But then adulthood had come and nothing had been easy between them.

'I have figs,' he said, 'and fine grapes from eastern Ofzib, which have been discovered to be far more elegant than one might expect. Bread too, and—'

'Nothing,' she said. 'No food.'

'Are you feverish? Come, the pool has been freshly refilled. Let's dangle our feet in the waters and enjoy the air. Sipon the Younger assures that the female spirit has an affinity for water. I'm sure you'll find it soothing.'

The pool had changed since she'd last seen it. It had once been tiled with a fine mosaic of flowers, but Renar'd arranged for a pamphlet to be circulated a few months back decrying such decorations as the ostentation of the overambitious. It had been aimed at Naklum the Level-Headed, a political rival of Bruyar's preferred candidate for Aquator, but clearly her sib had taken it to heart. Now the pool was a uniform, restful blue.

It was indeed soothing to dangle her feet in the water, which she saw had replaced decoration with a school of small silver fish. They nibbled at her toes in a not unpleasant way.

'Thank you,' she said grudgingly.

She looked up to find her sib studying her with unusual seriousness. 'Something is amiss, Renar, I know it. Will you not tell me? We used to be close.'

'When we were children. Our paths have diverged.'

'La! Not so very far, have they? I perform for the edification of the public and you for the advancement of your clients.'

'But you don't . . .' She stumbled into silence and shook her head. How could she possibly explain to him how wide the gulf between them truly was?

His feet slipped into the water beside hers. He dabbled his toes like a child, frightening the silver fish away. 'I miss our mother,' he said. 'Father died so long ago, and our maker has never much cared for us. But Mother's so close and yet unreachable. Why, she could be beneath our very feet as we speak!'

The brief moment of peace passed and her lips tightened. 'Mother is dead,' she said firmly.

'Well, yes, in a way.'

'In the only way that counts.'

He lifted one leg from the water so he could rest his head on his knee and study her. 'You won't admit it ever, but I know it's harder for you. I have the house and her art at least to remember her by. You have nothing.'

His words scratched the wound open again, as perhaps he'd meant them to. Even a man of his poor intelligence could boast a low cunning. How else had he persuaded their mother to pass the family fortune to one so manifestly unworthy?

'Well,' he said, 'the past is beyond reach, as the poets have told us. And your present has made you quite golden in Bruyar's eyes, or so the gossip tells me. This visit of Prince Krishanjit is the talk of the town!'

How? How did he always twist the knife deeper, even when he couldn't possibly mean to? She gritted her teeth and stared at the fish so her mind wouldn't wander back to the scene that played over and over inside it: the crystal spear sliding into his flesh, piercing it more easily than she could have imagined; the moment of stillness before the blood came. The trickle of gore from the corner of his mouth . . .

'La! You hardly look glad of it,' Lanalan said. 'Has there been some news I haven't heard?'

'So you can spread it to your friends as the freshest gossip?' She forced her voice to sound light, with only the sourness her sib must have come to expect from her.

'Mere weeks till he crosses the border.' His face took on the dreaming look she'd seen during the poetry recitation that had begun this whole thing. 'Do you think he'll bring a retinue with him?'

It was intolerable. What was she doing here? If things had gone to plan, the prince *would* be visiting soon, and Bruyar would be making preparations. What if *oms* sent for the God Killer and found Krishanjit's body before Renar had told *omas* its tale? She was wasting time with a man who'd never understand.

She stood abruptly. 'I have to go.'

'Oh. Will you not stay for a light meal first? We so seldom talk as sib and sib.'

'That's because I have nothing to say to you,' she told him, before striding from the house.

★

When she came to Bruyar's street, the house wasn't there. Although it was now late afternoon, no frames had been refitted after the burning and *omas* possessions lay scattered over the lawn in their boxes. The road outside was crowded with burden-beetles hitched to carts. The clacking of their feet on the lacquer was a loud irritation.

She'd always had a horror of the larger insects. Everyone knew, though no one admitted, that they were the legacy of Mizhara's rule. Gross, unnatural things, their mandibles nipped at her as she pushed through them. She was sweating in her borrowed clothes by the time she reached the garden.

She stopped as she saw servants boxing everything Bruyar owned, labelling the boxes and stacking them on the carts. This was no mere rearrangement after a burning. Bruyar was leaving *omas* home. But Bruyar hadn't told her *oms* meant to move. Renar hadn't even heard a rumour of it.

The inter sat in comfort at the centre of all the bustle, *omas* children arrayed around *omas* feet, the eldest leaning on the chairback. Bruyar's brow raised as *oms* saw Renar and *oms* gave a brief look of irritation before *omas* customary broad smile.

'Why, my darling, I wasn't expecting you today,' *oms* said. 'Had you given notice, I would have informed you it was a less than ideal time.'

Face to face, Renar found she didn't know what to say. She hadn't prepared her words, as she usually did. She hadn't given much thought to anything, besides getting here ahead of the news. 'Why are you moving?' she asked, for want of anything better.

'No, dearest, I don't believe you came all this way to ask me that.' Bruyar turned to *omas* oldest child. 'The young ones look thirsty. Take them to the fountain to refresh themselves.'

The oldest child, a boy, gave Renar a careful, considering look before leading the noisy gaggle away. Definitely a boy who took after his maker. But now she and Bruyar were alone and she had to decide what exactly she should say.

'I don't care for that expression one bit,' Bruyar said, studying her. 'The last time I saw it you were about to tell me that Kusadäb the Wise intended to vote for the wrong Triumvir. You'd best tell me straight out. I will be angry, and perhaps I will rant and rave – you know how my temper is. And then we will fathom how to fix it.'

'It's Prince Krishanjit,' Renar said, in the sudden relief of confession. 'He's here. I mean to say, he chose to come here before we invited him. He didn't trust us and I failed to read him.'

Bruyar stood abruptly, all traces of humour gone from *omas* broad face. 'You are telling me that the moon reborn is here, in Täm, right at this moment?'

'Yes. Well, no. I mean to say, in a manner of speaking.' Renar drew a deep breath, aware that she was gabbling. 'He came here, and I tracked him down. He'd come in search of the God Killer and he went to find it, in the Garden of Yron.'

With every word, Bruyar's expression darkened. Before she came here, Renar had felt an uneasiness that made food sit ill in her stomach. But this was the first time she felt true fear. She'd made a mistake in coming. She knew it now that it was too late.

'And did the prince find the weapon?' Bruyar asked, each word enunciated with deadly clarity.

Renar swallowed. 'No. I set a trap for him. I'm sorry, Bruyar, I should have told you as soon as I realised we'd failed to fool him. But I know you prefer to be handed solutions, not problems. So I set a trap for him, and when he came for the spear, I used it to kill him. The moon reborn is dead.'

There was a long silence between them. The shouts of the servingmen and the chittering of the burden-beetles filled it, but made it no less icy.

'That was your plan, was it not?' Renar offered tentatively.

'Never presume to know what I'm thinking,' Bruyar said. 'You fool. You fool! The God Killer was to be used at the last, not the beginning. I invited him here to study him, to . . . But that's not for you to know. Where is the God Killer now?'

'It's . . . It broke. I'm sorry. It shattered when I used it.'

Bruyar was no taller than Renar, but now *oms* somehow contrived to loom over her. 'You broke the only weapon that can kill a god?'

Renar nodded jerkily.

She expected rage. She found that she'd set her feet, braced for a blow. But rather than enrage Bruyar, Renar's words seemed to deflate *omas*. *Oms* sank back into the chair, face draw into taut lines that made it look suddenly old.

'The moon is dead,' Renar said timidly. 'Has not the weapon served its purpose? That is surely why it broke.'

'The moon is dead,' Bruyar told her, 'and now his sister the sun is upon our doorstep. I received news of their army this morning, crossing our eastern border. The sun is coming, the moon who might have stood against her is dead, and the one weapon that could have stopped her is destroyed. Shattered. Shattered!'

It was too much to absorb. There had been no word of a new sun god, none at all. Renar had never thought to weave such an occurrence into her plans. And now the event that the people of Ofiklanod most feared, the fear that had defined them, was coming to pass.

'What shall we do?' Renar asked. 'We must . . . we must rally our defences. Call the guard back from the southern lands. We can – maybe we can find weapons in the City Below. Use the sun's own devices against her.' But then she remembered what was going on around her: the household being packed away and placed on carts. 'You're leaving. You're fleeing before news of the invasion can break.'

'I'm not foolish enough to think I can stand against a god.' Bruyar shook *omas* head as if to clear it, and then waved a hand at Renar, a contemptuous dismissal. 'Täm is no longer my concern. Now go. Go and cower where you can. Your actions may have doomed us all.'

24

Eric thought he might turn into a mushroom himself, if he spent much longer in the damp and dark. He felt ill, an unpleasant ache in all his joints and a pounding in his head that stayed with him even in his dreams. Arwel seemed to be suffering too. He grizzled when he wasn't held and wriggled when he was. No amount of blood soothed him.

It was funny really, when you thought about it. It was the sun Eric was yearning for, but he was sure as he could be that it was the same sun making them both feel so ill. This was her city, filled with the dregs of her power, and she wasn't too fond of him or his son. Most folk came to the City Below to be cured. It felt like it was doing its level best to kill him.

He'd have to leave. For Arwel's sake if not for his own, he'd have to get out of here soon. But he still hadn't found the missing God Killer, and he didn't much fancy leaving without it. The sun's magic might be hurting him down here, but it wasn't meant personally. If Mizhara herself ever got her hands on him and his boy, it wouldn't be pretty.

'We need a strategy,' the Hunter had said to him, because that was the way she thought: warlike. She'd gone off to ask questions, but he had his own plan.

Seemed to him if the God Killer was gone, it was because someone had taken it. And if someone down here had taken it, they'd probably sold it on to someone else in Täm. It was only above they'd have use for something like that. And it hadn't escaped him that there was stuff down here that couldn't have been dug out of the muddy corridors. Food for a start, green and fresh, and nice juicy meat too. There was trade going on, and not just the mushrooms he'd helped farm. Someone was selling something a sight more valuable.

Of course, down here 'someone' meant 'some family'. That was one rule they did take seriously: the families down here each had their own domain and stuck to it.

He'd ruled out Mother Gesinde, whose family made their home in the old palace of Mizhara at the heart of the City Below. He'd heard too much gossip about them. The others said they'd been corrupted by their home, that they'd even started to worship the sun. He remembered the unfriendly cullies he'd met after he'd first come here, the ones who guarded the golden machine, and thought the rumours were probably true. They'd definitely been folk who'd had something to hide. But why would a man who worshipped a god be looking for a weapon that could kill her?

He thought he could cross Mother Ebibowale's clan off his list, too. They were learned coves. Most of them had been students or teachers in their lives before, and they still dedicated themselves to study. As far as he'd ever seen, thinkers weren't usually doers. Look at the mages of Mirror Town, who'd left all the work to their slaves and cowered in their homes when war came to them. They didn't seem the types to want a weapon.

He'd start his hunt with Mother Afonja. That lot were artists, apparently. It didn't sound too promising, but some of the folk of Smiler's Fair had called themselves artists too, and there hadn't been many crimes they weren't willing to commit. Besides, artists were dreamers and what bigger dream was there than killing a god?

He'd heard the family made their home to the east, not that sun-directions were much use buried down here. But he'd had hands waved vaguely leftward when he asked, so that was where he headed.

Arwel slept peacefully for once in a sling across Eric's chest. He was growing so fast Eric wouldn't be able to carry him that way much longer. It already made his back ache, but there was comfort in the fast fluttering of his heart against Eric's.

Now Eric had been given a vision of the City Below in its

youth, he understood it better. The streets were neatly laid out in grids and ovals around what had once been gardens and were now mud. When he looked in his mind's eye, he thought his path might be taking him towards a tower of gold he'd spied in the distance of his magic dream, the sun glinting on its spire.

The buildings around here were drab, some of them still half-filled with mud and most with their walls cracked and their decorations long faded. He remembered them painted with flowers. Curious, he scraped away at the earth caked on one. When he'd gone deep enough, his fingernails rang against something that sounded like porcelain. He spat in his hand to wash it clear and grinned to see the faded outlines of petals.

Not much further on from the flowery houses, he found the beginning of Mother Afonja's domain. Leastways, he thought that was what it must be. There were three statues in the road, far too clean to have been here a thousand years. Naked as they were it was clear one was a man, one a woman and one an inter, as these folk called it, boy parts and girl parts both between its legs. But the man had a bird's head, feathered and wide-eyed. The woman's was worse, some kind of insect with nasty jaws and antennae. He couldn't say what the inter's head was. Not quite a wolf, though the long jaws and dangling tongue were similar. But there was something more vicious and cold-hearted to its looks. It was fine work, unpleasant but well done.

Beyond the statues he saw his first people. They turned to stare at him as he walked past. One sat at a potter's wheel, fingers buried in moist clay as it spun. It didn't seem to Eric that this was a place in need of any more mud, but the old man had a pile of sturdy pots at his feet. Now Eric thought about it, he recognised the style. He'd eaten out of similar at breakfast today.

The people clustered more thickly after that, in the streets between the excavated houses. He could see beds and tables through glassless windows. But most folk chose to do their work outside. He supposed artists liked their genius to be seen. Look at Lanalan. He hadn't been able to go two sentences without mentioning some well-loved performance he'd given.

As if the thought had conjured it up, Eric stopped short at the sight of a face that was the twin of Lanalan's. Or no, not its twin. This wasn't Renar; it was an older woman. But if she wasn't Lanalan's mother, Eric would eat both his shoes.

She caught him staring and looked up, frowning beneath a neatly tied scarf. Her dress was patched and old, not like the finery Lanalan had worn, but now Eric had a plain look at her there was no mistaking it.

'Can I help you?' she asked.

'No, sorry. Or actually maybe yes. I don't know your name but I know your son and daughter. Lanalan and Renar, right?' The words in the Ofiklander tongue came easier to him now. Sometimes he felt as if the City was whispering the knowledge to him in his sleep.

'My children,' the woman said. 'Why yes, for I am Xion Afonja, who was known as Xion the Stonecarver in the World Above. And are they . . . are they well? Did Renar send you?'

'No, she don't know I'm here.'

'So they have no message for me? La, of course they do not. A foolish thought. But then what brings you here? A godlander with a baby in his arms. Such a pair have never been seen in this place in my lifetime.'

He shrugged. 'Just looking around.' He did just that and noticed what she'd been working on for the first time. 'Oh, those statues at the entrance – those were yours.' She was working on a smaller version of the bird-headed man, her hands smeared with clay. This one looked wilder somehow, the bird's beak savage and the limbs coiled as if he was getting ready to pounce.

'They're good,' he told her. 'Sort of ugly – or not ugly, but not *nice* if you know what I mean. Definitely lifelike though. I mean each half of them. I ain't never seen something like them walking around.'

She smiled. 'They were a commission from a wealthy man in Nesevadan.'

That seemed like as good an opening as any. 'From outside, you mean? I thought that sort of thing weren't allowed.'

'It isn't, which is precisely what makes it so appealing. You have a cheeky look about you, young man. I'd wager you understand the joy of rule-breaking. But alas my client died before the work could be delivered. I heard it was the Warp that killed him, a nasty business. So here the statues remained. They've proven rather popular. In fact, I would not be exaggerating to say they've begun a fashion.'

She gestured around them, and he saw that what he'd taken for market stalls lining the square were workplaces for artisans: painters and potters and jewellers and more. Everywhere in their work, the three animal-headed figures were repeated. He saw them woven into tapestries and carved out of marble and made into little golden earrings.

'But who are they?' he asked. 'They ain't no gods I've ever seen, not even in the Worshippers' hall, and the Worshippers follow all the gods there are.'

'You think them gods? How interesting.' She looked at her own creation as if seeing it clearly for the first time. 'To my people they are no more than ornaments. And in a week or a month or a year the fashion will change and we will be carving something else. It is strange that we should care for what is current down here, where nothing ever changes and even old age only approaches at a creeping pace. But I suppose that people are people wherever they're to be found.'

'Yeah, I reckon they are and all.'

She studied him. 'But I don't believe you just wandered through. You have the look of a boy on an errand. No, more serious than that. A mission.'

'Well, if I'm honest—'

'If he is honest, he will tell you he is looking for something that is already gone,' a voice said at his elbow. The Hunter had slunk up to him in that stealthy way of hers.

'Gone?'

Her face was hidden beneath its veil, but he thought the material caught the corners of downturned lips. 'Sold to the Mortals in the City Above. I have been speaking to Mother

Awosusi's people. They found it years ago. It was gone before
we ever arrived.'

Xion looked between them in fascination. 'How very intriguing
you are,' she said. 'And how very mysterious. There is intrigue
down here, but no excitement when there can be so little at stake.
But your face, young man, tells the story of a matter of grave
concern. I'd forgotten how bracing it was to care.'

'Would you know anything of this matter of the sale?' the
Hunter asked.

Xion shook her head. 'Family matters stay within the family
and only the Awosusis still concern themselves with matters in
the World Above. It doesn't surprise me that they are the culprits
in this theft of yours. This has always been the way of our people.
We speak promises out of one side of our mouths and break
them from the other. Why, look at me.' Her tone was light, but
there was a bitter edge to it. 'I was as obedient a follower of the
Mortal way as any while I was in health, but when the sickness
grew in my lungs, I took the path down here and the cure from
her we do not name. No doubt my children blame me for it still,
but our whole nation has made the same bargain. We eat the
crops that grow in fields where no crops should grow, and drink
the milk from cows far larger than any cow naturally should be.
And we travel everywhere with the sun's wind at our back. We
are hypocrites and always have been.'

'Yes,' the Hunter said gravely. 'The gods' gifts are too great
a temptation for most to resist. But this thing the Mortals
have taken, I must have back. How might I find the one who
bought it?'

Xion smiled, her moment of seriousness gone. 'La, to find the
name of the buyer would be easy. Gossip is rife down here where
there is so little to gossip about. But the name will do you little good.
They are no longer in Täm.'

'How do you know that?' Eric asked. 'Do you know them?'

'Not in a particular way, no. But the Mortals have all left the
city. Have you not heard? Why, it's as if you don't care for gossip
at all. Every single Mortal has packed up their home and gone.

Some say they're heading for the Cinderlands for some great conclave, although I cannot see that it could be so. They have never before removed themselves so thoroughly from the affairs of the land. Imagine the mischief we might get up to in their absence!'

Eric looked at the Hunter, although he couldn't see what she thought with her face hidden away. He didn't know what to make of it himself. Had they found Krish and taken him with them? Had they already killed him? But Arwel was still a warm and breathing weight against his chest, and he didn't think his boy would be thriving if Krish was gone from the world. He found himself surprisingly relieved by the realisation. He hadn't known he cared about the prince at all.

'If they have gone then we must follow them,' the Hunter said to Eric. Her veil stirred with the breath of her words and he realised that he could see the outline of her lips beneath, shaping them.

It had grown brighter. In the moment he realised it, others did as well. Xion squinted at the ceiling from which the mellow light of the City Below came. It wasn't mellow now. It was growing crisper and brighter, as bright as the naked sun. There was sound too: clanking and whirling echoing down the road-tunnels that led to the square. And something coming from the square itself.

He looked up and saw what had been hidden in the roof of the place: a great machine a little like the one in far-away Salvation. Its mechanism was caked with mud, but the mud flaked away as the cogs spun until it was entirely clear, gold and spinning in the centre of the roof, hanging improbably in empty air. The low soundless vibration of it set Eric's teeth on edge and started Arwel grizzling in his arms.

'What's happening?' he asked the Hunter. 'What's done this?'

'The City is waking.' She pointed to his left, where a narrow alley led into the square. It was widening by the moment, centuries-old mud flaking away to reveal the bare stone beneath.

And from the alley figures were coming: the man-machines he'd seen before, but as he'd seen them in the dream, whole and smooth and very alarming, not rusted and broken as they should be now. The people of the City Below stumbled out of their way. Some ran, while others stayed, seemingly frozen with fear.

'Oh no!' Xion said. 'Oh, my work!'

There was a loud crack, and the clay figure of the bird-headed man split neatly in two and fell to the ground in pieces. The air filled with cries from all over the square, from the other artisans. To Eric's left, a deep-red tapestry caught fire, the flames starting in the insect head of the woman stitched on it. Other statues were shattering: fingers and legs and strange animal heads all falling to the ground and breaking into pieces.

It was, he realised, only those three particular figures that were struck down. Paintings of flowers or of people remained untouched. But some force was wiping out every image of the three beast-headed gods.

'What's happening?' he said to the Hunter. 'Why is this happening?'

'It is Mizhara,' she said. 'The sun is returning to her birthplace.'

*

Only the fact that she slept so lightly saved Renar's life. She wasn't sure what it was that woke her. The assassin was silent, a professional at her work. When Renar's eyes opened to the pale light of dawn, the woman was already leaning over her, a thin wire stretched between her hands.

Renar kicked upward in panic. Her legs were tangled in the sheets and sluggish from sleep, but her assailant was already unbalanced. The woman staggered back and Renar tumbled from the bed. A hard lump jabbed in the small of her back where she fell. As the assassin leapt towards her, she rolled away and saw what she'd been lying on: the blackjack she'd kept for a defence she'd never truly thought she'd need.

The assassin's knife slashed for Renar's throat and caught her arm when she raised it in desperate, instinctive defence. It bit sliced into her skin and she screamed, but as she screamed she swung the sap.

It struck the assassin's temple with a horrible, wet, cracking thump. One moment her dark eyes were glaring into Renar's and the next all light was gone from them. She fell forward onto Renar's chest, her slight frame still enough weight to feel crushing.

Renar lay and gasped, fear turning to relief and then very quickly into horror as blood began to drip from the body onto her skin. The corpse pressed against her as intimately as a lover. She pushed it away and scrambled to her knees, clawing at her skin to wipe away the blood. Every part of her felt defiled by the corpse she'd touched.

The assassin was a young woman, Renar could see that now. Her face hadn't a single line on it and her teeth, gritted in the rictus of death, were painted with flowers. It was a fashion among the florists of Gad that had begun to make its way into the city.

She was quite dead, cooling already, with the noisome stink of her loosened bowels filling the room. For a long while all Renar could do was sit beside her corpse and shiver. She'd killed twice now. Two people were gone from the world because of her. The thought felt too big to fit inside her head. And another thought came snapping at the heels of it: that *she'd* almost been gone from the world. A moment's more sleep and the assassin would have killed her.

There was no doubt who'd sent the killer: it must be Bruyar. It was so very typical of *omas*. Even in the hurry of leaving Täm *oms* made time to punish Renar for her failure. Bruyar had always believed examples must be made.

Renar heard the soft whoosh of her door opening and her fingers closed convulsively around the blackjack, slippery with sweat.

But it was only Lanalan. She recognised his scent a moment before he strode into the bedroom and smiled wider than she'd ever smiled to see her sib before.

'La! What happened here?' he exclaimed. 'Are you hurt?'

'Only a scratch. That woman came to murder me in my bed, but . . .' She shook her head, unwilling to say that she'd killed her, though the evidence lay sprawled on the ground in front of her.

'Why, Renar, if I'd lost you I don't know what I should have done,' Lanalan said with every appearance of sincerity.

He dropped to his knees in front of her, taking her face between his palms. It was a gesture their mother had often used, and she tried to twist her head free of him, but his hands tightened convulsively around her.

'What's . . . what's happened to you?' he said.

'Nothing, I told you. I'm fine.'

'No, Renar, your eyes!'

She finally managed to pull away from him and stood, turning her back on him. She hated the thought that he might be able to see into her. 'You may go. There's little you can do to help and no need for you to be caught up in this business.'

'La, will you not listen! There's something amiss with your eyes. Their colour . . .'

He touched her shoulder to turn her and this time she let him, a sick feeling of dread building in her gut. 'What's wrong with my—' She broke off with a gasp when she saw *his* eyes, the unnatural silver colour of them. 'Lanalan, you have the moon's eyes!'

'No, not mine, yours. They're . . . Oh. Oh, I see. But Renar, your eyes are the sun's.'

There was a mirror to one side of her bedroom. She drew Lanalan with her to stand before it. She'd seen the eyes that her sib now wore before, in the head of Prince Krishanjit. But her own were something entirely new: bright golden circles without any visible pupil, though she could see as clearly as she ever had. She might have considered them beautiful, if she'd seen them in someone else's face.

'What's happened to us?' her sib asked. 'I don't understand.'

Renar thought she did. They all knew the stories about twins. For centuries in Ofiklanod they'd been killed at birth, in case they became what Renar and Lanalan now were. In these enlightened days it was no more than a joke, something to rib them with at boisterous dinner meets.

'The moon god came,' she told him, 'and now the sun's joined him. And because they came, we're becoming their servants.'

★

Krish woke to the fierce sensation of pain in his chest and the gentler one of water falling against his face. Opening his eyes took every morsel of strength he had. When he did, it was to see Dinesh bowed over him. The boy's face was shadowed, but he was making a strange sound. Oh, he was sobbing. The water falling on Krish's face must be his tears.

The effort of the thought wore Krish out, and he closed his eyes again. The pain stayed with him, banishing sleep. He drifted, unable to form thoughts, but aware something was wrong. His body was wrong. A command sent to his fingers brought only a twitch and the twitch sent another spike of pain through him.

His chest, that was the centre of his agony. It was such a relief to be able to identify it that he felt himself fade, drifting finally into sleep.

When he woke again, it was once more to the sensation of something falling on him. Not water, this time. There was a smell he recognised: earth. He forced his eyes open, saw only gloom and gratefully let them slip shut. The pain was a little less. Whatever was wrong with him, it seemed to be getting better.

The earth kept falling against him, though. It was irritating. A clod fell against his nostrils, blocking his breath, and this time when he ordered his hand to brush it away, his hand obeyed. But the moment his nose and mouth were clear, another shower of earth fell on them. Someone must be throwing it at him. He would ask them to stop.

'Please,' he said. 'Don't.' His voice was a rusty croak and he couldn't seem to make it louder. He'd already lost the energy to form words. But from somewhere above him he heard a yell. There was a thump and a vibration of the earth beneath him as something heavy landed.

'Krishanjit! Lord Krishanjit!' It was Dinesh's voice, but it sounded wrong, too thick and hoarse. Oh yes, Krish remembered now. Dinesh had been weeping.

'My chest . . .' Krish said. He reached out to touch the area
that hurt and found his hands touching something slick and
smooth instead. Was there . . . ? He forced his head to lift
and his eyes to focus. There was something crystal growing from
his chest.

'I'll, I'll, I'll, I'll, I'll take it out,' Dinesh said.

Other hands joined his on the crystal thing. There was a
wrenching sensation, searing pain and then nothingness.

★

When his eyes opened the next time, he was sitting up and the
pain in his chest was far better. His hands obeyed him easily this
time. He felt all around the area where the crystal thing had been,
but it was gone. There was only bare flesh, tender and scabbed.

Dinesh gave a cry and crouched in front of him, face far too
close. 'Lord Krishanjit. You're alive!'

Memory woke with Dinesh's words: the confrontation with
Renar and the crystal spear through his chest, the God Killer.
He looked around. He was still in the Garden of Yron, though
Dinesh must have carried him away from the tree-building. To
one side there was a deep pit with a pile of earth beside it. Dinesh
had been trying to bury him. *Had* almost buried him. He remembered the feeling of the earth falling against his face and
shuddered. What if Dinesh had finished before Krish had woken?
Would he have lain down there, buried alive for ever?

'I *am* alive,' Krish said.

'But the God Killer.'

A piece of it lay by Dinesh's side, smeared with Krish's blood
and jaggedly broken at one end. There was no question it had
gone through Krish's heart. He'd felt it there. And he *had* been
dead, or at least as close to death as it seemed he could come
these days.

'It doesn't work,' he said. He laughed suddenly, although it
pulled at his still-healing wound. 'She didn't kill me. She can't.'

His head felt bright with elation – and something else. It wasn't
a sensation he'd felt before and he couldn't say if it was closer
to happiness or sadness. It was an awareness: a sense of something

very powerful, very close. He thought he could even tell which direction it came from: somewhere to his left. He looked and saw nothing but more of the endlessly varied Garden.

'What is it?' Dinesh asked. 'Are you in pain?' His hands fluttered over Krish's body and Krish pushed them aside impatiently.

'I'm fine. Stop fussing. It's . . .' He tilted his head back and closed his eyes, concentrating on the feeling. It was important, he knew that much about it. There was an urgency to it that unsettled him.

The sunlight shone red through his closed lids and the red of the light blended inside him with the bright glare of the feeling until all at once he recognised it.

'It's the sun,' he said. 'Mizhara is coming. Here. I think she's coming here.'

'She can't be! She's, she's, she's dead.'

'So was I. So was Yron, I mean.' Though the distance between Krish and Yron felt the shortest it had ever been. Perhaps that was what gave him his certainty when he said, 'Mizhara is coming here to fight me, where I have no army and no friends. And the God Killer doesn't work.'

25

Eric thought with the Mortals gone, the path back up to Täm would be left unguarded. He wasn't the only one with the same bright idea. When he came to the place where they'd given him his sun-mark, there was quite a crowd. But the Mortals had left them a parting gift. The tunnel's mouth had been sealed with rocks, each bigger than a man and ten times as heavy. It was clever work. The crowd could have tried to move them, but then they'd risk setting the whole lot free to roll down and crush them.

Eric scurried backwards, clutching Arwel to him as he saw a couple of the more desperate cullies getting ready to do just that. He *had* to find a way out for them. There must be other paths. Hadn't Lanalan's mother said there was trade with the outside? Smugglers were cunning coves. The Mortals were bound not to know all their ways.

He squared his shoulders, determined to find a way if he had to shake it out of someone, and almost walked headlong into the Hunter.

'Ain't no use trying to get out that way,' he told her. 'Unless you can move a rockfall, which I suppose maybe you could.'

'We are not leaving,' she said.

'Speak for yourself. I ain't gonna sit here and wait for the worst. If I'm gonna get killed, I'd prefer for it to happen while I'm running away. Least that way folk could say I died sensibly.'

'You will not escape,' she said.

'But I've got to try, don't I? For him. She ain't gonna let my boy live and I can't stand by and watch anyone hurt him, even a god.'

'There is nowhere you could run to, nowhere far enough to

take you out of her reach. I went to the very end of the world, and even that proved not far enough.'

'Then what am I supposed to do? Just give up?' Eric had never enjoyed anger, how helpless it made him feel. But he was furious now. It wasn't right of her to try to take away his hope.

'We need the God Killer,' she said.

'It's gone. The Mortals took it.'

'No, I do not believe they did. I have spoken to many here who have contact with them. The Mortals fled the city in terror at the coming of Mizhara. That is not the action of those who possess a weapon that could destroy her.'

'If they ain't got it, where is it then? Cause it weren't where we went looking for it.'

'Come,' she said, turning back to the tunnel that led to the City Below.

Eric found himself following her, despite himself. She'd been a god for a thousand years and an army commander for who knew how long before that. You couldn't blame a boy for finding her difficult to disobey. 'Do you think you've found out where it is?' he asked, trotting to keep up with her long stride.

'No. But I believe there is a place that will tell us *what* precisely it is. I thought I understood. There were whispers of it in the last days of the last war: the thing that would stop the gods, which years before had been made as a safeguard. I was so sure I understood it that I never thought to question myself. But now I doubt. And how can we hope to find that which we do not even comprehend?'

'Right. And I suppose you need my boy again to help you get to it.'

'Not your son but only you. If there is information to be found, it will be in one of the ancient temples of sun or moon. That was where the priests kept their records and their secrets. And because they kept them there, they warded the place against intruders. Against us, the Servants. Their gods made us, but they never trusted us. Mizhara and Yron they were foolish enough to believe they could control. They knew that our loyalty was only to our makers.'

'So you're saying any normal person could get in there, just
not you?'

She nodded.

'Then you don't need me. You just need someone.'

'But you are the only one I trust.'

He stopped to stare at her, startled. It seemed such an obvious
lie that he thought he'd see her smiling, but she looked entirely
serious.

'You didn't trust me back at Salvation,' he said.

'Because I knew then there was some truth you were keeping
from me. I know that truth now.' She reached out a finger to brush
against Arwel's head. He flinched away from it, and sorrow flickered across her face. 'I understand that he is all your world and
that you will do whatever it takes to save him. And I know you
are wise enough to understand that in this we share the same aim.'

'Yeah, except I ain't sure you and me have got the same idea
what's best for him.'

'In this too you are wise. I am a betrayer, and for a thousand
years I lived a lie. But I promise you this: I will never knowingly
harm you, Eric, you or your son. And all that I have done, every
betrayal, has been in service of your kind.'

★

Eric had learned the City Below well in the time he'd spent there,
but the Hunter still managed to lead him by paths he hadn't
taken. Or maybe he had, and he just didn't recognise them. Things
looked very different in the bright light that lit them now. Cleaner
too. Over the last day the mud had started to flake from the walls
and ceiling, revealing the marble and granite and the curlicues
of gold paint beneath.

The old city that was slowly coming out of its shell was
beautiful, but Eric thought he preferred it the way it had been
before. The broad colonnaded avenue they were walking down
was too grand for the likes of him, and he'd never have felt at
home in the five-storey-high houses with lions guarding their
doorways and rotting wooden shutters over their long windows.

They passed beneath one of the vast cracks in the mud that

criss-crossed Täm. Eric looked up for a glimpse of the sky. It was the washed-out blue of midmorning and he realised that the light below was now brighter than the light above.

He knew they'd reached their destination before the Hunter said so. The building couldn't have been free of mud before, or someone would have stripped it clean. It was too grand by far to be ignored. The front rose in a high thin arch – so high it was a wonder the point of it didn't poke through into Täm itself. All along the arch was a golden script just like the one he'd seen in Salvation. Runes, of course, though more complicated even than the ones that had kept the sun from setting in the far north of the world. Above the grand doorway there was a sunburst made of a buttery yellow metal that could only be gold. It must be forty paces from side to side, and set all over with red gems the size of his fists.

'They wasn't exactly shy about showing their coin,' Eric said.

The Hunter smiled one of her rare smiles. 'No, indeed. Mizhara made her people very wealthy, but her priests did not want them ever to forget to whom they truly owed their prosperity. When I first came into this world, here was the centre of all power. But they had created something they could not control. When Mizhara assumed command of the Empire that bore her name, she lived far more simply. Wealth and ostentation never meant anything to her.'

'You make it sound like she wasn't so bad.'

'She was not born a monster.'

'But she turned into a killer, didn't she?' Eric said. 'That's what you told me. You said she meant to kill every one of Yron's people.'

The Hunter sighed. 'Yes. Her belief, like her power, was too pure. It would admit of no doubt, and a person without doubt will always be dangerous. Come, we cannot delay. You must go inside and see if you can find that which we seek.'

'That's a big old place. I could be there all year unless you tell me where to look.'

'I cannot tell you. But . . .' She swept her finger across the skin of his forehead in a pattern too complex to follow. 'When you enter, you will know the way.'

The skin she'd touched began to burn and he yelped and put his hand to it, but there was no heat beneath his fingers. 'You ought to ask a boy before doing magic on him. It ain't polite.'

'My apologies. Now you must give me your son for safekeeping. He, like I, cannot enter there.'

Eric's heart lurched at the thought of letting Arwel out of his sight. Worse, of trusting him to her. She was a monster-hunter, and too many people had called his boy a monster.

'My oldest son was very like him,' she said. 'He had the same way of pouting his mouth when something displeased him. I think it was for him most of all that I killed Mizhara.'

When she reached for Arwel, Eric didn't resist. Together they released the sling from around his shoulders and put it around hers. Arwel whimpered and Eric bent to kiss his cheek, then quickly turned and marched towards the building. He knew if he looked back, he wouldn't go at all.

The inside was just as grand as the outside: all marble and gold and tiles polished to such a brightness he could see his face in the darkest of them. They formed scenes on all the walls, pictures of a people and a way of life a thousand years dead. He caught glimpses of ashen-skinned men riding two-wheeled chariots drawn by bulls, of children dancing in a ring around a pole wrapped around with honeysuckle, and one huge image of a man with his arms crossed, bare-chested and with diamonds of red painted all over him.

Eric didn't linger to gawp. Whatever magic the Hunter had worked on him drew him on. He weaved through corridors and dining halls and one room that seemed designed entirely to hold a collection of multicoloured feathers framed behind glass. The way was easy to find, until finally he came to a door that didn't open.

The handle was a metal ring fashioned into a grotesque face, lips drawn wide and tongue lolling out. Eric didn't like to touch it, but he gave the door a good strong tug. It didn't budge, and when he peeked between the wood and its frame, he saw a dark shadow that might have been a lock.

The door was twice his height. There was no way he could break it down. But the magic inside him was insistent. His path lay forward.

'That's all well and good,' he told it, 'but I need a key.'

It made him shudder, the way the magic seemed to answer him. He found his eyes drifting without his say-so towards a table in the left-hand corner of the room. Its surface was empty polished wood, but below was a drawer and in the drawer was a key.

It was heavy iron, cold against his fingers. Flakes of rust drifted from it and he worried it was too worn away to work, but when he put it in the lock, it turned with a solid *chunk*, satisfying as you like.

When the door opened a crack, the stench hit him. It was so choking he had to back away and cough, swallowing down the bile in his throat. He knew that smell. Once you'd learned it, you'd never forget it. It was the smell of death.

He didn't want to know what had been locked away rotting behind that door for all those years. He turned away and tried to walk back the way he'd come. In this maze of a building there was bound to be another way. But the power that had guided him forward stopped him going back. Every footstep he took felt like he was walking through a tub of honey, and he was gasping for breath after only three. It was even worse inside his head. The silent voice that had told him he was on the right track screamed at him now that he was doing something terribly wrong.

After five steps he fell to his knees in defeat. It was no good. He'd have to go through that room. And how bad could it really be? He'd seen death before. It was the living that hurt you.

When he pushed the door, it stuck halfway open. No matter how hard he shoved, it wouldn't shift, and he was forced to squeeze himself sideways through the gap, breathing shallowly through his mouth to try to stop the stench overwhelming him.

Inside, he saw what had made it. The room was huge, larger even than the Temple of the Worshippers, and it was filled with bodies. They must have been down here a very long time, but they hadn't rotted, they'd *dried*. The skin was stretched tight over the framework of their bones and their faces were still faces, human enough that he could read the expression on them. It was terror. The pile of bodies near the door was the biggest. They must have been trying to get out. Others had tried to scale the walls, but there'd been no hope for them. With the door locked, they'd been trapped.

Their clothes had survived too, only a little frayed. They all wore some version of a white robe embroidered with suns. It was easy to guess who they were: Mizhara's priests from the olden days. He'd heard that after the war, the survivors had buried the City Below in mud on purpose, so they could put their past behind them. But no one had ever told him they'd buried its inhabitants with it. He supposed he should have guessed. Killing ideas generally meant killing the people who held them. The long-ago people of Täm must have locked the priests who ruled them into this room and left them to slowly suffocate when their city was buried.

He had no choice but to pick his way across the carpet of bodies. It was horrible the way the eyes seemed to stare up at him. He could almost fancy there was malice behind them, as if they blamed *him* for what had happened to them. And some of them were so young. He hadn't known they took children as priests, but some of the bodies couldn't have been any older than eight when they died. He stepped over one small corpse and was forced to place his feet on its delicate hand or else step on another body and cave in its ribcage.

It made it worse somehow that the room was so beautiful. Some of the places he'd passed had been a bit too gaudy. This place had been made by people of taste, he could tell. The walls were painted all over in light, delicate colours. Some scenes showed Mizhara among her people, some Yron. There were some panels that had both of them together, smiling and holding hands. What would it have been like, looking at those pictures as you died? It would have seemed like mockery, he supposed. A terrible joke with you the punchline.

He was damp with sweat by the time he made it to the far side. When he unlocked the door, a gust of wind swept past him, almost knocking him off his feet. After him, it swept over the bodies in the room: over and through. Whatever force had been holding them together shuddered and gave out and one by one they softened into dust that swirled and danced in the breeze and then settled on the floor in a deep carpet.

He didn't loiter anywhere after that. He let the force pulling him forward drag him into a run. And finally he knew he must have come to the place he needed, because all at once it drained out of him, and he sagged to the ground, exhausted.

He'd thought it would bring him to some kind of library, or maybe a place like the map room in Ashfall, where generations of kings had planned their wars. But this was only a bedroom. The mattress had long rotted away, but the wooden bed frame was still standing and beside it a small cabinet.

He opened the cabinet drawers to find nothing but perished cloth. The walls were bare of decoration too, except the merest faded outline of what had once been paint. If this place was the answer to their question, he didn't understand it.

His eye was caught by something twinkling under the bed frame. He knelt to pick up a locket on a delicate gold chain. Gold didn't age like mortal things. He supposed it was no wonder Mizhara used it for her symbols. He snapped the locket open to find two pictures, one on each side. Though their features had faded with age he could see that one was a man and one a woman. They weren't young, but they seemed happy. A married couple, he supposed, the couple who'd slept in this bed – and probably died in that awful room.

They weren't much of an answer either, but now he was low down he saw what he hadn't noticed before: a piece of parchment wedged beneath the frame of the bed. It was terribly delicate, and he bit his lip as he tried to ease it out, afraid it would crumble away to nothing.

Pieces flaked from its edges, but somehow he was able to work it free without destroying it. One side was covered all over with text he couldn't read. On the other there was a picture that made his chest loosen with relief: a drawing of the stand they'd found in the place that was meant to hold the God Killer.

Whatever or wherever the God Killer was, this piece of parchment might be able to tell them. It might even be able to help them find it before Mizhara came to Täm and it was far too late. He held it as lightly as he could and turned to make his way back to the Hunter.

★

The city knew the threat that was coming. When Krish and Dinesh reached its outer streets, they were thronged with carts piled high with possessions and racing to leave. Other people hadn't even bothered to pack. They walked or rode beetle mounts, hectically mixing with all the rest and clogging the roads so that no one was going anywhere with any speed.

'Maybe we should leave too?' Dinesh said, looking longingly at the crowds.

'We can't leave Eric behind,' Krish said. 'He's still in Täm somewhere.'

'We, we, we could,' Dinesh said stubbornly. 'We *could* leave him.'

Krish pulled him to the side as a panicked bull galloped past, nostrils frothing. 'We can't leave his son for Mizhara to find. And I can't . . . I can't ask people to be loyal to me and then not be loyal to them. My father told me that.'

He found to his shock that he missed his father, longed for his cold, steady, reasonable presence. Having a father allowed him to be a son, as the da who'd raised him never had. His father might have known what to do, but Krish didn't. He only knew that fleeing with the panicking masses would do him no good. His former self had fled to the end of the world and even that hadn't saved him. He'd been an idiot to come here, but now he was here, this was where he'd make his stand.

'It's no good,' he said to Dinesh. 'We'll not make any progress through these crowds. We'll have to go through the gardens.'

He grabbed Dinesh by his arm and dragged him sideways,

over the low fence that circled the house to their left. It was a modest building, made of only half a dozen or so cubes, but flowerbeds ringed it. They were easy enough to walk through, their feet crushing delicate yellow blossoms beneath them.

It wasn't all easy going. Some of the houses had no gardens and others were guarded, forcing them back into the maelstrom of the streets. The sun was bright and pitiless by the time they reached the peak of one of Täm's many bridges. Krish thought it must be that light that was blinding him. But when he pushed his way onto the high wooden arch, he saw that the light was shining from below. The city buried beneath the city was alight, blazing and golden.

'That isn't good,' Dinesh said, looking down. 'That's bad.'

'Yes,' Krish said grimly. 'Yes, it is.' When he'd come into this world, it had been as a baby, no knowledge of his other life and not a hint of power. It seemed his sister had experienced a very different reawakening.

'What are we going to do?' Dinesh asked.

'We're going to rally the city to fight, the same as we did in Mirror Town. What else *can* we do? At least we know I won't be easy to kill. I'll take the front line if I have to. I'll fight every one of my sister's soldiers.'

'But *how* will we rally the city?' Dinesh asked. 'Nobody knows us. It's, it's, it's not like Mirror Town. They won't know that they have to listen. Here you don't have us, you've only got me.'

'I know. That's why we need to find Renar. She's important here. They'll listen to her.'

Dinesh stared at him open-mouthed as they reached the tree-crowned top of First Hill. 'She tried to kill you,' he said at last. 'You can't go to her. She'll try to kill you again.'

'How? She doesn't have a weapon that can do it. And now she knows my sister is here. She's clever – that's how she found us. She's clever enough to realise she can't save Täm without me.'

Beneath the hill they came to one of Täm's many parks. Krish had expected this would be one of the hardest places to cross, with its huge crowd. But nobody was moving. Though they must have known what was coming, the poor of the park still sat in their groups or lay sleeping in their pitifully small paper shelters. When Krish looked into their faces, he expected to see the sort of dull despair he'd known in his own childhood. But that wasn't what he saw. Mixed in with the listlessness there was hope and even a sort of savage glee.

He thought he understood. These people had been crushed beneath the boots of the city, discarded more readily than its paper houses. Now a force was coming that would do to others what had been done to them, and why shouldn't they enjoy it? But he wasn't sure his sister was here to offer the salvation some of them seemed to expect. He wasn't sure either he or his sister was capable of bringing anything but strife.

He'd learned the location of Renar's house when he first arrived in Täm. He'd meant to be sure of avoiding it, and he'd never walked these broad, lacquered streets. The houses here were large and their gardens formal and neat. Renar's place was the delicate pink and orange of sunset with a garden made of rocks. Water flowed over them in carefully guided channels and settled in pools. It suited her, though he couldn't quite have explained how.

It hadn't occurred to him until he approached that Renar might have fled too. The streets were already emptying, the bulk of those who'd chosen to leave well on their way. There was a feeling of vacancy, the sense that the houses had been deserted. Even the birdsong in the corkscrew-branched puzzle trees seemed muted.

Gravel crunched beneath their feet as he and Dinesh approached the door. He scratched his finger against the paper, the way he would have against the goatskin of the village tents. There was no reply. He hadn't really expected one, and he slid the paper door aside and walked in.

It looked as if the place had been ransacked. Clothes were strewn across the floor and a dark wooden desk had been knocked over, its inlaid surface scratched. A sudden raucous squawk of laughter came from further inside and he froze.

'Robbers?' Dinesh asked, but then another laugh came, lower and lighter, that Krish recognised.

He followed a trail of wreckage to find Lanalan sprawled on a heap of cushions in the largest room of the house. Someone else was beside him. It was dark here, shades drawn over the windows so that even the last light of day did little to dispel the gloom. But Krish recognised Renar's silhouette, the particular way she had of moving her head when she thought you were being a fool. It was she who'd laughed before. She did it again, a harsh sound more like a yell of pain than anything amused. Krish didn't need to see the empty bottles scattered around the cushions to know they were both drunk.

Renar flailed her arm, making some forceful point, and hit Lanalan in the face. He only laughed louder.

'Stop it!' Krish shouted. 'What are you doing? You're not . . . you can't do this now!'

They were both startled into silence. Renar dropped the bottle in her hands. It chinked against the tiling of the floor and rolled to a stop by Krish's feet.

'Don't you understand? My sister is coming,' he said.

Renar wasn't laughing now. She looked afraid. 'You're dead. You aren't real. Lanalan, do you see him too?'

Her brother rolled awkwardly to his knees. 'La, I do. Are we sharing the same dream?'

'He, he, he isn't dead,' Dinesh told them. 'The God Killer didn't work.'

Renar shook her head. 'I know it doesn't work. Why, I was the one who broke it!'

The twins both laughed, and Krish had to suppress the urge to hit them. 'Get a bucket,' he said to Dinesh, 'and get some water and then throw it over these idiots. They're no use like this.'

'That is unkind!' Lanalan rose to his feet. He stumbled one step towards Dinesh, tripped and fell face-first into the cushions.

'Mizhara is coming to take back this land,' Krish said furiously. 'Do you want that? You were willing to kill me, and I wasn't even planning to invade. Why won't you fight her!'

Dinesh came back before they could reply – if they even
meant to – and the splash of cold water in their faces at least
stopped their infuriating laughter. They both spluttered and
Lanalan shook himself like a dog, spattering droplets of water
over Krish.

'I need you to rally Täm's people,' he said more quietly. 'If
they don't make a stand here, she'll take the whole country. And
with all of Ofiklanod hers she can take Ashanesland too. This
could be our only chance to stop her.'

Renar rose to her feet. She had to steady herself against the
arm of a chair, but her voice was clearer when she said, 'And
why do you think *we* can rally them? Why not do it yourself?
You're the one who's a god. An unkillable god, apparently. Why
are you afraid? We're the ones in danger – and the fault is all
yours.'

'You have to rally them because I *am* a god. And I look like
one. The people of Täm don't know me and they won't trust me.
They'll think I want them to fight for me.'

'And don't you?' Renar asked.

'La, my sib is right,' Lanalan said. 'You want an army to fight
hers.'

'Belbog's balls, I want you to fight for yourselves! And the
people here know you, Renar. You're important, aren't you? High
up in the court or, what is it you people have? A powerful voice
with the Triumvirate, that's what you told me. If you speak, people
will listen.'

She laughed again, a bitter sound. 'People will listen to me,
will they? No, I believe not. I believe that thanks to you, I shall
never be listened to again.'

She walked forward until they were nose to nose and he finally
saw what the shadows had hidden. Her skin glinted in the darkness and her eyes gleamed golden. Lanalan moved to stand beside
her so that Krish could see the change in him too, his ashen skin
and the silver crescents of his eyes, exactly like Krish's own.

'You've, you've turned into Servants!' Dinesh said.

Lanalan bowed ironically, grasping Krish's shoulder as he

swayed. 'I am yours to command – apparently. What are your orders? I have never been good at playing the soldier, but I will give you my finest performance.'

Krish backed away, appalled. 'I . . . I'm sorry. I didn't know. I didn't want—'

A great rending sound broke off his words and the ground lurched beneath them, flinging them towards the cushions.

'What's happening?' Lanalan cried as the movement came again. This time the whole earth seemed to tilt, spilling them against the nearest wall and then through it as the paper tore with the weight of them.

It had been an outside wall. They found themselves in the garden made of rocks and pebbles. They had to fight to stand against the bucking of the earth beneath them. The carefully tamed water of the garden was wild now, flung into the air in sheets and gushing downward into the sudden gulf that had opened to separate Renar's house from her leftward neighbour.

The sun had set, but light blazed from the new rift and from a hundred others like it. What was happening to them was happening everywhere. The earth shuddered again and another rift opened – no, wider than a mere rift: a ravine from which the unnatural golden light shone in a beam towards the skies.

'It's the City Below!' Renar said. 'It's breaking free. It's unburying itself!'

The danger was obvious. They were on the highest hill with the furthest to fall to what lay waiting below. 'Help Lanalan!' Krish shouted to Dinesh. He grasped Renar's hand, ignoring her cry of outrage, and dragged her towards the road and their only possible escape.

★

They arrived in a great fleet. Dae Hyo had watched them build it at the foot of the raised waterway they travelled now. The Sisterband had done it, combining all the secrets of the tribes, and Dae Hyo had chosen to help them. He'd chopped wood and sanded it and helped to set up the hoists that lifted the timber to the water. All the while, he'd wondered why he was doing it.

Probably he just hated to be idle. Too many thoughts and no drink to drown them.

The ships weren't beautiful, but all they had to do was raise their sails and let the constant wind that blew along the raised waterway carry them. Dae Hyo liked to stand in the prow of the leading ship and watch the land as it passed. At first it had been nothing but old tangled woodland alternating with fields of stumps where the loggers had done their work. Lately they'd passed over fields of tall, broad-leafed plants with smiling yellow flowers.

Now the sun had set and the fields were only shadows, the deeper shadow of the waterway falling across them. The moon was bright tonight. Its reflection lay perpetually ahead in the clear water. They chased it but never caught it – except that sometime soon they would.

'My power is everywhere here,' Mizhara said. She'd made her way to his elbow without him noticing, as she often did. Her footsteps were soft for all that her presence felt so heavy.

'It's your land,' Dae Hyo allowed.

'Yes. I remember . . . I remember it differently.'

He shrugged. 'It was a thousand years ago.'

'But not for me.'

He turned to stare at her. 'Is that how it felt? You went to sleep, and then you woke up?'

She tilted her head, considering. 'No. I was someone else before I was Mizhara. My life before is a memory – a memory I never lived.'

'Krish doesn't remember at all,' Dae Hyo said. 'He's only Krish.'

'He's ahead. I can sense him at last. And his power is growing with mine. We are bound. We always were. The brother I find will not be the brother you left.'

Dae Hyo thought of Krish, sometimes keen like a young boy and sometimes gloomy like an old man. He pictured him laughing, which was odd, because it wasn't something Krish did much. His brother was so different from this Yron she spoke about. It was impossible to think they could somehow combine without Krish being lost.

Dae Hyo couldn't bear the thought of that. He'd come to have a sort of fondness for Mizhara. She seemed so in need of something, and utterly unable to ask for it. But Krish was . . . Krish was the one decision Dae Hyo had ever made and stuck to. His hand brushed against the tattoo on his cheek and found it cold to the touch. It often was, recently.

'There,' she said, pointing ahead, a sudden note of excitement in her voice. 'There is Dara Ilu, my city.'

It was no more than a speck on the horizon, but they were travelling fast. They'd reach it soon, and his guts stirred uneasily. 'We're here, then?'

'Yes, this is where he is.'

She started to turn away, but he stopped her with a hand on her arm, only dropping it when two of the nearby Servants reached for their swords. 'This person you were before you were Mizhara, what was her name?'

'She – I – had no name. Servants take none.'

'But she was a person, wasn't she? She wanted things.'

'Servants want nothing.' Now her voice was very cold.

'Then she doesn't want this revenge you're after, does she? You, that part of you, doesn't want this war?'

'You're mistaken. I want it more than anything.'

He let her walk away and went to his thin mattress in a corner of the deck by the smallest mast. He'd positioned it so no sails were overhead and when he lay down, he could stare up at the stars. He found it soothing to trace the shape of them with his eyes. Even here, so far from home, they were the same. They must even have been the same in that distant land his people came from.

His elder sister Eun had smoked too much of the purple grass once. She'd lain on her back beside him just like this, with the stars above. She'd told him a secret she wasn't meant to tell, that no man was meant to know: the Dae were the keepers of the charts that had guided the Fourteen Tribes to this land. His people's talent was for finding the way.

Jimin hadn't told anyone about the sun magic he'd used to save himself from her. He supposed she couldn't without revealing that she'd tried to kill him. She kept herself away from him and he kept himself away from her, but he couldn't forget it. What did it mean, that he could use the power of Krish's enemy?

Olufemi had told him that only worshippers of the gods were granted their power. He didn't worship Mizhara, but he felt sorry for her. It was strange. He'd never pitied Krish for the cursed power he'd been born to, even though Krish seemed to want it much less than this woman who'd become Mizhara. Now he thought about it, maybe that was it. His brother wasn't always wise, but he was wise enough to question this unasked-for gift he'd been given. Mizhara had accepted it too readily, like a fish swallowing bait.

The old priests had wielded the power of sun *and* moon. Olufemi had told him that too. And they hadn't loved the gods. They'd used them. Was he supposed to use them? He didn't see how. Krish had never been one to take instructions and Mizhara was even less obliging.

He knew the question at the heart of all this, beating too hard to be ignored. What was *Dae Hyo's* purpose? His people were dead, their killers were dead and he'd also been given a gift he didn't ask for. His fingers crept back to the rune on his cheek, rubbing at it as if he could rub it away.

The Sit-Still People were weak, so they saw him as a warrior of power. But among the Dae he'd only been one strong arm among many. He'd never been known for his good mind, even when it was clear of drink. And as a lover he'd been mostly unsuccessful. He'd never found the right words and he'd been more often laughed at than kissed. He'd never stood first at anything.

But now he had this . . . this huge clear emptiness inside him. And when the runes filled it, he felt strong. There was a rightness to it, to the way they fitted in his mind. It was as if his mind had been made to carry them, and all his life had only been about waiting for the moment when it could. He'd spoken to some of the mages after the Battle of Mirror Town, those who were still able to talk. They hadn't liked the feeling of the runes inside them. They'd said it felt as if they were trying to squeeze a lion inside a bucket. It didn't feel that way to him. He thought his emptiness might be large enough to hold any rune there was.

He'd never believed in fate. Some of his brothers had said that life was a rug and your thread was woven into it from the moment of your birth, its pattern already decided. He'd hated that thought. What was the point in anything if someone else had chosen the weft? And what sort of weaver would choose the threads of the Dae's death?

He thought he might believe it now. This, everything that had happened, it had a purpose. *He* had a purpose. But he had no fucking idea what it was.

★

Eric emerged from the temple into the light of dawn. It shone through a gap in the buildings, bright enough to blind. It took him a moment to realise it was shining where no sun should be.

Täm was gone. The thousand-year-old mud had been washed away and the city along with it. Now there was only the City Below. It was almost exactly as he'd seen it in his vision, except no trees or flowers grew anywhere. There was only bare earth between the grand golden buildings, as if the whole vast place had been put together in a day.

The square around him was far grander than it had looked on the way in. The building to his left was piled together out of curves, like a whole load of giant eggshells had been put on top of each other and painted red, and the domes were topped with long thin spires. A breeze stirred and a musical ringing came from high above: delicate bells too distant to see.

The Hunter had sat herself on a marble bench. Arwel was settled on her lap, but she wasn't attending to him, or to Eric's approach. Her eyes were fixed on the reborn city, filled half and half with wonder and fear.

She jerked her head around as his shoe slapped against the marble tiles of the square. 'You are returned.' She didn't sound as if she'd entirely expected it. 'And did you find what we need?'

He shrugged. 'Can't say, but – hold on, what's that terrible stink? Bloody hell, can't you tell Arwel's soiled his clouts?' The smell was pungent and unmistakeable, weirdly metallic.

'Oh!' She looked at the baby on her lap in surprise. He looked back up at her, solemn as a priest. 'I had forgotten . . . I had forgotten how children are.'

'Give him here,' Eric said. 'I've got spares, I'll sort him out.'

Arwel's wiry arms reached for Eric as Eric reached for him. It made the love flare inside him the way it always did. He'd never known he could feel that for another person, let alone one who ate and shat as much as Arwel did. The smell worsened as Eric opened Arwel's swaddling, and he wriggled at just the wrong moment so that Eric got a smear of the black shit all along his mutilated hand.

'You must hurry,' the Hunter said.

He wiped the shit as best he could on a cleanish section of the clouts, then set to fumbling in his bag for fresh ones. 'I'm doing my best. I'll give you what I found when I'm ready.'

'No, Eric, listen to me. You must hurry. We must go – now.'

He looked up, suddenly registering the tension in her voice, like the string of a viol tightened too far. There was movement at the far edges of the square. He couldn't quite make it out, but her eyes saw further than his.

'We must run,' she said. 'Hand me your son. We will travel faster if I carry him.'

'I ain't finished yet. You'll get shit all over you.'

'Now,' she said, and as the distant figures drew closer, alarmingly fast, he did as she said.

It was the lions, the statues he'd seen guarding dozens of homes on their walk to this place. They hadn't seemed so large when they'd been sitting on their haunches, looking ornamental. They hadn't been baring their glittering teeth and their claws hadn't been extended to the length of razors, clacking against the pavement as they ran. He could see their inner workings now, the metal rods and cogs that turned beneath their cracked marble shells.

The Hunter led him on, pelting to the right round the eggshell building. It was the only direction the lions weren't coming from.

'What *are* they?' he gasped as he ran.

'Hers,' the Hunter said.

Almost the worst thing was how quiet their pursuers were. They didn't growl or snarl like a real lion would. There was only the *click-click-click* of their long claws against the paving to let Eric know that they were behind him.

He was glad the Hunter was with him. He couldn't have carried Arwel at the pace she set. And he knew she'd protect his boy too, almost as fiercely as he would. He thought she might die for him. He hadn't realised it before and it made his uneasy truce with her warm into something else inside him.

But the fact that she wasn't turning to fight the mechanical creatures terrified him. He'd seen her take down an ice bear without much effort and she wasn't even trying with these. He didn't like to think how fearsome they must be if even the Hunter wouldn't face them.

He snatched a look behind him as they rounded a corner between two sharp steeples. The creatures were only paces behind, their jaws open. They had no tongues nor spit, only a gaping darkness inside them.

'They're catching up!' he yelled.

The Hunter didn't reply, but her long, strong legs opened their stride even wider. Eric fell a pace behind, then another. Just when he thought he'd fall all the way into the maws of the beasts, she grabbed his arm and yanked him sideways. He had no time to see where she was taking him before his face smacked into something hard and cold.

He couldn't have been out for more than a moment, but when he opened his eyes, blinking back tears of pain, he saw that they'd somehow gone up. They were twenty paces in the air and rising. They seemed to be spinning too, the view changing as he watched, first facing back towards the golden temple and then over what must have been the houses of great lords and ladies, a patch of bare brown earth that had probably been a park, and round to the temple again.

He was standing on a narrow platform with his back to a pillar, and he realised that the pillar itself was moving. The platform wound about it in a coil so that they rose as the pillar turned. The Hunter had her arm against his chest, holding him tight so he wouldn't fall. Below, the marble-and-metal lions stood on their hind paws and snapped impotently at the pillar. The platform wasn't wide enough to hold them. There was a nasty intelligence in their yellow eyes that told him they would have used it if they could.

'We're safe,' he said, as the platform reached the end of its journey around the pillar.

The Hunter stepped smoothly off and onto the high roof of a tower. It was edged with a fragile, knee-high wall and he backed away from it and sat carefully cross-legged in the very centre of the platform. From there he could see only the edges of the new-old city and the countryside beyond, with the wonderful blue bands of the canals striding across it.

'We are safe but trapped. I will think of something.' The Hunter settled neatly beside him, her legs crossed in some needlessly complicated way that left her feet poking up.

He took Arwel from her. The clouts were gone, left behind in the square when they'd fled, so Eric took off his own skirt and tore a strip to wrap around his son's nethers. It left him in nothing but his smalls, though the Hunter didn't seem to notice. She was peering over the rim of their perch, frowning.

'What were those things, anyway?' he asked.

'Mizhara's guardians. She had become very interested in putting life into lifeless matter, in the last years of her reign. It pleased her, I think, to make simple mechanical things that behaved just as they were told. She did not enjoy the wildness of natural life as Yron did. I believe this was why his experiments offended her so. The beings he made were even less amenable to reason than those that nature grew. I remember how the mere sight of your companion Rii sickened her. More of her creations will be coming. Those we have already seen were only the nearest.'

He reattached his skirt, shorter by several hands, and put Arwel back in his sling. 'Well, ain't you cheerful. What are we supposed to do now? Wait here till something arrives that's small enough to climb up and get us?'

'Give me the thing you found,' she said. 'The God Killer is our only hope now.'

She frowned when she saw how very little of it there was: just one sheet of parchment and maybe a dozen lines of writing.

'It's all there was,' he told her. 'The place your runes led me was just a bedroom. But I know that's it. Tell me what it says.'

She hesitated. Probably she'd meant to keep the knowledge to herself. He'd already learned what a miser she was with information. But then she nodded and began to read, slow and awkward as if she'd lost the knack of it. '"My beloved husband, our problem is solved. Laughingly" – no, that is not it – "ironically, it was Yron himself who offered the answer. He was asking about his other selves. He seems far more interested in them than his sister. I suppose curiosity is in his nature.

'"As soon as he said the words, I knew they were what we needed. Do you see? The crystals we have used cannot work as a focus because they are of the present time, the present faces of our gods. We must look to the past if we wish to enact a change that big, because what we do will ripple back to the past as well as forward into the future. We are attempting to make the world not-be something that it *has* been for a thousand thousand years.

'"They say the western mountains have roots of a peculiar iridescent quartz. It was mined once for its beauty, but ill-luck followed and the practice ceased. This is where we will find our focus. And if the – no, I cannot say the gods, can I? If luck is willing and my theory is correct, we will finally have a focus for our runes and a way to unmake the gods.

'"I am afraid, my love. Are you? A world without gods. Without divinity itself. But we must finish what we have started. I have already begun to fear him."'

'I don't understand,' Eric said. 'That wasn't helpful at all. They ain't even mentioned the God Killer. Are you sure you read it all?'

He was shocked at the despair on her face. 'There is no weapon,' she said. 'I was wrong. That empty room, the marks upon the walls – they were a rune more complex than any I have ever seen. And that rune *is* the God Killer.'

'Oh.' He stroked Arwel's head, the terrifying warm softness of it. 'But what does that mean? What does the rune do?'

'It matters not. The focus through which the rune must be viewed is lost. And such a tremendous working is beyond me, and therefore beyond anyone living in this late age.' She reached out to the chain around his neck and placed the delicate bone whistle between his lips. 'Summon the beast Rii and flee from here, Eric of my people.'

'No, I ain't leaving. I swore an oath of loyalty to Prince Krishanjit. It was my choice – not like anything else I done these last few years. I won't break my word. And I won't leave you to face her alone. We're friends, ain't we?'

She looked shocked at his words. Well, so was he, but he found he meant them. He and Arwel owed her their lives.

'You do not know enough to make this choice,' she said. 'There is something I have not told you. I believed . . . I still believe that it was better for you not to know. But now you must. As Yron was not made from nothing in this new age, but born into the body of a man, so Mizhara returned into already-living flesh. And the person she once was is not your friend.'

'You're saying that I know her?'

'The fault was mine. I meant only to save her from an untimely and undeserved death. But I gave her Mizhara's power and in so doing I gave her to Mizhara entire. It was always the way of gods to take more than they were offered and call it their due.'

Eric felt a terrible sinking in his stomach. It was like that moment before the blow fell when you could already feel the pain. 'Stop talking around in circles, will you? We ain't got time for riddles.'

She dropped her head, as if she was ashamed to face him. 'It was your wife and the mother of your child. The one whom you called Drut has become Mizhara, and she has forgotten none of what transpired between you. To Mizhara you are merely one of her brother's allies. To Drut you are the worst of all betrayers – a man who stole her love and her child and left her to die in the ice. If she ever lays her hands on you or your son, there will be no hope for you. So I beg of you, do as I say. Take your son as far and as fast as you can, and you may yet buy a few months of life for him before the whole world is lost.'

26

Olufemi woke to a loud click and Yemisi's yell of triumph. The room was lit only by the very first hints of dawn and she stumbled over her shoes as she hobbled towards the sound of Yemisi's voice.

'What is it? Have you found a way to break the runes?'

'Better,' Yemisi said, 'I've opened the door.'

There was a lamp on one of the cabinets. Once Olufemi had sparked the wick she saw that Yemisi was kneeling beneath the door handle, a bent wire clasped in one hand.

'You picked the lock?' Olufemi was simultaneously impressed and deflated. She'd expected a less mundane breakthrough.

Yemisi grinned girlishly. 'My cousin Adetola taught me how when I was ten. He was a famed lockmaker. You remember him, don't you?'

Adetola had died before Olufemi was born, but she didn't think it would be helpful to say so.

'Come on then, let's get out of here,' Yemisi said.

Outside, the sea-washed eastern horizon was lined with pale yellow, but the dawning sun did little to lighten the dense black rock all around. The heat was everywhere already, stored in the rocks overnight and pouring back out like a clinging fog.

'We'll have to leave by sea,' Olufemi said. 'I believe we're on an island. You remember the map we saw in the orange house by the sycamore tree?'

'I don't pay attention to maps. I'm not an Eze like you. Look, it's growing brighter. If we don't leave soon, we'll be caught.'

The sun was already showing its upper edge and their shadows stretched long behind them, black against black. The jagged landscape offered few hiding places. Their only hope of escape was to be gone before their captors returned for them.

The dark rocks made distance hard to judge and the harbour was closer than it looked. They'd barely walked for half an hour before they were forced to fall into a crouch, and peer round crumbling boulders at their destination.

'Oh,' Yemisi said, 'is that good or bad?'

Only two small vessels lay at anchor in the harbour, seemingly deserted. But further out at sea, where tall waves set them swaying and plunging, an entire fleet was heading towards land.

'If we hide ourselves aboard the docked ships now, we should be safe,' Olufemi said. But she didn't move. A nagging curiosity held her back, the driving force and fatal weakness of her life. How could she leave now, when she knew so little of what was truly going on here?

'I thought you said it was safe?' Yemisi complained as Olufemi turned her back on the sea and its ships.

'It will be even safer later,' Olufemi lied. 'And we may as well use the time we have until then wisely.'

There was a path that led from their prison towards the lush valley at the island's centre. They kept it always to their left and made their way over the rocks in the heat of the climbing sun. It was midday by the time they'd scaled the peak and Olufemi's joints screamed their unhappiness at her. But she felt a thrill of joy and fear intermingled as she once again saw the green landscape that lay below, the thousand new species the new magic had made.

'Won't they notice us if we go back there?' Yemisi asked.

Olufemi had already considered this. 'We'll make a fist of our hands and hide them in our sleeves. Unless we meet the very people who brought us here, they won't know us from others of themselves, especially with all these newcomers arriving. And look, do you see down there? I believe we were taken to that red building on the left. I remember those broad-leafed trees that surround it. If we go right, where the tall grey hall is, we should be unobserved.'

Yemisi looked unconvinced, as well she might. It wasn't much of a plan. Yet something drew Olufemi onward. What was happening here felt wrong to the core of her bones, but she couldn't rest until she'd understood it.

The walk through the jungle was harder than over the rocks, and insects were profuse. Yemisi yelped when a mauve-winged creature bit her cheek but Olufemi stared, fascinated, at its lopsided body and the buzz of its many wings. There was fruit hanging from some of the branches, pale-skinned bulbs a little like pears that smelled of vanilla. Long vines with yellow polyps bled sticky juice in which some of the many insects struggled, trapped.

The sound of voices warned them when they approached the settlement. Olufemi hesitated, but the plan she'd laid out to Yemisi was the only one she had. 'Look like you belong,' she hissed and then made herself smooth her own face before she strode onto the beaten ground that surrounded every building.

There were few people about. Perhaps these Mortals had adopted the same habits as the people of Mirror Town and slept through the fiercest heat of the day. She'd always imagined the Eternal Empire remaining frozen in time at the moment in which it had driven out the mages. There had been, unspoken but deep, a sense among the inhabitants of Mirror Town that one day their exile would end and they would be permitted to return home. But the home they yearned for had ceased to exist a millennium ago. And now the Mortals meant to change their lands, perhaps the whole world, more completely than Olufemi had thought possible.

The laughing voices of children drew her on, and tucked behind a low red building she found a garden arranged around a three-headed fountain. There were three children in it, just before the flowering of their adulthood. One was clearly female, another male, and Olufemi guessed the last must be this third sex that only the Ofiklanders knew, the people they called inter.

'Are these their gods?' Yemisi whispered as they hovered on the verge, watching. 'I thought they hadn't created them yet.'

'I suppose they've been trying.'

The children's heads turned towards them at the sound of their voices, and Olufemi hastily stepped away, pulling Yemisi after her.

'They don't look much like gods,' Yemisi said.

'Krishanjit was only a boy until he came into his full power.'

'His silver eyes, though. You said he was born with them. And the statues we saw in that temple – they must have been figures of their new gods. And they had the heads of animals. Those are just children.'

Olufemi peered back at them through the hedge. The boy was reading from a manuscript while the girl and the inter played some game that involved rolling silver balls over the grass and much yelling in triumph or despair. 'Rorön wanted our assistance. Most likely it's because the Mortals' experiment failed.'

'Not entirely failed.' Yemisi stroked the three-lobed leaf of a plant beside her. 'They've changed the world already. And that plague we saw back in the flower fields. Don't you think it was them who caused it?'

Olufemi hadn't thought it, but now Yemisi said it, it seemed quite obvious. 'Yes, of course. No wonder they need help, if that's the result of their experiments. Or . . . yes, I believe I see. They planted a seed of one variety in the soil of the south, and then Krishanjit came from the north, and he is another type of seed entirely. And the two hybridised.'

'You're saying the prince caused the plague?'

'His presence. The triple god and the double can't coexist easily.'

Yemisi shuddered. 'I know. I feel it. Something twisting its way inside me that doesn't like me. It wants to *change* me.'

Without quite realising it, Olufemi had been pushing down that same feeling all day, hiding her discomfort from herself. Now she felt it in full and more strongly than ever in the presence of these seemingly ordinary children.

'We shouldn't linger here,' she said. 'We'll have to hunt elsewhere for answers.'

They found a building that seemed to be the children's home, and another that must have been a dining hall. There was also a nursery where three far younger children were being kept. But nowhere did they find any hint of the magic she felt in her bones. The Mortals claimed to have created a whole new system of it, and yet she hadn't seen a single rune. If there was power here, she had no idea how the Mortals controlled it.

'We should go back to the boats,' Yemisi said. 'People are beginning to notice us.'

It was true. Their aimless wandering had begun to attract glances, but she wasn't ready to leave. There was a puzzle here, one deeper and more intricate even than the runes whose study had changed the whole course of her life. She couldn't leave without an answer.

In the end, they found the building they couldn't see by pure accident. Olufemi's shoulder brushed a wind chime that seemed to hang in thin air, there was a ringing note, and suddenly the building was beside them. Some part of her had always known it was there, and yet her eyes hadn't been able to catch it.

'I don't understand,' Yemisi said. 'How did that happen?'

'A working of their magic,' Olufemi said.

Now she could study it, the building looked quite plain. Only the ornamented wind chimes that circled it added any interest to the plain grey blocks of granite. But it was the largest place they'd yet seen, and seemingly deserted.

'We should go,' Yemisi said again. 'I don't like this.'

'We came for answers,' Olufemi snapped. 'I'm not leaving just when I'm on the verge of finding them.'

'The countryfolk tried to burn us to death the last time we came too close to their new gods.'

'Then the secret must be worth the finding, mustn't it?'

Olufemi kept close to the building, one hand resting against the gritty surface of the walls. The chimes sang delicately in the wind and she was forced to duck beneath them. In some way she didn't understand they seemed to hold the magic of this place. She didn't know what would happen if she touched them again.

The entrance was on the far side, facing towards the untended jungle. She listened at the door, but there was no sound of voices and it was easy to slip in without being seen.

It was disappointingly plain inside, a narrow white corridor with doors leading off. The first few led to rooms with simple cots and little else. The next seemed more promising. There were gleaming silver instruments of surgery hung on its walls, and two long tables darkly stained with blood. But whatever bodies had been dissected on them were long gone.

The next door led to a library. Many volumes were written in the incomprehensible script of Ofiklanod. But in a dark corner, shielded from the light of the windows, a section of shelves held far older volumes. Olufemi recognised a few: great works of history that were also to be found in Mirror Town. Next to them were volumes she'd only ever seen mentioned in other works: Taiwo's great work *Being a History of the Mountain Races*, almost as thick as it was high, and his twin Kenhinde's more slender *On the Management of Cattle*. And there were books about the runes, dozens whose titles she knew and many more she'd never heard of.

It was clear the Mortals had sought to understand the old gods before making their own. But this was all in the past. The secret of what they'd created wouldn't be found here.

Yemisi gasped when they entered the next room. But Yemisi had never been privy to Olufemi's own experiments in the years she'd sought to summon the moon. The work here was work she'd done. It looked far more sickening when performed by another hand.

The shelves were lined with jars, some filled only with liquid but most containing preserved flesh: a hand here, a foot there, human but strangely clawed, and in many of them foetuses cut from their mothers' wombs. Those were the most intriguing. The fluid that held them suspended was murky, but she could see that their heads were deformed in some way. Was that a beak sprouting beside the half-formed mouth of a baby girl? And those were certainly scales running across the back of another.

Yemisi looked appalled. 'When they said they were trying to make their gods, I didn't think they meant it so literally.'

Olufemi shrugged. 'What other way to make an idea flesh?' Yemisi's delicacy annoyed her. It felt like a judgement.

In the far corner of the room, dusty and neglected, were what she took for the earliest experiments. There were glass cylinders nearly as high as the ceiling and broad enough to hold the corpses of grown humans. The liquid was a sickly green but clear enough that Olufemi could see what had been done. Each body had been decapitated and the head of an animal sewn to its neck with neat stitches: a coyote's head on the inter, a many-mandibled insect on the woman and a bright-feathered bird on the man.

That didn't surprise her. She'd learned what form the Mortals meant for their new gods to take. But the flesh around the stitches had grown to half-cover them, the marks of the surgery healed into scars. Impossibly, the victims of these experiments hadn't died, at least not at first. The Mortals hadn't succeeded. But they were very close.

Intent on her study of the experiments, she only heard the footsteps behind her when it was too late. She turned, expecting to see Rorön, but it was a person she'd never met before – an inter, to judge by the style of *omas* clothing. And *omas* expression was far too unsurprised.

'You knew we were here,' Olufemi said, as Yemisi shrank behind her.

'Indeed.' The inter smiled. 'So allow me to introduce myself. My name is Bruyar, Remembrancer of the Mortals these last ten years. And you and I have a great deal to discuss. I can't tell you how pleased I am to find that Rorön brought you here. Why, he could not have chosen a more opportune moment. For I have been told that you are Olufemi, the one woman in all the world who knows how to birth a god.'

Bruyar held out the crook of *omas* elbow as if *oms* were a friend inviting another on a walk. There was not a hint of hostility or anger on *omas* face. But Olufemi knew without question that this was the most dangerous person she'd yet met in Ofiklanod.

After a moment, she slipped her own arm through the inter's. 'You wanted us to come here,' she guessed.

'Not here in particular, my darling, but wherever you chose. How can you help us if you don't understand our work? And Rorön, cunning as he is, knew you would be far more likely to believe what you freely found than what you were given.'

'We found your experiments,' Yemisi said. 'Why would we want to help anyone who'd do this?'

'All gods are born in pain,' Bruyar replied. 'One has only to study history to understand that.'

'You were watching us,' Olufemi said. 'Your magic, the wind chimes on this building, the illusion that cloaks it. It's *nothing* like the runes. If you're using sound somehow to work your will, I don't know that I could help you, even if I chose. And besides, the power is already here. You've made your gods.'

Bruyar had led them back to the library and gestured them to sit. Olufemi saw that tea had been laid out for them in some parody of hospitality. The little silver cup looked absurdly small in Bruyar's meaty hand as *oms* sipped from it.

'There is power in what we've done, it's true,' Bruyar said. 'But not enough. I thought perhaps that it was your Krishanjit's presence that suppressed its spread. It was certainly the mixing of the two magics that caused the unfortunate warp whose effects you've seen. But now Krishanjit is dead and yet our problems persist. Our gods are only almosts.'

A chill swept Olufemi, and something almost like grief.

Bruyar tilted *omas* head to study her expression. 'Did you not know? It's true, I'm afraid. Your god is gone.'

It could so easily have been a lie, but there was too much of an air of triumph about Bruyar. *Omas* small smile spoke not of a lie successfully told but of a truth strategically deployed.

'How . . . how did he die?'

Bruyar frowned. 'An error. We meant to study him and then – I hope you'll forgive my honesty – to kill him. But a servant of mine took matters into her own hands. She used the God Killer.'

'No, it can't be. I would have felt it. Surely I would have felt it!' But Olufemi had been in the lands where the three gods held sway and the power of the runes was out of her reach. It seemed wrong – cruel even. But Krishanjit might have left the world without her ever knowing.

'He is gone,' Bruyar said. 'Believe me, I wish it weren't so. The servant in question has been appropriately reprimanded. But Krishanjit is no more, just when we need him most. I've left behind a few Mortals to rally Täm's citizens to its defence, but it won't be enough.'

Olufemi shook her head, less a denial than an attempt to clear her head. There was too much, far too much to make sense of in one moment. 'Why would *you* need Krishanjit? Why does Täm need defending?'

'Because his sister has come to Ofiklanod, and he was the only one who might defeat her. Him, or the new gods. But they aren't strong enough, not yet, not without your help. So tell me, Olufemi, how did you make your Krishanjit into what he was? Tell me how to make a person into a god, and together we can save the world from the ravages of the sun.'

If Krishanjit was gone, what did anything matter? 'I wandered the world,' she told Bruyar. 'I went from nation to nation and I told them all about the lost prince and the power he wielded. I planted the idea. It's the idea that must grow alongside the man.'

Bruyar tapped a fingernail impatiently against *omas* tea cup. 'Indeed. That much we knew. We have worked on this for centuries, my darling, did Rorön not tell you? Each generation we tried again with new children, and each generation we tried to make them the perfection, the very epitome of what a man and a woman and an inter should be. One time we raised the girl a soldier, the boy a scholar and the inter a debaucher. We encouraged books to be written that instructed our people in how warlike women were by nature, how studious men and how louche inters.

'It worked, in a way we hadn't expected. Inters, who'd been no more than one in a hundred of us, became one in ten. And we changed our nature, too. Before, people such as I were caught between man and woman. Now we're fully both. For a brief while we hoped this was the start of the greater transformation we desired, the triumph of the triple over the dual. But it wasn't enough. We tried again with different god-children, different natures, different books. None sufficed.

'We resolved to be bolder. We planted the seed of god worship in the south and carefully tended it as it grew – pruning now and again so that none would guess our plan. The occasional killing of an idolater, the burning down of a temple, these were all that was required. And that achieved *something*. That was when the system came to us, the music that describes the gods and summons their power. And yet still this wasn't enough. These last few months the power has grown and I'd hoped that perhaps *these* children, *these* gods might be the ones. But their strength cannot match the sun's and their power shrivels in her light.'

'But how did you create the children?' Olufemi asked.

The tapping of Bruyar's finger stopped, a final musical *clink* as it stilled. 'Create them? Why, *we* did not create them – that task was their parents'. We merely raised them here from birth to be what we required.'

So here it was. The thing they *didn't* know. If Olufemi chose she could stay silent and the three new gods would remain half-born. But Krishanjit was dead, and even alive Krishanjit had been a disappointment. He'd never been what Olufemi hoped. She could admit that to herself now. Whereas here was something new, something remarkable, and others to share her work with.

'I needed a rebirth,' Olufemi said, 'the last god to be made flesh again. So I . . . I tried many things. But finally I took the closest thing that still existed to Yron. I captured one of the Servants of the moon, one of the worm men, and I ground up his flesh and fed it to a pregnant woman. The child that was born to her was Krishanjit.'

Bruyar studied her in silence, gauging her honesty. Then Bruyar clapped *omas* hands and stood. Where before the inter had been calm and calculating, now *oms* was all energy and almost desperate determination. Olufemi realised that the desperation had been there all along. Only Bruyar's self-control had kept it hidden.

'I see. Yes. I think I see what we must do,' Bruyar said. *Oms* stood abruptly and swept from the room.

The entourage of guards and Mortals who'd waited for Bruyar outside rushed to keep pace with *omas*, and Olufemi was forced to run to follow, round the hidden house and into the garden they'd passed earlier, where the three young almost-gods played. They smiled when they saw Bruyar and *oms* opened *omas* arms wide so all three could fling themselves at *omas*. The girl had jam smeared around her mouth. She left a dark smear of it on Bruyar's robes and the boy picked at it with fussy fingers as Bruyar pressed him to *omas* chest.

'My darlings, I've been too long away from you,' Bruyar said. Unseen by them, *omas* eyes took in *omas* people, standing in an uncertain, black-robed group. Then they turned to Olufemi.

Olufemi's stomach clenched with horror. She knew with sudden, absolute certainty that something terrible was about to be done.

'You've been very good,' Bruyar told the children, releasing them from *omas* hold with a last brush of *omas* fingers against the inter's shaved head. 'I want you to know this isn't your fault. You've done nothing wrong. The fault is mine.' Then *oms* turned to the guards and said, 'Kill them now.'

'No!' Olufemi shouted. She wasn't alone. The same protest came from many of the Mortals and several of the guards.

'Do it!' Bruyar snapped, then flinched as if *omas* own words shocked *omas*. 'Please make it quick and painless. I don't want them to suffer.'

The children seemed to realise at last that this wasn't some joke. The boy stood rooted in place by terror and the inter smiled uncertainly, but the girl turned from the guards and fled.

Like predators whose prey was running, the guards finally acted. In five strides the girl was taken, and others clustered around the boy and the inter. The children looked very small beside the tall, white-skirted guards. They had to stoop to hold the children, one to each arm. Olufemi saw them jostle for that position. They must have known that whoever held the children wouldn't have to deliver the killing blow.

Bruyar's face was set now, cold and determined as *oms* said, 'Don't waste the blood. We need that too.'

'Please,' the boy said, and as if that was the final spur – as if he couldn't bear to hear the rest of that sentence – one of the men drew his knife and slashed it across the boy's neck. A moment later the guards around the girl and the inter did the same. Blood gushed from the cuts over the fresh young grass.

Several people screamed. Yemisi was one of them. But others stumbled over themselves as they rushed to grab the bowls and cups the children had been eating from moments before. They held them beneath the necks of the children to catch what blood they could. The children's eyes were frantic as they shuddered in their killers' arms. Then they dulled in death.

Yemisi knelt beside Olufemi, losing her lunch on the ground. Olufemi's throat was bitter with bile, but she swallowed it down. 'Why?' she asked Bruyar. 'Why did you do this?'

There were tears on Bruyar's cheeks. Their tracks gleamed in the sunlight but *omas* face remained calm. 'You told me that the new gods must eat of the old. La, had we leftover servants of a former age I would have done as you did. But we do not, and this is the closest I can come – a trick of sorts, like the tales of Soalik the Lonely, who walked into the sky by using his hands as a staircase. They would have died anyway when Mizhara came. They might have died far more horrible deaths, and ones without purpose. It's better this way. Yes, indeed, far better.'

Oms turned from Olufemi as if sure *omas* words had won the argument. Or perhaps merely satisfied that they'd quieted *omas* own doubts.

The guards still held the children's corpses. At their feet, cups and plates held half-finished food topped with congealing blood. A woman bustled around, putting them all onto a tray while the guards watched Bruyar. Most of them looked sickened, a few as if they'd enjoyed their work.

'Take them to the kitchen,' Bruyar said, then turned to Olufemi. 'Do you think it best if each younger god eats only the flesh of their counterpart?'

Olufemi shook her head, a denial of the whole vile process, but Bruyar seemed to take it for a simple no.

'I think it best if we make them into stew,' Bruyar told *omas* people. 'We must ensure all the flesh is mixed together so each of them eats the flesh of all. Cook it long, over low heat. The meat must be tender. The blood you can bake into biscuits, but season them well so the flavour is hidden. When it's ready, feed it to the youngsters – and make sure they clean their plates. The sun is coming, and we *will* have gods of our own to face her.'

27

They were in the city now. Dae Hyo walked alongside the army's long, orderly column through the empty streets. The roads felt too smooth beneath his boots and glowed the orange-yellow of amber. With its low buildings and many trees, this would have been a peaceful place, if an army hadn't been marching through it.

'Where are my people?' Mizhara said. 'Why aren't they here to greet me?'

They've fled, Dae Hyo thought. It was obvious. There were possessions thrown everywhere. Some were in the road, trampled beneath the army's feet. Dae Hyo guessed they'd fallen from wagons or saddlebags. The rest were heaped in gardens. Their owners had probably found them too heavy to take.

They walked up a long hill and down it again before they saw the first people. They were ragged and dirty, crowded on the dry grass that lay in the crook of two hills. It was hard to imagine these people building the smooth roads and pretty houses they'd passed.

But Mizhara finally got the greeting she'd been hoping for. She smiled as the crowd roared at the sight of the golden army and surged to greet it. Dae Hyo stepped back from the front lines. He'd been to Smiler's Fair. He knew how a happy crowd could turn ugly on the spin of a coin.

As the crowd drew nearer, he began to see that there was more amiss with them than poverty. Many wore long coats to cover their deformities, but some couldn't be hidden. There was a head with hair that turned to fur and covered everything from nose to chin. A woman had the long antennae of a grasshopper in place of her eyebrows. A man's mouth had twisted into the beginnings of a beak.

'What's wrong with them?' one of the Sisterband asked, horrified.

Whatever it was, it got worse as they approached Mizhara. The shouts of greeting turned to yells of panic and screams of terrible pain. Dae Hyo saw the fur-faced figure writhe in agony as some unseen force pulled the hairs from his body and left bleeding, naked flesh behind. The beak that had twisted the man's mouth emerged fully formed at last, large and black like a pelican's. It tore out of his face, splitting his head around it so that his eyes fell to one side, the wreckage of his nose beside them, and the bones and sinew of his throat on another.

The crowd screamed and panicked. Those who were unhurt tried to flee, trampling the fallen beneath their feet. It wouldn't be long before the army was sucked into the same whirlpool of fear that swirled the crowd.

'We need to get out!' Dae Hyo yelled to no one in particular, but Mizhara seemed to have reached the same conclusion. The golden trumpets of her heralds sounded and the army began to march sideways, away from the horribly changing crowd.

There were yells for help as they left. Mizhara ignored them. The army was less orderly now. It hadn't been bloodied yet by battle, but Dae Hyo saw the same shock he'd seen on the faces of young warriors the first time they faced a real fight. It was the knowledge that this was no kind of game, and their own flesh was as vulnerable as their enemies'.

Mizhara's beautiful golden face looked drawn. Dae Hyo found it reassuring that she wasn't yet cold to the troubles of the world.

'What happened there?' he asked her.

Her golden hair shimmered as she shook her head. 'I don't understand. I felt something wrong as we approached. Something had shaped them whose very presence was inimical to mine. It must have been my brother.' But she didn't sound sure.

'I tell you what,' Dae Hyo told her, 'it doesn't seem like the kind of thing Krish would do. What's the point of it?'

'You may ask him when we find him. I sense his presence, like a dark hole in the world. We aren't far. Soon my brother and I will be face to face at last.'

*

Krish stopped running when they reached the outskirts of Täm, under the shadow of the Green Leaf Canal. The city behind them was a ruin. Only two hills remained intact. Probably they'd been built later and lay beyond the perimeter of the City Below. But the rest of Täm was gone as if it had never been. In its place, the great city of Mizhara shone as bright as it must have a thousand years before. It was undeniably a wonder, but Krish struggled to find it beautiful.

'Why did you do it?' he asked Renar. 'Why did you kill me? I didn't think you hated me.'

'I didn't. Why, I had no strong feelings about you at all. But you came here on your own and I knew Bruyar would kill me if *oms* learned it. I knew *oms* had the God Killer and I'd always assumed *oms* meant to kill you. I saved myself by bringing on a death that would have happened anyway. Except, of course, that I was wrong in every particular.'

'But why did you agree to this job with Bruyar?' Lanalan asked.

'For the money,' Renar said shortly.

'La, don't treat me like the fool you took the prince for! You never trusted Bruyar. You told Mother so. You were sure Bruyar had bloody hands and you swore you'd be careful never to bloody your own. If you were sure that Bruyar meant to kill Krishanjit, why did you take the work?'

Renar's face was easy to read: the decision to lie and then the choice not to. 'Because of you,' she said, her voice astringent. 'Because of my trusting fool of a sib, and because of our mother, who left our fortune to him and not to me. To you, Lanalan, when you were the joke of all Täm, and I a woman on her way to success. Bruyar promised me that *oms* would reverse the inheritance, as only *oms* could, and so I bloodied my hands!'

'I see,' Lanalan said. 'And did you not know that mother gave it to me *because* she knew me for a dreaming fool? She knew I would never make my own fortune in the world.'

Renar's mouth set mulishly. 'No. 'Tis a convenient excuse, but the truth is she loved you more. She always did.'

'It's no excuse, but the bare truth. She told me so herself.'

Renar had no reply to that.

'And did you not know,' Lanalan said quietly, 'that I would have given it all to you, had you only asked?'

Krish looked away, smiling bitterly. All of this, because a sister was jealous of her brother.

A cry sounded above him, a familiar sound. It was painful to start hoping again, but he made himself look up. He hadn't been mistaken. Rii was there, silhouetted against the sun like a black inkblot.

'Your monstrous bat comes for you!' Renar said. There were equal parts fear and hope in her voice.

Soon Rii drew so close that Krish could see the pointed leathery shape of her ears and the ragged outline of her fur. She carried something clasped between her claws: a huge crystal spear, gleaming in the daylight.

Rii's shadow followed her on the ground, growing darker and clearer as she descended. It was a hundred paces from them, fifty – and a great waft of mouldy cinnamon swept over them. But there was no swirl of air to signal her landing. She *wasn't* landing. Her shadow moved away as she flew obliviously past. A mile or two ahead, she finally landed.

'Where is she going?' Lanalan asked.

'It must be Eric,' Krish said. 'He had a device to call her. He must be alive after all. If we can reach him in time, we can leave with him when he goes.'

Krish felt his sister's presence ahead of him, a golden glow that burned in his mind. But Rii was his only chance to escape her, and he turned back towards the city at the centre of her power.

*

Eric had been near death before. He hadn't much liked it, but he'd met it face-on. The idea that Arwel might die, though? He couldn't even think it. But the creatures of Mizhara down below were thinking it all right, and there were more of them with every moment that passed. The marble-plated lions had been joined by clockwork horses. Their steel hooves crashed against the rock of the pillar and made chunks of stone fly out in showers of sparks.

The statues of people were the worst. Eric had watched from his perch as they marched towards him from all over the city: marble generals and boys at play and women in flowing robes cracked open to show the mechanism beneath. Those statues had enough sense to know they were better off trying to climb the twisted marble column than knock it down. A few had made it to the top already. It was only the Hunter who held them back. She stood with her face shining gold and her eyes bright, looking fierce but fragile. All Eric could do was curl his body around his babe and hope his flesh would be barrier enough to save him. He'd never felt more useless in his life.

When he saw the golden shapes winging towards them, he knew all hope was lost. They looked like herons from a distance, long-winged with spindly legs dangling beneath. But as they drew closer he saw the monstrous length of their beaks and the wicked jewel-bright teeth that glinted inside them.

'We got more company!' he yelled at the Hunter. 'Up above!'

The birds' beaks gaped, hungry for the kill. Eric tensed for the blow that would rip his flesh – and instead felt a waft of cinnamon-scented wind and heard a shriek of rage.

Rii's great dark body was like a thundercloud above him. She shrieked again and lashed out with her left claw. The golden birds seemed like fleas beside her bulk. They tore into shreds of metal as she raked them.

In her other claw she clutched a long shard of crystal. She swung it towards the stairs where the living statues were. He realised that he recognised it. It had been part of the vast statue of Mizhara they'd once camped beside. It was a fearsome-looking thing, but when it hit the marble casing of the statues, it shattered and fell to the ground in a thousand pieces.

But the tide of the battle had turned. Even without her stolen spear, Rii was a match for Mizhara's mechanical monsters. Their metal skeletons and marble shells were too soft to resist her claws, and her fangs left terrible wounds in their sides. One by one the horses and the lions stilled, their mechanisms wrecked or their bodies torn apart entirely.

The Hunter leaned against her spear and watched the destruction. There was an expression on her face he couldn't understand. It wasn't precisely happy, but it wasn't angry either. He thought perhaps she was looking into the past, to another battle where she'd seen Rii at work. In that battle she and Rii had fought on different sides. But when this fight was finally done, the Hunter lowered her spear and smiled.

'Your coming was timely,' she said, as Rii settled on the ground below them, leaving her face level with their platform.

'My coming was not for thee.' Rii bent her head so that her fanged mouth and squished-up nose were level with Eric. Her nose nudged his arms until he opened them and let her see that Arwel was whole and well.

'We need to get out of here,' Eric told her. 'Mizhara's coming with a bloody great army to kill us.'

Rii turned her head to look eastward. *'We cannot depart yet, morsel. Our master is not yet come.'*

★

Running through the streets of the ancient city felt like running through a dream. Krish remembered this place with startling clarity and the absolute knowledge that the memories weren't his. This fountain on his left, marble children frolicking in a waterfall of sapphires, was where his nursemaid had walked him and his sister, when he was still young enough to be free. The tall building to his right had been the home of one of his secret followers. Krish had visited in the depths of the night, sneaking from his Garden before his captors realised he was no longer its prisoner. In that square up ahead he'd faced his sister as her enemy for the first time.

It was *Yron* who'd done these things. Yron and not Krish. Yet the distance between the two seemed to be closing. He wanted to be himself, if only he could be sure who that self was.

'La – the beast is landing!' Lanalan shouted. His long strides had taken him ahead of the other three and when he turned back to them, Krish was shocked again by the changes. They seemed to be accelerating. His high cheekbones had grown sharper and there was an almost skeletal thinness to his face.

Renar flinched at the sight of her twin. Krish wondered if it was because of the changes in him, or what it told her about her own transformation.

They no longer had Rii to guide them, but they didn't need her. Her landing site couldn't have been more than a few streets away. Krish was weary to his bones, but he made himself run, and when they passed between two ivory gates he finally saw her.

Eric stood beside Rii as Krish'd expected. He had his son clutched in his arms and Krish felt an intense rush of relief at seeing them both safe. It was *him* who felt it, Krish not Yron, and he held on to the feeling as hard as he could.

But Eric wasn't alone. There was a woman beside him. No, not a woman – a servant of Mizhara with golden skin and eyes, and hair as tightly curled as Olufemi's. Her face looked familiar, though Krish was sure he'd never met her. He thought for one terrible moment it might be his sister. That couldn't be, though. He felt his sister's presence like a stone in his gut, west of them and drawing closer.

'I'm glad you're all right, Wheelheir,' Eric said, but his eyes were on Lanalan.

Lanalan turned away from the searching gaze, his shoulders hunched in shame.

'Looks like a lot's happened while I've been gone,' Eric said.

'Yes. For both of us, apparently.'

'Oh, sorry. I forgot you'd never met. This is the Hunter, though she also goes by Bachur. Either way, she's on our side. And she says we need to leave, fast as we can.'

'So you are Yron. You are . . . not very like him,' the Hunter said. 'I am on no side, and certainly not the moon's.'

'But you ain't his enemy,' Eric said. 'Least she ain't now. I told you how it was, Krish. How she turned against Mizhara and let me go free. She'll be in water even deeper than us if your sister catches us. So let's go. We can tell you about the God Killer while we're a-wing.'

'I know about the God Killer,' Krish told him. 'Renar tried to use it on me, but it broke.'

'What was used on you could not have been the weapon, but only its focus,' the Hunter said.

'It was?' Renar's expression might have been funny, if it hadn't been sitting on a face so strangely altered. 'So I never could have killed you anyway?'

'It don't matter – we got to go!' Eric physically shoved her, pushing her towards Rii. His face was white and strained. Krish could see there was more here than he was being told, but Eric was right. He wouldn't have the chance to learn it if he was still here when his sister arrived.

'Let's leave then, if Rii can carry us all,' Krish said.

'She's taken heavier loads than us, ain't you, Rii?'

'My strength sufficeth,' she said. *'I shall—'* Her words broke off into a screech so shrill and horrible that Krish could do nothing but cover his ears and wait for it to be over.

'Rii! Rii! What's happened?' Eric yelled.

'She must be hurt,' Renar said. 'Some weapon, or – are Mizhara's people here already?'

Rii screamed again, quieter this time as if her strength was failing. Eric ran his hands over the matted fur of her flanks. They flexed in and out with every panting breath, but there was no blood on them, no arrow or spear in her.

'There's something coming out of her!' Lanalan yelled, voice high with fear. 'She's – oh. Oh, I see.'

Rii's eyes were ringed with white and there was a yellow froth at her mouth, but her voice was full of joy as she said, *'At last! My children come at last!'*

Her body twisted and Krish saw what Lanalan and Eric had already seen. Crawling towards Rii's chest was a small, mucus-covered creature a hundredth her size. She screamed again and her whole body flexed, opening wide an entrance at her rear so that another blood-smeared form could force its way out. It fell to the ground beside her, feebly twitching its transparent wings.

Eric dropped to his knees and tenderly wiped the mucus from its gasping mouth. Then he lifted it up to latch on to one of her dugs. 'Rii, you great fool,' he said. 'Why did you have to go and do this now?'

All around her, the ground glowed golden. The light shone on her newborns' half-formed features, the delicate petals of their noses and the huge, half-blind eyes swivelling as each searched frantically for its mother.

'My sister is nearly here,' Krish said. *We have to go*, he thought, but Rii could never fly in this condition, and without her Krish could never flee fast enough. 'Go!' he said to Renar. 'You can join my sister's force. She'll take you – you were meant for her. At least you can be safe.'

'Truly I wish that I could do so. I wish it more than I can say, but I can't. You and your sister have made us into . . .' She gestured at her face, her eyes. '. . . into this. But you don't command us. I won't give up my freedom. I won't leave my sib. He's a fool, but he's a better man than I.'

As Eric stayed by Rii, tending to her young, the rest of them turned to watch the west, where they knew the sun was rising.

28

Alfreda didn't know what it was that woke her. It wasn't the pain. That had faded over the days of their journey. Hunger no longer gnawed at her belly, and her sand-dry mouth and raw throat felt very distant, as if they belonged to another body.

Maybe it was the stillness that disturbed her. She'd grown so used to the rocking of the boat. It had followed her into dreams, rocking the forest she always saw and setting a phantom Algar swaying on his feet.

She forced open her eyes, breaking the crust of sleep and illness. Her head felt thick, and the light was far too bright. She blinked the water from her eyes and saw that it was only sunlight, seeping between the slats of the crate in which she'd been trapped for so long.

Sunlight. That meant something, but her mind felt as slow as an overladen wagon. It had been dark before and now it was light. That was because . . . because the boxes all around them had been moved. She knew that was a good thing, although she couldn't remember why.

She wasn't alone here, she remembered that. There were other bodies beside hers. She prodded the smaller, but it didn't move. The larger one was Marvan. She felt glad to have remembered that. Her head was filled with a noise like fever, but colder. All of her was cold.

She shook Marvan. He groaned and his eyes opened, but there was no sense behind them. Her own head had begun to clear. She remembered where they were now, in the hold of the Mortals' ship. Or perhaps not. Perhaps they'd been unloaded along with the crate that had imprisoned them. It would explain the daylight.

There was pain with the new clarity. Her head pounded a loud beat of agony and her muscles spasmed as she tried to move. But she knew that she had to. She had to find water. Food too. Part of her weakness was hunger.

The room outside the box was empty. A storeroom by the look of it, filled with more crates likes theirs, some already emptied. The doorway led to a plain corridor. There was nothing to indicate which way she should go. But there was a smell, the thick, oily scent of meat cooking. It drew her like a lure, left down the corridor and then straight down a broader hall until she reached the kitchen.

There were people here. She stopped, swaying in the doorway at the sight of them. There were two women and a young boy. They looked shocked to see her. She expected the shock to turn to calls for guards or help, but they didn't move.

The boy was crying. Alfreda realised the women were too, though not as noisily. They must be the cooks. They wore long aprons over their dresses and one of them held a hatchet. Alfreda eyed it warily, but the woman made no move to raise it. Outside the room she could hear the sound of retching.

The results of the cook's butchery had been left on one of the surfaces: a pile of bloody bones. They were small, not from any animal that Alfreda recognised. A stewpot bubbled over the fire. It was clearly the source of the enticing smell. The dry retching she could still hear outside worried her, but she didn't have time to look for other food. She could already feel herself weakening.

Someone must have made a recent trip to the well. A bucket of water sat beside one of the cupboards. Alfreda yearned to drop to her knees and drink from it, but she knew she needed to leave before the cooks came to their senses. She picked the bucket up in one hand and used a towel to take the stewpot in the other. There were blood-biscuits on a plate beside the fire. They were a little burnt, but very like the ones her mother cooked that Algar had so loved. She freed a hand to drop them in her pocket.

It seemed to take a very long time to return to the room that held Marvan and Nabofik. Her mind drifted. A moment later – maybe longer – she snapped back to attention to find that she'd stopped and sunk to her knees. There was no strength left in her when she finally passed through the doorway, not even enough to take one step further.

She wanted a drink. Her thirst screamed at her and she allowed herself to lap twice from the bucket. But Marvan and Nabofik were unconscious. There was no knowing how close they were to death. She made herself scoop a handful of water from the bucket and crawl across the floor towards them.

Nabofik lay on *omas* side with *omas* mouth open. Alfreda tipped her hands and water poured into it, faster than she'd intended. Half of it splashed out, a quarter more over Nabofik's face. But some must have gone where she'd intended. She saw Nabofik's tongue stir in *omas* mouth, feeling for the moisture on *omas* lips.

It took two journeys before Nabofik was awake enough to mumble, 'Alfreda?' and three more before any reason returned to Marvan's eyes. After that Alfreda finally allowed herself to drink, great desperate gulps until she felt some of it rising back up her gorge.

Finally, she dragged the stewpot over to the others. She fed them lumps of the meat by hand: one for Nabofik, one for Marvan and one for herself. The sauce was rich. It hurt her stomach at first but after a while she began to appreciate its flavour. She remembered the blood-biscuits in her pocket and used them to scoop up the sauce.

The life and energy returned to her far quicker than she could have hoped. She felt as if she could run back across the sea all the distance the ship had carried them. She felt as if she could have carried the ship on her shoulders as she did.

She saw it was the same for the others. They were soon sitting up, scooping handfuls of the stew to stuff into their mouths. The flavour seemed to get better with every mouthful. Alfreda almost felt that she knew the source of it, but the name eluded her. She reached down for another mouthful and found to her surprise that they'd emptied the bowl. There was still some juice left, and she ran her fingers along the rim to lick it up.

Marvan smiled at her as he did the same. She'd never seen his smile look quite so bright. Nabofik laughed delightedly and Alfreda joined in, though she had no idea what either of them was laughing at. Nabofik's face seemed changed since Alfreda had last looked at it. Marvan's too. Or perhaps *changed* was the wrong word. Maybe *perfected* was better.

Inside her, Alfreda had the warm knowledge of a job done, an aim achieved. It scorched through her, burning all fatigue and weakness and any last doubts away. She'd travelled where she was meant to go and become what she was meant to be. And one day soon Krishanjit would be hers.

29

Dae Hyo wasn't sure what he'd expected to find when he finally saw Krish again, but it wasn't this. He'd hoped his brother might have gathered an army to defend himself. He'd hoped Olufemi would find him to lend her magic. He'd expected at least to be met with weapons. But when Mizhara's forces sighted Krish at last, his brother wasn't even facing them.

Mizhara's army was formed into ranks: her Servants spear-armed at the front, the Moon Forest folk behind and the Sisterband and all the rest with bows in the rear. Mizhara had her hand raised, ready to give the signal to charge. She lowered it uncertainly at the sight of Krish and the tiny group around him. There were just five people and that great fucking bat the boy Eric had brought, but even she only sat there on the ground, as much use as a saddle on a rat.

One by one they seemed to sense Mizhara's coming and turned towards her army. It was walking forward now in unnatural silence. A battle should come with yells and boasts. Every man knew that.

As they drew closer, Dae Hyo saw blood on the ground, gory streaks of it. Perhaps Krish had already fought a battle against some other enemy and that was why his force was so depleted. The ground was littered with shards of crystal and he heard the sound of young birds chirping for their mother, but far too loud, as if the birds were of monstrous size.

Krish stood and faced his sister. His hands were smeared with blood and his face was drawn. With his shaved head he looked almost like a child, shorter by several inches than Mizhara. He didn't look like her brother. He certainly didn't look like her equal.

Dae Hyo wanted to run across the fifty paces that still separated them to embrace Krish. But he knew if he moved he'd be killed. He sensed the tension from Mizhara's people, the fingers itching to pull bowstrings. They suspected a trap. Dae Hyo could have told them Krish wasn't that cunning, if they'd been willing to listen.

The mewling chirrups sounded again and now Dae Hyo could see what had caused them. The monster Rii had given birth. Her black tongue flicked out, long and sinuous, to clean the filth of birth from her young. There were near a dozen of them, bald as eggs but nothing like as beautiful, though no doubt to their mother they looked lovely enough.

The others moved to stand at Krish's side. Dae Hyo knew Dinesh, but the man and woman were strangers to him, though one appeared to be a moon servant and the other a servant of the sun. Then there was Eric. He remained seated beside Rii, looking as if he was trying to make himself small. And another woman, another sun servant, who'd placed herself in front of Eric as if she meant to guard him.

For a long moment there was silence. It didn't seem as if either Krish or Mizhara knew what to say, now they were finally face to face. They'd probably spent so long with the idea of each other, the reality was bound to be disappointing.

Finally Mizhara said, 'Brother.'

Krish shook his head. 'Am I your brother? Or am I Krishanjit of Ashfall? Whichever I am, I've no argument with you.'

Her eyes circled the square, studying the buildings, no doubt still hunting for the ambush she was certain would come. But she couldn't have found any sign of it, because when she looked back at Krish, she said, 'So you say when you stand defenceless before me. If I let you leave to find an army, how would you answer then? I see you've already made new servants of your own.'

'Them?' Krish nodded to the two standing beside him. 'I didn't make them that way. You did. That happened when you came.'

'It happened when the two of you drew close.' That was the other woman, the servant standing guard in front of Eric.

Mizhara's expression darkened. 'Bachur. I should have known you'd complete your treachery by siding with my brother.'

'Her treachery had nothing to do with me, nor is she mine to command,' Krish said. There was a growing, peculiar rhythm to his speech. It sounded like someone else speaking through his mouth.

'He speaks truly,' Bachur said. 'I am neither friend nor enemy to either of you.'

'You killed me!' Mizhara shouted.

'And brought you back,' Bachur said calmly. 'But I did not bring you back for this. A thousand years ago, this war between brother and sister had cause, though never a good one. Will you revive it now out of nothing but fear?'

'She won't suffer me to live,' Krish said, again in that strange him-and-not-him voice. 'She couldn't abide my way of doing things. Why should it be different now?'

'I wasn't the one who rebelled!' Mizhara snapped. She marched towards him, fury in every stride. A voice among her Servants called out and she seemed to remember herself, stopping halfway between her army and Krish's meagre collection of friends.

'You weren't the one who was imprisoned,' Krish said, smiling, but it was a smile that was meant to provoke.

'You wouldn't be controlled!'

'And you refused to accept disagreement!'

'This is foolishness!' Bachur cried. 'Remember who you are. Who you are *now*. You are no longer trapped together in one nation and kept for the benefit of others. The world is broad enough for you both.'

'She's right,' Dae Hyo said. 'The gods of my people are many, and they don't argue more than any man or woman would. You've done nothing to each other yet. I tell you what, I don't see any reason you need to start now.'

For the first time, Mizhara seemed to hesitate. She looked back at Dae Hyo, and he was glad he hadn't stepped forward to stand with Krish the way he'd wanted. Mizhara saw him plead with her from her own ranks. Her face softened – and then her eyes narrowed and all the softness was gone.

'Eric,' she said.

'Drut.' Eric's voice was little more than a whisper. 'I'm sorry for what happened between us. But see, here's our boy. I've looked after him for you.'

Mizhara shuddered with some terrible emotion and raised her spear. For an awful moment, Dae Hyo thought she meant to murder her own child right there. And maybe she did, except that was when the ambush Dae Hyo hadn't believed in chose to be sprung.

They came roaring down the streets that led to the square, a huge angry mob of them. The ones Dae Hyo could see already outnumbered Mizhara's force by two to one, and that wasn't the end of them. More were crowding in behind, some climbing over the statues and fountains that lined the square in their eagerness to reach Mizhara.

Krish seemed as surprised to see them as his sister. Dae Hyo had a moment to wonder whose army they were, and then the two forces clashed.

The newcomers weren't organised. They'd surprised Mizhara's forces, but that was the only advantage they had. Most of them didn't even seem to have proper weapons, and no bead or leather or metalwork to protect their bodies. Some leapt forward in nothing but long white skirts, bare-chested and bare-handed as they reached for their enemies. But it didn't seem clear who their enemies *were*. Those few who had weapons aimed at Mizhara and Krish both.

Dae Hyo felt the tug deep inside him of the runes being used. Flame belched from the Servants towards their attackers. It was blue in its centre and so hot it set alight the men and women it touched like candles. They screamed as they burned. The smell of it was hideous and many of those behind them tried to flee. But the press of the crowd was too great. They were pushed against their will to face the next gout of flame and to become candles in their turn.

Dae Hyo sensed movement on his left and swung to face it. Two men came at him, amber blades raised above their heads as if they meant to club him with them. He gutted them both in one swing of his axe, but he didn't feel good about it. None of these people were soldiers. The only chance they had of killing him was crushing him to death.

A hand grasped his wrist and he swung his axe towards it. He stopped it an inch short of murder when he saw that it was the Servant who'd stood with Krish, the one Mizhara had called Bachur.

'Let me go!' he yelled, but she only held on harder, both her hands working at the manacle around his wrist. With a click it fell free. He gasped as the power rushed back into him, filling him almost beyond endurance.

'You are Krishanjit's man, are you not?' Bachur said.

He had no time to answer. Another of the rabble was coming for him, a woman this time, yelling her fear and anger. His axe moved with reluctant slowness but she wasn't quick enough to stop its blade and it gashed through half her cheek and the thick veins of her neck.

Streaks of flame still flew from Mizhara's forces, but some of the mob had managed to push through, half-burnt and half-crazed. The Sisterband moved forward to face them. The air should have been scorching but instead it was bitterly cold. The ground beneath his feet was iced over and he saw the Sisterband and their assailants slip and slide as they fought.

'They do not know what they are doing,' Bachur said. 'They have not been trained. The sun's magic is an exchange: heat for cold, power for power.' She stood calm and tall in the midst of the slaughter, a spear of metal in one hand and a shard of crystal in the other, as long and thin as a spear itself.

Dae Hyo swung his axe towards another enemy, only to find that Bachur had speared him first. 'I'll be honest,' he said, watching the wall of fire that held back the thousands, 'it looks to me like they know what they're about.'

But even as he said it, he saw one of the Servants around Mizhara freeze in motion – literally freeze. Those behind her pushed forward and she rocked backwards, forwards and then toppled to the ground and shattered into bloody chunks.

'She took the heat from inside herself,' Bachur told him. 'But better there than elsewhere. It was said that Mizhara's power used unwisely could snuff out the sun itself.'

She pulled him from the path of a scythe and into the scant shelter of a fountain, its flowered bowl already chipped and half-listing off its stand.

'Why did those others come here?' Dae Hyo asked. 'All they can do is die!'

'I suspect they are the city's own, rallied to fight for their home. And they can do more than die. They can kill.'

It was true. Hundreds of them might have been burned to embers, hundreds more sliced apart by the trained warriors of Mizhara's army. But theirs wasn't the only blood spilled today. And while Mizhara's people injured themselves with their own magic, it was far from certain which side would win the messy battle.

And there was another force joining the fray, stranger and more deadly than any of the rest. They looked like living statues, but beneath their marble faces moved gears and cogs. They were human and animal and bird – giant eagles and small children with chubby cheeks and a beast like a mammoth with a long lizard's tail. Dae Hyo couldn't say what side they'd joined. They didn't seem to want anything but murder. As he watched, the children leapt onto the backs of two men locked in combat, tearing at their throats with small fingers until the blood gushed out.

Suddenly he couldn't bear it. He'd seen so many battles, who could have guessed that this would be the one that proved too much? But it all seemed so pointless. He had no idea what anyone here was fighting to achieve and he didn't think they knew either. It was too much like the senseless slaughter that had taken the Dae half a lifetime ago. No one should die to no purpose.

He knew so few runes. He had no understanding of how the glyphs were sewn together into useful cloth. But his memory these days was near perfect. He could picture the pages of the book Yemisi had once shown him. There'd been a rune there for separation. He seemed to remember it had been meant for turning milk into curds and whey. But he knew enough about the runes to know that they worked on principles. And if he only made his need and his thoughts wide enough, couldn't he perform a wider separation? Pushed apart, perhaps the people here would come to their senses.

It was hard to clear his mind amidst all this noise and death. Cold and the stench of burned flesh kept pushing their way inside the emptiness he made. He pushed them back with all his strength and it only made them stronger. Of course it did. Hadn't Yemisi once told him that the void was the absence of everything, including the will to make it?

In the moment he remembered, the space inside him opened. All he had to do was form the rune inside it, two perfect half-moon curves, a swirl just so and then three dots beneath it. He held the shape of it perfectly in front of him and called the power into it, all the moon's power and all the sun's power too, because this working was for both of them.

Distantly he felt Bachur grasp his shoulder. She screamed a word whose sounds had once been familiar, but which meant nothing to him in the void. The sound washed through and past him and he remained still in the centre of the world.

Release came as he let the power go. In the moment he did, thunder cracked far above. Something struck his head, and then again, and he thought they must be under attack, but it was only hailstones. Hailstones the size of fists falling all around.

'Did it work?' he shouted to Bachur above the roar of the new-come storm. He knew in his bones that some monumental working had been done.

Bachur didn't answer him. She stared, blank-faced, at the battlefield. Dae Hyo looked too and laughed to see how his intentions had been carried out. The fall of hail was heavy overhead but heaviest of all in the centre of the square. The mechanical statues stood frozen, their gears locked tight with ice. No person could cross that icy downpour and survive, and its presence had forced the two armies apart.

He looked back at Bachur to share his triumph, but she was gazing at the battlefield still, at the side where Mizhara's forces stood. Only . . . not all of them were standing. A swathe had been cut through their ranks where once the Sisterband had been.

He stared, unable to understand how they'd been slaughtered so completely. 'What happened to them?'

'Tell me, what cost has the moon's magic for you?'

'It's nothing – nothing bad. Just breaking the minds of a few animals. Birds. Fish. Making them forget how to fly or how to swim. Nothing that mattered.'

'For small magics, no doubt. And what do you imagine the cost of a working as great as this would be?'

It couldn't be true. He wouldn't accept it. He would have known if his magic had done such a thing. Except that in the centre of the void, he had felt nothing – could feel nothing.

The women of the Sisterband were still alive. He could see them now, lying on the icy ground. Their mouths were open, gasping. They must be trying to breathe, but they couldn't remember how. They were drowning in air.

He saw the rage grow among Mizhara's people at the fate of their comrades. They thought it was Yron's forces who'd done this. They blamed Krish and now nothing but his blood would satisfy them. The hail Dae Hyo had summoned was gone, its aim achieved, and the screaming warriors of Mizhara streamed back across the battlefield to begin the slaughter again.

'No,' he said. 'No, I take it back. I take it back!'

'You cannot take it back,' Bachur said. 'But if you come with me, I can show you a way to end it.'

★

Eric had never been in battle. He'd flown above one, high on Rii's back, but nothing had prepared him for this. It was the chaos that frightened him most. He'd always imagined neat ranks of soldiers and heroic duels between the greatest warriors of each side. This was screams and flailing weapons and the brutal hail that had come and gone so quickly. Anyone could die here, for any reason. It terrified him.

Two women ran screaming past him, knives in hand. He thought they might be kitchen knives. Fury carried them forward and when a spear-wielding Jorlith warrior tried to stand in their path they cut him down, the serrated edges of their blades leaving ragged wounds in his arms and face.

He fell near Eric's feet, still twitching feebly. He wouldn't need his spear any longer and Eric pulled it from his slack fingers, then looked at it in his own hands. What did he know about using a spear? He'd be more likely to gut himself than anyone else – but he couldn't let it go. Arwel was clutched to his chest, bawling the fear of a baby where no baby ought to be, and Eric would do anything, anything at all to save him.

He huddled against Rii's flank, surrounded by Rii's chirping young. There were seven of them here, as safe as anyone could be, but the others were too far away. They crawled desperately towards Rii as she swiped weakly at anyone who dared approach her babies.

To Eric's left, Krish stood raised up on a platform whose statue lay toppled and shattered, its fragments rimed with ice. Krish was like an island in the sea of battle, a clear area all around him. Only he didn't look like Krish so much, not now. His face was much happier and more sure of itself than Krish had ever been.

Krish didn't seem to be doing anything. His hands weren't moving. He was barely breathing. But everywhere he looked, bad things happened. When he glanced left, at a knot of fighting people, the flagstones beneath them seemed to soften like quick-sand and they all sank screaming into the rock. A look straight ahead and two men rushing towards him with a spear were suddenly one man, a mass of flesh with four arms and four legs and two screaming mouths.

A man fell against Eric and he almost speared him in the gut before he saw that it was Lanalan. He held his sister in his arms. She was pulling against him, struggling to break free.

'Please, I have to go to her,' she said. Her eyes were fixed on Mizhara, shining bright in the centre of her army.

'I won't let you,' Lanalan told her. The face that had been so handsome was horrible to look at now, all grey and bony with the same eerie silver eyes as Krish. Eric didn't know if Lanalan was trying to stop Renar out of love for his sister, or loyalty to Krish. Probably Lanalan didn't know.

It was impossible to tell who was winning the fight. It didn't seem the kind of battle anyone won. The best you could hope was to survive it. It had a sort of ebb and flow to it, currents and wild waves and strange moments of stillness. Right now the heart of the battle had flowed past them, leaving splashes of violence behind. There was a man who charged at Rii with an axe. She swatted him aside with contemptuous ease and left him, bleeding and short one leg, to scream on the ground. Two women fought with teeth gritted, one a golden-skinned Servant, the other an Ofiklander no older than twenty, oblivious to the mechanical tiger stalking towards them both.

And to Rii's rear, where her claws couldn't reach, a man raised a gutting knife to one of Rii's pups. He grinned and ripped it open head to tail. Rii's scream was like nothing Eric had ever heard: full of rage and a pain so terrible it couldn't be spoken. He knew it was the sound he'd make if Arwel was ever taken from him, and without thinking about it he drew back his arm and flung his spear.

It took the man through his chest, piercing clean through and pinning him to the ground beside the pup he'd murdered. Eric hadn't known he had that strength in him. He shivered with rage and shock and the knowledge of what he'd done.

'*Thou murderer!*' Rii cried and took the fallen man in her mouth, worrying at his corpse till there was nothing recognisably human about the shape of him. Her other pups chirruped their alarm from where they huddled to her chest, a few of them still latched to her teats.

Eric grabbed Rii by her fur, trying to pull her out of her madness. Her huge black eyes turned to him, filled with fury, and he thought she was going to tear him apart too. But she only shook his hand away impatiently.

'We have to go,' he told her. 'Can you fly yet? Can you get us out of here?'

The matted fur of her flanks stretched outward as she drew in a deep breath. *I can fly. I am ready now. I can carry them to safety, but morsel, I can carry no heavier a load than them. I cannot take thee, nor can I take Yron, and him I cannot leave without.'*

'Yes, you can!' Eric said fiercely. 'There ain't nothing you can do to help him, not in the state you're in. He'd want you to get them away from all this.' Eric looked across at Krish, still casting his awful magics at his enemies, and doubted his own words. But he stooped to pick up the pups anyway, placing them one by one on Rii's back so they could cling on with their soft, transparent claws while their cloudy eyes looked blindly at a world they couldn't understand. They didn't smell like Rii, the mouldy cinnamon scent that Eric had grown so used to. They smelled like dandelions.

He slapped Rii's flank when he was done. 'That's all your pups. Go now, while you've got the chance.'

Her head swung to look at him, ugly and blood-splattered and strangely comforting. *'Thou hast not given me them all, morsel. Hand thine own pup to me, and then I shall depart.'*

Eric's heart lurched in his chest. He couldn't. He *couldn't.*

He looked around at the battle, at the bodies. It had started to break up into groups, little knots and swirls of people trying their very hardest to kill each other. But it wasn't fading – it was spreading. The streets that led to this square were full of fighters now, and more seemed to be coming. Some had turned on each other, killing for the joy of it, filled with the craziness battle seemed to bring.

'Be careful with him,' he said to Rii. 'He don't like to eat unless he's sitting up, and if you don't sing to him, he'll never get off to sleep.'

'I shall care for him as one of my own, this I swear to thee.'

Eric couldn't bring himself to let Arwel go. His arms wouldn't release. It was Rii who prised them gently apart. She took the baby in his swaddling clothes to press against her chest, as gentle as any mother with her child.

Eric felt the downdraught of her wings, but he couldn't bear to watch as she took to the air. He closed his eyes and hoped it would all be over soon.

★

Dae Hyo shouldn't be following Bachur. He should be at the battle. He ought to be fighting beside his brother. But every time he thought of turning back, he saw the women of the Sisterband choking out their lives. And behind their faces he saw the faces of the slaughtered Dae and he kept walking through the empty streets of the golden city and then down into its lowest levels.

Finally, the Hunter stopped beside a door. 'Place your hand beside mine,' she said.

The stone was cool beneath his palm and her hand beside him warm. And then the stone was warm too – scorching hot as a bolt of power passed from it, through him and then away.

He gasped and pulled his hand away, but the door was already opening.

Beyond was a chamber, dark and wide with a dome that rose overhead. It would have looked grand if someone hadn't patterned the walls so messily, scribbling them all over with swirls and lines that were almost but not quite in the shape of runes. The sight of them bothered him, the way they didn't quite work. He knew that if only that line had been joined to the one above it, it would have been Yu, the glyph of falling. And over there was the one that Yemisi had told him was Dänt, for venom, only it was missing its bisecting line.

In the centre of the chamber there was a pedestal. When Bachur walked up to it he realised that the spear of crystal she held in her left hand was just the right size for her to slot into the hole. Before she did, she turned to him.

'You travelled to us over the mountains, did you not?' she asked.

'More dragged than travelled. But that's the way Mizhara came, and brought me with her.'

'And when you went that way, did you pass a city? A very ancient one. The easiest route from west to east leads past it.'

It seemed a ridiculous question to ask at that moment. Somewhere behind them a battle was raging. But he could see from the subtle shake of her hand on the crystal shard that it was important. 'Yes. But I didn't much care for it. The whole place seemed to be poisoned. The animals around it were ill. No one went close.'

'No, I do not imagine Mizhara enjoyed her proximity to the place.' Her voice was shaking now as well. He could tell she was getting to the crux of the matter. 'But tell me also, was there rock around? Rock veined with crystal?'

Finally he understood what she was getting at, though he had no idea why it mattered. 'Rock with crystal like the one you're holding, a sort of yellowish pink? I tell you what, I remember noticing it. I couldn't decide if I liked the colour.'

She let out her breath in a puff of relief. 'I thought so. I thought I remembered it, but it has been so very long. "Roots of a peculiar iridescent quartz." They made Mizhara's statue of the same stuff. I suppose that was how they explained their mining of it in a way that would not rouse her suspicions.'

She nodded once, as if settling the matter with herself, then turned to thrust the crystal shard into the pedestal.

Dae Hyo tensed, expecting some shock or fire or other sign of power, but there was nothing. 'It didn't work,' he said.

'It is no more than a focus for the runes you see scribed on all these walls. They can only be understood when seen through the prism of this crystal. And once understood they may be used. Yes, they may finally be used, but only by a follower of the sun and moon in concert, for so were they designed.'

Dae Hyo walked closer, until he could peer into the crystal. His eye caught flashes of some enormous shape in its depths and he stepped back, startled. 'You brought me here to work rune magic? Svarog's cock, didn't you see what happened before? I'll never touch the runes again.'

'Fear not, warrior. For this magic there will be no cost. Its working is its own price.'

'I don't believe you. How could that be true?'

'Because it is the God Killer.'

His hand fell to his axe, though truth be told he wasn't sure he could take her in a fight. 'I won't kill my brother, not even to stop the war.'

'I will not ask you to. The God Killer is no weapon. It is far subtler and more powerful than that. It is a working of magic to remove godhood from the world and with it magic itself.'

'How can magic remove magic?'

'Has no one ever told you what Mizhara and Yron truly are?'

'The sun and moon.'

'No. Although we have chosen to make them that. But both sun and moon and Mizhara and Yron are no more than shapes that their creators saw within the runes – a way of understanding them. The runes do not of their nature have a pattern; it is only you humans who impose it upon them, time after time. Because thus may you understand the world and through understanding, bend it to your will. This pattern: sun–moon, light–dark, order–chaos. It is one you are always drawn to. But it has no inherent truth. And so what is seen may be unseen, and what is known may be *unknown.*'

A restless energy filled Dae Hyo and he began to pace, though he couldn't tell if it was because he failed to understand her, or because he understood her all too well. 'You're saying you can make it so the runes don't work any more. So Krish goes back to being just Krish.'

'Yes. Is that not what your brother would wish?'

'I don't know. It's not for me to make that choice. A man has to pick his own paths. And how do you even know I can work this magic? I learned to use the runes less than a season ago.'

'But there is a perfect stillness inside you, a perfect emptiness. I sensed it the instant I saw you. The shape you saw within this crystal is a sentence perhaps only you and I together in all the world may speak. It says, in the language of the runes, that there are no gods. And if we can fill it with the gods' power, if we can force the paradox to become real, Mizhara and Yron will be banished from our world not just for now, but for good.'

He could see she meant every word of it. She reached for him to draw him closer, but he stepped away from her grasping hands. 'It sounds good when you say it, lots of pretty words. But what does it mean? What will it do to Krish to have the god taken out of him, or to the Servants? What will it do to the *world*?'

'Nothing worse than is already happening to them.'

He saw the choice clearly, the weight of it, and the fact he was the only one who could make it. That was a heavy burden to place on a man. And there was another argument against, one he was ashamed to put into words but felt to his core. Because this magic that he'd found had filled him when nothing else could. He was *good* at it. As a mage there was a point to him, a purpose to his life. What purpose did he have if even this was taken away from him?

Or was that his purpose after all? This one, monumental act.

'Please,' she said, the plea obviously coming hard to a proud woman. 'We have to act now, or it will be too late to act at all.'

★

Krish-who-was-Yron was enjoying himself. It should have felt strange to be two people at once, but to him it felt right. He'd always felt happiest in disorder, he remembered that now. He remembered a lot: the Garden cage they'd kept him in for so long, the joy of forbidden creation when he was freed from it, and the betrayed rage at his sister when she would have taken it all away from him. He'd hurt no one, but she must have the world in an order of her choosing. Well, not this time. This time the battle would end another way.

His body was pierced with arrows from thigh to neck but he couldn't feel them. Such weapons couldn't hurt him. Only his sister could wound him, and only he could wound her. This time he wouldn't hesitate when it came time to deliver the killing blow.

But the currents of the battlefield had pulled them apart. The ground was thick with corpses, yet still these people fought to make more of them. It was as if they didn't understand that the only conflict that mattered was between Yron and Mizhara themselves. They spent their lives for nothing and it made him sad and angry too, though he wasn't sure which of Krish and Yron was sad and which angry.

A group of golden-haired men placed themselves before him, spears raised. He thought of a rune he'd once designed to make the trees of his prison grow wild, and as he thought it, the men's spears turned to branches in their hands. Their roots, desperate to drink the water that was their life, pierced the men's bodies, drinking their blood instead, and he was able to walk past them.

There at last was Mizhara, only a few score paces away from him. She wore a face neither of him remembered, but both knew needed to be destroyed. It didn't matter that the same knowledge was in her eyes. He was stronger now than her. His human life had learned far more of the world than the Servant who was the other half of her.

The air was full of snow. It fell on all the corpses, hiding them beneath its drifts. If Mizhara's people went on as they were, this whole land might become as cold and desolate as their polar home.

He would transform her. It was what she'd always hated most in him: the power to change. He thought he might make her into an animal, a vulture, perhaps, like his marvellous airborne mounts that she so despised. He closed his eyes to make the working easier, emptied his mind – and screamed.

Krish-who-was-Yron was torn apart, forced by something more powerful even than him to become Krish alone. Something wanted to rip Yron away, to tear away Mizhara too and leave the world without them both.

Krish wouldn't allow it. The magic wasn't as powerful as it believed. If he *knew* himself to be Yron firmly enough, it couldn't take that knowledge away from him. It couldn't make untrue what he knew to be true.

He *wanted* to be Yron. Yron wasn't afraid and he wasn't uncertain. Yron was –

Yron wasn't him. For a moment Krish could think absolutely clearly. He had a choice, just for this moment and perhaps never again. He could hold on to the godhood that was his birthright. He might even find a way to banish the memories that belonged to another man and be only Krish, with all that power and a body that could never die. He'd never want for food or comfort or safety again. He could rule the world if he chose. Was that what he wanted?

It was too big a question to answer. Instead he found himself staring at a tiny fragment of memory, *his* memory: the moment when Renar had explained why she betrayed him to Bruyar. He'd been angry then, so much trouble over something so small. But now he saw that this was the heart of it all. The quarrel between Yron and Mizhara should have been as meaningless for the world as Renar's petty jealousy of Lanalan. The conflict between brother and sister would never have grown so large without the presence of gods. They changed everything just by their very being. They took the small and made it huge. The things they created could be works of wonder, but some things were only meant to be small.

The tugging came again, deep inside him, a wrenching at the part of him that had always been there, the part that was a god. He felt the immensity of what was being taken, the potential for such very great good and very great evil.

And then he sighed and let it go.

Epilogue

Jalena sat on the mound beneath the water cactus and watched the ants at work. They were very busy today, marching in a dark column from their nest to the place where a spine-apple had fallen from the cactus. Another column marched back again, improbably huge chunks of the yellow fruit held high above their heads. It was said that among the Ostatni Ludia, people marched in the same orderly way to go about their business, but she didn't believe it. Put two people together and there would be three opinions. No one would ever agree to such order. And besides, there couldn't be as many people in the world as there were ants in just one column.

She was supposed to be watching the plant-speaker. She was meant to see that no other obec had sent some sly crawling worm to lure him away. Everyone knew that Juh Obec had the best plant-speaker in all the grasslands. They'd only found him last year, when the grass sweetened, but they'd known at once that he must be of great power. A man who'd eaten so much must be filled with knowledge.

But no one would come to steal him away. It was also known that he would never leave without the Lucky Woman, who'd travelled from the non-world with him. And Jalena *had* been watching the Lucky Woman. She sat at the foot of the hill, winding flatgrass together to make a dress for Jalena's sister, who was welcoming a new person inside her and had grown large in the belly.

The Lucky Woman often worked on her own and didn't speak much. It was strange. If Jalena had been as lucky as her, she would have sung and danced and been very merry. But the Lucky

Woman wasn't merry. Jalena's father said that some luck was so great the person who possessed it couldn't always see it clearly, like a woman holding a puzzle tree in her arms who couldn't count its leaves. Maybe that was the way of things with the Lucky Woman.

Their new plant-speaker was very merry. Some said he was too merry for a man who dealt with the world-beneath-the-world, but Jalena thought he had much to be merry about. The grass had been rich everywhere he led them and the birds had to feed on seeds, because they left no carrion behind. The birds were angry but the people of Juh Obec were happy and gave much red beer to the plant-speaker. That probably accounted for his merriness.

The day was ending. They would soon have to gather the house-beasts inside the circle of watch and lock themselves inside their huts for the night. The night was a war-home not a peace-home and not a time for people to be about. Already the sky was red on one side of the world, the colour of blood. But the plant-speaker was still in his trance and it would be very bad luck to move him.

Jalena was wondering whether she should try anyway – perhaps a gentle nudge to his belly would draw him back to the grass-world – when there was a terrible scream. It was the plant-speaker's voice. Even when he screamed you could tell he hadn't been born as one of the true people.

This was bad. If the plant-speaker was hurt when Jalena was meant to watch him, she would be very much blamed. She might even be thrown from her hut and made to travel at the back of the obec, with the dust of the house-beasts' footsteps kicked up in her face till she looked like a horn-beast in wallow.

She was only the ninth fastest runner in the obec, but she almost winged over the ground to reach him. Even so, the Lucky Woman reached him first. He was on his back, arms flailing and ankles drumming on the ground.

'Quick – hold him down!' the Lucky Woman ordered. In her panic she'd used not-speech, but Jalena understood. Jalena had been learning it from the plant-speaker. The jagged sounds of it amused her, even though it was supposed to be bad luck.

She grabbed the plant-speaker's arm and put a hand against his chest, trying to hold him down, but he was very strong and even stronger when the voice of the plants was in his ears. He threw her off. After that, she couldn't even catch his hand again so that in the end she had to sit on his chest, just to stop him bouncing up and down and hurting himself.

The Lucky Woman sat at his head, watching to make sure he didn't swallow his tongue. That happened with plant-speakers sometimes. Any obec that let them die of it was considered very low by all the rest. A gift thrown away was the worst luck there could be.

Their plant-speaker was too wise to do anything so foolish. After a little while the frothing and the thrashing grew less. When a small crowd of people came to see what the screaming had been, Jalena waved them away. They had to obey, because she had been chosen as the plant-speaker's eyes today.

'What happened?' the Lucky Woman asked when he was finally still, but not yet awake.

Her skin and hair were so burned away it was easy to forget that she wasn't one of the people and didn't understand all the things even a child should know. 'The plants had big words to say to him today,' Jalena explained. 'Strong words. Don't worry, the plants don't mean to hurt him. And everyone will be very happy.'

The Lucky Woman didn't seem reassured, though it was never easy to tell what she was thinking. But she sighed with relief when the plant-speaker finally opened his eyes.

They were stupid, like a little baby's, and Jalena knew he was finding it hard to climb back up the path from the world-beneath-the-world. She sat behind him, circling him with her legs so that she could prop his back against her chest, and handed the Lucky Woman her flask of white-berry juice. It would make the climb easier.

She could no longer see his eyes, but she knew they must have cleared because the Lucky Woman said, 'What happened to you? You've never reacted like that before!' She spoke sharply, which was not how you were supposed to speak to someone so important, but maybe when you were as lucky as her you didn't need to worry about giving offence.

'It worked,' the plant-speaker croaked. Jalena could feel his words vibrating from his chest into hers. 'I saw the world-beneath-the-world. I really saw it.'

'I'm not surprised, the amount of that tea they gave you.' The Lucky Woman spoke in the tone of voice people used for mockery, although no one – however lucky – would mock the visions of a plant-speaker.

He wriggled against Jalena, pushing himself away and to his feet. The Lucky Woman reached out an arm to steady him, but he brushed it off. He seemed agitated and when he turned to face Jalena, she felt fear for the first time. That wasn't the face of a person the plants had gifted with happy news.

'It will be all right,' the Lucky Woman told him soothingly. 'You just took too much, that's all. Everything will seem normal soon.'

But that was a foolish thing to say and the plant-speaker clearly knew it. He shook his head. 'You have to listen to me, Mahvesh, it was real this time.'

'I'm sure it seemed that way.'

'It was. Will you please just listen! I saw the world-beneath-the-world and then I saw the world above it. I saw what was coming. *They're* coming. They're coming here.'

Now the Lucky Woman seemed to understand. She gasped and stepped back. Her hands knotted together, perhaps to stop their shaking. 'That can't be true. Why would Yron and Mizhara come here?'

'No,' the plant-speaker told her. 'Not them. Something far worse.'

Acknowledgements

This book has been a long time in the writing, and before anything else I'd like to thank those who've waited patiently (or possibly impatiently) for me to finish it. I hope it was worth the wait.

If it was, there are a lot of people to thank for it. My friends have, as ever, provided invaluable advice and plot suggestions as well as much-needed support during a difficult time. In particular I'd like to thank Naomi Alderman, David Bailey, Kathleen Bryson, Peter Griffiths, Matt Jones, Carrie O'Grady and Adam Wantman, without whom this book might well not exist. Also my mum, who's always there when I need her, even when I don't know it myself.

And last but definitely not least, my editor Oliver Johnson and my agent James Wills. You've both been more forbearing than I could reasonably have expected, and I'm enormously grateful.

WANT MORE?

If you enjoyed this and would like to find out about similar books we publish, we'd love you to join our online Sci-Fi, Fantasy and Horror community, Hodderscape.

Visit hodderscape.co.uk for exclusive content from our authors, news, competitions and general musings, and feel free to comment, contribute or just keep an eye on what we are up to.

See you there!

NEVER AFRAID TO BE OUT OF THIS WORLD

 @Hodderscape   @Hodderscape   /hodderscape